Other books by
Joe Coomer
The Decatur Road
Kentucky Love
A Flatland Fable
Dream House
The Loop

Beachcombing for a Shipwrecked God

Joe Coomer

Scribner Paperback Fiction
Published by Simon & Schuster

SCRIBNER PAPERBACK FICTION
Simon & Schuster Inc.
Rockefeller Center
1230 Avenue of the Americas
New York, NY 10020

First Scribner Paperback Fiction edition 1997
Published by arrangement with Graywolf Press
SCRIBNER PAPERBACK FICTION and design are
trademarks of Simon & Schuster Inc.

Designed by Will Powers
Manufactured in the United States of America

1   3   5   7   9   10   8   6   4   2

Library of Congress Cataloging-in-Publication Data
Coomer, Joe.
Beachcombing for a shipwrecked god / Joe Coomer. —
1st Scribner Paperback Fiction ed.
p.   cm.
1. Archeology—Fiction.   2. Women archeologists—Fiction.
I. Title.
[PS3553.O574B43   1997]
813'.54—dc20   96-38328
CIP

ISBN 0-684-82440-X

for the women

"Gracious heavenly Father, . . . Please let me stay at Green Gables; and please let me be good-looking when I grow up. I remain,

> "Yours respectfully,
> "Anne Shirley.
> *Anne of Green Gables*
> L. M. MONTGOMERY

GLINDA   Are you a good witch—or a bad witch?
DOROTHY   Who, me? Why—I'm not a witch at all.
> *The Wizard of Oz*, screenplay
> NOEL LANGLEY, FLORENCE RYERSON
> EDGAR ALLEN WOOLF

What meanest thou, O sleeper?   JONAH 1:6

I came across a love of moving water, an ebbing tide parting on the plumb bow of an old boat, and the sea passing swiftly along the waterline carried bits of seaweed, the body of a dead bird, a dark brown leaf, and a love that seemed necessary to me, to be near that abrasive current, the green swell and nascent gurgle. I thought I'd never be able to love anything again, anything other than the memory of my husband, and so I felt ashamed and queer kneeling there on the dock, my bag over one shoulder and a kitten inside my coat, looking down into the water of Portsmouth Harbor, and feeling for a moment, not sad. He'd died at Christmas, nine weeks earlier.

The kitten mewed and, using my skin as a boarding net, tried to crawl up between my breasts. I reached for him but didn't take my eyes from the water till I had him nose to nose, round pupil to narrowing pupil, and said to him, "We'll stay here for a while." I'd found him at a rest stop in West Virginia and hadn't named him yet, though I was leaning toward Peytona Pawtucket, two small towns near my home: PP for short. Jonah never liked cats, and at the roadside it suddenly occurred to me that I could rescue this kitten without any recrimination. It wasn't the kitten's fault that Jonah had died. It was, I realized, his dumb luck. But perhaps this kitten had somehow killed my husband so I'd save him from his miserable abandonment. Maybe Jonah had died so I'd rescue the kitten. If Jonah had been there at the rest stop I wouldn't even have considered . . . well, it was another strange hallucination of my rage. I was still mad at my dead husband for dying. I like to lay blame and it seemed as if something as huge as Jonah's death ought to be someone's fault.

I tucked the kitten's angular tendon-taut body away again, and stood up, walked back in the March cold to my car. I'd driven east till I beached at the ocean and then splashed north along the coastline till I decided there wasn't any reason to turn away. We indulged ourselves that first night, the cat and I, and stayed at the Portsmouth Sheraton in a room that looked out over a monumental pyramid of salt to the river, the tide-wracked Piscataqua, whose mouth was the old harbor. I'd asked an old woman on the street what all the salt was for. I learned later it was simply road salt. But that afternoon she looked at me sadly and explained, "Why, dear, when the rains are heavy and too much

7

fresh water flows down to the sea, we add salt back to the ocean so the fish won't expire."

≈

I came across a love of moving water kneeling in the current of Caudel Run, the small creek behind our home in Kentucky, whose waters were as clear and cold as my fear, falling over black ledges of slate, gathering in white sluices of anguish, numbing my feet, blueing the skin. I could hold the water in my hands and bring it to my mouth.

≈

By morning I'd changed the kitten's name to Piscataqua. He'd scratched up a few carpet fuzzies and taken a dump under a chair. After I cleaned it up I hid him in the bathroom and ordered room service: eggs and milk. We ate at the window and watched the working of the gulls over the river, trailing behind a boat. It was warm in the room, but I could tell it was cold beyond, cold on the street below and colder still at the water. So I bundled up and put Piscataqua between my shirt and sweater, where he dropped to my stomach and soon fell asleep. When I reached the sidewalk it dawned on me that there was nothing I had to do. There were things I should have done and things other people wanted me to do, but nothing necessary beyond breathing.

I felt as if I'd escaped. I hadn't called it that before, but an escape it was, through a tunnel, over walls. I'd left home with a wad of cash, to avoid using my credit cards to buy gas or food so I couldn't be tracked by the bills. I felt guilty. I'd left my parents a note saying I was just getting away for a few days, but I knew at the time that I had no intention of returning permanently. I'd even contacted a real estate agent to list the house. I'd call Mom later, I thought. It wasn't fair to Mom and Dad, because I wasn't running from my parents, but from his, Jonah's, the Montagues. If I told my folks where I was, I knew Richard and Mary would somehow find out. They were ravenous, and I no longer had the strength to fend them off. Jonah was their only child, and after his death they fed off my memories. I'd seen them every day since the wreck. They drove the thirty-two miles from their home to mine to keep me com-

pany, but I soon realized they were scavengers and I was their last hope for food, the only carcass on an endless stretch of desert, and that they wouldn't leave me till my bones were hollow and bleached. They seemed to have no memory of their own. Mary washed all of Jonah's clothes, even those that were already clean, going through the pockets in search of a scrap or seed that might be explained by some story I could tell. A ticket stub from a movie was a mine to her and in her grief she'd torture me asking question after question: "How was the movie? Did Jonah like it? Did you have popcorn? Where did you sit? Did he laugh? Tell me where he laughed. We could rent the video and watch it, the three of us. You could tell us where he laughed." I found Richard in the attic reading my letters to Jonah and Jonah's to me. I left the day after Mary, blowing into a cup of coffee, her eyes on the cup's rim, said, "There in the hospital, before he died, when we knew he was going to die, we should have had the doctors take the sperm from his testicles. We could have frozen it. You could have had his baby yet." I left. I loved him too.

I looked over my shoulder, Richard and Mary weren't behind me, and then walked up the street into old Portsmouth. I'd been here before as an undergraduate, attending an archaeological field school at the Isles of Shoals, five miles off the coast. I spent two weeks uncovering the foundations of a seventeenth-century fishery. The ferry to the islands left from Portsmouth, so I had frequent opportunities to roam the streets and waterfront of the city, to visit Strawbery Banke (Portsmouth's original name and now a museum collection of early houses near Prescott Park), to sit in the many restaurants and cafés, to browse the used and rare bookstores and antique shops. But most of my spare time was spent with my eyes on the water, simply watching the tide and the boats. That's what I'd come back to. And although I knew I should have begun to search for a place to live, my feet carried me back toward the piers on the river. I wanted to see the sun's reflection off the water. I crossed Market Street in front of the Moffat-Ladd House, passed through a small garden to Ceres Street, eighteenth-century warehouses turned twentieth-century gift shops on one side and tugboats on the other, climbed up along Bow Street, more waterfront brick warehouses that were now restaurants and boutiques.

Portsmouth seems to be washed with age, worn by touch and breath. Its streets, like animal paths, lead down to the river and then mimic its banks. The city is comfortable here, relaxed, as unconsciously nestled in this point of land as the last bone in my finger. What's brick is red and what's wood is white and what's stone is gray granite. Cobbles and sills are footfall worn, cupped like waiting palms. The glass of many mullioned windows flows toward the river, distorting interiors. The shops and cafés are small and eclectic, with merchandise-weary walls and light-poor corners. Layers of old patina, layers of faded paper over horsehair plaster, levels of plank flooring, all seem burnished like the head of a cane. Behind the counters, in between sales, clerks read with cats in their laps, dogs at their feet. Above them, copper dormers modeled to frame a human face look out to sea. Slate roofs, rust streaked, widow's walks and witch's peaks: the skyline crouches under the lighted steeples of old churches.

I whistled past St. John's Church with its sidewalk-level burial vaults, and finally crossed Daniel and State Streets to Prescott Park and a clear view of the river. This city is so close to the sea it's hard to put your hand in the water.

When I was here before, during the summer, the streets of Portsmouth were thronged with tourists, but in early March at eight in the morning I was alone in Prescott Park. Wind came in from the sea and down the mouth of the harbor, blowing patterns in the bare branches of the trees above me and rasping the surface of the river. I leaned on a railing at the seawall and looked down into the green but bright water, looking through shards of light and scattered leaves on the surface to the current beneath, the tide coming out of its slackness. Lobster buoys, lolling with broken necks and then swinging upright, began to take the strain. Boats tugged at the lines holding them to the dock below, and the dock itself with rusty groans moved as far seaward as its pilings would allow. All the water was being pulled from the river. It happened, high tide and low, every six hours or so, this great back and forth, the earth shuddering, a slow shake of cleansing, over and over. Here the tide was particularly strong, the current as fast as six knots, the rise and fall as much as nine feet. I never knew a more active environment, as if the skin of the world was loose as a cat's. If the creek behind

our house in Kentucky turned around and raced uphill as fast as it coursed down, and rose and dropped eight or nine feet in the process, if it did this just once, the entire human species would come and sit on its banks in hopes to see it happen again.

The sound of steel on steel came across the water from Seavey's Island and the navy yard. There were submarines flanking each side of a pier. Men stood on the rounded black hulls, pulling lines, gesturing. They seemed to have purpose.

A lobster boat puttered through the gut between Pierce Island and Prescott Park past me to a buoy on the edge of the main current, just off tiny Four Tree Island. A man in yellow bib overalls turned the bow of his boat into the ebbing tide and adjusted his speed to match the current, leaving the boat at a standstill. He reached down, picked up a buoy, and wrapped its line around a small winch. Spray flew, and soon a green rectangular metal cage appeared alongside, and he stooped over with gloved hands and pulled it aboard. He reached inside the cage and brought forth a lobster waving semaphore and then, to my great dismay, chunked it overboard. He proceeded to throw away three more, rebait the trap, and drop it back over too. I thought, perhaps lobstering is not only a business but also a sport. The smell off his bait rose to me on the wind that moved against the tide and I walked away along the railing.

The gangway to the Portsmouth Public Landing led down to a dock. Entrance was allowed only to boat owners and guests, but the small guardhouse was empty, so I crept down the aluminum incline to the green lumber of the dock. Most of the slips were empty. Two small sailboats nested near shore and further out a lobster boat was backed into its berth. I walked past *Elizabeth Ann II* to the end of the dock, kneeled down, held one palm under the weight of the kitten, and plunged my free hand into the water. It was colder than I could believe, colder than ice cream in the sinuses, so cold I jerked my hand back and hit myself in the face with my already blue knuckles. It didn't seem to me that anything could live in such extremes and that perhaps the lobsterman had been throwing back dead, frozen lobsters. I smelled my fingertips after rubbing them dry on my coat. It was a precise smell, thick, pungent, like moss or loamy soil but not those, more like the worm it-

self, like fur and skin and pee and death and rocks, but beyond all of these, on top of and suffused through them, was a sense of cleanliness. I took a handful of water, bearing the needles of pain, and saw it clear, unlike the body of the river, clear and without movement, as clear as the whorls and lines of my palm, as if it didn't exist at all without the rest of the ocean and so I threw it back.

There was a shrill peep and I looked up to see two tugboats nosing a huge ship around Henderson Point on Seavey's Island. I'd read in a guidebook at the Sheraton how the big ships came up and down the river at slack tide, when the water was at its deepest or shallowest. A loaded ship came in at high tide so her bottom would clear the rocks and an empty ship left at low tide so her superstructure would clear the bridges. As I watched the tugs push the ship around the tight corner, a great blast from the horn on Memorial Bridge lifted me an inch off the lumber of the dock and brought Piscataqua alive between my shirt and sweater. He crawled, marsupial-like, up the front of my blouse to my neck, peeked out at the collar of my coat, and so we watched the show together. After a moment or two, gates dropped in front of the traffic on the bridge above us and the center section slowly rose on steel cables. The tugs, alternately whistling and tooting in their spare, plaintive language of air, guided the ship with what seemed like inches to spare between the twin towers of Memorial and on up the river to meetings with the two other bridges that cross the Piscataqua between Portsmouth, New Hampshire and Kittery, Maine. The ship was out of Venezuela and didn't seem to have a soul on board. I couldn't conceive of what might be in its hold, but thought myself blessed to welcome it after such a long journey.

I rose and turned back up the dock, gazing into the cockpits of the lobster boat and sailboats as I passed to see if there were any secrets there. I walked to the north end of the park and watched, for at least an hour, the tide backing out from underneath a restaurant, the Smarmy Snail, perched over the river on pilings. The receding water left mudflats and shallows, blanched barnacles, tires and splintered lumber, the remains of two wire traps, and still the water fell, revealing a tattered nylon fishing net clinging to the pilings like a forgotten web, a fragmented Styrofoam buoy and plastic bottles caught in its filaments. I

could think of no word to weave in my web that would have saved him.

Another dock led out from the Smarmy Snail's deck, a private float where two larger boats were tied. I'd explored that dock the evening before. I entered the glass-enclosed dining area of the restaurant, ordered a cup of hot tea, and sat with my face to the sun looking down on the boats. Downriver was the old prison, a stone Victorian edifice now used for storage by the navy, but whose prisoners once must have looked forlornly out to sea. It was warm here, and Piscataqua began to purr heavily. I dropped two dollars on the table and carried my tea out on the restaurant's deck. One of the boats alongside the dock was obviously a work boat of some kind. There were coils of rope on board, buckets and plastic bins, nets on a huge reel. The boat across the dock was an old motor yacht, perhaps fifty feet long, varnished mahogany gleaming in the sun. On the sternboards: *Rosinante* and *Palm Beach, Fl.* There was an even older woman on board, in bright orange galoshes and jacket, hosing down the deck of the boat. As she moved around to one side, bending over with a sponge to wipe woodwork, I saw a small sign leaning on the sill of one of the many windows of the raised cabin. At first glance I thought it read, BOAT FOR RENT, but it clearly became, ROOM FOR RENT. I hadn't seen the sign the evening before because I'd been down on the dock next to the boat. This sign was intended to be seen by patrons of the restaurant. I thought for a moment, and then somewhat awkwardly yelled, "Room for rent?"

She didn't hear me. Maybe the sign meant she had a room in her house for rent. Maybe there wasn't a room on the boat at all. I looked for more evidence that the boat was a live-aboard. Electrical lines leading from the dock plugged into an outlet at the base of the cabin. There were curtains behind all the windows and portholes. A small air conditioner, similar to one on a motor home, sat on the roof of the raised cabin. Weathered clothespins hung from a stretched line like dead sparrows.

"Room for rent?" I yelled again.

She rose up slowly from the deck and looked up at the railing of Memorial Bridge, thirty or forty feet above her.

"Over here," I yelled, and for some reason held my tea high in the air.

She looked at me, and cupped her ear while she walked with the

running water hose. If it was possible, her skin was whiter than bone, so translucent it seemed glazed like ironstone. Then I realized her face seemed brilliant because her hair was like the soft blue glow of a television in a house across the street. I could make out the bones in her hands, even at that distance, and the blue veins tracing over them. She walked all the way around the cabin with her mouth open and turned off the water. Then she screamed, "What?" at me with such force the hot tea sloshed over onto my wrist.

"Room for rent?" I said again, gesturing toward the sign. "Do you still have a room for rent?"

"Yes, yes," she nodded, "There's the sign."

"I'm looking for a room."

"Well, come have a look," and she swept the sky with a hooked arm. I put the cup on the railing and walked down the ever-increasing steepness of a gangway in an ebbing tide. The dock itself rose and fell with the water, sliding on iron hoops around pilings, so the boats and the dock were always at the same level. The gangway rolled on rubber wheels farther out on the dock as the tide rose, lessening its angle, and back toward the restaurant as the tide ebbed, increasing its angle. There was a set of steps for boarding the boat and as I moved up them the old lady held out her hand. I took it as gingerly as I would a bird's wing, and put the sole of my shoe on a brass step plate that said, ELCO. I felt the boat move under my foot. It was hardly perceptible, but the boat gave when I stepped on it, as if it were alive. It made me tremble. I stepped down to the deck, looking for handholds. Still grasping my hand, she tapped the back of it three times with her index finger, and asked, "Honey, can you swim?"

"Yes," I said.

"Should have asked you before you stepped aboard. Life jackets are in the deck lockers forward and aft. Fire extinguishers in the main salon, engine room, galley and under the awning aft."

She was thin, her nose so fine it seemed brittle. Her skin wasn't loose but relaxed, as if it were thinking of something other than skin.

One of the intrusive and particularly rude habits I have acquired as a result of my work is my interest in teeth: overbite, underbite, caries, fillings, etc. This old lady was missing both of her upper canines, the

dog teeth. These teeth are frequently missing in archaeological specimens and are often found in trash pits. They have only one long root. Her teeth would leave a telling bite. I thought if she were a vampire, she'd pulled the evidence.

She slid open the door that led into the many-windowed salon, and stepped over the high sill. "Bilge pump switch is here. I leave it on automatic." She pointed to a toggle next to the ship's wheel. The cabin, or salon, was the only living area above the boat's deck. A settee filled one corner, behind a table mounted on a brass pedestal at eating height. "OK, that's the safety drill. Room's below." I followed her down a flight of five mahogany steps past a bathroom and the door to the engine room, to a cabin that filled the rear third of the boat. There was a bunk on the port and the starboard, and a dresser at the stern with a large mirror above. A closet, or hanging locker, stood at the head of each bunk. The room was paneled in a rich red mahogany.

"You'd share this cabin with Chloe. She's at work now. You'd get this bunk, half this dresser, this locker, and use of the head of course, and have galley and salon privileges. The galley is forward of the salon, down the companionway, and my cabin is forward of the galley."

She demonstrated how a curtain could be drawn between the two bunks to provide some privacy.

"No smoking is allowed on board. The rent is fifty dollars a week. If you're prone to seasickness, this isn't the home for you. We do get some wake at times from the speedboats. If you're religious, that's fine, keep it to yourself. Do you drink?"

"No, not really," I said.

"That's a shame; I do. Do you use profanity?"

"A little."

"It's welcome on board," she said. "Sometimes it gets cold or hot. Do you complain a lot?"

"I've got a sweater."

"Do you have the two hundred a month?"

"Yes, I can manage that."

"Do you want to live here with Chloe and me? We're good people. Chloe's some fat and inclined to inquisitiveness, but she's all right. She's

been here for three months and likes it fine. She pays two hundred a month too. I pay eight hundred a month to keep the boat here so it's a good deal for you. I wouldn't try to cheat you."

"Oh, no," I nodded. "It sounds fair." I could hear water gurgling around the hull and feel the bumping of the fenders between the boat and the dock.

"Men," she said, but didn't continue.

"What about them?" I asked.

"You're young," she said.

"Yes, but I'm not . . ."

She'd already turned, hadn't heard me. "Aren't they pleasant?" she said, and she turned back to me smiling. "Just try to keep it down past eleven, and remember: this is a boat. It rocks."

I wrote her a check for a month's rent on the table in the salon. Her name was Grace. As I stepped out onto the deck, going after my suitcases, I asked, "What happens when you go out on the boat?"

"Honey, *Rosinante* hasn't left this dock in four years, not since Sweet George passed away."

I paused. My eyes whispered the name.

"Sweet George was my husband," she said, and turned away again, stepping down the companionway into the galley. I closed the door behind me and trembled again over the six inches of falling space between the boat and the dock. It was the next morning before I realized I'd written her a check, and by the time I offered Grace two hundred in cash for its return, she'd already deposited it. I didn't want to make anymore of it, afraid that she'd be suspicious. Instead I sent a change of address to my bank, asking them to keep this information confidential. I'd asked my mother in my note to pick up my mail but I knew there was a possibility that Richard and Mary were waiting for my postman to intercept what information they could.

I was, on that afternoon of moving aboard *Rosinante*, as happy as I'd been in two months. I'd hoped to find an apartment close enough to walk to the river, but hadn't even considered living on the water itself. I took quick short hops, interspersed with frantic searches for Piscataqua in my clothes, back to the Sheraton, packed my soft bags, threw them in the trunk of my car and raced back to Prescott Park as if I'd lose my place if I

didn't hurry. Piscataqua barely had time to establish himself on the car's headrest before I was tugging his sprung claws free from the upholstery again. I shouldered all three of my bags and my knapsack but decided to leave my box of tools, trowels, brushes, and dental picks in the car.

The car itself would be my biggest storage problem, I thought. I'd have to find a place for it. I agonized over the quarters the meters would cost me and over the price a garage might charge for a permanent space. I still wasn't used to having money. Jonah and I had struggled from month to month to pay the mortgage on our old farmhouse and the twenty acres around it, not to mention car payments and the usual bills. Ironically his death left me financially comfortable. Jonah's health insurance had a twenty thousand dollar accidental death rider and insurance at the bank not only paid off both of the cars, but the remainder of our house mortgage. I had assets totaling over one hundred and fifty thousand dollars, thirty thousand of that in cash, and didn't owe a penny to anyone. I just didn't have a husband.

For the moment I filled the parking meter and then thumped my way down the wooden sidewalk that led around to the Smarmy Snail's deck and on down the gangway to *Rosinante*. I tapped lightly on the pane of glass in the door. When no one came, I let myself in, almost tripping over the coaming. I found I couldn't go down the narrow companionway with all my bags and so pitched them below one at a time. I pulled back the curtain partitioning the cabin and set about filling my three drawers in the dresser, and hanging shirts and one dress in my locker. There were more drawers under my bunk that I put papers and notebooks in, and a bookshelf above my bunk, beneath a row of three windows, where I put field manuals and a few cherished texts. The bathroom, or head, had the smallest toilet I'd ever seen, a porcelain doll's throne with a mahogany seat. There was a tiny brass corner sink with four small shelves above where I put my soap and toothbrush behind low railings. I opened the door leading into the engine room but found only a huge diesel engine there. I was looking for a bathtub or a shower and was beginning to worry that I'd be walking to the local Y every day for the next month. I walked back across the eighteen-inch hallway to the head, closed the door and latched it, unbuttoned my pants to sit down, whereupon Piscataqua fell to the floor. I was sitting on the cool

mahogany, watching Piscataqua's ears flit about when I glanced up and saw the shower head in the corner near the ceiling, pointed directly at me. This was the shower too. There was a drain set into the floor between my feet. To say the least I was surprised. I searched for the toilet paper and found it wedged under the rim of the sink, the only place in the room where it would avoid the spray from the showerhead. As I spread my legs to wipe, I bumped one knee into the sink drain and the other into the inward curve of the boat's hull. There was hardly enough room to pee in there, much less turn around while showering. It didn't take me long to appreciate the efficiency with which space is used on a yacht. When I stood up and turned around I had to hold my arms at my side like a tin windup soldier. There was no obvious flush handle on the tank, because there was no tank. A long brass arm protruded from the toilet's base though, with a shiny knob at its end that looked like it had been rubbed by human hands for good luck. I pumped on this, slowly once and then more quickly as I felt the suction, and this seemed to do the job. The bowl emptied and refilled. It would be hard to explain the satisfaction this gave me.

I wanted to explore the rest of the boat so I left the kitty in the head and closed the door. The engine room was large but with a low ceiling since it was directly beneath the raised salon. There were electric lines stapled to the walls, a bank of huge batteries, a generator in one corner, a tool chest in another. The center of the room was occupied by the engine itself, a gray brooding behemoth with a shaft leading out toward the stern of the boat. And although I could tell the engine was pristine because there was no rust or oil or grime of any sort, I could also see that it probably hadn't been used in years. There was a thick coat of dust on its upper surfaces and limp cobwebs swung from the engine to the floor. The belts were cracked and dry.

The floor, or sole, as Grace corrected me later, of the salon was covered with hooked rugs: sirens on a rock, a forested island, a sailing ship, all from the thirties and forties. Blue vinyl covered the corner settee. The curtains above were also blue, but lighter, faded and stained, a watercolor sky. The windows themselves slid in tracks; every other one could be opened. On the left side of the salon hung a mahogany ship's wheel about two feet in diameter with a big brass compass and other instru-

ments between it and the flat, vertical windshield. Two control levers were clearly marked FORWARD/REVERSE and THROTTLE. It seemed simple enough. The only things that looked complicated were three modern instruments mounted on the ceiling over the compass. One was clearly something like a CB radio, another had the logo SEALORAN and the third was a radar. What looked like the original brass key, worn smooth but dull from disuse, was in the ignition. I wanted to run my hands over everything here to come in contact with some of the experience. It was such a tiny room to contain so much possibility. I felt it was coming and going at the same moment that it had arrived.

Stairs on the right front of the salon led down in an L turn to the galley, which surprised me because it was completely modern. The sink was almost full-size; a microwave hung from an upper cabinet; a three-burner gas stove with oven and a small but modern refrigerator sat below a tile counter. All of the upper cabinets were fronted with stained glass.

As I poked through the cans in a lower cabinet, and just as I spotted three large bars of chocolate, I heard a muffled something, a squelched . . . something, a snore or a gurgle, but surely a sound made by a living creature other than me. I thought I was the only one on the boat. Grace hadn't come to my knock and I hadn't heard a sound till that moment. I stood up and stepped forward. Another head to starboard and a large locker to port. There was a door between this area and Grace's cabin, but it was wide open. I stepped in. Two bunks, one above another, to my left; a small desk and chair and another built-in dresser to my right. There weren't eighteen inches between the back of the chair and the bunk, and the aisle narrowed forward. I stopped here and listened. I could hear the cries of gulls outside, intermittent and sharp, sounding more like warnings than anything else at that moment. Occasionally I heard the faint murmur of water against wood. Perhaps, I thought, I had heard only the groaning of the dock against one of its pilings, or the compression of one of the fenders that protected the boat. But then I heard the sound again and I was almost unnerved. It was a guttural choking, a gasping futile rush of saliva, a slick wheeze of viscous air. There wasn't anyone in either of the bunks. No one beneath the desk. Four portholes, two on either side of the cabin, let in stark

shafts of light that veiled the far end of the room and a short narrow shutterlike door that led forward to the bow of the boat. The space beyond it couldn't be very large, I reasoned. The door itself wasn't more than a foot wide. Its brass knob was worn bright. I crept forward, stepping through the shafts of roiling dust motes, my hand trembling toward the knob. I felt like a great cowardly boob. As I held my hand inches away from the door I heard the snuffle again, lips sliding grotesquely over toothless gums, a dozen straws sucking out the last lick of blood in a paper cup. No light exited the slatted door.

"Is there anyone there?" I said, my voice breaking.

The snuffling stopped. There was instead a brushing sound of wire over wicker and then a muffled thumping

"I'm the new boarder, Charlotte," I said. "Are you OK?"

No answer. I touched the doorknob.

"I'm coming in, OK?"

Nothing, but the now persistent brushing and then a snort or a fart, air over mucous. I couldn't get the movie reel out of my head, the one flashing, "Perhaps Sweet George isn't dead." I turned the knob, opened the door outward a crack, and held it with a stiff arm in case someone tried to rush me. Then I pulled lightly back on the knob and let the door swing open. I leapt back to the far end of the cabin, even though I knew that anyone beyond that door had to be near death. It was dark in there. At first I couldn't see anything, but after a moment I made out a large coil of what must have been anchor line, a few old life jackets and some cardboard boxes. Then, from just inside the doorway, from the height of the door latch, a red satin pillow about a foot and a half square dropped to the sole with a dusty thump.

"Hello?" I said.

No answer. Then I heard a great rousing of a body, asthma ridden, corpulent. There was a groan, a flash of something white and hairy. I uttered a faint but crisp gasp, as if I'd just swallowed a bug. The spit slathered, strangled gatherings reached a new more awful level and I was on the verge of bolting, and vomiting as I bolted, when I came to the realization that the hair was in many ways similar to the shape of a dog, an obese pug-faced dog, a bulldog. He had jumped down off a locker and now sat on his satin pillow trying to look past his nose at me.

His upper lip was too short to cover his teeth and his teeth couldn't keep his tongue in his mouth. His nose was so high it had to drain into his eyes. There was drool. The fur wasn't actually white but sallow, like a nicotine stain. He shifted his rear haunches and suddenly I could see between his legs two inches of an unsheathed and almost fluorescently pink penis, glistening beneath the roll of his distended stomach. Before he could move again I rushed forward and slammed the door on the beast. I'd never been more disgusted by a living creature in my life. If I had to live like that I'd simply do away with myself. I'd excavated dozens of dog graves in my work, but none of them approached the horror of this dog's simple act of breathing, and when I thought of the possibility of his sneezing or drinking from a bowl of water I could only shudder. I closed the door to Grace's cabin, closed the door to my cabin, and tried not to think of the sounds on the other end of the boat.

I laid down on my bunk, little dry silent Piscataqua on my chest, and listened instead to what my life in that room would be like. It seemed as though I were lying upon another living being who was as mindful, as tense, as I was. The boat had been alive, of course, constructed as far as I could tell entirely of wood. It reacted to the slightest change in both the wind and water with movements I could feel in the same way I could tell when Jonah moved beside me in bed. There was a floating sensation, as if I were being rearranged or adjusted. When the tide ebbed *Rosinante* was pushed up against the dock, tubular PVC fenders protecting the hull, and held there with, I suppose, the force of several tons of pressure. When the tide flowed, the boat went taut on the lines stretching to the dock's galvanized cleats. I could hear these lines creaking and the slow groan of the boat's timbers, each fastener taking its turn to moan. Some form of friction was constant. The current sliding off the hull, perhaps four inches from my head, gurgled, shushed, and occasionally popped. As I lay there a small electric motor turned on somewhere beneath me, beneath the sole, and I heard a stream of water falling into the river outside the hull. It lasted for perhaps thirty seconds and the motor shut off. The boat had peed. It was silly, but it made me smile.

Across the compartment, on the foot of my roommate's bunk, was a mound of dirty clothes, mostly blue jeans and T-shirts, but also a huge

bra, pink socks with silver stars on them, and a pair of leopard panties, a really large pair. There were a couple of snapshots jammed into the woodwork near the head of the bunk: one of a rather scraggly young man in beard and overalls, and one of diminutive figures on a stage far, far away. Probably a rock band. I thought about looking into her dresser drawers and her locker but I didn't. There was very little else of a personal nature in the cabin. No books or magazines, posters or letters. Perhaps she knew Grace was showing the room and had cleaned up. I didn't think much more about her because I thought I'd meet her that evening after work. The only thing that worried me was that Grace said she was inquisitive, and I wasn't particularly in the mood to disclose the history of my anxieties at the time.

I'd left home, quit my job. I was the only person on the planet, outside of Grace, who knew where I was. It felt safe. I'd left at least some of my grief a thousand miles away. Another delusion, another pretty thought, shimmering above my head like the reflection of light off the water that entered through the windows of my snug cabin, my constantly shifting home.

I put Piscataqua back in the head after a while, with a dish of water and some food. I hoped he wasn't going to be a problem. I hadn't intentionally kept him a secret from Grace; I'd simply forgotten about him. I'd have to set up some kind of litter box so he wouldn't stink the place up. It was still too cold for him to live outside.

Before I went up to the restaurant for lunch I walked *Rosinante*'s deck. There were doors leading out both sides of the salon. Stanchions with lifelines ringed the boat. I walked up two steps to the raised forward deck. The roof over the galley was curved slightly so water would run off. There was a stained glass skylight over the forward cabin that I hadn't noticed from below. At the bow, over the lair of the dragon, were two anchors, a big Yachtsman and a smaller Danforth, and a capstan to help lower and raise them. I couldn't have named these anchors at the time. I picked up the nautical terminology from Grace over the next few months; she actually grimaced if I called the head the "bathroom," or the bow the "front." The roof over my cabin was curved also; storage lockers and a life-raft canister were mounted on one side and there was a bench that resembled a church pew on the other. A canvas awning on

brass standards extended over all this and six ten-gallon propane tanks bolted to the deck. The afterdeck was flat, with a hatch leading below. A ten-foot dinghy or tender hung on davits off the transom. It was a varnished shimmering jewel, this little boat, with lapstrake planking and an undeserved name, *Dapple,* Sancho Panza's donkey, in gold leaf on the mahogany transom. All of the woodwork on *Rosinante* was varnished as well, but most of the brass railing around the stern was dull, although its surface hadn't yet weathered to verdigris. The forward half of the deck was fiberglass, painted white; the stern was decked in natural teak. She was a beautiful old boat. The understanding that she was sound as well would come later.

I went forward as far as I could, leaned on a stanchion at the bow, and looked up and down the river. What made Portsmouth so interesting, beyond its picturesque colonial homes and history, was its working harbor. It was small enough that I could watch the whole of the port and not feel overwhelmed. I could follow individual lives moving back and forth, going out with the tide and coming back in, scooting between the islands and up into the estuaries, gunkholing along the riverbank, arriving for work at dawn or dusk and going home. I had no other desire for the next few months than to do the job of this scrutiny. I was spying, of course, in the safety of my aloneness, behind the veil of my unhappiness, whispering secrets to myself. I thought, at times, that I missed Jonah so much that I was gone too. What brought me out of this misconception was the ability to experience a pain beyond that present one, to know that pain comes to you in levels of understanding, that your mind won't let you proceed to the next level till you're comfortable with the present and accumulated anguish. I came across a love of moving water, and thought it would heal me with its simple movement, substance and time under the bridge, its persuasive argument of endless beauty. But I found that you have to drown before you can be saved. The water below me moved constantly, was never stagnant. Living this close to it, I hoped I wouldn't be either. The very briskness of the water, current and cold, made me feel clean. I whistled at a gull that swept under Memorial Bridge and beyond me toward the sea. I waved at a boy on a boat across the bay. And I wept down into the tide, and whispered names into the depths.

Part of the reason my mother-in-law's last suggestion upset me so was I did want to have Jonah's children. But it was his argument that we should be ready for them, fiscally responsible. I came to tears many times over the years with Jonah, but never more so than during our arguments over children. "We have to be able to afford them, Charlotte," he said. "It's not them," I said. "They usually come one at a time. We don't have to have the baby's full college tuition in the bank the day it's born." "Soon," he said. "Please, let's not put ourselves in a place that we'll regret. Please give me some time to make a home." And I'd relent. I let him have his way. Over and over. I don't know what I would have done if I'd known he was going to die. I mean, if he'd had a terminal illness rather than the accident. Perhaps he would have let me become pregnant then. Perhaps I wouldn't have wanted to. At any rate his death seemed to leave me terribly alone and terribly conscious of the things that could have been and the things that would never be. I don't know why we love people who refuse us things, but my love for Jonah was uncontrollable.

I knew at the time that I was turning, spiraling up or down, but when you're in the eye it's hard to tell the direction you're taking and therefore impossible to know which way you'll be facing when you spin slowly to a stop. I tried not to think of the future or the past, especially not my past, but concentrated on the rush of the present, the quick skid of the moment in and out of my peripheral vision. I relied heavily on bodily functions, letting my hunger, my bowels, and my weariness tell my mind where to move next. There was an odor of chowder from the restaurant above and suddenly I wanted a cracker so badly I'd have fought for it. I thought about a saltine, dimple stippled with unleavened undulations, the piquant and instant satisfaction of salt crystals, the flaky matrix of flour that softened between tongue and tooth, and finally of the broken perforations of a cracker's borders and the poignancy of the complete holes in its center, an artwork of food, a perfect bite. I bolted from *Rosinante*, felt her shy when my sole left her deck, and took two steps at a time up the gangway to the Smarmy Snail.

"A bowl of chowder," I told the waitress, "and crackers, lots of crackers, don't hold back on the crackers." She looked down at me quizzically as she left; there was no way that she could know I was indulging myself, having the world just as I wanted it, if only for that moment.

Grace walked by the windows of the restaurant as I ate, carrying a bag of groceries and apparently talking to herself. I couldn't hear her of course, but her lips moved as if in the midst of a virulent quarrel, point and counterpoint. She looked down as she walked and spoke, so I wondered if there weren't someone under the restaurant in a boat. She kept up the argument the length of the sidewalk and through the empty tables and chairs scattered on the deck. As she stepped onto the gangway she turned and pulled a small chain across the entrance, and then, I'm sure of this, nodded her head in a quick thrust of disdain to someone, something, directly behind the chain she'd just latched, a nod that somehow completely vanquished whatever apparition that had the audacity to argue with her. This was somewhat unnerving for a new boarder. Immediately after her nod she seemed to focus, saw me in the window, smiled broadly, and pointed to her sack of groceries mouthing the word, "dinner." Her face was once again the unstrained, composed model of septuagenarian grandmotherhood I'd met that morning. She held her coat closed and shuddered mockingly, gesturing kindly to me about the weather, and then with a quick wave turned to *Rosinante* below. My smile in return fell away to a slack jaw, open mouth, lip drool that I soaked up with my last cracker. My teeth came together with the realization that I was soon to spend the night with two people I didn't know, on a boat in a town where no one knew me. Grace and her boarder could have popped me into the Piscataqua at midnight and no one would ever have been the wiser. My mind took wide swings at that point in my life. As I paid my bill, I told the waitress, "I'm moving into the old boat at the dock. It's my first night. I was just wondering what time you open for breakfast?"

"Seven," she said.

"I'll be here," I said, and tried to smile, as if I were looking forward to my return. "7 A.M.," I said. "Look for me."

"Right," she said.

"It's nice to have a restaurant so close to my new home down at the dock below."

"Yes," she said, somewhat desperately, anxious to get back to her tables.

"And your name is?"

"Melissa."

"Melissa, see you in the morning. I'm Charlotte."

"Good-bye," she said.

"Bye bye," I replied, looking directly into her eyes, and burning my impression into them. If she didn't remember me in the morning, I thought, I'd beat her with a stack of their heavy laminated trifold menus.

I spent the remainder of the afternoon conducting new business: opening a checking account, renting a post office box, and acquainting myself with the stock of the two used bookstores on State Street. I wanted to fill the bookshelf above my bunk in a random order and then spend the next few months reading them from right to left. As I finished each one I'd date and initial the last page to show I'd been there, passed that way, a literary Kilroy. I bought a book at each store, and managed to tell the clerks my name, that I was new in town, and that I lived on *Rosinante* below the Smarmy Snail.

I didn't want to hide from the city I'd run to. I wanted to not only live in the landscape of Portsmouth and the river, but also to be a part of it, to establish myself. I'd never lived in a city before, or even a town of much size. I grew up on a small farm outside of Parksville, Kentucky and went to school in Danville, five miles from home, at Boyle County High School and later at Centre College. Jonah and I lived on the outskirts of Lexington in an old farmhouse on just enough land to call it a farm. I'd always driven a car to buy groceries, mail letters, to do any sort of errand, but here I was within walking distance of almost anything I desired. I found a small newsstand on Market Street and resolved to buy a newspaper there every day rather than subscribe. I made mental notes of places to get my hair cut, places to sit and read with a cup of tea, of benches, water fountains, public restrooms, and even of the location of a tattoo parlor. I had the thought that a little silver trowel on my ankle might be cute. I imagined relationships with shopkeepers, policemen on the beat, waitresses. I'm Charlotte: I'm one of you. There goes Charlotte with her *Portsmouth Herald*, down the sidewalk of Congress Street, waving at Freddy in MOES sub shop, standing at the river's edge to watch the ferry *Thomas Laighton* slide under Memorial Bridge. I wanted to leave an archaeological layer in Portsmouth to be known later as the Charlotte

strata, bits of my hair, skin, and nail, the broken dishes and other by-products of my existence: enough trash that I'd be recognized as a culture, a unique and once thriving way of life. People had lived on this point of land for perhaps twelve thousand years, most thickly for the past three hundred and seventy, and I was now one of them. I wondered if Portsmouth had a brick-buying scheme as part of its preservation-funding efforts: donate ten bucks and your name is impressed into one of the bricks that pave the streets and sidewalks. I'd splurge for a dozen and press my thumbprint into the soft clay for good measure. I'm here. I'm Charlotte. You don't know that my husband is dead, that I've been too sad lately almost to speak. But I've changed the subject. The subject is me alone, beginning again, setting up a new life, reading my own story out loud as it happened. On my walk back home I bought a bouquet of cut flowers for *Rosinante*'s salon table.

It was almost dark by the time I stepped back aboard the old cruiser. A passing boat rolled over a wake that rocked *Rosinante* at her berth, and I had the same queer sensation that she was alive when my foot touched her deck, that I'd stepped on something that breathed. The windows of the salon were fogged, but a dim light still shone from within. Heat and a faint smoke issued from the stack over the galley and was blown up-river. I pushed down on the brass lever with my free hand, and let myself in as quietly as possible. The mahogany table in front of the settee was set with silver, china and crystal, cloth napkins. Above the table an oil lamp that I'd thought merely decorative was burning. From the galley there was an odor of chicken and onions. The door to my cabin was closed, but there was a bar of light issuing from beneath it. I'd unbuttoned my coat and stepped toward the door when Grace spoke to me from the galley. I couldn't see her.

"Hello, Charlotte."

"Hello." I waited.

"You didn't tell me you had a cat, dear."

I froze. I couldn't tell if the electrical hum of her tone was one of annoyance or teasing. If I were to say simply, "I'm sorry," it would sound as though I'd meant to deceive her. I hadn't. The table was set for three. Grace hadn't come up the companionway to face me. I said, "You didn't tell me you had a dog, either, Grace. He's adorable."

Silence. The stirring of food.

"Fair enough," she said. "Chloe has already fallen in love with him anyway. Dinner in a few minutes."

"It smells wonderful," I said, and knocked on my cabin door. I'd been holding my breath since I stepped inside and thought I might faint. There was no answer. I knocked again. Still no answer. I opened the door slowly and crept down the stairs into the cabin. It was brightly lit with electric light. Chloe was lying on her back, in her bunk, eyes closed. A Walkman plugged into her ears. I could hear the tiny voices of the tiny band in the photograph above her head. Piscataqua was sound asleep, cradled between her breasts. When I dropped my books on my bunk, Chloe shot up, pulling the earphones off her head and sending the cat spread-eagled out into the center of the cabin.

"Oh, oh, oh," she yipped, dropping to her knees. "I forgot all about him." She stroked Piscataqua's arching back. "I'm sorry, kitty. Did stupid Chloe throw you across the room?"

"Hi," I said.

She looked up at me, almost cowering.

"It's OK," I said. "He's had much worse tumbles than that. Has he been much trouble?"

"Oh, no, not at all. Well, he pooped the cutest little turd you've ever seen over there in the corner, but I cleaned that up, no problem. He's a doll."

She stood up, holding Piscataqua in the nape of her neck.

"I'll get him a litter box tomorrow," I said.

"Sure. But when he gets older we'll teach him to go over the side, like Pinky."

"Pinky?"

"Grace's dog, Pinky. He just backs up to the gunwale. No mess, no bother. Grace says Pinky wouldn't know what to do with a patch of grass. He's always been a boat dog."

"I met him earlier. I thought he was dying," I said.

"No, not yet. But it's something you have to get used to. I mean, Pinky's existence. But he's a sweet dog. Grace took him from another couple on a boat when they thought he was dying years ago. It's just that his packaging isn't all you could hope for. I understand him because my

package isn't all it could be either. I'm Chloe." She held out her hand.

"Charlotte." Holding her hand was like grasping a link sausage before it's cooked. Her legs were proportioned to her height, but her torso was oversized, almost blocky. She was very young, perhaps seventeen, and her face, although pudgy, was beautiful, glowingly pale with patches of peach in her cheeks. Bright green eyes. Unfortunately her hair was in a crew cut, dyed blond over a quarter inch of brown roots. Her ears were as tiny and bunched as a baby's fist. She wore faded overalls over a yellow T-shirt. The arms protruding from the shirt were thin but muscled. Hers seemed to be a body built of spare parts. I couldn't help but wonder how differently her parents must have been modeled, a Laurel and Hardy union producing Chloe, light limbed, heavy bodied, angelical face.

"It will be great to have some company in the stern quarters," she said, smiling, her teeth white and as evenly spaced as the rows of tombstones at Arlington National Cemetery. I couldn't see any caries, filled or otherwise, and the third molars, or wisdom teeth, hadn't yet come in. The third molars are genetically unstable teeth that may erupt at any time from age eighteen till death.

"How long have you been on board?" I asked.

"Since I left home, about three months." She looked down at the sole when she said this, and handed Piscataqua to me. But after only a moment of silence she turned back up, smiling her marble memorial smile.

"Do you like it here?" I asked.

"It's great. I'm close to work. It's cheap. I mean you can't beat a hundred dollar a month waterfront apartment, can you?"

"I couldn't," I said.

"Dinner, dinner, dinner," Grace chanted, banging in time on a black pot with a wooden spoon.

We sat down to settings of antique flow mulberry stoneware, the Eastern Birds pattern by Davenport. Staffordshire potters produced it from about 1830 to 1850. Mulberry can sometimes fool you because the color can range from a light purple to almost black, and many of the patterns were also done in flow blue. The crystal was recent K-Mart and the flatware by Towle, the Paul Revere pattern. We each had a cut glass

open salt of the Victorian period, and a linen napkin with corners of hand-sewn lace. Each piece was set off by the dark red grain of the varnished mahogany table and the soft oily light from the lamp above. In the center of the table, on a crocheted doily, was a mangled and burned pot holder on which sat a huge black steaming cauldron. I set the flowers next to it.

"How nice. Help yourselves," Grace ordered.

Chloe bowed her head and rushed through, "God is great, God is good, let us thank him for this food."

"No religion at the table, Chloe," Grace said.

"Oh, nynh," Chloe snipped. She took the big wooden spoon, stirred the contents of the pot and scraped chicken, broccoli, onions, carrots, and celery out onto her plate, and I followed her at Grace's nod. There was some garlic in the stir as well. I believe it was the best meal I've had in my life. The chicken was braised till it was almost crisp at the edges, and the broccoli snapped off with a clip of the incisors. Chloe drank milk while Grace and I drank a white wine of uncertain vintage. The Smarmy Snail had given Grace several bottles that had lost their labels.

"It's warmer in here than it was this morning," I said.

"Heat's on now," Grace said. "We've got propane heat that Sweet George installed before he died. I try to conserve during the day."

We didn't speak for a few moments. There was only the clink of forks against the heavy old plates, and the wind buffeting the windows of the salon.

Grace put down her glass, tilted her head slightly, then said with some nonchalance, "Oops, I've let the stink bird fly."

I stopped in midchew, a slice of carrot saved momentarily from the crush of molars.

"Mildred," Grace added.

Milk began to dribble out the corners of Chloe's mouth. She pressed her lips harder together and little jets of milk sprayed out across the table. I smiled, still holding the carrot in abeyance. Grace now smiled. Chloe lowered her head, opened her mouth and what was left of the milk drained onto her plate, which allowed her finally the relief to gush with laughter, to pinch her nostrils closed with one hand and to

touch the middle of her forehead with her hitchhiking thumb. After this, still holding her nose with the one hand, she pointed at me and said, "You ate it."

"Did not," I said, looking from one to the other of them.

"Did too," Grace said. "Chloe clearly beat you. You ate it."

I decided not to argue but did choose to pinch my nostrils. In a few seconds Chloe tested the air tentatively and nodded an "all's clear" to me.

"Are there any other rules I should know?" I asked.

"A boat's concentrated," Grace explained. "When you birth one you own it, and must give it a name. It gives the rest of us a chance. When you go number two, always light a match afterwards."

"I'm still learning," Chloe said. "One of my favorites is, 'Never load a gun on board with the barrel pointing down.'"

"I'll remember that if I ever get a gun," I said.

"It's not just rules," Grace added. "It's a way of life, living on the water, and you'll have to adapt. Over at Strawbery Banke there's a family of sparrows that hop from grille to grille of the cars in the parking lot. They enter the grille, and come out fatter. They're eating the insect roadkill off the cars' radiators. They've adapted, making themselves a rich easy life off a parking lot. Here, on *Rosinante*, you'll learn to conserve your movements, to live in a smaller world, but it has its rewards."

"Shorter trip to the fridge," Chloe said.

"I love the water," I said unblinkingly.

"It smells bad sometimes," Chloe said.

"Me too, I love the water too." Grace slid about half of her food back into the pot. "Just not hungry," she said.

"You need to eat more than that, Grace," Chloe whispered harshly.

"You eat it." Grace poured herself more wine and called, "Pinky, Pinky, Pinky baby."

I swallowed quickly. "Why Pinky?" I asked.

"Oh," she said, "It's just an obscene reference to his pistol. He never has been able to keep the thing sheathed." Grace put her plate on the salon sole and called again, "Pinky, plate on the sole."

There was a sickening, bowel emptying slush of air over tongue from the companionway as Pinky flushed over each step. He reached the

salon, paused to rest with a great asthmatic gasp for breath, sneezed once and again, and then finally stumbled toward Grace's dish as if he were falling off a cliff. I even looked to see if he had all four of his legs because his walking seemed so uncoordinated and painful.

"Pinky's a little past his prime," Grace whispered.

"He had a prime then," I said.

"Oh, he was at stud for a couple of years. Won shows."

"Really?" I said. I felt at that moment something horribly akin to being groped, listening to the simple act of a dog licking a plate. It was one long unbearable slurp with gaseous ejaculations of dog pleasure at its beginning and end.

"Gross, hunh?" Chloe said, her hand over her nose and mouth.

"He can't help it," Grace cooed and bent down to stroke his flaccid skin. Pinky looked up at her then and I saw, unmistakably, absolute love in his eyes. I was immediately humbled. I apologized.

"He's beautiful, isn't he, Grace?"

"Of course he is. He's Pinky." She wiped his chin and jowls with her linen napkin. "You can go back to your pillow now, baby."

Pinky turned, took one heavy step back toward the galley. And paused. Piscataqua was in his path.

"Piscataqua," I whispered. But it was too late. He arched his back, hissed and spit at Pinky twice. Then he freaked, bounced off the ship's wheel, the settee cushion, clawed his way up a curtain, and finally leaped across a third of the cabin and landed in Grace's blue hair. He dug into her scalp with all claws sprung and held on for fear of a slow-moving dog. Grace calmly uttered a fifteen second screech of pain, like a siren in the distance, and reached up, pinching the loose fur of Piscataqua's neck. He released his grip and allowed himself to be put in my lap. Pinky had never moved from where he'd paused when he first saw the cat. Once Piscataqua was in my lap, the dog continued on his mizzling fall back to his pillow.

As Chloe poked through Grace's hair, looking for wounds, I apologized. "I'm so sorry, Grace. I guess Pinky's the first dog Piscataqua's ever seen. Or maybe another dog traumatized him. I'm sorry."

"That cat's going to end up in the middle of a river in more ways than one," she said. "Out of my hair, Chloe."

"I'm just trying to help," Chloe pouted.

"Well, the damage is done. Raking my hair won't improve things."

Chloe continued to dig through Grace's blue wisps while I held the cat. I could see Grace's face reaching a boil. Her eyes narrowed; her lips worked themselves up under her nose; her nose began to whistle.

"Lean over into the light, Grace," Chloe said, and she tugged at her hair as if it had burrs lodged in it as well.

Grace reached for the big wooden spoon. She yelled, "Girl, you're about as deep as a cookie sheet," and whapped Chloe on the back of her hand, and then whapped her on the hip, and when Chloe rubbed her hip Grace took advantage of her and whapped her on the shoulder.

"Stop it, you crazy old woman," Chloe screamed, and ran to the far side of the table.

Grace held the spoon at her side for a moment, then dropped it back into the pot. "I'm not crazy," she said.

And quickly, too quickly I thought, Chloe answered, "Of course you're not, Grace. I'm sorry."

"Did I hurt you, Chloe, honey?"

"No, of course you didn't."

"I didn't mean to hurt you."

"Well, you didn't, and that's all there is to it, Grace."

"I try to keep all the demons off the boat. They usually don't follow me into the water," Grace said.

"This wasn't a demon, Grace," Chloe answered. "It was a person pissed off at another person. It happens to lots of people. Lots of people get mad at me. I annoy them somehow. I don't do it on purpose. But I'm deeper than a cookie sheet. I know what's going on. I'm at least as deep as a saucepan." Chloe parted her lips enough to show a single row of tombstones, sheepish privates and corporals.

"The hardest part is understanding what's happening to you," Grace said. She was looking directly at me. "If you went completely senile at the snap of a finger it would be all right. Little harm done. But when it's gradual, when you slip in and out, when you lose moments, that makes it hard. I'm always trying to remember something I've forgotten, trying to resurrect a little death, to make myself immortal by the power of my memory. It's all very humbling."

"Grace is an artist," Chloe said.

I noticed the remains of food beginning to dry on our plates, a momentary flicker of the oil lamp.

"Really?" I said, turning from Chloe to Grace and back to Chloe.

"She paints things that are so real they fool you."

"Like trompe l'oeil?" I asked.

"I used to do faux work. You know, grain painting, painting a baseboard so it looked like marble or a different kind of wood. I worked on some of the houses at Strawbery Banke. But now I've gotten into Harnett: dollar bills, ticket stubs, more detailed things."

"But she doesn't work on canvas much, Charlotte," Chloe said. "She paints on walls and on tables, on sidewalks, stuff like that."

"The best way to fool someone is to paint something they want to see: a twenty dollar bill protruding from a street grate works because almost everyone expects to be lucky someday. Why else would they play these lotteries? Another way is to paint something they only see peripherally, such as a light switch. You paint a switch, you paint a smudge around the switch as if it's been used, then you go back in a year or two and if your work is good you'll find the painted smudge replaced by a real one. I want to paint a puddle of water on a street, with a nickel in the middle of the water. I want to paint it so persuasively that people break their knuckles putting their hand in the puddle going after that nickel. Water—that's the hardest—getting water down just right. You have to know it's there but still be able to see through it."

"There's a window on the side of a brick building downtown. But when you get close enough," I said, "it's just the brick wall."

"Grace did that," Chloe said.

Grace nodded. "How close did you get before you knew?"

"I don't know. Six or seven feet, I guess."

"If it had been good work, you would have bumped your forehead on the masonry trying to see inside," Grace sighed. "I had a lot of trouble with that wall. The brickwork was so uneven it cast shadows."

"But isn't it great that she can make a living at something she likes to do?" Chloe said, looking at me. "She gets offers all the time to paint people's entrances, their kids' rooms, all kinds of stuff."

"What do you do, Chloe?" I asked.

"I work up at Small World on Market Street. We sell all sorts of cheap, funky gimmicks: windup penises, toys, environmental bags and books, sandals, posters of Marilyn Monroe. We get lots of tourists. I'm just a clerk but I try to make it interesting by asking the customers questions, taking polls."

"She asks the same question of everybody for a whole day, and keeps track of their answers in her journal," Grace explained.

"I just try to get a consensus," Chloe said.

"What do you ask them?"

"All kinds of things. I ask them when they check out, so my results are sort of skewed. I mean, the only people in my polls are people who'd buy the things we sell, and it's not run-of-the-mill stuff. I mean, there's no Polo or Mattel logos. We sell a lot of breast coffee cups, the kind where you drink from the nipple. A lot of it's from overseas."

"Well, do you ask them who they're going to vote for, or what?" I asked.

"Oh, no, nothing like that. For instance, one day I'll ask everyone what their favorite color is, or if they believe in angels, or if they think there could be any reason their house might be burning down at that instant. A different question everyday. It keeps things interesting."

I nodded, stared down at Piscataqua.

"Where do you work, dear?" Grace asked.

With each moment that evening I better understood the compactness of a boat, how you were always squeezing by someone. I didn't want to lie to them. I wanted to continue listening, to hear how other lives worked.

"Well," I said, "I'm not working anywhere right now. I just moved here from Kentucky. I quit my job a couple months ago after my husband died. I was, I am, an archaeologist. I worked with the University of Kentucky Anthropology Department as an excavator on digs."

"I'm sorry about your husband," Grace said, and she slid her palm across the table and touched the back of my hand.

"Thank you."

"Do you have family here?" Chloe asked.

"No. To tell the truth I came here to get away from them for a while."

"We're the only people you know in Portsmouth?" Chloe asked.

"Well, yes, so far."

"Maybe you can get work at the University of New Hampshire in Durham, or maybe at Strawbery Banke. They do some archaeology," Grace suggested.

"I think I'm just going to take it easy for a while," I said.

"Sure," Chloe said.

"How long were you married?" Grace asked.

"Six years."

"And his name?"

"Jonah," I said.

"Sweet Jonah," she said.

My eyes began to burn, but I looked straight at Grace and said, "I'm sorry about George."

"Yes, me too," she said, smiling. "I'm sorry to say it won't get much better for you, I mean if you miss him. I'm almost dead and I still miss George."

"Grace and her husband were sailing *Rosinante* from Florida to Prince Edward Island when he had a heart attack," Chloe said. "She's been right at this dock ever since. They'd sold their house to buy *Rosinante* when he retired, so Grace just decided that this would be her house."

"You don't know how to drive the boat?" I asked.

"I was first mate, cook, and deckhand. I might be able to get the engine started, but I wouldn't know what to do next. I like it here. I feel like George is still on board."

"I wish you wouldn't say that, Grace," Chloe shushed. "It gives me the creeps, ghosts and stuff like that."

"He's a good ghost, though," Grace insisted.

"This old boat creaks and groans too much already, Grace. I don't want to hear another word."

"Even so, if you ever hear anyone on deck at night, especially during the middle watch, that will be Sweet George, protecting the three of us."

"Grace," Chloe almost cried, "I'm going to bed, right now."

"He wore a soft rubber shoe," Grace said, "so it sounds like a mouse squeak against the teak."

"That's it." Chloe rose with her dishes and carried them to the galley. Grace and I followed her. I offered to do the dishes but she wouldn't hear of it.

"It's late. You go on. It's your first night on board. You'll sleep like a baby. No better sleeping than on a boat. Besides, if you chipped my Mulberry I'd have to sic Pinky on you."

I followed Chloe to our cabin and closed the door behind us.

"Do you really only pay a hundred dollars a month, Chloe?" I asked.

"Yes, but I think my father pays her more. Grace won't admit it, but I think he does."

"Why?"

She sat on her bunk and blew air between her teeth. "Well, I was living in sort of a bad place when I first left home. My folks knew about it and didn't like that part of my life either. I left home because they didn't like my boyfriend. But anyway, in walks Grace at work one day, and wants to put up a room for rent sign. I snapped this place right up. After I moved in, I remembered my father talking about Grace. He's got a lobster boat. I guess he met her somewhere. Anyway, after I paid Grace once I saw a deposit slip for two hundred sticking out of her wallet the next morning. You're paying two hundred, aren't you?"

"Yes."

"My folks and I fight a lot, but they worry about me. It's part of why they're so mad at me, because they have to worry. I tell them not to. It's not my fault that they worry. It's my dad's way of caring for me."

"Why aren't you in school?"

"I've graduated. I took summer courses and got out in three years. I wasn't very happy in high school. You know, fat girl in a skinny-girl world."

I smiled because she was smiling.

"You didn't have any children?" she asked.

"No," I said. "We were going to. Someday."

"Maybe it's good that you didn't," she said. "They would have missed their father."

I didn't know what to say to her, so I said what I thought most people wanted to hear, how Jonah died. "He was killed in a car wreck.

37

His car went off an embankment. He drowned in a shallow creek. He was coming home."

"You and Grace are both widows," Chloe said. "But you can start over."

She said what she said with such sincerity, such openness, that it was hard for me to feel that she was intruding. I didn't believe there was an insensitive bone in her big soft body. She seemed to be glaringly honest. I nodded at the sole and began to undress.

"Do you mind, Charlotte, if I pull the curtain to? I'm sort of shy."

"Of course not. I've undressed in front of so many people I forget it's not the norm. Out in the field there's not much privacy. Come here, Piscataqua."

Chloe slid the curtain across our tiny apartment and I finished pulling on my flannel pajamas. I crawled into my bunk, dragging the cat with me, and after a moment Chloe opened the curtain again. In the split second it took her to reach for the light switch I saw her blocky form shrouded in floor length white chiffon, then there was darkness. I heard her situate herself in the bunk with many sighs of satisfaction.

"Have you ever heard Sweet George?" I asked.

"I don't know. Once I thought I heard someone on deck. It was very late and I'd awakened from a dream about my boyfriend. It sounded sort of clumsy for a ghost, so I think it was my boyfriend."

"Is he the guy in the picture?"

"Yeah."

I tried not to sound provisional when I said, "He's cute."

"My mother thinks he looks like an ax murderer," she said. "Did your parents like your husband?"

"They said they did."

"What does that mean?"

"It means they said they did."

"Oh."

Light oozed in through the portholes on either side of the dresser mirror, a viscous industrial light from Memorial Bridge. As my eyes adjusted, I could make out Chloe lying on her back, only the blanched oval of her face above the blanket, as if it floated on dark water. Occasionally cars thrummed over the steel grating of the central section of Memorial.

It sounded like many birds suddenly taking wing. This is what it's going to be like, sleeping here, I thought: this light, these sounds. There was a thick thud then through the hull of the boat. I sat up.

"It's OK, Charlotte," Chloe whispered. "It's just the tide. Sometimes things come along and bump into the boat, a board or maybe some ice from upriver. The ice in the creeks is starting to break up."

I laid back down then, waiting for the next frozen moment of sound, waiting in the dark till I descended into an immaculate void of sleep, floating above the water.

≈

I did sleep well on *Rosinante*, whether the cause was the action of the water or the weariness of my bones. I came home from my made-up errands around the city to her warm wooden womb and slept as if unborn. Chloe said she slept the same way, but analyzed it as a reaction to the constant strain put on our bodies by the rocking of the boat, however minimal it might be; our attempts to remain level required us to always exert one muscle, then its opposite, as if we were continually climbing a steep hill. Even in our sleep we constantly worked, every minute degree of heel in *Rosinante*'s hull counteracted by a muscle exerting an equal force to keep the body in place. At any rate it was a blessing, a full night's sleep: no crashing cars, no cries for help, no one following me everywhere I went.

≈

I called my mother after a week, told her I was OK and where I was, begged her not to tell Richard and Mary. I asked her to forward my mail and check on the house occasionally. She was concerned in her way, but we'd always trusted one another, my parents and I. Richard and Mary had contacted the police, claiming I was missing, but Mom had refused to allow a search. My mother knew I was only sad, not lost. She said it would be hard for her to keep my whereabouts from them, but that she'd try. They'd called her twice a day since I left. When they saw the FOR SALE sign go up in front of the house, they caused a scene at the

realtor's office and threatened a receptionist with a lawsuit if she didn't give them the keys to my home. So I didn't tell Mom where I was living, not the particulars, gave her only the p.o. box address.

"I can't tell them if I don't know, can I?" she said. "Charlotte, you can come back home. I mean, live here with your father and me again."

"I know that, Mom. It's beautiful here. Maybe you and Daddy can come up this summer. I just feel like my past is further away here. That it's easier to deal with."

"Call again soon, when your father is home so he can talk to you. He's been so worried about you he doesn't sleep."

"OK." I paused for a moment.

"What, honey?"

"Would you take some flowers to Jonah's grave for me? Maybe you could do it tomorrow morning and I could think about you doing it then."

"I'll do it tomorrow morning. I'll do it at ten o'clock sharp."

"Thanks, Mom."

"Please be careful, Charlotte."

"I will."

"I don't want to hang up from you, honey."

"Mom, I'm fine. I'm feeling better. I'll call again soon. This weekend sometime."

"OK."

"Bye bye."

"Bye bye, baby."

I hung up quickly so she wouldn't hear me crying.

≈

I enjoyed the routine, and the lack of routine, of those first few weeks in Portsmouth. Of the three of us, only Chloe had to be somewhere at a given time, but even her schedule varied through the week. Usually we were awakened by the other boat on our dock, by the clomping of the fisherman's boots or the rumbling of the engines. Harry owned *Fern*, a big steel trawler, and when he cranked her engines over, my teeth

vibrated in their sockets. Harry and Grace were neighbors and good friends. When she introduced me to him one afternoon, he immediately lumped me in with Grace and Chloe, saying, "There's three of you now, is there? The Three Graces." And he smiled a full-denture smile at me, pumping my arm like the knob on a head. Later my hand smelled like raw fish and I thought, well, I've met a fisherman. Harry always wore tall rubber boots that came up to his crotch, and a gimme cap sporting a fishing co-op logo of a dead cod. He never failed to ask Grace if there wasn't something she needed. Usually it went something in the form of, "How's the old girl, old girl?" Which was an inquiry into the health of not Grace but *Rosinante*. He and his crew might be out for days or overnight, and often as not he brought us something from his nets, wrapped it in newspaper, and left it on *Rosinante*'s deck. He was far too young for Grace, but acted as if he weren't. "Christ," he'd yell, "Don't tell the wife, Grace dear." Then he'd stomp up the gangway, leaving his crew to wash down the boat.

In the mornings, while Chloe dressed alone in our cabin, Grace and I would pack her a lunch, usually leftovers from the evening before, but always with a healthy chunk of Hershey's chocolate, broken off one of the big bars in the cabinet. We'd all have breakfast then, cereal and toast or English muffins, and over our food we'd try to come up with Chloe's poll for the day. Her journal was thickly bound accounting paper, pea green and ruled, so she could accumulate totals of yeas or nays. More particular responses, say, to a question like, "Do you think the death of one bug changes the course of world events and why?" were written in longhand on the backside of the ruled columns. Sometimes we took poll questions from the morning's paper. "If the navy yard closed would you stay in this area?" or "Do you think gays should be allowed in the military?" or "If Jesus were to return, could you recognize him?" There were times when Chloe's poll was more or less personal. One of these was an entire page of positive responses to the question, "Do you think I'm pretty?"

"I needed to give myself a lift," Chloe explained.

Grace and I looked at each other, knowing that if she'd gotten even one negative response it would have been disastrous. Chloe was overweight and apologetic, acutely aware and inexcusably forgiving. Occa-

sionally Grace told her, "You know, the most long-term side effect of eating is dying."

"It's all right, Grace, I understand how the world treats fat girls."

"But you've got a boyfriend," I said. I hadn't met him yet, but Grace told me he did exist.

"I'm not talking about Roger. Besides, Roger is as skinny as I am fat. Who else would have him? I'm not mad at the world. I understand it. Hell, I walk down the street myself, see an ugly person or a big fat one, and think, cripes, what a cow. People can't help it. So you have to get to know them. You have to snake your way into their psyches so that they have to deal with you as another intelligent being and not a lump of flesh. It just takes work to be fat and happy. More work than it takes someone like you, someone pretty. But it's not your fault you're pretty anymore than it's mine that I'm fat. I just have to smile more than you do to get results."

Grace said, "When I was young, if there was a man I was interested in, I'd walk right up to him with an apple in my outstretched hand and just hiss, 'Sssssss,' like a snake, and if he was brave enough to take the apple I knew he was worth the effort."

"You were a vamp," I said.

"I was faithful to my desires."

"Did many of them take the apple?" Chloe asked.

"Very few. Most of them backed away, asking questions. They were afraid."

"Did George take the apple?" I asked.

"He took my hand, with the apple in it, pulled me toward him, and bit my arm." Grace grinned with pride.

"Wow," I sighed.

"You see," Chloe said, "You have to take the initiative."

"I could never do something like that," I said. "Even in response. I'd be one of the ones who backed away. I'm afraid of snakes."

"But you're so beautiful," Chloe said. "You could be forward all the time and always be successful."

I blinked. "It's just not in my nature. Living people frighten me. I'd much rather deal with things, artifacts. I'd much rather deal with dead people."

"You weren't afraid of Chloe and me," Grace said.

"I was terrified. But I wanted to be near the water so badly I overcame it. I'm going to stick to you like glue now. I'll never move away."

"What are you afraid of?" Chloe asked.

"Oh, I'm really not afraid of you two. I'm afraid I won't confront my fears."

"Why are you afraid of that?"

"Because I've done it before, failed to face things."

"What do you fear?" Grace asked. "I'm sorry for asking."

"Now?" She nodded. "My past."

"Why?" Chloe asked.

"Chloe," Grace chided.

"Because it won't come together," I said. "It won't take a shape I can handle. And I can't change it."

Grace said, "Why do people treat the past as if it's fact? Why not confront it with an imagination. I think the past is as malleable as the future."

"What are you afraid of, Grace?" Chloe asked.

"Dying, maybe," she shrugged, almost happily.

Chloe said, "I'm afraid of love. Isn't that romantic?"

"You're both silly girls," Grace said.

"That's another thing," I said. "I don't feel like a girl anymore. I feel old. I mean, no offense, I just feel tired a lot."

"That will go away," Grace said. "You've got an ice jam of emotions. With time it will melt and you'll feel young again. I promise."

I looked over at Chloe, took her journal and pen, and put one more tic in the yea column. "You're very cute, darling," I said.

≈

I read in the mornings: Mays's *Early Portsmouth History* (1926), Brewster's *Rambles About Portsmouth* (1859), and from a fine leather-bound 1825 edition of Nathaniel Adams's *Annals of Portsmouth*. The area's written history began as early as 1603 when Martin Pring, an Englishman, visited the coast and rowed up the Piscataqua ten or twelve miles. I wanted to familiarize myself with the old city so that on my afternoon

walks I'd have some historical sense of the things I saw. Portsmouth seemed to be full of opportunities for an historical archaeologist, almost four hundred years of recorded occupation. Many eighteenth-century residences and commercial buildings were still standing. Portions of the city had been burned and rebuilt on three separate occasions, in 1802, 1806, and 1813, which should have left substantial debris over which new structures were built, predominantly of brick. Puddle Dock, a tidal creek extending into Strawbery Banke, had been completely filled and built over at the beginning of this century. In my mind it formed an almost perfect time capsule, every artifact pickled in mud beneath a protective layer of dirt and debris. I supposed that one could dig on any square meter of the city and find some evidence of culture. I had worked mainly at prehistoric sites in Kentucky but also on a few historical salvage digs in Lexington, before a new structure destroyed what information could be gathered about an old. I found myself intrigued by the vast variety and amount of debris found at historical sites, and how far removed we are from our own culture at a distance of only a century or two. I felt a poignant connection to every sherd I came in contact with, almost as if it were a personal message to me, asking me to understand. As I walked through Portsmouth, stepping to one side of the sidewalk for the living, I walked arm in arm with the dead, among the tangible evidence they'd lived lives: their homes and shops, the names of their streets, our stony and silent inheritance that requires a true diligence to decipher. I knew I was only walking on the surface of the past. All of the houses and shops had been rebuilt many times over the years, and even the names of streets had changed. The only material that remains in the same state as it was left to us by our forebears, when you can find it, is their trash. Trash is honest. Graves are sometimes honest, but you can't always rely on their veracity. They may have been plundered. They may contain artifacts far more or less meaningful than those used in everyday life. I've never yet excavated a trash pit that lied to me about the people who made it.

So I read in the mornings, with a pencil behind one ear and a trowel behind the other. And from time to time I'd look away from the page and think about what Jonah and I had left behind, what an archaeologist might find in three hundred years. She'd find very little. After searching through historical archives and straining every spoonful of

soil at our house site, after noticing the date on Jonah's headstone and the one on mine, if she's thorough and intuitive, if she used all the power of her empathy she might understand dimly that I cried over the ebb of the tide, over the mud and shell and rock revealed.

After Jonah was gone all there was left to do was analyze our marriage. I didn't need Richard and Mary to remind me of him because he was continually on my mind. His presence seemed unavoidable. He filled my consciousness more completely dead than alive; before his death he'd leave for work, or I would, and the next eight or nine hours were mine alone: afterwards he was always around the house, underfoot, constantly calling, asking. And I wanted to think of him, felt that I owed this at least to him. But it was painful, because I couldn't leave it at memory, wasn't able to cry or smile and be done with it for the moment. I ate my remembrance and regurgitated, ate and cramped with poisoning. In the end I was able to see it as a healing process, but during its interminable excavation and reburial it seemed anything but a coming to terms with understanding. The heaviest cross was allowing myself to understand. Because what I most wanted after all of my agonizing research was simply to deny my conclusions.

≈

As the temperature rose through the day, and my eyes began to water and blur with reading, I came out of my cabin wrapped in swaddling clothes and put myself on the river. Jumping from my basket I walked the banks of the Piscataqua at low tide, searching for signs of civilization, clues to my past. I frequently walked down Marcy Street to Mechanic, past Point of Graves, an early cemetery, and over the bridge to Pierce's Island, where the shore was rocky and firm. In places here the beach is more brick than rock, chunks and halves of what I call Portsmouth red, abraded and broken but still retaining the semblance of building blocks, heartbreakingly man-made. They scatter the shoreline and reach out into the murkiness of the river. There isn't a trace of the mortar that once held them together in the shape of a house or building or bridge, no imprint of a maker or even the paw print of the brickyard dog. I wandered over the beach, occasionally bending over to pick up a

sherd of pottery or a bit of rusting iron. Rivers, up until very recently, were most cities' cheapest ash bins. The Piscataqua, at six knots of current, would carry off a dump-truckload of garbage quite rapidly. The sediments would be deposited up- or downriver, depending on the direction of the tide. So although provenience will always be in dispute, a river's banks are good beachcombing, if you're looking for something someone else has thrown away, be it a body or a bowl. The shores of Pierce's Island have been pretty well picked over because the island is also a park, but I was still able to come up with various sherds of nineteenth- and twentieth-century pottery, a piece of eighteenth-century creamware plate rim, and what really surprised me, an inch and a half segment of kaolin pipe stem, which dated sometime prior to the Revolutionary War. Kaolin pipe stems are very important to the historical archaeologist; if found in sufficient quantity, in situ, there are dating methods that can be applied. Through the years the pipe stem lengthened and its bore became narrower.

Over those first few weeks, I know I walked every street in the old part of the city several times, and ventured farther out to New Castle and Little Harbor, to Odiorne's Point in Rye, where the first settlement recorded along this part of the coast was established, and across Memorial Bridge to Kittery and Eliot. On all of my journeys I took pains to walk as close to that point of contact between the water and land as I could, trying to use the ebbing tide to my advantage so I could actually be where the water and the soil disputed rights. Through the spring and summer, I gathered a gallon jar of beach glass, brought home in pocketfuls of coldness and sand. I'm sure I trespassed on occasion, but the lure of a stoneware sherd with a line of cobalt across its salt-glazed surface was to me stronger than my fear of an owner-terrier stomping onto the front lawn with offended newspaper. Besides, I did try to stay to the tidal zone, free range to navigators, fishermen and hunters. If you're willing to walk shin-deep in waves or mud, very few property owners are likely to come in after you.

≈

As I walked through the city I became alarmingly familiar with Grace's work, finding it when least expected, underfoot or in my peripheral

vision. It was there all along but she was so good at suggesting the real that it took several glances to question the authenticity of window boxes full of blooming flowers in March. Her work was in shop windows: new trunks grain-painted as antiques and new furniture worn with paint to represent the greasy hands and abrasive bottoms of two hundred years' use. On Bow Street, on the sidewalk in front of Points East Properties, there was a wallet lying open, the corners of various credit cards exposed. I bent over. Grace had lost it there. It looked as if a thousand people had tried to pick it up, the paint chipped by fingernails at a shadowed corner. In front of the Portsmouth Athenaeum, her canvas a grainy concrete, she'd painted a fat pigeon trying to dislodge a cigarette butt from a crack. If it had moved when I stepped over it, I wouldn't have been surprised. Down on the dock in front of Harbour Place there was a series of U.S. bills and coins protruding from splits in the lumber or blown up against the granite base of the building, and a receipt for paint and brushes lying among other real litter near a trash can. I stopped at each dollar bill or silver quarter, alarmed and then full of wonder. It was outright deception, with all the brashness of a con artist. It made me wonder if the planking I stood on was real, or was merely boards painted on cheesecloth, boards painted on water.

Everyone in town knew Grace or knew of her. She'd painted murals in several shops and restaurants, worked at Strawbery Banke on restorations, as well as her street projects, which, as far as I could tell, were gifts to the city. But her work was overshadowed by her idiosyncrasies. She always walked the streets briskly, head down, gesturing abruptly with her hands and arguing with someone who seemed to tread at her heels. At her heels because she stopped occasionally, turned and held her hands out as if to fend off this person who'd blundered into her, as if he or she walked with head lowered as well and hadn't seen her stop. I'd see her at errands, and she might pass within inches of me on the sidewalk and never know I was there. Her tone wasn't of rage but rather of exasperation, as if she were arguing with an idiot or the sidewalk itself. No one in town seemed to be afraid of her, except perhaps the tourists. They gave her a wide berth on the streets and pulled their children closer. I stopped her once in Market Square, under the tall steeple of North Church, when she stepped past me muttering, "No, no, no, that's not it at all."

I had to skip to catch her because she walked so quickly. Taking her arm I said, "Grace." She jumped as if I'd been a flock of birds taking flight at her feet.

"Charlotte, dear," she smiled.

"Did you say something to me?" I asked.

"I don't think so."

"You passed me and said something," I said.

"Oh, well, I was probably talking to myself. I do that." She looked completely lost. "I'm sorry, dear," she finally said, looking back down at the sidewalk.

"You weren't talking to yourself," I said. "You were talking to some-body."

"I'll be all right when I get back home," she said meekly. "Let me get back to the boat."

"Do you want me to go with you?"

"If you'd like."

I took her arm and we walked back to *Rosinante* together, at a leisurely pace, and we talked pleasantly of dried flowers and the wind and of dinner. Whoever she'd been speaking with had left. Apparently she was able to keep these "demons" away while she was with someone or while she worked. And *Rosinante* seemed to have a soothing effect as well, safe harbor in a boat. And although I was intrigued with the iden-tity of her pursuer I never again pressed her because it seemed to con-fuse and upset her so.

≈

Occasionally on my afternoon walks I stopped in to see Chloe at work. I'd tell her of something found, a turn of a street or the cut of a shutter, something that intrigued me so much it allowed me to think only of it and nothing else, nothing past or future, a moment of presence. She'd show me an interesting entry in her journal or some new piece of stock, a glow-in-the-dark condom, or a ball that never bounced true. We'd talk about dinner because we both seemed to think about food a lot. I'd put on eight pounds during March, which I rationalized as a sign of health because it was mostly in the form of leg muscle.

I met Chloe's beau, as she called him from time to time, at her shop one afternoon. He was sitting behind the counter on her stool, and playing with a tiny BB pinball game. Chloe introduced us. He said, "Hi," and returned to the high intensity pressure of his game. He didn't seem unfriendly, just incapable. He was easily a foot taller than Chloe, with long limp black hair that needed to be washed, and long limp arms and legs that almost seemed emaciated but for the bumps of biceps, like socks wadded up under the skin. He wore a black nightwatch cap, a paint-spattered T-shirt and jeans so tiny at the waist they seemed childish. Roger still lived with his parents, although he was out of school and worked at a restaurant as a busboy. Chloe would meet him at his folks' house, or they'd leave from her job on dates, but she was always home early, by ten or eleven o'clock. Neither of them owned a car. We'd all be in bed by midnight, sleeping our deep sleeps.

Chloe seemed to be fond of him, but I was predisposed at that first meeting to dislike him. He was the great scandal of our boat: banned from setting foot on it again by Grace herself. While aboard he'd done two things within Grace's presence that she couldn't suffer. He'd thrown trash from *Rosinante*'s deck into the river, and a bare half hour later he'd struck Chloe. Grace forced him off the boat, down the dock and up the gangway at the point of a boat hook. Chloe, of course, was behind Grace all the way, forgiving him. I never brought the subject up, but Chloe did, and explained it in the same way you might explain a traffic accident. "I ran a red light and he hit me."

"What was the red light?" I asked.

"Well, he was just pouting really. He really tries to control this basic instinct he has of lashing out. I told him I wouldn't do something he wanted to do, and he'd just had a fight with somebody else and so he just reached out and slapped me. It only took an instant and then he was sorry for it. It was his last resort. It didn't have anything to do with me. I thought Grace was going to run him through."

"It had everything to do with you," I said. "He hit you."

"Well, he apologized, and he hasn't gone that far again."

"What does 'that far' mean?"

"Sometimes he shakes me. It doesn't hurt. Jonah never hurt you?"

"I don't think he ever considered it."

49

"But Roger is just passionate. If I have to put up with a little shaking, it's ok."

"You don't have to stay with him, Chloe," I said.

"Of course I don't. I want to. I know it's not good, what he did, but Charlotte, he likes me. He keeps me company. I'm not alone when I'm with him."

And so I broke the conversation off, turning back over in my bunk that night, partly because she was intractable and partly because of jealousy. I realized that for much of my marriage, even when Jonah and I were in physical contact, I was alone. Perhaps he was more alone than I was. At any event, it seemed supremely unfair at that moment that this fat girl and her hostile boyfriend should be happy together, while Jonah and I couldn't. I missed him a great deal then, wanting to make things up to him. Because at heart he was a good person. I loved him with an almost suicidal fear.

Early in April I woke in the middle of the night and heard the faint but rhythmic squeak of what I thought at first must be Sweet George pacing *Rosinante*'s decks. I lay listening for moments and when the sound didn't stop, I turned and whispered Chloe's name. She didn't respond. "Chloe," I whispered more harshly, turning in my bunk. As my eyes became accustomed to the dark I realized she wasn't in her bunk. I sat up in bed. Piscataqua was already at the door to our cabin, listening intently. Holding the latch firmly, I opened the door. The clock at the steering station read 1:30. I was worried about Chloe. She'd come home in one of her silent moods, disappeared behind her curtain, and was in bed before Grace and I had washed the dishes. Something must have been bothering her deeply for her to be pacing the deck in the middle of the night. The temperature was at freezing. I slid the salon door open silently on its brass track and stepped outside. The night was clear, with little wind, bright with a half-moon whose reflection ran down the length of the river. The only sound was that of the tide piling up against the hull of the boat. I looked forward but she wasn't there. I started to walk aft but I halted in midstep. At first I saw only Chloe's pink glistening knees over the aft bulkhead of the salon. She was lying on the church pew, her raised knees bare to the frigid air. But as I stopped I also saw the full but cleft moon of Roger's rear rise between her knees and fall again, rise, and fall.

It wasn't the soles of Sweet George at all but the squeak of the foam cushion on the pew. They themselves were both perfectly silent. The scooped-out, almost hollow cheeks of Roger's rear caught the light of the moon like craters. My stall in midstep felt like falling down a ladder, as if I'd never stop. But in between the thumps of my heart I kept looking, catching details, the taut skin of Chloe's knees, the steam rising from their silent breathings. I turned, picked up Piscataqua at the open door and slipped as noiselessly as I could back to my bunk. Minutes later I heard the creak of the companionway stairs under Chloe's weight, and I felt the boat sway to the loss of Roger's, and with one eye I watched her sweep across our cabin and slide into bed, leaving only a short sigh hanging in the air above her head before she fell fast asleep.

≈

The next morning I stepped down into the galley to help Grace with breakfast. I'd lived with her and Chloe for almost six weeks at that point.

I said, "Good morning."

And she jumped, let out a little yip of surprise.

"Who are you?" she asked.

I paused on the steps, looking at her eyes. She didn't know me.

"I'm Charlotte, Grace," I said slowly.

She put her spatula back into the skillet then and said, "Of course you are, dear," and neither of us said another word about it.

≈

In April I changed Piscataqua's name to Midden, an archaeological term for a stratum of refuse, which described his food preference. Midden didn't seem to mind the name change: he didn't respond to it when I called in the same way he hadn't responded to PP or Piscataqua. The cat ate anything and everything. As he grew he ventured forward to Pinky's lair and ate his food as well, and eventually came to prefer it, a mixture of dog food and human leftovers ground to gravy in a blender because most of Pinky's teeth were loose. Midden's potty training was coming along nicely, though. I was so proud. We'd moved his litter box from

our cabin to the salon and then out on deck. It was now screwed to the gunwale, literally hanging over the river. We were progressively cutting slices off the plastic box. As it was, Midden now had to place his front paws on the deck and his rear in the litter box to go. The idea was to eventually remove everything but the box's plastic lip screwed to the gunwale. Midden would back up to it and deposit his load overboard. I was so pleased with his ability to adapt. He didn't seem to miss all that covering up business afterwards.

As Midden became more tolerant of Pinky so did I, although I wouldn't share his gruel. Pinky wasn't a yapper, which I admire in a dog. And while I wasn't able to use the epithets that Grace did to call him, Lovelick, Darling, Pretty Baby, I did come to appreciate his devotion to life. Each of his living moments was a struggle to either eat, breathe, or defecate, yet he seemed to hold no ill will toward those around him. I believe I'd have been biting people. He lived on his pillow in the chain locker for the most part, and appeared from time to time when Grace or Chloe or I called to offer him some small pleasure, a rub or a soft treat. Of course, there were portions of his loose body that you didn't let your hand near for fear of liquids, but midway between his jowls and his rump there was an area of fur relatively dry for scratching. As long as you gave him one bounce he was still unusually adept at catching food. In late April and on into May, if there were an hour or two of warmth, Pinky would lay out on deck, lolling in the sunshine, while Midden stalked him from behind the capstan or galley hatch.

On one of these afternoons I lost them both and was nearly in tears by the time Grace returned from an errand. I'd searched the entire boat, every locker and storage bin, and was sure they'd chased each other overboard and drowned. Grace went directly to the dinghy, and lifting a loose canvas cover found Pinky and Midden, blinking and snuffling to our intrusion. They were lying between the thwarts, using oars for pillows.

"Pinky used to love to go for a row with Sweet George," Grace said.

It suddenly dawned on me that I was getting to my beaches the hard way.

"Could I use *Dapple*, Grace?"

She paused, thinking. "Of course. If you'll promise to carry a life jacket. There's a small engine up in the chain locker. You can row if you want, but you'll need help if you go head on into a tidal rip." She gestured toward Henderson Point downriver. "The current's so strong there they call it 'Pull and be damned point.' I think it's that point. It may be some other point. But we need to drop her down into the water for a couple days so she'll swell up. She's been hanging dry all winter."

After we took Pinky and Midden from the tender she showed me how to lower *Dapple* on her davits. Her hull smacked the river with a pleasant plop.

"You'll have to climb down and bail her out every once in a while till she swells up," Grace said.

"Thanks, Grace," I said. "I'll be careful with her."

"I like a good row myself," she said, and for perhaps the one hundredth time since we'd met she took my forearm between both of her hands and squeezed it. It made me shiver.

Later that week she got Harry to check out the little motor and show me how to operate it. He took me on a spin behind Pierce's Island so I could get the feel of the boat, all the while cautioning me about the water, how easy it was to die in. Then he set me loose on the ocean, wishing me great adventures. I couldn't keep from grinning. At first *Dapple* and I didn't dare to cross the main current of the Piscataqua. I was afraid that it was too strong for my arms or the motor and I'd get carried, if not out to sea, then at least into the restricted waters of Seavey's Island and the navy yard. Small patrol boats circled the island to warn off craft that came too close. I could imagine putting a scratch on one of their nuclear submarines with *Dapple*'s bow, and then trying to explain I was an archaeologist looking for sites. So I kept to the back channels and shoal waters behind New Castle Island for the most part, gunkholing estuaries and coves off Sagamore Creek and Witch Creek, gawking at the yachts docked below Wentworth by the Sea, a huge white Victorian hotel that overlooked Little Harbor and the ocean. I did feel as if on adventures, sneaking under low bridges when the tide was high, taking *Dapple* as far inland as she could go, to the doorsteps of colonial mansions and into quiet salt marshes, where I had to use an oar to push myself through the grass. *Dapple* had a very shallow draft; she

was light and so was I, and we ventured far beyond the limits of most boats. I tried to use the tide wisely, timing its ebb so it would carry us to our destination and using the flow to carry us back to *Rosinante*. But occasionally I misjudged, and found myself dragging *Dapple* through the grass and mud and shell of some cove, chasing the receding water on foot. I might tie up to a tree overhanging a creek to explore the bank and lose track of time and return to find the water a hundred yards away. Try as I might to become accustomed to a vertical eight-foot rise and fall of water over a six-hour period, I couldn't. It still awes me. Growing up in Kentucky, with its lakes and ponds, I came to understand and trust a body of water, its surface, almost as a solid. If rain fell it would always be there. The Piscataqua was deceiving. If its surface was undisturbed by a storm or the wake of boats it seemed serene, reflecting a broad sky with only minor imperfections, the blur of some entanglement below, a small rip of embroiled currents. The only way to know the river was to set something on it and watch it be carried away or under. It was never static. It never treated you with indifference.

From time to time I'd take Midden or Pinky along, and on several occasions, as the weather grew warmer in May, Grace and Chloe and I dressed in sweaters and took a picnic to one of the tiny granite islets off Goat Island. We didn't dare go far because with all three of us aboard, *Dapple* came dangerously close to dipping her sheer strake. There was an abandoned and dilapidated house on one of these rocks. One Sunday afternoon, we spread our blanket out on its front yard in short stiff grass growing out of sand and wave-washed gravel. I remember Grace in a fine mood, smiling at a remark she'd made about a house on the far shore. The house had unfortunate coloring, a milk chocolate base with a bright yellow roof.

Grace had said, "Well, you can tell all their taste is in their mouth," and left it at that.

But nothing we said seemed to appeal to Chloe, who sat on the edge of the blanket continuing a funk she'd been settling into for almost a week. Grace made her a turkey and cucumber sandwich, but before handing it to her chomped a section out of one corner, leaving her telltale bite.

"Thanks, Grace," Chloe frowned.

"You're an evil child," Grace answered, "keeping Charlotte and I from your secret."

Chloe's mouth opened. There was a secret. "You do have a secret," I said. "How did you know, Grace?" I asked.

"I've never known her to be quiet for this long. You usually can't shut her up."

"I don't have a secret," Chloe said, her eyes brimming with tears. She held her sandwich up in front of her face to hide them. "I don't have a secret," she said again. "You took a bite from my sandwich," she mewled. And then, in full cry, she added, "It was my sandwich and you bit it."

"You can have my sandwich, Chloe," I offered.

"What's the matter, baby?" Grace asked, handing her a paper napkin.

Chloe's face was choked, wadded up like wet Kleenex, reddening to a rubric. She cried with enviable abandon, I thought. I'd never in my life cried as wantonly, as thoroughly, as she was doing at that moment.

"I just can't take it anymore," she managed to say, her words issuing like bubbles, one at a time, from a clogged drain. And then with a great eruption of emotion, she burbled, "I'm pregnant," and fell over on the blanket, dragging half of it and most of our picnic up over her distraught face.

Grace leaned over and patted her heaving body, whispering, "Shh, shh," over and over, till she seemed to cry herself dry, gasping one last burp of anguish into the blanket. I couldn't touch her.

"How pregnant are you?" Grace asked.

"What do you mean?" Chloe said, looking up from her hands in confusion. "I'm completely pregnant."

"She means how far along are you?" I said.

"Maybe a little over four months," she said, her eyes slapping back and forth like windshield wipers.

Grace gasped this time. "Four months?"

"Yes," Chloe cowered.

"What took you so long to find out?" Grace asked indignantly.

"I've known for ten or twelve weeks," Chloe said.

"Well, why have you waited till just now to get so upset?"

"I told Roger last week."

"Oh. I see," Grace answered. She picked up a metal spoon and began popping its bowl in her open palm.

"Ever since I told him he's stopped making love to me, as if he could get me pregnant again."

"I'm not going to say a word about him," Grace said.

"You want the baby, then?" I asked quietly.

"Of course I do."

"He wants nothing to do with you now, I suppose," Grace said.

"It's not that, Grace. He wants me off the boat. He wants me to move off *Rosinante* and move in with him."

"But doesn't he live with his parents?" I asked.

"He's looking for an apartment," she said.

"So it's just the sex thing?" Grace asked matter-of-factly.

"No," Chloe answered, "It's the moving thing. I don't know if I want to move in with him. I like living with you and Charlotte. I like living on the boat."

And with this she fell to tears again, nodded over and covered her face with the blanket, as sliced cucumbers rolled down the folds to Grace and me.

"Well," Grace said, musing, "It's not as if we can add on to our home. We'll have to turn the salon into a nursery."

Chloe woke up. "What?"

"The salon, the salon," Grace said again, exasperated. "Just listen, girl. The baby would be best kept in the salon during the day, where it's warmer. And then at night, if it's all right with Charlotte, we'll move the baby to your cabin so it will be near you."

"Oh," Chloe said. "That sounds simple enough." She wiped tears off her cheeks and squinted.

I found myself nodding, assenting, caught up in two lives that were no longer distinct from my own. I picked up a stone, worn smooth by innumerable tides, and held it in the palm of my hand till it grew so warm I couldn't distinguish it from my hand.

"It can be your baby too, Charlotte," Chloe said.

And I found myself continuing to nod, finding my gratitude almost

unbearable, almost didn't know how to say thank you, how to accept trust because I wasn't used to being included. I cried almost as inconsolably as Chloe had earlier, with a sense of gain and loss. Grace could do no more than frown at both of us.

"I'm OK," I said after a while. "I'm OK."

We finished our lunch. I took *Dapple*'s oars in my hands, and they felt comfortable there. I felt the tug of the water through the blades, as if the river needed me, and I rowed the full increase of our numbers home to a larger vessel.

≈

I volunteered at Strawbery Banke that month, offering my services free of charge to the archaeological staff. I've always been lucky enough to enjoy my profession. I needed to get my hands back into the dirt and then into a lab, where three-quarters if not more of an archaeologist's work is done. Fortunately Michael Hall, the staff director, had heard of some of our work at the University of Kentucky. That first interview was especially enjoyable, in part because I wasn't asking for a job but volunteering.

≈

In the meantime my house had sold. I'd signed papers. All of my things were in storage in Kentucky. My folks had been great in attending to all the details that I couldn't, or wouldn't, do. Mom said that Mary and Richard's inquiries had abruptly broken off after she'd given them my letter, which was included in an envelope to my mother so they wouldn't see a postmark. I was beginning to feel badly about the way I was treating them, but had absolutely no desire to see them. So I wrote, apologizing for my behavior, asking them to understand my need for solitude and a new beginning, a time to mourn on my own. I said they could write to me through Mom, and that I'd probably come back to Kentucky for Thanksgiving or Christmas. They didn't respond, for which I was both grateful and ashamed. By my silences, my omissions, by running away, I'd accused them of harassment, and as the weeks slipped by I began to feel as if I'd done them an injustice. If I'd lost my husband of six years,

they'd lost their son of twenty-eight. I was beginning to understand that by keeping them from me it was as if we'd both died in that car crash. Yet I couldn't bear to tell them where I was.

I felt people couldn't now see Jonah's death on my face, that I was an individual again, and not just a widow. I still wore my ring, still thought of Jonah almost unceasingly. Finding him alive but silent in my dreams, I almost wanted to kill him a second time, kill his memory. It seemed unfair that he should die and my memory of him live on to torment me.

Grace's memory of Sweet George seemed to give her comfort. Often I'd see her touch the ship's wheel and run her fingers lightly along the curved mahogany. Many times she'd turn and tell us something of Sweet George, some honest pleasure that she was able to glow with. She promised me that I'd come around, that I'd get bored with melancholy. Then I'd say something stupid, like, "But you had forty-five years, Grace. I only had six."

"You're right, dear," she'd say. "I'm sorry. But is that difference supposed to make life easier or harder for me?"

Chloe, who found any discussion she wasn't participating in almost unbearable, would usually appear at this point and say, "Cookies. Can we make some cookies?"

And Grace and I were both grateful to her.

I had the conscious understanding that many people had suffered more than I, that individuals lost entire families, children and babies, to tragedies of unbelievable horror, but this understanding offered little solace to me. I tried to bear my suffering gracefully, but at times I was selfish, bitter, silent, and reproachful. I'd never been particularly religious, and so being angry with God came easily. I told Him I didn't believe in Him, which gave me a perverse pleasure that in turn frightened me. I told Grace this and she said, "Well, of course. Who in the hell are you, not to believe in God?"

Her reaction was much stronger than I'd anticipated. She was the one who told Chloe and me to keep our religion to ourselves. "I don't know what to believe," I said in defense.

"That's a belief, not knowing what to believe. It's a belief in ignorance," she said. "Anybody can believe in ignorance."

"Grace, I don't want to argue about this," I murmured. "I haven't got the strength for it."

She was pounding dough on a wax sheet at the time, and talking in puffs of flour. "That's all right," she said. "Don't you worry. I've got enough faith to carry you across with me."

Chloe, who'd been trying to jump into the conversation, now paused, relinquished what she was going to say, and said instead, "Grace, bring me too."

"Yes, dear. I'll see Sweet George first thing then I'll turn around and wait on both of you."

Which, queerly enough, made me feel better, because I had much more faith in Grace than I did in God.

≈

In late June, during the night, a storm blew through the city, rocking *Rosinante* at her pier so that we all thought heaven was closer than we'd imagined. The mooring lines held solidly though, thanks to Harry, who'd added additional spring lines and some fishing buoy fenders to keep the boat off the pilings. Wind hummed through the rigging on *Rosinante*'s short flag mast, and rain lashed across her decks as in old sea tales. We looked out through the salon windows but could only see sheets of spray over the river and spindrift on its surface. The tide rose higher than I'd ever seen it, with swash slapping over low seawalls. Many lobster traps were lost that night, their buoys torn from the warp. We heard that two small sailboats in Pepperal Cove broke free from their moorings and were beached on the rocks below the old prison on Seavey's Island. The Coast Guard, stationed at the mouth of the harbor, had rescued the crew of a trawler that foundered five miles outside the Isles of Shoals. There were shingles, leaves and tree limbs strewn about the city but the most visible damage was in Prescott Park, across Mechanic Street from Point of Graves: three large old elm trees, part of a row that lined the street, were blown over, roots and all, into the park.

I'd been working in the lab at the Joshua Jones House and in the Cummings Library at Strawbery Banke for a couple of weeks, getting acquainted with the work already done there, reading back issues of the Banke newsletter. The second floor of the Jones House already con-

tained thousands of artifacts excavated from the Puddle Dock neighborhood. I had spent several days trying to familiarize myself with these artifacts and the digs they'd come from, their cultural associations, when Michael announced we had some unexpected work.

The morning after the storm, a city worker investigating the damage at Prescott Park had found a long section of kaolin pipe stem and several sherds protruding from the roots and earth disturbed when the trees fell. Sensitive to the area's history, he brought them first to the offices of the *Portsmouth Herald* who sent them on to Michael. He was extremely excited because the artifacts appeared to be early eighteenth century, and the pottery sherds were similar to those already unearthed at the Samuel Marshall site, an early Portsmouth potter of the seventeen thirties and forties. The city was going to use federal funds to run pipeline through this area out to Pierce's Island and by law had to investigate for archaeological remains before doing so. The damage to Prescott Park encouraged the city to go forward with this work earlier than expected, and they contracted with the staff at Strawbery Banke to conduct the salvage archaeology. We were given three weeks to do our work because the tourist season was already in full swing. Prescott Park was the focus of most of the outdoor cultural activity in town; tourists naturally gravitated to the waterfront view and botanical displays.

The area was the site of the 1631 Great House, a large timber structure that was the focus of the original colony established by John Mason. Through Portsmouth's years of growth, Water Street (now Marcy) was lined with riverfront wharves and warehouses, which eventually gave way to shops, apartments, and a red-light district. The Prescott sisters wanted to clean up and preserve the old neighborhood where their father had owned a provisions store in the 1850s. They bought many lots and deeded the park to the city in 1940. Trustees of Prescott Park continued to extend its grounds and the park now stretched for several hundred yards along the river, from the Smarmy Snail to Point of Graves. Puddle Dock once flowed out through the clustered wharves here. The shallow estuary was filled with ashes and debris between 1899 and 1907, and so much of Prescott Park is fill too. What's now solid ground was once only wharves and the water between them, and the mouth of a tidal creek.

An 1812 map of Portsmouth, however, did show that solid ground had long existed on the north side of Mechanic Street, then called Gravesend Street, between the road and the mouth of Puddle Dock. While other volunteers searched through abstracts, looking for ownership records of the lots we'd be working on, Michael and I and two other volunteers moved quickly to cordon off the site, using a bright yellow roll of POLICE CRIME SCENE tape. Michael had picked up what was left of the roll after a murder investigation.

Our first order of business was to have the city remove the bulk of the fallen trees. We'd already knocked and scraped off the earth that still clung to the roots. Before the intact roots were cut we carefully searched the base of the tree and the root system to see if there were any artifacts embedded in the wood itself. It's not unusual to find trees that have grown around artifacts in the same way that they can envelope a rock or strand of barbed wire. After the tree's limbs and trunks had been cut up and the great carcasses of the base and root systems had been hoisted onto a flatbed truck and carried away, we went to work in earnest. We chose a datum point and laid out a meter square grid system across our excavation area using a surveyor's transit and tape measure. Our site extended from forty feet inside the park to the edge of Mechanic Street, and forty-five feet along the street, level ground bordered by a slight incline that led to the roadside. City records indicated that all current water and sewer lines were run on the far side of the street, so we hoped to find undisturbed strata below, once we got through the plow zone and the area disturbed by tree roots. Roots can, in their growth, push artifacts and associated features either deeper into the soil or lift them to the surface. In the center of our site was a row of three holes left by the felled trees, as deep as three feet. The artifacts recovered by the city worker had come from the bottom of one of these holes, so we knew we had a lot of overburden to remove to get to the earlier levels of the site. But the upper strata were important too, and even though we had severe time constraints (many digs take season after season to complete), we didn't want to lose any scrap of information.

Once a site has been excavated it has also been destroyed, so it's imperative that nothing be missed, that the location of every feature and artifact be recorded and mapped, and that soil samples be taken at each

level for later analysis in the lab. Excavation is physically challenging, hour after hour on your knees. You must be ever alert to some subtle change in the color or texture of the soil that might indicate the location of a hearth, a refuse pit, a well, or even the path someone took to the privy. The reward of scraping through several feet of clay or mud, or chiseling through earth as hard as concrete, is seeing something no one else has seen for perhaps several hundred if not several thousand years. You become intimately connected not only with the past but with the human being who sat before the hearth, or who lost the marble, or who died the death of a disease told in their bones.

In the first week of June, on what locals across the river call a "Maine Day," bright sun, light winds, we set up sieving screens just off our site on the green grass of Prescott Park. Along with Michael and his staff of two part-time professionals there were seven students from the University of New Hampshire, six locals who'd volunteered on previous Strawbery Banke digs, and myself. Posthole tests revealed at least eighteen inches of what we called Prescott Park topsoil toward the northern border of our site, which trailed off to only a few inches at the roadside. This topsoil seemed to be barren of any cultural remains and so we surmised it was brought in to cover and level off debris when the park was created. We used a backhoe and grader, loaned to us by the city, to remove most of this topsoil from the site. While a pair of surveyors argued over the measurements and language of several abstracts, we volunteers were given our choice of grid squares to excavate. Records were somewhat incomplete as to what had existed here over the past three hundred and seventy years. We were west of the site of the Sheafe Warehouse, which originally sat at the mouth of Puddle Dock on Gravesend Street. It was later moved to the waterfront of Prescott Park, and is now used as a museum. Much of the rigging and sails for John Paul Jones's ship, *Ranger*, were made in this seventeenth-century building. We thought we might be near a site notated as "Bell's Wharf" on Brewster's 1850 map of the city. Without evident features such as a foundation or a settling of the soil over a cellar, Michael thought we might as well start moving dirt while we waited on the surveyors to give us some idea as to where houses or shops or wharves might have been located. I chose a square between the tree line and Mechanic Street which was

shaded by an elm left standing. Experience told me that working in the sun for three weeks on end was best left to inexperienced students and volunteers. But I also knew that the original landscape sloped from the street down to the bank of Puddle Dock, filled ninety years earlier. There would be less fill up the slope. I hoped to get to undisturbed strata much more quickly than those working further into the park.

I sharpened the leading edges of my favorite pointing trowel, a six-incher that I'd worn down to four and a half, put my knees into the cool, damp earth. I began the simple backward scraping motion, an eighth of an inch at a time, that eventually uncovers pyramids, and which, incidentally, has over the past ten years given me trowel elbow and aggravated a bit of arthritis in my wrists. The natural inclination is to stab the point of the trowel into the heart of the earth and pop out the goodies, but it's best to move slowly, a layer at a time, in order to discover artifacts in situ, where they were dropped or laid down, and to look for relationships between artifacts and features. Most artifacts are pedestaled, brushed clean, and left intact on a mound of soil, until any connection with lower levels can be ascertained. Once everything is measured and mapped, artifacts are bagged and labeled. After all soil samples are collected from a level, the dirt remaining is sifted through screens in order to locate small artifacts that may have been overlooked. This sifted material, what some archaeologists call the spoil, makes excellent window box soil, devoid of even the smallest sticks and stones. Grace visited the site on several occasions and stole away with a small bucket of the stuff for her potted flowers on *Rosinante*.

I scraped through a couple inches of Prescott Park topsoil, a dark rich humus, raked it into a dustpan with my trowel, and emptied the pan into a five-gallon plastic bucket. Michael was kind enough to drop by occasionally to carry my full buckets to the screening area. He walked around with a clipboard full of level forms and squatted next to each volunteer's square to note progress and make sure nothing was missed. As soon as I was through the topsoil, I began picking up fragments of brick. When Michael brought back my bucket he bent down, picking up a small piece of brick, and crushed it between his fingertips.

"It's very friable," I said.

He looked up at me, and said, "It's certainly not any kind of fired

stuff," which was a rather obvious statement, since I'd just said as much, but what made it interesting was that while he spoke, and while I was assessing his teeth, I realized I was appalled by the fact that he was obviously doing the same to me.

"You're looking at my teeth," I said.

"No, I wasn't," he lied.

"You were too," I said. "It's OK. It's a professional thing, I think. I do it myself."

"Did you wear braces?" he asked.

"They came in this way. Look," I said, opening my mouth widely so he could see my molars, "I've got a Carabelli's Cusp."

"Really?" he said, holding his head laterally and peering up into my mouth.

Carabelli's Cusp, a tubercle located on upper molars, appears to be a rather late evolutionary development, occurring in all modern populations with varying frequency. No fossil hominoids have been found with an undisputed cusp.

Michael pursed his lips and suddenly I thought kissing him might be like kissing the seams on a baseball, and he said, "One of my maxillaries is almost peg-shaped."

"Really?" I said.

"Yep." He opened his mouth and threw back his head.

"That's congenital, right?"

"They think so. Neither of my folks have pegs," he said.

I smiled. He smiled. I turned back to my digging because a great wave of hot guilt was sweeping through me, and even though I was in the shade I was beginning to sweat. I felt nauseous for a moment, and if I'd been alone I think I would have thrown up just to relieve the bitterness of the tension. As it was I simply bent over further into my work and rubbed the saliva off my lips with the sleeve of my shirt. My eyes began to burn and tear. I was so mad at myself over this flush of emotion, unnecessary, and at last, tiresome. Jonah would be among the last people to mind my thinking about someone else in that way. He was as dead as the brick dust beneath my knees.

≈

I was always the first person to arrive at the site each morning, and among the last to leave in the evening. I was close by. It was about a three-minute stroll from *Rosinante* to the site. But I also hated to miss anything. Chloe wanted to hear every word of every conversation and often asked what someone had just said to be repeated, not because she hadn't heard it, but so she could savor it, roll the words over in her mind again. I was the same way toward the dig. I wanted to see or know about every nail and button pulled from the earth. So I usually came home to *Rosinante* late in the evenings, with soiled clothes and dirty knees and forearms, the dust of bricks and bones in the creases of my neck and the wrinkles around my eyes. I'd shower in the tiny head and then collapse on the salon settee in my bathrobe with a towel over my head. Chloe would rub my shoulders and then pummel my lower back, while I huffed and puffed about the day's finds.

Chloe's doctor thought her pregnancy was coming along nicely and had predicted a September twenty-fifth arrival. She still, at five months, didn't show, at least as far as I could tell. I'd return the favor of her backrubs and find it almost impossible to locate the epiphysis, the knobby end, of any long bone. She always had some form of food nearby, and had taken to helping make her own lunch. Grace and I weren't packing it full enough. She and Roger still hadn't come to any agreement. He didn't want to get married, but did want her to live with him. Chloe wasn't sure. She didn't want to be alone, but she also had an inkling that she didn't want Roger for the rest of her life. Grace still didn't allow him aboard, so he'd come down and pace on the pier while waiting for Chloe, or he'd sit on the Smarmy Snail's deck with a soda and glare down at *Rosinante*. The most acknowledgment he'd offer me was a "Yuh, hello," in an embarrassed undertone. I tried to engage him in conversation, although anyone who brooded as much as he did scared me. Chloe said the baby was his only topic of conversation, but that he still seemed to reside in a state of bewilderment. He'd yet to tell his parents, but neither had Chloe, though Grace and I had begged her to.

I came home late that first week of the dig, and found Chloe and Roger at a table at the Smarmy Snail. Grace was down on *Rosinante*'s afterdeck, sweeping. I could tell that something had happened, or was about to, from Chloe's downcast face. When Grace stood up I saw a

dustpan in her hand with two or three cigarette butts in it. Roger, one hand gripping a cigarette, the other gripping the sleeve of Chloe's shirt, looked up at me and said, "Get off."

"What?" I said.

"Mind your own business," he said.

I looked at him, then to Chloe, "What's going on, Chloe?"

"Leave her alone, Roger," Chloe said. "She doesn't have anything to do with it."

"Come with me, Chloe," I said. I reached down and took her hand.

"She's staying here," Roger said, and I realized that the tone I'd taken often for embarrassment was actually one of suppressed rage. Chloe still looked down into the table.

"Just come down to the boat, Chloe," I said, and I tugged on her hand, lifting her forearm from the tabletop.

"Listen, lady," Roger hissed, but before he could finish, Grace was standing over him, dumping the cigarette butts in his lap. He let go of Chloe's sleeve and pushed himself back from the table. It was then that I realized the butts were still lit.

"You crazy witch," he screamed at Grace.

Chloe stood too, and moved over behind Grace and me. I held her forearm and put my other hand on the trowel in my back pocket. Everyone on the deck had stopped eating and was looking at us and Roger.

"Go on home, young man," Grace said.

"Roger, I want you to leave me alone," Chloe cried.

He turned around, as if to leave, but instead picked up his plastic chair and flung it at the table in front of us. "You know what the facts are, Chloe. You just can't get rid of me." And with that he shoved his way off the deck and down the sidewalk around the Smarmy Snail.

I helped Chloe down the gangway. She was crying and it was low tide so the walk was steep. Grace walked behind us, slapping the dustpan on her hip.

"This is not a good thing," she said, "for someone in your condition, Chloe. Too much stress. Too much stress."

"I'm OK," Chloe cried, "I just need to cry some and I'll be OK." And she stepped down into our cabin and proceeded to do just that. Her protracted wall-banging wail of pain forced Midden up from the cabin

with fur prickling, and brought Pinky up from the galley to see what the fuss was. Grace and I sat in the salon with the animals trying to calm them while we all listened to Chloe cry.

"What can we do?" I asked.

Grace shrugged. "Make her something to eat?"

"Maybe we should tell her parents," I suggested. "They'll find out sooner or later."

"Maybe," Grace said, "Chloe and I should tell your in-laws where you are. They'll find out sooner or later."

She was old, forgetful and blue-headed, but she could still stick a pin through you as if you were a bug.

"Bad idea," I said.

"It's her secret to tell," Grace said.

"Perhaps brownies," I said and a particularly high-pitched yell of painful assent shot out from the cabin below.

"I think that was an aye," Grace said.

So we descended to the galley. There I whispered, "He frightens me."

"He's unbalanced, out of level. He's just a kid," she said. "But if he ever puts another cigarette burn on my teak, I'll put the hex on him, boyfriend or not. Wash your filthy hands."

"What's the hex?" I asked.

"It's bitter," she said, and would say no more, would only shake her head sadly, as if even brownies wouldn't help someone so afflicted.

≈

The Prescott Park dig was proving to be less interesting than Michael had hoped. At the end of our first week it looked as if most of the site had been destroyed by heavy machinery, or buried under fifteen to twenty feet of debris that really had no provenience. We were merely salvaging artifacts that had little to say other than that they were brought there from somewhere else as fill. Michael had already abandoned the area furthest into the park, realizing that undisturbed strata was just too deep to reach within the limited time available.

So we were concentrating on the ground between the row of trees

and the road, where the pipeline to Pierce's Island would eventually run. At eighteen inches below the surface, beneath brick debris that rarely was larger than my fist, we hit what seemed to be a largely intact level. It seemed to be the site of a blacksmith shop. We uncovered a cut granite foundation, eighteen inches wide, reaching ten feet back toward the thick debris fill and lost there. We surmised that the building probably extended further on pilings, eventually hanging over the tidal bank as a wharf. The artifacts in this level consisted of scrap iron: bits and pieces of flat bar left over from making something else, heavily worn hardware from wagons and carriages. Much of it was heated at one end and bore a cut from a big chisel. One leg of a pair of tongs was found, many worn horse and mule shoes, and a large brass platter that had four rectangular sections, an inch by three inches, cut from its center. One of the older volunteers, a man immensely satisfied with each horseshoe uncovered, suggested the strips cut from the platter were used as shims for worn bearings. "We used to cut up tin cans and slide them over the worn-out kingpins in Model T Fords." His eyes were large with memory. Fauna, mainly pig bone, was almost wholly contained in a set of shallow depressions just outside the foundation, one bone to a depression: a dog's hidden caches; he'd either forgotten or died before returning to them. There were four separate areas of waste product, slag from the forge, dumped on the northern side of the building. The only other features at this level were a line of very shallow postholes that showed up as slightly darker patches in the soil, like bruises, paralleling Mechanic Street: perhaps a fence of some sort. Most of the soil here contained charcoal, but not enough to suggest that the building had been burned. And although many bent horseshoe nails were found, we located very few construction nails and so we hypothesized that the building may have been moved in its entirety or was dismantled and carried off.

We found no privy, which disappointed me, because privies were often used as a repository for refuse of all kinds, and this refuse can be well preserved due to the moist conditions. Cloth, leather, and hair will survive very well in an oxygen-free, watery environment in which the pH is acidic. Acidity acts as a preservative (the bog bodies of Northern Europe survived in heavily acidic peat bogs) and the lack of oxygen prevents the growth of microbes that eat organic material. Michael sug-

gested the privy was probably a hole cut through the floor of that part of the building that hung out over the river.

All the artifacts of this level suggested it was occupied no earlier than the 1860s. The nails were all machine-cut and the few sherds found were white ironstone, popular in the late nineteenth century. I was most intrigued by an area just inside the wide doorway, an area thick with iron filings, cinders, and horseshoe nails. In the very middle of this artifact field was a circular patch, two and a half feet in diameter, almost devoid of these finds. I couldn't help seeing our blacksmith hammering on an anvil securely mounted on a section of oak tree trunk, a mass of wood and iron too heavy to move on a whim: the center of activity marked by a complete absence of remains. Once every feature had been measured and photographed and the foundation stones had been numbered and moved off-site we proceeded to the next level.

I don't want to give the impression that archaeological layers are as ordered as those of a cake. They're often lopsided, off-centered, and spill over into one another. A posthole may extend through several levels. A well may extend through three or four historical occupations, descend through six feet of barren soil, and then plunge into a paleo site. Specialized conditions can turn the entire cake upside down, with the most recent icing on the floor, so to speak.

Our second week of excavations led us through what seemed to be one hundred and fifty years in the life of a vacant lot: sixteen inches of midden, thin lenses of refuse of all sorts, but no single long-term use of the site.

We'd had several guests at the dig already, reporters and city officials. Michael used much of his valuable archaeological time to pamper them and give short tours. It's really one of an archaeologist's most important jobs, to educate the public, to get them on our side, to entrust them with our history so they'll come forward with sites they've found, and more importantly, so they'll recognize that once a site is dug it's destroyed. Pothunting, or ravaging an archaeological site for its "treasure," does irreparable damage, and renders the site a complete loss because everything that's left is out of context, turned over and raked through. Tourists and locals also stood beyond our crime-scene tape watching our dig, frequently offering us work in their gardens or asking

if we'd found anything yet. Often I showed them my tray of bent nails, broken shell, bits of glass and bone, and often they were unimpressed and showed in return obvious sympathy for me.

Late in the afternoon in the middle of the week I put my trowel down, wiped my hands on my shorts, and sat up to pull my hair back out of my eyes. As I held an overworked barrette in my teeth and combed my hair with my fingers, I looked out past a couple of onlookers at a man standing across the street in the cemetery. He'd just taken my picture. I'm not sure how I knew this but I was positive. He was still holding a 35mm camera with a telephoto lens in his hands. Perhaps it was because his face was turned away from his camera, which pointed at me. He walked around Point of Graves for a while, took a picture of a couple of early gravestones, which I knew wouldn't come out because he was still using the telephoto lens and he was too close. He crossed the bridge to Pierce's Island on foot, but moments later came driving by slowly in a blue sedan, an Avis sticker on the bumper. He never turned to look at me as he passed, but stared straight ahead. No tourist stares straight ahead when driving through Portsmouth. There are too many interesting things off to the side. Throughout the rest of the day and for days afterward, I'd pop up out of my hole at the site like a prairie dog and scan the horizon for predators. I was constantly uneasy and had the feeling that someone or something was bearing down on me. So I cowered in my burrow of sorts, digging it deeper for better protection.

As the dig progressed, deeper and earlier, the artifacts began to play out. We'd gone through successive layers of scattered refuse, creamware and pearlware sherds, glass sherds of case and wine bottles, an occasional button and even a George I farthing dated 1720. The sherds found by the city employee turned out to be from one redware milk pan, shallow, with a narrow rim, that Michael finally concluded may or may not have been produced by Marshall, the Strawbery Banke potter. The faunal assemblage was large and diverse, including bone from sheep, goats, pigs, cattle, geese, chickens, and many species of fish. The great majority of the artifacts came from lower down the slope, as if they had been pitched into the river from the roadside. All we were finding was the trash that didn't make it to the high water mark. The deeper we went, the lower Portsmouth's population, and the less refuse produced. At the end of our

second week Michael began to make plans for backfilling the dig and gave everyone the weekend off. It looked as if we'd have plenty of time to finish during our last week of work. Our last level was an artificial one so designated because we couldn't see any sign of occupation.

≈

On Sunday morning of that weekend, we sat in lawn chairs on the bow of *Rosinante* and watched from afar the Blessing of the Fleet celebration at the State Commercial Wharf on Pierce's Island. All the fishing boats were decorated from stem to stern with flags and balloons and made extravagant use of their bells and horns. On Sunday evening, Grace was arrested.

Chloe and I were standing on the afterdeck, glasses of iced tea in our hands, when a policeman escorted Grace down the gangway and up *Rosinante*'s boarding steps.

"There you go, ma'am," the officer said.

We met Grace at the steps with open mouths.

"When do I get my paints back?" she asked the officer.

"They'll be held till your hearing, ma'am."

"What is it?" Chloe asked.

"Well, I'll be going now," the cop waved. And with that he turned and stepped back up the gangway to the Smarmy Snail, but not before Grace caught him by a loop in his pants with her yell.

"You caught me in confined quarters. It won't be so easy next time."

"Grace!" I whispered harshly, tugging at her sleeve.

She turned to us. "I was arrested for defacing public property. If I own it, I ought to be able to deface it."

"What public property?" Chloe asked.

"The post office at the Federal Building." She put her hands on her hips and looked up and down *Rosinante*'s length.

"What did you do, Grace?" I demanded.

"Well, I didn't get away with it, for one thing," she said. "I thought they were going to put me in the slammer, but all they did was set a date in court next week and take my paints. It's all right, though. I've got more paints."

"Grace," Chloe said, confused.

"Oh, shut up. Everything was closed at the Federal Building but the door that leads into the post office boxes. They've got that stamp machine on the wall in there that's constantly taking everyone's money. I was just painting a long roll of stamps, issuing from that little slot, down the wall and coiling on the floor. I thought I'd be in and out of there in a few hours on a Sunday afternoon and that would be all there was to it. Maybe four or five people came in to check on their mail. One of the zealots must have squealed on me. Cops swarming all over the place."

"Did they hurt you, Grace?" Chloe asked.

"No, no, no. They were very polite. And they took pictures of my work. That boy who brought me home had very kind things to say."

"Grace," Chloe and I both said.

"It wouldn't have been so bad but they called my daughter," she sighed, and then she stamped her foot on the deck.

Chloe and I looked at each other.

"You have a daughter?" we said.

"She's my next of kin. Called her like I was some kind of nut."

"You've never mentioned her, Grace," I said.

Grace smirked.

"You've never mentioned her," Chloe reminded her.

"Not much to mention. She's my daughter. She lives in Florida. I haven't seen her since we put her father to rest. We don't get along." She shrugged. "I need to get another box of paints together."

"We need to get you a lawyer," I said.

"Well, all right," she said, almost absentmindedly, "I asked them what would happen if I pleaded guilty and they said I'd probably just get a fine, but I've about decided to plead innocent."

"I think they've got you dead to rights," Chloe said.

"I don't know," she said. "Their case hinges on that 'defacing' word. Most people like my work. They pay me for it. I didn't deface that machine as much as I enhanced its appearance."

"I'll go down and take some pictures of it," I said. "Before they remove the evidence."

"Good girl," she said and squeezed my forearm.

"It all just makes me nervous," Chloe said. She touched her head lightly. She'd just had a haircut and her scalp had burned in the sunshine while we watched the Blessing of the Fleet. Grace had offered her one of her many big floppy hats but Chloe had refused to wear it.

"No need to worry," Grace whispered. "I'll talk it over with Sweet George tonight and we'll decide what to do."

"You should have talked it over before you went and did it," Chloe pouted.

"Look who's talking, Little Mother," Grace snapped.

Chloe burst into tears, and so Grace and I put an arm each around her and escorted her to her bunk. Grace apologized continuously and I ticked off the ingredients to a chocolate cake out loud.

≈

In the late evening Grace and I watched Harry bring his boat into the dock, parking the big trawler in tight quarters amid a swirling tide. He'd been rafted alongside other fishing boats at the State Commercial Wharf, and while his crew lowered the dress flags and readied the boat for the morning's work he joined us on *Rosinante*.

"What are the Graces up to this evening?" he called, and, taking a chair next to Grace, squeezed her knee.

"We're just watching the boats go by," I said.

"Unhunh," he nodded. "The laymen are out."

"The laymen?"

"The pleasure boaters," he explained, and pointed toward the sailboats milling in the harbor below the bridge. Memorial opened on the hour and half hour during the summer months. There was only twenty feet of clearance under the center span and most sailboats' masts were much higher. As we spoke the warning siren sounded, the gates swung down in front of the motorists, and after a couple of minutes the center span began to lift. All the boats scurried under. We waved. The span soon dropped back into place and the cars sped across. Another sailboat arrived then and began to circle off Badger's Island.

"Now there's a fair craft," Harry said. "She's a motor sailer but she's old and designed on a fishing hull. Very seaworthy."

73

"They're going to have to wait half an hour for the bridge to go up again," I said. "Their timing is off."

"Nope," Harry winked. "Look."

As the little boat swung around and put its bow to the flow of the tide, someone walked forward and loosened the shrouds, the wire rigging on either side of the mast. He stepped under the mast and seemed to snap it in two at the deck, and then he let it drop forward, walked it back to a cradle on the bow pulpit.

"There's a turnbuckle on the mast," Harry said. "This boat can duck when she needs to. Here she comes." As the boat motored under Memorial we all waved and received a wave in return. A raised deck supported a little doghouse so you wouldn't bump your head as you went below. Her green hull knifed through the water with a plumb bow, and left us a view of a mahogany transom with a carved board on one side of the rudder.

"*Yonder*," I said.

"Sweet craft," Harry said. "She's even towing a little lapstrake tender."

"Does it have a name?" Grace asked, leaning over. On her lap was a thick notebook, filled with thousands of boat names and their home ports, vessels that had crossed *Rosinante*'s bow or stern, years of ink and pencil scribblings blotched and stained with coffee and salt spray.

"*Hither*," I said.

"Of course."

"I'm jealous," I said.

"Why?" Harry asked.

"Just of their ability to go, to slip under the turnstile and be off."

"Wouldn't take much to get this old girl on her way again," Harry said.

"Really?"

"A couple hours of maintenance, oiling, changing the old hoses and belts," he said.

"Who'd steer her?" I asked.

"Not me," Grace said. "Sweet George was captain. I handled dock lines and helped with the navigation."

Harry said, "Well, she's young, but that Chloe's been on lobster boats with her father since she was old enough to bait a trap. He works

a forty-four footer and I've seen that girl at the helm for six or eight years now."

"Chloe?" I asked.

"Yup."

"I'm not staying on any boat that girl steers," Grace shook.

"Dear old girl," Harry confided, "this old ship's been here for four years now, dockside. I know she's copper-bottomed but she needs to be hauled, hosed off, and checked over just in case any deterioration has set in. She's a fine old girl and you'd hate to be the owner who let her go."

"Grace takes good care of her," I defended.

"Of her topsides," Harry said. "That's important, but it's not essential. Her bottom's essential."

I looked at Grace, and never saw her with an expression so dismal, so strained with guilt. "I don't like leaving the dock," she said, her fingers crocheting excuses in her lap.

"If you'd like, Grace, dear," Harry suggested, "I'll have my mechanic come by and see what he can do. It would just be a short trip, upriver to Patten's Yacht Yard or around Seavey to Dion's. They'll haul her and wash her off with a power hose. Whole process wouldn't take more than a few hours. I'd come aboard as pilot."

She looked at him, at me, then back to Harry. She seemed almost anguished over the prospect of moving *Rosinante* from her berth.

"Sweet George would have me say yes," she finally said. "And so I'll accept your offer. Thank you."

"Nothing to it. It's the right thing to do." Harry stood, waved at the river, and left us on *Rosinante*'s bow.

"That Harry's a good person," she whispered to me.

"He sure is," I said.

"I wish Sweet George could know him," and she sighed, settling into her chair, looking more like an old woman than I'd seen her before, her eyes waning, as if she were dissolving in this decision, or wearing away like an old Mulberry plate.

≈

On Wednesday morning Chloe and I both took off work to go with Grace to court. She'd decided against a lawyer when she discovered the

price of his services were more than the fine. She pleaded not guilty, and although the judge was attentive he was also unforgiving, and fined her one hundred dollars above court costs plus the cost of the cleanup at the post office. He also advised Grace against painting any more public buildings without permission. "While I realize," he said, "that you aren't the typical graffiti artist spray painting 'Dick loves Jane' on a bridge overpass, the result was still the destruction of public property, which I cannot tolerate. Your motive seemed to be one of revenge, not artistic enhancement, as your defense would suggest."

Grace replied, "It wasn't revenge. It was sarcasm. And art is art no matter the motive. And for that matter I'd rather see 'Dick loves Jane' on an overpass than 'State Liquor Store Next Exit.'"

Which got her only a frown and a final bang of the gavel. Grace stood up, called out, "Let's go, girls," and Chloe and I marched out behind her in single file, quick time. Grace had her head down, and by the time we were out of the building she had Chloe and me skipping to keep up. She was talking almost as rapidly to herself, sloshing through the judge's reasoning, his appearance, and hypothesizing about his lifestyle choices. People stepped out of her way on the sidewalk. A dog, searching through a trash can, was so thrilled with her pace that he bounded along beside her, expecting her to break out in a game of Frisbee or chase.

"Grace!" we called out after two or three blocks. "Slow down."

She turned and was actually startled to see us. Her head fell back, her eyes widened, and she smiled her vagrant smile. "Why, girls," she said, "where are you off to?"

Chloe clasped Grace's hand in both of hers. "We're going with you, Grace."

"Of course," she said. "Look at this silly dog."

"Yes," I said.

"Where are we off to?" Grace asked.

Chloe never flinched, but said, "Well, we're on our way home to make grilled cheese sandwiches. And we'll have some kosher dills and some potato chips and maybe some peanut butter ice cream."

I walked along behind them, watching Chloe swing Grace's hand back and forth in stride.

"Then," Chloe said, "this afternoon we're going down to the Federal Building and pay our fine, and we'll pick up some groceries on the way back."

"I need to get a tube of titanium and a tube of cobalt," Grace said.

"That too. We'll get those too. This afternoon."

I realized then that Chloe was going to be a fine mother, that empathy was beyond understanding; it was almost as if she existed in each of us, rather than someone else existing inside of her.

"Charlotte?!" Grace yelled.

"Yes, yes, I'm here," I said, and hopped up beside her.

"Get on the other side of Chloe and hold her arm. This girl's five and a half months pregnant."

"Right," I said.

We walked arm in arm, the three of us, down the incline toward *Rosinante* and grilled cheese sandwiches, and I listened to our conversation as closely as I could, trying to divide up the vowels and consonants, sorting syllables, seeking to fathom this link between human beings, each of us alone but connected by a common language that allowed us brief glimpses into each other's lives. I don't think Chloe or I felt any pity whatsoever for Grace at that moment. I think we felt we were her, Grace old and young, Grace in memory and pain and joy and loss. I think we loved her.

≈

On the Thursday morning of our last week of excavations, as we were cleaning the site preparatory to final photography and backfilling, I came upon a stain in the soil of one of my units. This pit was a bit deeper than the rest. I'd merely been scooping dust from the bottom of the square so it would look nicely finished for the camera. The last few trowel swipes revealed a slight but positive change in soil color and consistency. The stain was darker than the surrounding buff, but mottled as well, with eyelashes of lighter earth. It extended from the far corner of the unit in a curved line to the near corner. Grinning, I showed it to Michael, and he dropped his hands to his side and groaned.

"We've only got two days left, Charlotte," he said.

"We can't leave it, Michael," I pleaded. "By the arc of the circle it could extend into three or four more units. It might be an early well."

"If it's a well we won't have time to dig it."

"Start backfilling on the far side of the site. Give me half a dozen of the volunteers and we'll know by Friday afternoon what we've got here. It might just be a shallow midden. We can't just cover it up. It might be prehistoric."

"Dig to bedrock, then?" he sighed.

"Just till the stain is removed," I said.

"OK, Kentucky," he said.

One of the first clues a guy's interested: he calls you anything but your given name.

≈

Jonah began by calling me, embarrassingly enough, Iddybit, a reference to the fact that I was a half inch shorter than him. It became an endearment as we dated and after we married: every birthday and Valentine card came in an envelope so addressed.

"Don't worry, Iddybit, I'll protect you. Hide behind me," he'd say, and I'd pound his shoulder for the chauvinism, and then chide myself for the gush of pleasure and security I felt with him. He wasn't much bigger than I was, but he took up twice as much space in the world. I met Jonah during the fall semester of my senior year, after I'd returned from the Isles of Shoals. There was a core requirement I'd put off my entire college career, a business class, and there I found Jonah. He excelled in school, although he disliked it, and this carried over into his work later. Soon after we graduated he went to work for a bank in Lexington and although he earned regular promotions, and would have become an officer if he hadn't died, he went there every day with some sourness and returned in despair. I loved my work, but I couldn't communicate it to him, because he accepted it as a reproach. It came to the point that I only told him the irritating aspects of my day, rather than the overriding joy I felt through it. I hardly saw him smile for perhaps a year before he died. But he always remained committed to me, atten-

tive, responsible. And although there were times I didn't understand him, I always cherished him. I still feel that he deserved my love. My past is buried in levels of emotion and in one of these levels is an artifact, the word Iddybit. And although it's been months now, and it's overlaid with many other joys and sadnesses, I cannot yet unearth it without tears, and the always new and sudden understanding that I existed before the present moment, that I am intimately connected with that girl in the past who was married to Jonah.

≈

By Friday we'd taken six units down to a level three and a half feet below the original surface of Prescott Park. This six by nine foot rectangle was only eighteen inches off Mechanic Street. The circular stain in the soil was contained in this rectangle and was approximately five and a half feet in diameter. At one edge of our rectangle, however, near the street, another stain of similar color had appeared. Only a segment six inches across and three feet wide was revealed. It seemed to extend further under the roadbed. While the tractor scooped up buckets of our screened soil and dumped them back into our other excavations, we hurriedly photographed and measured our latest feature in preparation to excavating it. Our stain was very clearly delineated. All the volunteers gasped when they first looked upon it. Once a hole has been dug in the earth and refilled it will always be a different color than the surrounding soil. Whatever you put in the hole, what blows or falls into it, changes the color and texture. The rotting post darkens the soil and makes a fence line of three hundred years earlier a simple job of connecting the dots. Even if you were to dig a hole and immediately refill it with the same dirt, you couldn't get it back to the same consistency as it was originally laid down by the millennia. The earth forgets no intrusion. There's always the possibility that an animal, or some other act of nature, a falling tree, created a hole that was filled in later over time, so all stains aren't necessarily man-made. But now that we had two stains, I was hopeful that we'd find some evidence of early human occupation here.

We decided to quarter the main feature, cutting our pie into four big slices and excavating two quarters on a diagonal from each other.

This would leave the two remaining sections standing and give us a good profile of the strata in the feature to analyze and refer to. Almost immediately we came upon our first find, a tinned-brass hook, part of a hook and eye that anchored a man's doublet to his breeches. Jason recognized it from a photo he'd seen in Hume's *Martin's Hundred*, the excavation of an early English site near Jamestown. The hook was about an inch long and of the style fashionable during the mid 1600s. Down another sixteen inches we came upon a fragment of white clay pipe stem that looked very old, judging by the diameter of its drawing hole, which was very large. But beyond that we found little else in the way of artifacts for a while, although the soil seemed to darken. We were beginning to hope we had an early privy, from the first years of Strawbery Banke's occupation, and would find hoards of well preserved artifacts at its base.

I don't know why I didn't consider the possibility of what the feature eventually turned out to be. The large size of the stain was perhaps a component. Yet if I'd only looked across the street I might have guessed. I had my head buried in the earth just as much as any ostrich. Almost simultaneously Michael and I, working in opposite quadrants, came upon human remains. I looked down and softly brushed soil from the coronal suture of a skull, while Michael was looking down at a first and second row of phalanges. At first we thought we had one individual but soon realized there were two people buried here, in shallow graves, side by side.

"Someone misplaced the walls of the cemetery," I said.

"Hell," Michael said softly.

"I don't think they're prehistoric, not with the artifacts," I said. The volunteers looked down on us silently.

Michael stood up and brushed dirt from his khakis. "Shut the dig down," he said.

"What?" I said, struggling to my feet.

"Shut the dig down."

"You can't be serious," I said.

"We've just entered a maze here, Charlotte. You know that. Before every paper in the country announces we've found bodies, I want to be prepared. I want to bring in the state archaeologist, the local coroner,

and the police, and we have to get more time from the city. We're supposed to be out of here by tonight. There's no way we can properly excavate two grave sites in that amount of time."

I was nodding in agreement long before he finished. "You're right, you're right," I said. I'd momentarily forgotten our time constraints. And too, the grave wasn't just another feature to the society at large but carried religious associations and ethical considerations in its disturbance. As an archaeologist, I looked upon grave sites as a huge source of information, not only from the burial items often interred with the body, but from the body itself, the message in the bones.

We covered with dirt those small areas of bone we'd revealed, and then laid a heavy vinyl tarp over the entire six-unit hole and pinned its perimeter with stones. While we worked on cleaning up the rest of the site, backfilling and raking everything smooth, I began to realize the prickliness of the situation. Clearly these graves should have been enclosed within Point of Graves directly across the street. The city certainly would never have approved of digging within those limits, which contained many of the area's forefathers. The graves, I thought, must have been so early that by the time the cemetery was large enough to enclose within walls they had been long forgotten. The land for the cemetery was given to the city in 1671 by Captain John Pickering, Jr., who stated that Strawbery Banke should "have full liberty to enclose about half an acre upon the neck of land . . . where the people have been wont to be buried . . ." Perhaps people had been buried on the point since the Great House was built in 1631. There is no marker earlier than 1682 still existing within the walls, but stonecarvers were rare during the early years of settlement and wooden markers may have been used.

The reason Michael wanted the police and coroner there was so they could see the bodies for themselves and understand they weren't evidence of recent homicides. The bog bodies in Europe, and discoveries of ancient skeletons all over the world have many times led to murder investigations. Even if these bodies had been found to be the result of foul play, the guilty would have escaped prosecution through death long ago. It was important that the community not think we'd discovered the shallow graves dug by a mass murderer.

Michael returned late in the afternoon and said that the city council would hold an emergency session Monday morning to take up our request for an extension. He'd notified all appropriate authorities and would spend the weekend gathering burial recovery forms and investigating city archives for clues to who these people below us might be. The city was adamant that the graves not be opened without official consent. In the meantime, over the weekend, he needed volunteers to stand guard round the clock at the site. He asked us all to keep mum about our discovery to limit sightseers and the possibility of vandalism. We drew up a schedule with four-hour shifts and I accepted two watches, one each on Saturday and Sunday nights.

≈

Chloe and I went to our first birthing class on Saturday morning. Grace would have gone along but stayed behind to hover over Harry's mechanic, who was working on the old engine. I felt sorry for him as she led him to the engine room. I knew that one slip, the slightest hesitation in his work, and Grace would nail him to the sole. Chloe had become extremely conscientious in the past few weeks. She was giving up her occasional cigarette on the pier, struggling with her weight, and walking a two-mile circuit of Portsmouth every evening. Roger had been keeping his distance since the scene on the deck of the Smarmy Snail, but Chloe still received his calls at work. She said he always asked her how she was, but wanted her to make a decision about their relationship.

"Why does he want you to decide?" I asked her.

"Because he can't. He isn't able to."

"But I thought you had decided," I said

"Well, I have. I just haven't been able to tell Roger in so many words," she said.

"At least he isn't running away."

"It's weird though," she said. "He doesn't want anyone to know I'm pregnant, or that he's the father."

"I thought he wanted you to move in with him."

"He does. I mean he says that one minute and the next he says that it's impossible. He's confused. I think if he were honest he'd admit he wants out. I'm trying to help him."

"Then why don't you tell him? I mean, that you don't love him and that you'll raise the baby on your own."

"He gets so ashamed that he gets angry," Chloe said. "I know Roger looks like he doesn't care about anything, but he does. His appearance, the way he dresses, everything but what he says when he's mad, is calculated. He has a sense of self-importance. I mean, you'd think he was the Prince of Wales when it comes to his sense of how other people look upon him. At least until his anger overcomes him. And I hate to hurt him. You know, I've told him before that I loved him, and now he says it and waits for me to repeat it. So I do."

"When are you going to tell your folks?"

"Soon."

"When soon?"

"Soon," she said. "As much as my mom and I don't get along, I feel like I need her help somehow. The thing is, I know she'll be disappointed."

"Maybe she'll be happy," I said.

"No, no," Chloe shook her head firmly. "She'll be pretty upset. She and Dad saved a long time for me to go to college. When I left, she said I was no daughter of hers."

"She didn't mean it, Chloe," I said.

"My brother has two degrees and works down in Baltimore for Hewlett-Packard. They wanted me to do that. I didn't want to go back to school. I worked hard to get out of it as fast as I could."

"But college isn't like high school, Chloe. People aren't quite as childish there. I loved college. You'd love it too. You could be a psychology major."

"You see. That's what my folks said. And I suppose it could have been true. But now there's the baby and the baby can't go to college. And besides, I'm much more interested in the baby than I am in school. Wouldn't you be if you were pregnant?"

I half-smiled at her, neither agreeing nor disagreeing. She held her stomach while she practiced her breathing, and I counted for her, "One,

two, three, four, exhale, one, two, three, four, exhale, one, two, three, four, of course."

"Charlotte?"

"What?"

"I'm taking a poll."

"What kind of poll."

"One . . ."

"Breathe," I said.

"One that only I can take part in."

"Why?"

"Because then there will be no margin of error," she said, and she smiled broadly at me. She flew my hand across the sky to land on her surprisingly firm belly and held it there under her damp palm.

≈

By late afternoon the mechanic had installed two new marine batteries, replaced two belts and several hoses, changed the engine and transmission oils, flushed the block with new coolant, and replaced glow plugs, zincs, and a half dozen additional components. As Chloe and I looked on expectantly from our relay position at the engine room door, he said, somewhat solemnly, "OK, tell her to put the boat in neutral, and then turn the key, but just for a moment. I want the engine to turn over once or twice before we start her."

I spoke these instructions loudly up the companionway to Grace at the helm. Chloe added in explanation, "Scotty says he wants impulse before we go to warp." I pinched her elbow because Grace was already about to shoot through the ceiling of the salon.

I watched her ease the key over from the warming position as if it were going to give her an electric shock. Almost before the starter could make a full revolution, the boat began to tremble beneath my feet. There was no intermediate cough, no chance to become acclimated, but a sudden and thronging rumble as the engine took its first opportunity at compression and came alive, vibrating with possibility and power. It never seemed startled. For a few moments white smoke poured from the exhaust at the stern, and fogged in the diners assembled on the

Smarmy Snail's deck, but soon that cleared. Up on deck it was hard to feel the engine running, but the river seemed to know. It rippled at the hull as if the boat were magnetic, and the expanse of water seemed smaller somehow. The mechanic had walked around the engine two or three times, as if he were lost. We all gathered in the salon with him. He held a wrench in his hand, the hand held against his heart.

"She shouldn't be running," he said.

"Why not?" Chloe asked. "It sounds great."

"The fuel," he said. "I brought a five-gallon can that I meant to run directly into the engine, but I haven't done it yet. She's running on fuel that's four years old." He shook his head, but his eyes remained fixed. "My boat won't run on last year's fuel."

"Grace?" I said.

"I don't know," she said, her eyes wide, the pupils narrowing.

The mechanic went to the throttle and backed it down to an idle. Then he turned back to us. "Let's shake some seaweed," he said, and popped the gear lever down into reverse.

"We're still tied to the dock," I warned.

"Not to worry, just at idle," and he stepped out of the salon and down to the engine room, where we all watched the slow turning of the propshaft. He looked up at us. "This is a good thing," he said. He said the stuffing box wasn't leaking, and then he led us all to *Rosinante*'s transom and we looked overboard and saw there bits and scraps of seaweed rising up slowly from below, and the gentle stream of cooling seawater expelled from the exhaust. "I was worried that an old piece of line might have been wrapped around the prop," he said. "But she looks OK. I can't get over that fuel. Somebody must have put a gallon of preservative in it."

"Sweet George," Grace said, looking down into the water. "He took care of everything." She seemed to suppress a deep moan of recognition, as if she'd confronted some detail, a remote possibility, at last. "I was perfectly happy right here," she said, and turned away from us all. "Leave your bill on the chart table," she yelled back at the mechanic, and then she said something else and slipped inside *Rosinante*. It was the first time I'd ever heard her speak to herself on board.

≈

Over dinner that evening, in between Chloe's recitations of the calories and grams of fat in each course, an attempt to lower her intake of them, Grace talked about her husband.

"We tied up to the dock here in late September. It was getting very cold at night by then and since our destination was further north, Sweet George thought it was a good place to end the season and begin anew in May. We'd come all the way from Palm Beach that summer. It never seemed fair to me, that he got only the one season on the boat. Sweet George was fat too, Chloe, but he was quiet."

Chloe stopped chewing, the corners of her mouth dipping.

"He hardly ever raised his voice and even on the boat we'd communicate by hand signals when anchoring or docking because he didn't like to yell. I remember that season. We saw so many things. Our whole lives were spent apart before that summer, in work and social activities. When we came together on *Rosinante* after forty-five years of marriage we weren't unfamiliar with each other but unaccustomed. We'd always had some separate life to communicate to one another and now we led the same life. I was afraid at first that we might not ever say anything to each other again. Sweet George wasn't a recluse or even introverted, but it didn't bother him to go without speaking for hours on end. He was fascinated with the machinations of cruising, the details of the boat, with navigation. I always thought it superfluous to remark upon the beauty of our surroundings. So to keep in contact, I began to add Sweet to his name every time I called it, and he began to hold me close to him at odd moments. It was as if it took him forty-five years to gain the courage, the confidence. He never missed an opportunity to touch me in some way in passing, to brush my arm in the companionway or to move my hair from my eyes while I cooked. It almost seemed as if we were courting. We met friends at a couple of places on our journey, and then Sweet George and I would open up, burst with speech, exclaiming on the beauty of our lives, expounding for hours on what had been only a few moments' occurrences aboard *Rosinante*. It was during those times that I realized we hadn't spoken aboard ship not because we had nothing to say, but because there had been no time. But we always slept well, and we saw many things together, cracks of lightning, whales. When young you're always afraid you're going to miss something, and then

when you're old, you realize you spent too much time being afraid. Sweet George died that winter. He was old and fat. But he was full of plans, like you, Chloe."

"How'd he die, Grace?" I asked.

"He went quietly. It was like him. A heart attack. He died on a bench in Prescott Park. I thought he was asleep. There were birds all around us. We'd been feeding the pigeons. I think they knew before I did. We intended to go on to Prince Edward Island the next spring. Sweet George read all the *Anne of Green Gables* books to our daughter when she was young, and he wanted to see that setting, to arrive there from the sea the way Anne did, to walk in the fields of his and his daughter's youth."

"Why don't you ever talk about your daughter, Grace?" Chloe asked.

"We don't get along. I told you," she said.

"Why not?" Chloe could be incessant. Grace frowned at her. "Well," Chloe said, "my mother and I don't get along either. I'd just like to know why. I hope we're still not fighting when she's seventy-five."

Grace sat up straight. "Well, Chloe," she said, "good for you. But your problem with your mother won't end up like mine. Because my daughter is the express bitch from hell, and you're almost rather pleasant."

"The bitch from hell?"

"I suppose it's my fault somehow, but I've stopped trying to analyze the situation. She was an only child."

"I'm an only child," I said. "I get along great with my mom."

"You see," Grace said, "there's no understanding it. I just try to keep my distance from her."

"But why, Grace?" Chloe insisted.

"We've just never seen anything eye to eye. We can't agree on gravity. When we decided to retire in Florida, she threw a fit. When we decided to buy *Rosinante*, she threw a hissy fit. When I decided to live on the boat, she threw a raging hissy fit. She's a control freak. She was spoiled. She wants to be responsible when there's nothing to be responsible for. Can you believe she wanted me to move in with her after Sweet George died? I'd sooner move into a rat's maze. She'd have put a

87

bell and a trapdoor for my food in my room. Her children and her poor husband are automatons. She thinks the ocean is inherently dirty, and that I live in a septic system. I saw her four years ago. It was the only time I seriously thought about leaving the dock."

"Oh," Chloe burped.

"What?" I asked.

"I saw Harry this afternoon. He said if everything turned out OK with *Rosinante*'s engine, he'd be here Monday morning to take her up to Patten's Yard in Eliot."

"Monday morning?" Grace said.

"Yes."

She looked at both of us, her eyes sadder than Pinky's.

"What?" we asked.

"I'll probably cry," she said.

"But why, Grace? It's just a short trip. It will be good for *Rosinante*."

"I know, I know. Its just that no one's moved the dock lines since Sweet George tied us up here. The knots in those ropes are his. It just seems that once they're untied, I'll have lost that much more of him."

And so by then Chloe and I were both bleary eyed, while Grace looked on at us, dry and apologetic, shaking her head back and forth. "It will be all right, girls. There, there."

≈

Another volunteer and I had the eight-to-midnight watch over the grave sites Saturday. Although there were chairs and a lantern next to the dig we sat in her car. There was a chill off the river, and she'd brought a small TV that plugged into the cigarette lighter. We watched Alfred Hitchcock's *Rebecca*.

"I know he's Laurence Olivier," she said from behind her steering wheel, "but he broods too much for me. I'd tell him to open up or get happy, one or the other." She'd brought a basket of snacks and her teeth clicked together as she chewed and spoke.

"She can't tell him that. She's hopelessly in love with him," I said.

"That's what I'm saying. It's her fault."

"It's her fault?" I adjusted the horizontal.

"Sure," she said. "He's hiding behind this rich in sadness nobleman facade crap, and she's letting him, while she hides behind this hopelessly in love, ignoramus crap. It's not real. If it was real she'd smack him." Her teeth went clickety, clickety, clickety.

"That's really how you see it?" I asked.

"Yeah, but I've seen this movie dozens of times."

"Me too. But she can't help the things she doesn't know," I pleaded. I yanked the bag of pretzels from her grasp.

"She takes too much crap: from her boss and then from her own housekeeper. She takes too long to come to a decision, and when she should hesitate, she doesn't. How could she be so sure he didn't kill his wife? Even he isn't sure that he didn't."

"Maybe she felt that his wife deserved it. I mean even if he did kill her, she deserved it. She needed to be killed. At least Rebecca wins in the end. She gets her man."

"You call that winning? The mansion's burning down. Those thin little lips on his face? This is the guy who put his wife's body on a boat and sunk it, burying her at sea to protect himself." Her teeth had to be made of stainless steel.

"You've completely destroyed this movie for me for the rest of my life," I said. I turned away to the graves.

"We're archaeologists," she said. "We find that gods break down in dirt too." She took the pretzels away.

"But she loved him," I said.

"You say that like it's a cure-all. You're like some saint invoking God as the flames crawl up her socks. Anyone can see she should have smacked him and half a dozen other people in the movie."

She switched off the TV. Our watch was almost over. I motioned toward the blue tarp over the graves and said, "I wonder what kind of an end they came to."

"Oh, I don't know," she mused. "I don't think the dead have as much to say to us as we might hope. I think they're probably just dead."

I looked back at her, this matter-of-fact housewife I hardly knew, and opened my mouth to speak but my courage faltered and I turned away.

≈

Midden woke me Sunday morning by mewing plaintively at the cabin door, and trying to reach the salon by sliding his paw underneath the door and grasping at a hooked rug on the other side. Chloe and Grace were already in the galley. Midden shot across the salon when I opened the door, cleared the galley steps in a carom, and slid to a dead halt in front of the stove and whatever its contents might be.

"Morning, grave watcher," Grace said.

"Good morning."

"See any ghosts?" Chloe asked.

"Just Laurence Olivier's," I said. "He was barely six inches tall, shades of gray and black and white. He kept going in and out of focus."

"Get out," Chloe said, staring at me.

"He was on TV, Chloe. It was so cold we sat in a car and watched a portable TV."

"Oh. Wouldn't have been much of a ghost at six inches anyway. I'm off tomorrow. Can I come watch with you tonight?"

"Sure. But I've got the midnight to four shift."

"That's OK."

"Well, I won't be there," Grace said. "Poor dead people. Why can't you just leave them alone?"

"They don't care, Grace," Chloe said. "They're dead, laid low, worm food, RIP."

"That stands for 'Rest in Peace,' which they certainly can't be doing, lying there with half the dirt off them. I'll bet they're cold," Grace said.

"Some of the dirt that covered them is in your flower pots," I said, and then thought better and added, "Well, I'm hungry."

Chloe wouldn't let it go. "They're dead. We get to make the decisions now. Charlotte can study their bones and tell all sorts of stuff. Can't you, Charlotte?'

"We might be able to learn something about their health, their diet, burial customs, things of that sort."

"Can you tell what killed them?" Chloe asked, narrowing her vision.

"Maybe, but I wouldn't get too excited. Usually people die of fairly mundane ailments. Aren't you hungry, Chloe?"

"We're both starving," she said, rubbing her stomach.

Grace poured batter onto a lightly greased cast-iron griddle, dollops that spread to four inch circles. She said, "I wouldn't want anyone digging up my grave to put my bones in some box at a university. I'd want my bones left in the dirt to go back where they came from."

"I'm gonna be cremated," Chloe said, watching the pancakes bubble. "I've never liked the idea of rotting. Sweet George is buried at sea, Charlotte. Did you know that?"

"No," I said. "I didn't."

"It cost twice as much," Grace said proudly.

"But that's what she thought he would want. Right, Grace?"

"Right, Chloe," Grace said.

Grace flipped the pancakes and then ladled them onto plates that we carried up to the salon. Midden was quick on our heels, and mewing furiously. When we sat down I asked, "Where is he, Grace?"

"Oh, a few miles off the Isles of Shoals. Sleeping on the bottom." And then, with a three-layer thickness of pancake poised on her fork she added, "Just deep enough that no archaeologist can get to him."

"These are great pancakes," I said, pouring more syrup over them. "How do you make them?"

Grace started to list the ingredients but I motioned her to stop while I ran below for a pen and paper. When I returned she completed the list and explained how the beating of the egg whites to a fluff was the most important step. I include the recipe here not only because it was good. No matter how delicious pancakes are I can take them or leave them. It's Jonah who was fond of them. It was only after breakfast, after we'd washed up and I was returning to my cabin with the slip of paper in my fist that I remembered. I include the recipe here as a sign, or marker, of this lapse in memory, the one in which I thought I could somehow go home and make my husband pancakes he would like.

Grace's Pancakes

2 c. flour	1 t. salt
4 t. baking powder	2 eggs, separated
2 and one-quarter c. milk	2 T. sugar
one-third c. melted shortening	

*Measure sifted flour and resift with salt and baking powder and sugar. Beat
egg yolks, beat in milk and add melted shortening. Remember to add flour
mixture all at once, and beat vigorously until smooth. Stir in stiffly beaten egg
whites. Cook on hot griddle. Serve with real maple syrup.*

≈

Chloe and I stood in the middle of Point of Graves, a little before midnight, reading inscriptions by flashlight. The tombstones, half-sunken,
tilted, moss-weary and lichen-worn, were intricately carved with
death's-heads, skulls and crossbones, weeping willows. "Here lyes
buried. . . ."

For Jonah's tombstone I'd chosen a dark granite. But it seemed so
thick, so heavy that when it was finally placed on his grave I wished I'd
chosen the flat bronze plaque that was easily mown over. The inscription I'd ordered was simple: his name, the dates, and below these in
smaller block capitals the words BELOVED HUSBAND. All of it carved
deeply in stone so it might last. A week after the burial the director of
the funeral home called to ask if I'd like to reserve, purchase, the plot
next to Jonah. I was at a loss for breathless moments and after what
seemed like several minutes of silence he said he'd call back later. I
couldn't even say good-bye to him. I put the phone down and walked
into the kitchen and looked into the refrigerator, as if the answer might
be in it.

When they caught the beam of our flashlights, the low stone walls
that gathered in the graves glistened with dew. Chloe clung to my sleeve
and read the inscriptions aloud as we came upon them, those of sea cap-
tains and their wives and children. I noticed how often the wives outlived their husbands, counting the years of their widowhood till their
own deaths.

"All of these children," Chloe whispered.

"Almost any infection could kill you," I explained.

"Look. Here's three kids in the same family, all at the same time,"
she said.

"Cholera, maybe," I suggested.

"Here's one that was just a month old." Chloe sniffed and I turned

the flashlight to her face. She put one hand to her cheek and another over the flashlight so I lowered its beam to the grass.

"Do you believe in Jesus, Charlotte?" she asked.

I wanted to comfort her. "I believe in everything," I said. "Why not? Belief is cheap. I mean it doesn't cost you anything. Why believe in nothing when everything is the same price?" My tone and delivery were somewhat glum. I swung the beam of light over the pairs of headstones, the grave markers of spouses tipping closer or father apart with centuries of settling and frost heave. I couldn't help but think they were reflections of their marriages. "It's almost midnight," I said. "Let's go across the street."

"OK, but there's nothing like having a baby to scare the living daylights out of you," Chloe said. "I used to think spiders were pretty bad. Here I am in the middle of a graveyard and I'm not even flustered. But I think about the baby and I get knock-kneed."

"You're a good kid, Chloe," I said, and led the way through the turnstile.

Although my watchmate hadn't arrived, we relieved the earlier crew. I really hadn't expected her, an undergrad taking summer classes at UNH, to show. She had an early class on Mondays and I think she only signed up because Michael was standing there over the sheet. Chloe and I settled into two lawn chairs, and draped the blankets we'd brought over us. It wasn't cold but damp, and we wanted to keep the dew and mist from the river off. I turned down the burner on the Coleman lamp to a gentle glow, then sat back, holding the blanket up under my chin and gathering my legs beneath me.

"Four hours," Chloe said.

"Why don't you go home and go to bed, Chloe?"

"And leave you here alone? Not on your life."

"I'll be fine."

"Forget it."

"Four hours," I said.

"Maybe I'll just try to sleep a little here."

"I promise to wake you if anything happens," I said.

"What could happen?" Her head snapped forward.

"Nothing. Nothing could happen."

She leaned back, her head swung around in two slow orbits like a top dying till her chin rested on her chest, but bare seconds later she popped up again and said, "I can't sleep. Let's talk."

"About what?"

"I don't know. Anything but Roger. That gives me a headache."

I said, "Grace was still up when we left. She's going to get less sleep than we are tonight."

"She's just trying to make sure everything's secure for tomorrow. If we catch a wake on the beam, we'll rock and everything that's not tied down will end up in the sole."

"Why didn't you ever tell me you could pilot a boat?"

"I don't know. It never came up. I've been doing it for so long it doesn't seem unusual. It would be like telling you I can spit. Lots of kids around here are raised on boats. My father hauled traps on the side for a long time, then when I was six he lost a job at the navy yard and so he started lobstering full-time. My family's on boats more than we're in cars."

"I really like the water," I said, yawning.

"Me, I like getting off it. It's just a place to work. It's always cold. The bait stinks. It can scare the pee out of you. On land the weather is a daily thing. You watch the news: it's going to be seventy-five degrees and partly cloudy. Out on the ocean it's a momentary thing. The tide, the wind, the pressure. You always have to be on the lookout. And if it's not the weather, it's other boats, running over you or kicking up a wake, or it's your own boat, losing your engine or your radio or your winch. The only time I don't worry about my dad is when I'm on the boat with him and I'm worrying about both of us."

"Does he like it?"

"Most days he loves it. He likes the details: painting the buoys, repairing the traps, washing down the boat. He likes being his own boss. He talks to the lobsters like they're old friends. Sometimes he gets upset if he loses a trap. In the summer when the pleasure boats really get going they cut buoys up pretty bad. Occasionally he'll hear of some gold plater being hauled or hiring a diver to cut thirty feet of warp wrapped around their prop and it really hacks him. He's working and they're playing. But I tell him those are the same people who're buying his lob-

sters. He doesn't want to see that side of it. My dad, when he gets an idea, that's it. There's no swaying him. He's wicked stubborn."

"What's he going to do when he finds out you're pregnant?"

"I don't know. He'll be disappointed. I feel like I've let him down, but what can I do? He'll be ashamed probably."

"Are you ashamed?"

"Of course not."

"Then he doesn't have a right to be either."

"What does right have to do with what your parents think?"

"I don't know. I get along with my folks. They always seem to be fairly rational."

"Did you ever go home pregnant?"

"No."

"With your head shaved?"

"No."

"Earring in your nose?"

"You don't have an earring in your nose."

"Did when I was fifteen. Boy, that sent them up."

"What happened?"

"Oh, it got infected so I let it heal over."

"No. What did your parents say?"

"My mom yelled and my dad said my name softly and then he walked down to his workshop real slow. All that over a pierced nose. I mean I've never done hard drugs, never got a speeding ticket. It's true my room was always a mess. There were periods when I sulked and took it out on them. It was the only power I had, to sway their emotions. I can be mean."

"What happened? Why'd you leave home?"

"I started spending nights out with Roger. At the time I didn't see how I could live without him, and they didn't see him at all. Roger sort of skulks wherever he goes. He has a permanently guilty conscience. There are times when I've wanted to put my knee in the middle of his back, grab his shoulders, and really straighten him up. Anyway, their last power play was living at home. Home or Roger. They even put a curfew on me. I'm wicked stubborn too. So I left. Haven't spoken to them in almost eight months now."

"Maybe, Chloe, you could introduce me to your parents. I'm fairly respectable. I could be there when you tell them about the baby. Then you could tell them Roger's out of the picture. That might mollify them."

"They'll be happy to hear that, sure."

"Whenever you want," I said.

"OK," she whispered.

She pulled her lower lip into her mouth and stared into the folds of the blanket. "I know my dad loves me," she said. "I know he can't help the way he thinks."

"But your mom can?"

"My mom," she sighed, "she's . . . she's hard to cut any slack. She says she knows me, and I tell her if she knows me it's only because she knows herself. There's this way she has of twisting her lips. Her eyeballs get real big and she tries to drive them right through me and so I yell at her, 'Your eyeballs are big, Ma! Your eyeballs are gonna explode!' I think she feels she has to be hard because it's impossible for my dad to be that way with me. He just can't do it. He'll establish a position, like a rock in the river, but all you've got to do is move around him. Mom, she keeps stepping in front of you till you have to shove her or turn around and go back the way you came. But it's probably not her fault either. I'm such a black sheep. Fat, pregnant, and poor."

"Sometimes," I added, "your feet smell really bad too."

"I wasn't very good in algebra in high school, either."

"Your roots are showing, even in this light."

"When I wake up in the mornings, Charlotte, my underwear is always giving me a wedgy," she sissed.

We laughed, swaying in our lawn chairs, rollicking over the dead. When our laughter died down to the same muffled hiss of the Coleman, Chloe whispered, "We should hold a seance. To see if they have anything to say to us." She nodded toward the tarp.

"There's only the two of us, though," I said.

"That won't matter. As long as we hold hands, it's still a circle." She grabbed the arms of her lawn chair and bumped toward me, folding and unfolding with an insect crackle and leap. Her hands were warm and moist. If I'd touched them in the dark I'd have screamed.

"What now?" I asked.

"Well, I'm not sure exactly. I only know what I've seen on TV. We hold hands. We call forth the dead by name. And we must have faith in their presence or they won't come."

"But we don't know their names. We don't even know if they're male or female."

"We'll call them, 'O ye buried below ye blue tarp.' They'll know who they are."

"Don't we need a candle and a big oak table?"

"There's the Coleman. It's a couple thousand candles. As for the table, let's just hold hands over the blanket."

I couldn't think of any other hindrances.

"OK," Chloe whispered, "here goes." Her grip tightened on my hands. It was as if I were being clutched by an entire can of Vienna sausages with knuckles. "O ye buried below ye blue tarp, we beseech thee to come forward and give us, Chloe and Charlotte, a sign. Remembering," she added, "that I'm a pregnant woman."

"A sign?" I asked.

"A sign," she said.

"How will we know?"

"We'll know, Charlotte. It will be a goddamned SIGN. Shut up. You'll frighten them off."

"It's me that's frightened," I sprayed.

"O ye buried below ye blue tarp," she began again, "give us a sign of your presence."

No cars moved nearby. We seemed to be alone in the park. Only the lap of the current at the seawall and the fizz of insects around the Coleman broke the silence. I looked down at the tarp. A slight breeze moved over it, caused the tarp to swell upward momentarily, then reside. I suddenly remembered the mound of earth next to Jonah's open grave was covered with a green tarp. Why? So the mourners would think of it as grass rather than dirt? I wanted to get him in the ground so badly at the time. He seemed vulnerable in the sun. I wanted to send everyone away and bury him myself, alone.

"There's no sign, Chloe. Let's stop."

"Wait, wait," she said. "Give them a chance. Do you feel it getting colder?"

"No," I said, somewhat abruptly. Then added, "It always gets colder after midnight anyway."

"It's awfully quiet," she said.

"Chloe," I said.

She began to hum, or rather, moan. Then chanted, "O ye, O ye, O ye, O ye."

"Chloe," I whispered, my voice cracking.

The wind bloated the tarp once again. Something moved in the branches of a tree.

"Give us a sign," she said, "just an idea."

I found myself losing my grip on her hands and squeezed harder. Somewhere on the Southside a dog barked, and barked again. I closed my eyes.

"Please," Chloe said, "we want to help. Some sign. A word. Just give us a. . . ."

The warning siren on Memorial Bridge sounded then, a shriek into the night. We both stood up, still clenching hands, and moved closer together. Chloe's breath glanced off my neck in quick hot bursts. Even though she'd heard the blast a thousand times before, she asked almost breathlessly, "What was that?"

"It was the bridge. Someone's going under the bridge."

"Right," she gasped. "That's it. It wasn't a sign at all." Then she dropped her hands, pulled them back up to her face. "Or was it?"

"Oh, Chloe. Look, it's 1:30. It opens on the half hour when someone wants to go through."

"Right," she said. "Right." Then, changing her mind she said, "No, no. That's only during the day. At night you have to ask for it to be opened. Someone asked the bridge to open just as we called for a sign."

We collapsed back down into the webbing of our chairs and exhaled when someone put a hand on both of our shoulders. I heard all the air go out of Chloe's body as she rose from her chair. Her body turned. It seemed as if I saw it all in slow motion: the rapid flash of her eyelids, her little teeth frost-heaved in abject fear, the twisting of her legs as she rose, unable to catch up with her torso, and the beginning of her fall into the excavation. She held out her hands to me and I threw myself toward her and came up with the swing of fat beneath her armpit. My

fingers dug in but we'd already passed beyond some fulcrum of hope and weight and she pulled me over. Together we screamed the scream of falling into an open grave in the depth of night. We crashed through the taut tarp and landed with a wump on the clay, our arms entwined, our legs and feet still looking for traction, spinning like the wheels of an overturned car. Before I had a moment to move, Chloe was scratching her way out of the grave, fighting me, the tarp, and her own unfamiliar proportions. It was Grace who finally pulled her up and free.

"Jesus Christ, Grace, what'd you do that for?" Chloe screamed.

I pulled myself up over the lip and put both hands on my chest, trying to keep my heart tucked in. Grace was in her nightgown and robe.

"Do what?" she asked. "I just wanted to see if you girls were all right before I went to bed."

"Well, why did you slip up on us like that? You nearly scared the baby out of me."

"You've got the wildest imagination, Chloe. Here, I brought you a snack."

Grace reached inside her robe and magically produced two huge cinnamon muffins. Chloe's expression was completely transformed.

"Look, Charlotte," she said, "muffins."

"Thanks, Grace," I said.

We lifted the tarp and pulled it taut again. It was going to be hard to explain the six-foot rip in the middle. No rain was forecasted so I wasn't worried about that. But I was worried that we might have disturbed some of the overlying earth. I raised the edge of the tarp and held the Coleman up.

"Be careful," Chloe whispered, as if I were leaning over to look under the bed.

Some dirt had spalled from the quadrants we hadn't yet excavated onto those we had, but there didn't seem to be any great damage. I couldn't yet believe I'd done exactly what I was put there to prevent others from doing.

I gave Grace my chair and sat down on an upturned five-gallon bucket.

"Why don't you girls come home?" she said. "No one's going to bother these people."

"People vandalize archaeological sites all the time, Grace," I said. "They think they'll find some fabulous treasure. For some reason people think burials are just loaded with loot. They think every grave is another King Tut. It usually isn't. They miss the treasure by destroying it. The burial itself, the methods of interment and the bones themselves, the data, are the treasure."

"So that makes you the treasure hunter," Grace said. "Charlotte, honey, maybe these people have secrets. Why not let them alone?"

I wanted to just tell her OK, but every nail on my hands longed to scrape the dirt from those bones, to know their faces. "I don't know, Grace. It's an intrusion, I know. On one level digging a grave is the ultimate voyeurism. We just can't help but look. On the other hand it's an attempt to understand ourselves. We're looking at someone else's grave but we're really looking at our own. It's one of the few times we look into someone else's face and see it as a mirror. It's voyeurism but it isn't as titillating as it is humbling."

"So why do it?" she insisted.

"Because we're like dogs, Grace. We've always considered the earth to be the safest depository for our valuables, but we've got to keep digging up our bones to make sure they're really safe. I don't know why, Grace. I wouldn't want to dig up my grandmother, but these people seem removed. Besides, we weren't looking for them. If we'd set out to dig people up, we'd have picked a likely spot in front of a tombstone across the street. These people presented themselves to us."

"You're digging them up, as you say, because they're valuable. Whether the value is in the knowledge you gain, or the rings off their fingers, it's still vandalism and thievery."

"You can't equate a search for knowledge with one for money, Grace. That's not fair."

"Hmph," she snorted.

"Aren't they going to run a pipeline right through them?" Chloe said.

The three of us looked out into the darkness. Chloe finished her muffin so I broke mine in two and handed her half. A car thrummed by on Marcy Street.

"This is where Binny Wallace washed up," Grace said, rather lugubriously.

"What?" Chloe asked.

"Binny Wallace. A little boy swept out to sea in a small boat. A squall came up and well, he washed up right here at Point of Graves."

"When was this?" I asked. "Did you know him?"

"I read it in *The Story of a Bad Boy*," Grace said. "Thomas Bailey Aldrich wrote it."

"That's eerie," Chloe said. "Him washing up right here at the grave-yard."

"It's fiction, Chloe," I said. "It didn't happen."

"It's in the book," Grace said.

"That doesn't mean it happened," I said in exasperation.

"It doesn't mean it didn't," Grace said.

"She's got you there, Charlotte," Chloe affirmed.

We were silent for a moment when Chloe added, "Washed up right here. A little boy."

"Criminy," I huffed.

"Was he the bad boy?" Chloe asked.

"Oh no, he was a sweet little thing. Mr. Aldrich was the bad boy."

"Swept out to sea," Chloe whispered.

"Well, I'm going to bed," Grace said, and pushed herself up from the chair. I was still pouting. "You girls lock up when you come in. To-morrow's a big day. Going upriver. Big day."

And Grace walked off, quietly for a bit, but then we heard her speaking in conversational tones again, and saw her speed increase as she gathered her robe and nightgown up and disappeared through the trees.

"They're after her again," Chloe said.

"Who could they be?"

"I don't think they're people. Well, maybe. But mostly I think they're Grace. I mean her doubts and misgivings, her regrets. I think it's queer that she can get through a whole lifetime like she has and not yet be sure of herself."

"Grace?" I asked.

"Grace," she said.

"I don't see it," I said.

"It's hard for you to see anything, Grace says."

"What does that mean?" I threw back.

"She says that it will take you a year or two to stop thinking continually about yourself."

I was appalled. "What? I don't think about myself continually. I'm trying to be active and involved."

"That's just outside stuff, Grace says. She's not saying you're egotistical or anything, just self-absorbed. She says you can't see anything as it is right now because you're so bewildered by your husband dying. I shouldn't have told you. She thinks the world of you."

I didn't know what to say so I put my hands in my hair. I felt accused but didn't see any form of defense that didn't begin with the word "I." Finally, I said, "Are you OK, Chloe? You're not hurt anywhere are you?"

"I think I've got a wicked bruise on my butt."

"But the baby's OK? I mean you don't feel funny or anything?"

"I'm fine," she said. "Just no more seances."

"Right," I said. "Let's leave the dead where they are."

"Well," Chloe said, "I'd rather they come to us than we go to them. I can't believe we fell in someone's grave. I mean, with them already in it."

"When the next shift shows up," I said, "let's not mention that."

"OK, but what about the rip?"

"I'll tell them the wind did it."

"Good idea," Chloe yawned.

We sat for the next hour or two, listening to the wind and current, the occasional passing car or boat. Chloe dozed off from time to time, her mouth falling open, her hands distractedly smoothing the mound of her belly. I distinctly made the effort not to think about myself, but found it almost maddeningly impossible. Crazy old woman. She'd given me a monkey's puzzle. The harder I pulled, the tighter my brain's orbit became. Under the strain, I too, fell asleep.

I woke to the crunch of gravel under tires. Michael was parking his small truck on Mechanic Street between two other cars. It was 3:15 A.M. We had another forty-five minutes till the next crew would show up.

"I couldn't sleep," he said as he walked nearer.

I held my finger to my lips and shushed but it was too late. Chloe climbed out of her sleep with whimpers and kicking feet.

"It's OK," I said, "it's OK."

"I'm sorry," Michael whispered.

"Chloe was just keeping me company. Chloe, this is Michael, the archaeologist from Strawbery Banke."

"Hi," she sniffed.

"I didn't think I'd see you till later this morning, after the council meeting," I said.

"I thought I'd just check on everything," he said. "I knew you'd be here."

Chloe leaned toward Michael, yawned at him, and asked, "Will you be here till the next shift comes on?"

"Yeah, sure," he said.

"Then I think I'll go home and go to bed, if that's all right with you, Charlotte?"

"Go home," I said. "Michael, will you walk her? It's just across the park."

"Sure."

They set off, Chloe wrapped in her blanket, Michael's hands stuffed deeply into his pant pockets. I rubbed the sleep from my eyes and the corners of my mouth and tried to shake some life into my hair. When Michael returned, he sat in Chloe's chair. I braced myself as he began to speak, spreading my feet so I could lie more staunchly about the torn tarp.

"I thought she was half asleep, your friend, but she startled me," he said.

"Why?"

"I was just saying things, trying to make her feel at ease as we walked. She doesn't know me. I was saying things and all of the sudden she tells me that I'm fond of you. I thought she was half-asleep."

I was so startled I told the truth just to change the subject. "I tripped and fell into the excavation. I ripped the cover. It's my fault."

He looked over at the excavation. "Was anything hurt?"

"I don't think so. I looked with the lantern. I don't think so." I

pulled my feet up underneath my butt and looked at the rip in the tarp.

"I'm sorry," he said. "I didn't mean to make you nervous. I know where you are, and I won't push it, but I needed to tell you. I've been lying in my bed for the past few hours, wide awake, not because I'm concerned about the dig but because I've been thinking about you out here. It wouldn't be fair if I didn't tell you. I mean fair to me. But I want you to know I won't push it because I know where you are."

"Where am I?" I asked.

He moved uncomfortably in his lawn chair. "I mean it's only been a short time since you've been alone, since your husband died."

"If he were here right now he'd kick your ass," I lied.

"I'm sorry, Charlotte. I didn't mean. . . ."

"You did mean."

"It's not my fault that I've met you now. Forget it. I didn't expect you to jump into my arms. I mean, nothing would be possible if you didn't know how I felt."

I leaned forward, both of my hands in fists in my lap. "I loved my husband," I said. "I still love him. No one can change that." And I almost added, "Not even he could."

Michael slumped back in his chair. "I'm sorry, I'm sorry," he whispered. "I don't want to take anything from you."

I knew I was being unfair to him, but his was the first assault upon my past. I wanted it intact and whole. He wanted to confuse the issue.

We sat silently for a few minutes and I'd begun to say, "I'm sorry" when he held up his hand.

"It's OK. I've gotten it off my chest. I'm sorry I upset you. I hope this won't interfere with your work. You're very good and I'll need you when we get the OK to proceed. Maybe your husband. . . ." Michael began.

"No," I broke in. "You shouldn't say anything about him. You shouldn't even guess. I'll say anything that needs to be said about him."

"OK," Michael nodded, "You're right."

"He deserved my love."

"Yes," Michael said. "It's OK, Charlotte." He stood up then and stepped toward me. He reached down and took my hand. I felt my knees give and almost simultaneously his hand on the small of my back

to hold me up. I turned my face toward his and although I did not meet his kiss I did not draw back either. His lips felt so strange, so unfamiliar. It was only for the briefest moment that we touched. I was shaking uncontrollably with grief. He let me back down into my chair and he sat down on the edge of his and that's when we both heard the automatic whir of a self-winding camera coming from one of the cars parked along Mechanic Street. It stopped almost as soon as it had begun, then the car behind Michael's started, backed up, then shot forward down the street and around the corner.

"What the hell was that?" he asked.

"Someone took photographs of us," I said.

"But why?"

"I don't know. But it scares the shit out of me." Michael looked at me, and turned his head back to where the car had been. "That car has been there all night," I said. "I had no idea there was someone in it."

"Are you in some kind of trouble, Charlotte?"

I shook my head. "I don't know." Perhaps it was absurd, but it suddenly occurred to me that I might be asking him the same question. If someone was taking our photograph in the middle of the night, why shouldn't I assume that he was in some kind of trouble? Maybe the man I'd seen taking pictures in the cemetery a week earlier hadn't taken a photo of me. Maybe he'd been shooting for Michael over my shoulder. The yellow crime scene tape still hung around our excavation. I stood up then. "The next crew will be here in a few minutes. Can you cover for me? I'm going home."

"Sure I can, but, Charlotte. . . ."

"I have to get up early. I'm helping a friend take her boat upriver in the morning."

"Charlotte."

"I have to go now."

"Charlotte."

"I'm sorry," I said and I walked away, lowering my head and speeding up, and halfway home heard myself speaking aloud, "You don't need that now, you just don't need anyone else now," speaking with authority, as if I knew exactly who I was talking to.

≈

The roar of *Rosinante*'s engine woke me in the morning. I hurriedly dressed. Midden sat in the middle of the floor, his eyes wide and whiskers twitching. He knew something was up. Chloe was at the helm with Harry, and Grace handed me my second muffin in the past eight hours.

"I'm handling the dock lines," she said. "No time for a sit-down breakfast today." She put her hand on Harry's forearm. "Just tell me when."

"OK, Grace, dear. It'll be a bit. We want to let this old girl get comfortable."

I got the impression that Grace had asked several times already. She looked back at me, her lips parted in an attempt to smile, but they could only reveal impatience. Now that she'd decided to go, she wanted to be there and back.

Harry went down to the engine room, came back shaking his head and said, "What a beast."

"It's very reliable," Grace insisted. "Not once has it ever let us down."

"I believe you, dear," he said. He tested forward and reverse, throttled up and down, then gave Grace and me the go ahead. "Release your lines girls. This boat's been here so long she'll break from the dock like an iceberg."

No one was on the dock to see us off, but I was as excited as if there'd been thousands, waving and cheering. I jumped across open water to the dock and unwrapped the stern line from its cleat while Grace pulled it aboard. We did the same for the bow line, and as I flipped it to Grace, I realized that the gap between *Rosinante* and the dock was gradually widening. She was free and the incoming tide was taking her already.

"Jump," Grace said, and so I did, landing with a thud and an enormous grin that vibrated up from my shoes. "We're away," Grace yelled into the salon at Harry and I said it again, just so I could enjoy the roll of the words across my tongue too. I smiled broadly at Chloe who suffered me kindly.

Harry pushed the throttle forward and we began to churn into the current. I stepped back outside and ran to the stern to watch our wake. As we reached the middle of the river, Harry turned *Rosinante*'s bow. The current took her nose and spun the boat around and we were off at seven knots. We slipped under Memorial Bridge and past the rafted tugboats, past the Sheraton and beyond the scrap metal yard. Long Bridge lay before us, too low to pass under, except for a section near the Maine coast where the railroad track had been hoisted and moved over.

"We could scoot through there," Harry said, "but it's tight."

Grace lifted the mike to the marine radio and her voice took on a clipped but clear tone, "Long Bridge, Long Bridge, this is the motor yacht *Rosinante* coming up river requesting a lift at your next scheduled opening. We need twenty feet."

The radio crackled back, "We see you, Captain. Be about three minutes."

She replaced the mike. I said, "Grace, that was great."

"Nothing to it," she said. "Parts of the Intracoastal Waterway, I was doing that every ten minutes. Sweet George always said the bridges opened sooner when I asked."

"No doubt, Grace dear," Harry affirmed.

The siren soon sounded on Long Bridge, the traffic stopped, and the central span rose straight up on steel cables. Harry applied power and we slipped under.

"Give'm our thanks, Grace," Harry said, and she walked over to the helm and pushed the air horn button. *Rosinante* emitted a short blast, like a dumpling shot across the water.

"She does cut through the water," Harry said. "Hardly any wake to speak of. Fine craft." Grace beamed. All of her agitation over leaving the dock seemed to have gone. It returned when Harry said, "Chloe dear, you take her, would you?"

She stepped up to the big mahogany wheel without the least hesitation, and as Grace brought both hands up to her mouth Chloe took one hand from the wheel and pushed the throttle forward. "What do you think, Harry? About eighteen hundred?"

"She ought to cruise nicely there," he said.

Rosinante swept under the I-95 bridge, almost a hundred and twenty

feet above us. Turning with the current as the river narrowed, we passed colonial and Victorian houses on the Maine side. As we came around a swirling bend at the power plant the river opened up again. There were small boats moored beyond the channel markers: lobster boats, sloops, a bright blue dory, and the green-hulled *Yonder* that we'd seen before. They all bobbed on their chains with promise, like dogs in the park.

"This is what they call Long Reach," Harry said. "Straight shot all the way to Dover from here."

We passed another power plant, the fishing co-op where Harry unloaded his catch after every voyage and finally Chloe and Harry eased up to the dock at Patten's Yacht Yard on the Maine side. We threw our lines to a man on the pier, Grace and I, but she followed hers with a dozen admonitions, half orders and half threats that *Rosinante* not get dinged. Harry jumped down to the dock to help Grace and me down. Chloe remained aboard to guide *Rosinante* onto the lift.

"This is the owner," Harry said, introducing Grace. She shook the man's hand, almost as if she'd been forced to.

"You'll be gentle?" she affirmed.

"Yes, Ma'am."

"I'll be watching," she warned.

"Yes, Ma'am. We've done hundreds of boats," he said.

"This is the only one that counts," she said.

"Yes, Ma'am."

Harry said, "Steve, she's pretty foul, I think. Hasn't been out of the water in four years and you can feel every bit of it dragging as you go along. We just want to knock everything off with a pressure hose and have you go over the hull to make sure everything's in order."

Within ten minutes a semi had winched a special trailer down the ramp and Chloe had positioned the boat over it. Hydraulic arms rose from the bed of the trailer to brace the boat and the trailer was winched back up to the truck, which pulled forward slowly up the incline. The great bulk of *Rosinante*'s girth slowly left the water. Green moss, long strands of brown seaweed and gray barnacles clung to her hull and glistened in the sunshine. She seemed monstrous out of the water, towering over all of us and dwarfing the semi. We all walked under her sea-draped sheer, looking at the walls of our dripping home. The prop and rudder

were massive but were almost hidden under a thick curtain of marine growth.

Grace said, "Sweet George would be ashamed. I should have done this long ago. I've let her go."

Steve used a heavy wand to direct the pressure wash. The algae and seaweed fell away quickly, revealing a sometimes green, sometimes brown and occasionally shiny copper hull. The barnacles left small circles of brightness, like new pennies, on the sheathing. As the growth fell away, the beauty of *Rosinante*'s lines became apparent. Graceful and slim, she was a work of art in design. She had the same organic sense of line that airplanes and cars had in the thirties, as if beauty were just as important as utility. She seemed full and sensuous, like a sail ripe with wind.

"She's gorgeous," I told Grace.

"Sweet George was in love with her," she said, and then, not seeming to expect an answer she added, "How many owners do you suppose she's outlived?"

It took little more than an hour to clean the bottom, and another hour to inspect the hull and replace several sacrificial zincs bolted to the prop and rudder. The various metals used to construct a boat, when immersed in salt water, can act as a weak battery and the resulting electrolysis can corrode the weakest metal present. Sometimes, according to Harry, the weakest metal is the prop, sometimes it's the fasteners holding the boat together. The zincs are more prone to electrolytic action than most metals and therefore, if they're replaced before they completely deteriorate, they'll save the rest of the boat from corrosion.

"I wish there was something like a zinc I could wear on my wrist," I told Harry.

"Don't you know it, girl," he said. He looked down at his wet boots for a moment, then spoke lightly, "My mother and father took it all on themselves. Wouldn't let a hair of harm come my way if they could help it."

"Well, Harry," I whispered, "you're a poet."

He visibly shied. "Not me, little girl. I'm a fisherman," and he moved away from me, my presence almost unbearable I suppose.

As *Rosinante* was lowered back into the river, Grace's shoulders drooped with relief. "I didn't like that one bit," she said.

"All better now," Harry told her and squeezed her arm as he passed.

We moved back out into deeper water and Chloe turned *Rosinante*'s bow into the flowing current toward her berth. The tide was against us now and we moved slowly back downriver. I went forward and laid on the deck between the two anchors and looked down into the spin of water lifted by the bow. It curled up from darkness, became clear and buoyant, was sustained with speed and light and fell away beyond with a bare whisper, the same way recognition gives way to knowledge. I pushed myself up and walked back to the salon where Harry and Chloe and Grace were standing.

"We could go anywhere now," I said.

Harry smiled. "All you need is three feet of water."

Grace, weary of the morning and her worry of memory, knocked three times on the mahogany of the helm, and said, "If we can just get back to the Smarmy Snail, I'll be happy."

"I've got to go to work this afternoon, so no transoceanic trips for me," Chloe said.

"Can I go out with you sometime, Harry?" I asked.

Chloe looked at me and sneered.

"Of course," Harry said.

"You'll be sorry," Chloe followed.

"I will not."

"Let her go," Grace said.

"You'll have to work," Harry added. "No room on a trawler for tourists."

Chloe began to giggle.

"What?" I asked.

"You'll see," she said.

"Don't let her scare you off," Harry said. "Anytime you want just say the word."

"I'm not afraid of work," I defended myself. "As soon as I'm finished at the dig, Harry. I'll let you know."

"Good girl."

Chloe giggled once more. I kneed her in the butt. Grace sighed. "When are you two going to grow up?"

"I'm grown up," Chloe laughed. "I'm having a baby."

Which left me without a response. I went back out on deck and watched the water swirl by.

"There are too many things that torment you," I said aloud. "You've got to let some of them go." I turned and looked through the windows of the salon, at Chloe and Grace, who were looking back at me, trying to read the words on my lips. I smiled a lying little smile and turned my face back into the wind, so that my hair could blow from my mouth and eyes.

≈

We were so busy when we returned, tying up to the dock, that I never noticed the man looking down on us from the deck of the Smarmy Snail. Grace and Chloe and I gathered on the dock after *Rosinante* was secure to thank Harry.

"Think nothing of it," he said, refusing to look us in the eye and turning up the gangway. He passed the man in the suit on his way down. And although Harry said, "Hello," the man just brushed past him.

The man strode directly to me and spoke my name.

"Yes?"

"Would you sign for this, please." He handed me an envelope.

"What is it?" I asked.

"A summons. The contents will be self-explanatory. I need your signature."

"What is it?" Chloe asked.

"Just a minute." I signed my name and he strode back up the gangway. I read for a few moments, then read again.

"Well, honey?" Grace asked.

"I'm being sued," I said.

"By who?"

"Richard and Mary, my in-laws."

"But why, what for?" Grace asked.

I looked up into the bewilderment of their faces and explained, "For the murder of my husband."

What Richard and Mary propounded was so completely removed from my conception of the events surrounding Jonah's death that their

suit took me completely by surprise. It was their contention that I owed them damages for the loss of their son, that his death was a direct result of my actions and behavior; that, in short, I withheld affection, which led to his depression and ultimately his suicide. I stepped back aboard the security of *Rosinante* and sat down on the settee. Grace and Chloe followed, at a respectable distance, and stood in front of me.

"I'll make some tea," Grace said. She went below.

"Charlotte?"

I looked up at Chloe. The wrinkles on her forehead plunged into her hairline like waves into salt grass.

"I didn't kill my husband, Chloe."

"Maybe you need to get a lawyer," she said.

"They're forcing me to see them," I said. "I've been free of them for a few months and so they're forcing me to meet them. They just won't let him die."

"They're parents: they're crazy," Chloe said.

I raised the envelope and shook it. "They're saying I didn't love Jonah," I yelled. "They say he committed suicide because I didn't love him."

"He committed suicide?" Chloe asked.

"I don't know," I said softly. It was the first time I'd acknowledged the possibility.

Grace brought a pitcher of iced tea up from the galley and she and Chloe sat across the table from me. I took a tumbler, held it firmly while Grace poured and then rolled it between my palms on the tabletop. It was cold and wet.

"They've probably been watching me for a week or two. I saw a man, some kind of detective, I suppose, at the dig last week and I think again last night after you left, Chloe. He took pictures of me and Michael."

"Why would he take pictures of you and Michael?" Chloe asked.

"Probably," I hesitated, "because we were kissing," and I began to sob.

"There's nothing to kissing," Grace said. "It's not against the law."

"But I know what they'll think when they see the photographs," I said.

"Who?" Chloe asked.

"Richard and Mary. They'll take it as proof that they're right. That I didn't love him. And I did. I still do." I had my hands over my eyes, but I could feel my tears squeezing through my fingers.

"Charlotte," Grace said, "calm down. Jonah's been dead for almost six months. It's all right for you to kiss someone."

"I'm not in love with him," I burbled. "I just wanted the kiss. I wanted someone to want to kiss me."

Chloe and Grace moved around the table, sat next to me, and put their arms around my shaking shoulders. "I'll stop, I'll stop," I said. And I began wiping my cheeks with the back of my hands.

"It's all right," Grace said.

"Yeah, it's all right, Charlotte," Chloe said.

I cleared my throat. "Oh, God."

"There," Grace said, rubbing my forearm.

"There, now," Chloe said.

"Oh, God," I said. "I need a plan."

"You need a lawyer," Chloe said.

"What do they want?" Grace asked.

"Well," I said, dabbing my eyes with my sleeve, "I can't go to jail. It's a civil suit. They obviously couldn't get anybody to go along with any kind of criminal charges. They want a million dollars."

"A million dollars?" Chloe screeched.

"It's ridiculous," I said. "I'm sure they know to the dime how much money I have. There's no way I could pay it. They'd get what I have and I'd file bankruptcy."

"But they can't win, can they?" Grace asked.

"I don't think so. I hope they don't believe what they've suggested. Maybe they're just trying to force me to meet with them."

"Why wouldn't they have just come here?" Chloe asked.

"I don't know. Maybe they're too mad."

"They're nuts," Chloe said.

"I just can't believe they would say those things in a courtroom. In front of my parents and our friends. In front of me."

"Don't count on it," Grace said. "If they feel scorned, they'll do just about anything. And you did, in a way, abandon them."

"Just to save myself. I hadn't married them."

"I know, I know," she said. "I'm not saying what you did was

wrong. But in a way they're unrequited, and they're hurt. Maybe they feel they're saving themselves too. Or maybe they feel they're protecting their son in the only way they have left."

"You know," I said softly, "Never once did any of us suggest that Jonah had killed himself. I think we all thought about it. But the authorities ruled the wreck an accident. There was some evidence of skid marks that showed he was trying to brake before he went off the road. But we all knew that he'd been depressed for months. We couldn't help but think . . . of course there's no way to know."

"I'm sure it was just an accident," Chloe said. "Thousands of people are killed every year in car accidents. Odds are it was an accident."

I looked at her and nodded. "He didn't leave any kind of note to me or his parents. He was alive one minute and gone the next and no one was with him. The last time I saw him was when he left for work that morning. He kissed me and said good-bye, like always."

"Why do you think he was depressed, honey?" Grace asked.

"Maybe he was having trouble at his work," Chloe suggested.

"No. Everything was OK at the office. I mean, he didn't care for his job, but it alone wasn't the cause of his problems."

"What was?" Chloe asked.

"Chloe," Grace admonished.

"I'm sorry, I can't help it," she apologized. "You asked her in the first place, Grace."

"It's OK," I said. None of us had taken as much as a sip of our tea. I lifted my glass and knocked off a third of it, then wiped my mouth with my hand. "I don't know. He was just depressed. It was getting to the point that he didn't even eat much. He never smiled. He never raised his voice. He just didn't seem interested in anything. He functioned. He got up and went to work. He could sleep. I tried to get him to go see a doctor but he wasn't interested in that either. He said it was just a phase. He even made jokes about it. He said if he just watched enough TV he'd get over it. And then he wouldn't smile at his own joke. He died in a car crash." And then I told Chloe and Grace the most bald-faced lie I'd ever told them, but I was only then beginning to understand it as a lie. "One morning Jonah and I were in love with each other, and that evening there was only me left to love him."

We sat silently for moments, sliding our tumblers in slow circles on the varnished mahogany, through pools of condensation. The glasses refused to leave wakes.

"I just can't figure out what they want," I said at last.

"They want their son back," Chloe said matter-of-factly.

I shot back, "The thing is, I want him back too. I didn't take him. I haven't got him. I don't know where he is, either."

I hated to cry, especially in front of other people. I'd rather be morose than gushing. Although Chloe cried without any provocation, easily and with abandon, Grace never shed a tear. Her eyes seemed to be as dry as dead spiders at moments when anyone else would be underwater. Perhaps she'd used them all up, I thought, her tears. But I found out later that there isn't any specific allotment. I should have guessed because Chloe dipped out of an endless river. Or perhaps they were just the same tears, the tide coming in and going out, and we use them over and over.

With the arrival of the suit I'd completely forgotten about the dig. I was supposed to be at the site with the rest of the volunteers and crew at noon so Michael could give us the news on whether we could continue. I looked at my watch and said, "I've got to go."

"What are you going to do, honey?" Grace asked.

"I'm going to think about what to do. But I'm going to think about it later. I'm tired of it now. I'm going to the dig."

Grace said, "OK, but get yourself a better lawyer than the one I had." She smiled.

"OK," I smiled back at her.

"Charlotte?" Chloe called as I stepped off the boat.

"What?"

"I'm ready. I know it's not a good time for you, but I'm ready."

"For what, Chloe?" I'm afraid, even though she'd been more than generous with her ear, that I sounded exasperated. "I'm sorry, Chloe. Ready for what?"

"To go see my parents. You said you'd help."

"When?"

"Tonight?"

"OK." I ran up the gangway two ribs at a step.

≈

A knot of people stood close to Michael. He'd just arrived. "OK," he said. "Here's our mandate. Sometime this afternoon representatives from the Portsmouth police and the coroner's office will come by to inspect the site. Tomorrow we'll have a visit from some people from the University of New Hampshire. The city said to take all the time we need. According to their surveyors, our two friends here would be cut in two by the pipeline. So we'll remove them, and it looks like the university will do the lab work. As to the ultimate disposition of the remains: that will be decided when we have more information. There's lots of variables, whether they're Native American, European, or African, whether we can find some kind of archival material on them. So, let's clean up the site, and settle down into some slow, detailed, exacting work. I'm expecting the state archaeologist any minute. He wants to monitor and help out with the excavation. Any questions?"

"The other stain," I said. "What about it? It might be a grave as well, Michael."

"I presented that possibility to everyone concerned. Since we'd have to tear up the street to excavate it, and since it won't interfere with the pipeline or work in the park, the consensus is to leave it undisturbed. To include it in the report of course, in case future work is done in this area."

I understood the reasoning but it still bothered me to be this close and to turn away. It might be decades before another archaeologist worked here. The only consolation, and it's considerable, is that she'll have better techniques and more knowledge. That's why many sites go purposefully unexcavated. We know their exact location but restraint will prove the better part of archaeology. It's an odd science, waiting to ask why, in hopes we'll be more capable at a later date. It's a luxury that most sciences aren't blessed or humbled or cursed by. Patience is a virtue, but it's not innate. Me, I want to know the cause of the Big Bang right now.

We spent the afternoon mapping the stratigraphy of the quadrants we hadn't brought down to the level of the bones, and building a boardwalk around our much-reduced site so spalling would be kept to a minimum. Bones are quite fragile and the last thing we wanted was a visitor kicking a clod down onto a cranium.

I spoke to Michael briefly and only about the dig. We were surrounded by other volunteers and crew. I owed him an apology for leaving so abruptly. And I wanted to tell him I wasn't ready.

I was distracted most of the afternoon, thinking about the lawsuit, how incredibly outrageous it was, and how I could deal with Richard and Mary and come out with my life intact. Jonah would have been so angry with them. Perhaps I could tell them. But if they really believed I killed him, my resurrecting him to provide a defense probably wouldn't be very convincing. I wanted to get out of the whole ordeal without seeing or speaking to them. Maybe lawyer to lawyer was the way to handle it. I decided to make phone calls first thing in the morning.

≈

Late in the afternoon, as the day's work was breaking up and volunteers were being scheduled for night watch again, I took Michael aside. I held a clipboard with a level sheet as I spoke with him.

"I'm sorry," I said. "I ran off and I'm sorry."

"It's OK," he said.

"No, it wasn't. You were being honest and I wasn't. But I'm being honest now and what I need to tell you is I'm not ready."

He looked down at the ground, holding his face loosely, as if all he cared about at the moment were his shoes.

"I just need more time to get away from where I've been. I'm glad you need me; I'm glad you like me. I need this work and I need people like you around me."

"So we're free to date other people?" he asked.

I laughed, and I reached out and squeezed his forearm.

"As long as you don't tell me about them," I whispered.

"Deal." He looked up and smiled, pegged tooth and all. It wasn't such a bad kiss, just unusual for me, as if I'd kissed the toe of a boot. And that's unfair too, but I'd kissed only Jonah for the past eight years and I suppose any other pair of lips would have seemed as foreign as Michael's.

"We'll uncover the bones tomorrow," he said, walking away from me.

≈

Grace had set up her easel in the salon when I got home. The canvas faced upriver to catch the western light. There was an eight by ten color portrait of Sweet George on the table and Grace was clearly working from it.

"You're doing a portrait of George," I said.

"Yes. I don't do many humans, but I've been thinking of him all day long and I thought this might get him out of my hair."

"Get him out of your hair?"

"Yes, I'm tired of thinking about him. Every once in a while is fine but today's been ridiculous. I mean," and she emphasized her point with a jab of her brush to the canvas, "he's quite dead." She went back to her work, using a length of dowel rod resting on the easel to steady her hand.

"Can I look?"

"Well, there's quite a bit yet to do. All right."

I squeezed between the helm and the edge of the canvas and stood next to her. She was really very good. There was no background as yet and George's shirt was still only sketched in, but his hair and face seemed almost photographically exact. I looked from the canvas to the picture and back again. I checked one more time.

"Grace?" I said softly.

"Yes, dear?"

"His eyes. They're brown." I pointed hesitantly to the canvas.

"Oh, yes," she answered, and with her brush, bent forward and made a tiny stroke representing a faint eyelash.

"But, Grace," I said. "In the photograph his eyes are blue. He had blue eyes."

"Oh, George's eyes were blue, but I've never liked blue eyes, especially on him, so I've changed them. I've always loved dark brown eyes."

I tried to smile but my lips couldn't carry it out. I wanted to run and tell Chloe. I looked at Grace again. "It just doesn't seem right, somehow."

"It's my picture," she said forcefully.

"I know, I know," I said. I stood silently for a moment until I couldn't stand it any longer. "But they were his eyes, and they were

blue. You've put brown eyes in your dead husband's head. Don't you feel guilty?"

"He knew I liked brown eyes. I tried to get him to wear some of those colored contact lenses but he wouldn't do it."

"Grace," I coughed, "that's like some creep asking his wife to wear a blonde wig to bed."

"Don't knock it if you haven't tried it," she said, throwing her shoulders up in the air and shaking her head. Then she began to work on his collarless shirt, a deep red along the arch of his shoulders. She asked, "Haven't you ever said anything about your husband that wasn't true? Never told anyone he was taller, handsomer, nicer, richer, better, than he really was?"

"No," I insisted, trying to wear outrage.

"You've never omitted some detail, some imperfection he had when describing him to a friend or relative, to your mother?"

"Of course not," I said.

"There was nothing about him you would have changed?"

I was stunned. "Grace, that's not fair. I don't even want to think about a question like that."

"Why not?"

"Because I don't."

"You don't want to speak badly of the dead," she mused.

"I don't have anything bad to say about Jonah."

"Then you're a fool. No one, not even Sweet George, is an angel. I'm not trying to say you didn't love him, faults and all, but to say he had no faults is trying to impress someone who's been there and brought back pictures. Was he good in bed?"

"That's it," I said, and started for my cabin.

"Wait a minute," she said, and slapped her brush down on the helm. Specks of red paint splattered across the wheel and onto the photo of Sweet George. "Who's it more important to get along with now?" she yelled, "Me or your dead husband?"

I stood on the first step of the companionway leading down into my cabin. Midden came up from below and began to mew at my feet. Grace looked down at him.

"Your cat or your dead husband?" she asked. She stared at me, her

hands on her hips, and finally, when I wouldn't respond in any way, she said, "Bless it, Charlotte. Now I won't be able to work for the rest of the evening," and she turned and stamped down into the galley and on into her cabin.

I reached down and picked up Midden, the cat my husband would never have tolerated, and went below to my bunk where the cat laid on my chest, alternately sniffing the snot coming from my nose and licking the grit from between his toes.

I didn't think it then, but I imagine that Grace, at that moment, was similarly comforted by Pinky and whatever tenderness or offense he might show her.

≈

Chloe bumped down the companionway later, carrying the results from her latest poll. As she spoke she changed clothes behind the drawn curtain, out of the overalls and black T-shirt that said, I HAVE COMMENT and into a pair of stretch jeans and a man's long-sleeved white shirt.

"I asked everyone if their life was more like a sitcom, a soap opera, or a movie."

"How many responses?" I asked automatically.

"Thirty-two." She picked up her journal she'd dropped on the sole. "Two people refused to answer, twelve said sitcom, eleven opted for a soap opera and only five said movie."

"Were those five old people?" I asked.

"Not necessarily."

"Well, how did they know their life was a movie then?"

"Maybe by the tone it had."

"Tone?"

"Yeah. Maybe their lives have a mood."

"What's your answer?" I asked.

"Well, I think this evening could turn out to be either a sitcom or a soap opera, depending on how it goes."

"Are your folks expecting us?"

"No. I thought we might just show up."

"Why not," I humphed.

"What's wrong with you?"

"That old witch just chewed my butt."

"Grace?"

"Yes."

"Why?"

"You tell me."

"What'd she say?"

"She, well, she. . . ." I was whispering so Chloe pulled back the curtain and came closer. "She was painting Sweet George's picture. I don't know. Something set her off. She thinks I think my husband was perfect."

"Do you?"

"Of course not."

"Did you tell her that?"

"Of course not. It's none of her business."

"You just told me."

"Well, you didn't ask me."

"Are you on the rag or something because maybe we should go to my folks some other day."

"Go to hell," I said.

"Are you mad because she was right or because she wasn't gentle? Part of her problem is she waits till she's dead on before she lights into you. There's nowhere to escape."

"Let's go," I said.

"Are you sure?"

"Let's go." I grabbed my car keys and on our way through the salon I yelled down into the galley, "We're gone, Grace. I don't know how long we'll be." I didn't wait for a response.

We drove across Memorial Bridge to Maine, then took 103 to Kittery Point where Chloe's parents lived in a white cape on Chauncey Creek. She pointed out her father's dock and lobster boat. The house was small with almost no front yard. Roses bloomed under the windows and a gravel driveway led off to a garage and workshop behind the house. Everything was meticulously cared for, the grass freshly mown, hedges trimmed, the house so clean it seemed just washed. Nothing looked as if the people inside hadn't spoken to their daughter in months.

"Do you want me to sit in the car at first?" I asked.

"No. I want you with me. Maybe things will at least start out politely if you're there."

Chloe was so nervous she was sweating. I was beginning to feel uncomfortable myself. I reached into the glove compartment and pulled out a wad of fresh Kleenex.

"Insurance," I said.

Chloe got out of the car and adjusted her clothing. She ran her finger around the spandex waist of her jeans, adjusted both bra straps, and with the tail of her untucked shirt dabbed at the wetness above her lips.

"Do you think they'll be able to tell?" she asked as we walked around the side of the house.

"That you're pregnant?"

She nodded, her eyes wide with terror.

"Maybe not."

She knocked on the back door, and turned to me. "They're here. Both cars are here. Feels funny knocking."

I turned around and looked down into the creek. It was almost low tide. In the middle of the narrow channel a black cormorant stood on the blanched half-moon of a mooring buoy drying his outstretched wings. The door opened. I swung around and heard Chloe say, almost hoarsely, "I've come for a visit."

The woman in the doorway didn't frown or smile. She showed no emotion. I wanted to kill her.

"Come in," she said. "It's perfect timing," and the woman turned back into the house.

Chloe looked at me and whispered, "I'm sorry. Maybe you shouldn't come in."

"She's pissed me off already. I'm here for the duration," I said.

We stepped inside. The house smelled of potpourri and incense. It was almost overpowering. There were empty boxes on the dining table and the contents of the upper kitchen cabinets were stacked on the countertop. There was a sheaf of blank newsprint on the floor, dishes piled around it.

"Thomas, come out here," Chloe's mother yelled.

A balding man, sunburnt came out of a hallway. He wore a khaki shirt and pants and black socks. He held a screwdriver in a short-fingered, pudgy hand.

"Chloe, baby," he whispered, and stepped over the dishes, the loose toes of his socks swinging, and opened his arms. Chloe moved into them without hesitation, but turned her stomach to the side at the last moment.

I looked at her mother. It was all she needed.

"What now?" she said.

"This is my friend, Charlotte," Chloe explained. "She lives with me."

I shook her father's hand, firmly, and smiled at her mother. Chloe wiped tears from her eyes, then she took her father's hand.

"What's going on?" she asked. "Are you moving?"

"Well, baby," he said, "your mom and I have decided to be separated for a while. We think it's the best thing for us."

I thought Chloe was going to faint. Her father and I moved her to a chair.

"What?" she said. "Why?"

Her mother took the boxes off the tabletop and sat down across from Chloe. "If you'd been here you'd know why," she said.

"Daddy?"

"It's been coming for some time, Chloe. It's nothing to do with you. You and your brother are both gone now and it was just us and we decided this was best. It's the best thing."

"Why didn't you come get me, Daddy?"

"Aw, Chloe, there was no sense dragging you into it. It was our mess."

"But you'll both be alone," Chloe said, and she bowed her head and put both of her hands on her stomach, and cried unmercifully. Her parents looked at each other and then at me and finally back at Chloe. When the crying finally seemed to be abating and Chloe looked up from her lap, her mother stood up from the table and leaned against the kitchen counter.

"How far along are you?" she asked.

Chloe's father looked up at his wife and then back down at the tabletop. He closed his eyes. Chloe stopped sniffling almost immediately.

"Thanks, Mom," she said.

"Chloe's been pregnant for a little more than six months," I said. "She's healthy and the baby's healthy. She's due in September."

There was a moment of silence. "What about Roger?" her mother finally asked.

"I still see him every once in a while," Chloe said. "But you'll be glad to know he's pretty much out of the picture."

"He's what?" her father asked.

"Is he the father?" her mother asked.

"Yes," Chloe said.

"He doesn't want to marry you?" her father asked.

"I don't want to marry him," Chloe answered.

"You should get married as soon as possible," Chloe's father said. "You and that boy owe it to the baby. That boy owes you. I'll talk to him."

"Daddy, I don't want him. You never liked him anyway."

"How are you going to raise a baby alone?" her mother asked. "Working in that gimmick shop twenty hours a week? Roger has a responsibility to you and the baby. And the baby needs a father."

"I can't believe this," Chloe screeched. "You hate Roger and then you want me to marry him."

"Jesus, Jesus," her father said, "How did you get yourself into this, Chloe. It's the rest of your life, the rest of your life." He pushed himself up from the table.

"Daddy," Chloe whimpered.

He walked back down the hallway toward a dark room. Chloe looked up at her mother.

"Your father is going to stay here. I've got an apartment up in York. I'll stay there for a while till everything is finalized. Do you need any money?"

Chloe shook her head.

"Well," her mother sighed, "Quite an afternoon. We haven't told your brother yet. He'll be pretty upset."

"You should have tried harder, Mom," Chloe said. "What'll he do without you?"

"Your father? He's lived most of his life alone already. He'll be OK.

You should come see him more often, though. But this thing with the baby is a failure, Chloe. You should have had enough sense to do something about it."

"I'm leaving now," Chloe said. I stood up and followed her out without saying good-bye to her mother.

Chloe was crying again by the time we reached the car. "Well, that was pleasant. Just like the Waltons."

"Maybe they'll come around," I said. "Maybe they'll. . . ." and I stopped short.

"Well," she said, "at least it's over with."

"I'm sorry," I said.

"What are you apologizing for?" she asked.

I shrugged. "I don't know. I just thought it might help."

"She's wrong about my father. She's wrong about herself. I can't believe they're getting divorced."

I put the car into gear and headed back toward Portsmouth. Chloe cried for a few more miles. Her body was hunched forward till her nose almost touched the dash. We had to wait for a boat to pass through at Memorial Bridge. All we could see from the car was a single mast slipping through the open span, a solitary, slow procession. I reached over and rubbed Chloe's back. She looked up.

"I'm just seventeen," she said. "Maybe I can be adopted."

"We've both had pretty crummy days. I'm getting sued for murder and your folks split up."

"It's only Monday too," Chloe added.

"Maybe Tuesday will be better."

"I've got to try harder," she whispered.

The gates on the bridge swung up and we began to move forward.

"Look," Chloe said, "Grace is standing on the bow of the boat."

"She doesn't look old at all from up here, Chloe," I said.

"I want to go stand out there with her, Charlotte."

≈

I lay in my bunk that night listening to the muffled patter of rain on the deck, to the water's gathering runoff through the scuppers and into the

river. It was somehow unnerving to think of a drop of rain falling into the depths of the ocean, becoming so involved. The rain seemed to calm the waves and *Rosinante* wallowed gently as she was washed. Lightning came later, though the rainfall never increased, spotlights burst into our cabin, casting brief tangled shadows. I woke later, in the middle of the night, and thought that the storm was still moaning and the arcs of lightning still wasting our room. I realized in moments that all was at rest and the light I thought intermittent was a steady beam, the full moon through a porthole, and that it was I who'd been blinking. Chloe slept peacefully in the moonlight with Midden under her pale arm. I missed my mother for a rending moment.

≈

Rain fell lightly the next morning and was to continue for the next couple of days. Michael postponed any more work till things dried out.

I spent the rest of the morning with Malcolm Laury, of Orcutt, Chambers and Laury Attorneys. He explained I'd probably want a lawyer in Kentucky, since that's where the suit was filed. I explained I didn't want to go to court, that I wanted to settle with Richard and Mary, and to settle with them, if possible, without meeting with them personally. I wanted Mr. Laury to act as an intermediary.

"But," he advised, "this suit is ridiculous. I don't see how you could lose if what you tell me is true. It'll probably be thrown out of court."

"I don't want to be put on a stand," I said. "I don't want to have to answer their questions. I don't want to be under their thumb."

He sat still for a moment, bouncing the eraser of his pencil off a legal pad. "OK. Why don't I call their attorney and see what they have in mind? If they're even willing to settle."

I wrote down the amount of cash I had in the bank on a notepad and handed it to him. "This is how much money I have," I said. "They can have all of it. They can have the contents of my house that are in storage in Kentucky too. They can't have any letters, photographs, or any of the personal belongings I have here with me in Portsmouth. And they can't have me."

He looked at the figure on the pad. Then he looked back up at me,

stopped rapping his pencil, and asked, "Is there anything else? Rather, are any, or any part of their allegations true? Do you think that there's any possibility that your husband might have killed himself because you withheld affection?"

"I loved my husband, Mr. Laury. I gave him everything I had."

"Very well. I'm not going to offer anything at first. We'll see how serious they are."

"Thank you," I said. "I don't have a phone, so I'll have to contact you."

"Give me a few days."

I left his office and walked the six blocks home down Market Street. I felt the secret I held from them all was worth far more than everything material I owned.

≈

Within a couple of days the dig was dry enough to continue excavating. I'd been pacing the length of *Rosinante* in the meantime with Midden and Pinky on my heels. I went back to my trowel anxiously. The work would take my mind off the suit and all the memories it brought back. Michael and I began to take down the two quadrants we'd originally left for profiles so both graves could be exposed in the same level simultaneously. Other volunteers handed me my trowel, dustpan, tape measure, or brush as if I were a surgeon. Artifacts again were lean. There were some anomalous iron fragments in my unit, perhaps what was left of nails. But I found these high up in the grave and they didn't seem to be ordered in any way so we didn't think they were the fasteners of a casket. A few inches lower I came upon a nice sherd of sgraffito, floral patterns incised through a slip. The sherd was light yellow, the pattern a light milk chocolate. Michael pronounced it North Devon, probably dating from the latter half of the seventeenth century. He thought he could come closer by typing it against similar finds at Jamestown.

Michael's unit was even more barren than mine. However, what had originally appeared as a rusty stain in the soil, perhaps the size of a dime, turned out to be some sort of iron rod greatly decomposed. It seemed to have fallen into the grave almost perpendicular to the earth.

When the first few inches were exposed we were trying to come up with some idea of its use as a piece of coffin hardware. The further down he proceeded, the further the rod went. By the time we reached the level where we'd earlier found bone, the rod was standing a full twelve inches high. It resembled more than anything else a length of half-inch concrete reinforcement.

"It could be anything," Michael said.

"If it's part of a coffin," I suggested, "the individual in the grave is either very short or in a fetal position. The only problem is the disturbed area of soil. It goes beyond the hardware."

"OK," Michael sighed. "From this point on let's just work on one individual. I don't want anything to get away from us. Let's get a photograph of what we've got now, then we'll expose some bone."

We set up a tripod, placed a small chalkboard in each unit that indicated the grid designation, depth, direction north, and took photos. Now that we knew the limits of the grave sites we used shovels to remove the undisturbed soil adjoining the two graves so we wouldn't have to work on our stomachs.

"Let's begin with the grave with the rod," Michael suggested. "It bothers me standing there like that."

We started at the end of the grave that Michael had exposed earlier. Almost immediately phalanges and metatarsals appeared as the earth brushed away easily. A small foot. There was no evidence of a shoe buckle or any leather. The further we proceeded up the length of the grave, beyond tibia and fibula to femur, it became clear that the skeleton wasn't flexed. The individual was laid out on its back. But what was most interesting was the degree of deformity in the long bones. The load-bearing bones seemed to be twisted.

"This person was clearly crippled," I told Michael.

"From birth?" he asked.

"I don't think so. It looks like Paget's. It's an older person's disease. Hard to tell with half the bones still in the dirt."

As I brushed soil near the patella, I suddenly drew in a rush of air, an audible gasp.

"What?" Michael yelped. A half dozen onlookers bent lower.

"A thimble. I found a thimble. It's tiny. Look at it." I sat up on my

knees and pointed with my brush. Everyone cooed appropriately.

"That's not in there by mistake," Michael said. "I'll bet it was in a pocket of some sort, or a small bag."

We left the thimble in place and continued with the excavation. The dirt flaked so easily off the hard bone that a small whisk broom did all the work. The gray bone was blatant against the dark earth. We swept away a dustpan of soil, slid it into a bucket, and handed the bucket up to the sifting crew. Michael told them to be on the lookout for anything of bone or brass that might be a clothing fastener. It was clear by now that the iron rod would interfere with the grave. It seemed to be planted squarely in the upper abdomen. I worked carefully on the pelvis, looking for aids in the determination of sex. The length of the long bones and certainly the thimble pointed to a female, but the greater sciatic notch, a notch in each pelvic half near the sacrum, is a better indicator. In females the notch is usually wider and shallower than in males. After forty-five minutes of careful probing and sweeping it seemed we had an aged female. It would take careful measurement in the lab to be more sure. Michael began to work around the iron rod. He was certain that it would begin to tip over and fall at any moment so he had me hold its upper end gently as he worked at its base. But before he got to the end of the rod he encountered more bone, the lower ribs and vertebrae. Soon we realized the rod went completely through the skeleton, passing just to the side of the backbone.

One of the crew asked, "Could that be what killed her?"

"Surely not," Michael said. "They would have removed it before burial."

"Maybe it's a surveyor's stake. Put there long after the burial, after it had been lost," I suggested.

"Yeah," somebody above me agreed. "That's possible. We are at the edge of the road. This could be the corner of two property lines."

We left the rod in place, although Michael and I both felt some instinctual reluctance to do so. We hadn't stopped for lunch and it was now late in the evening.

"Let's call it a day," Michael said. "No use in screwing something up because we're worn out. We'll expose the rest of this skeleton in the morning and then begin on the second."

The screening process had failed to turn up any small artifacts. We'd hoped to find some type of clothing fastener or personal adornment, but it was quite possible that these were made of string or leather and hadn't survived. We took a close-up shot of the thimble with a Polaroid. Michael wanted to see if he could type it that night.

Only three-quarters of the skeleton lay revealed, from the eleventh rib down. A thin sheet of earth still remained over the rest of the rib cage, the skull, and arms. I estimated she wasn't more than five feet tall. The deformation in the bones would have made her even shorter. If she walked at all, it would have been with great difficulty and an obvious limp, a struggling shamble. I expected to find her upper vertebrae and clavicle similarly deformed, and perhaps also an enlarged skull, another characteristic of Paget's disease. The disease disrupts the body's bone-replacement system, substituting strong bone with fibrous tissue and blood vessels. The pain produced when the bones become misshapen or enlarged is virtually continuous. Bones are more likely to break, and if the skull enlarges around the auditory nerve, deafness will ensue. There is, even now, no known cure.

It was unsettling somehow, to find a specimen in that condition. As I walked home that evening, my own legs felt weak, disarticulated. I realized too, that it wouldn't be a pleasant task to tell Grace what we'd found. For some reason I knew it would make her feel, if not violated, vulnerable.

≈

As it turned out I didn't have to tell her that evening or for several more. I brushed the last dust from my jeans on the dock, stepped aboard *Rosinante*, and was met by Chloe in the salon, her eyes wide with fear, her voice a bird's shrill call.

"Charlotte, Charlotte, something's wrong with Grace." Chloe clutched my wrist and dragged me forward to Grace's cabin where she lay on her back fully clothed, wrapped in her painting apron. I bent down, my knees on the sole. Her eyes were vacant, pale as the moon in the morning. She brought one arm up distractedly and tugged at the skin of her cheek. She hadn't noticed me at all. One side of her face was completely slack, the corner of her mouth turned down.

"Grace?" I said.

She didn't respond, didn't even blink.

"She's had a stroke, Chloe," I said. "Go now. Go up to the Snail and call an ambulance."

"Charlotte?" she whispered.

I stood up. "Chloe, you go right now and call an ambulance. Go." She left at a run. Tears were already forming in her eyes. I could feel her weight clear the boat and hear the thud of her boots up the gangway. I moved Grace's hair off her face, and untied her apron. "Can you hear me, Grace?" I asked as I rubbed her arms and cheeks. She didn't look at me, but tried to speak. It was completely unintelligible. Then she turned her head slightly in my direction, and I saw her looking at me, her eyes passing over the features of my face. "Hi, baby," I said. "It's OK. It's me, Charlotte." But there was no recognition. She had no idea who I was. And then, as her eyes went beyond me, to the cabin around her, I realized she also didn't know where she was. Her entire life was suddenly unfamiliar. "It's OK, it's OK," was all I could say, and I held the hand that could still move, that gripped mine with all the strength it had left.

≈

Chloe and I both sat up with her that first night in the hospital, as she was given a brain scan, chest X-ray and an electrocardiogram. I tried to examine the X-rays but found myself turning away from the bones. She remained incoherent. Her speech and the right side of her body seemed to be affected, although she did occasionally move her hand and foot slightly. The initial diagnosis was a cerebral thrombosis. The blood supply to part of the brain had been cut off by a clot. She was put on anticoagulants to thin her blood. The doctor said it would just take time to tell how much damage had been done. There didn't seem to be much swelling of the brain. She slept a great part of that first day, and when awake she made motions and sounds but never really focused on us or anything else.

I'd called Grace's daughter, Anne, but it took her almost thirty-six hours to arrive. I waited downstairs in the lobby for her, knowing approximately when she'd arrive, and recognized her immediately. She looked exactly like Grace. She didn't look like she'd been in a plane and rental car half the night. She was about forty-five years old and her hair was styled in a close salon-kept curl. It hadn't touched a headrest or pil-

low. Her makeup wasn't spare but wasn't caked either and she was dressed conservatively in a long Laura Ashley skirt and pressed white blouse. She carried a large Louis Vuitton bag. The sight of her made me uneasy. About the only makeup aboard *Rosinante* was Chloe's discount-store black eye shadow, and she wore it only once or twice a week. None of us owned a purse that wasn't gathering dust. I'd given her the basic outline of my relationship to Grace on the phone, so after we shook hands I led her upstairs to intensive care. Grace wasn't there. In the twenty-five minutes I'd been downstairs, she'd been moved to her own room. Anne made no attempt to hide her annoyance, either with me or the nurses. She did this with an abbreviated snort and a brief search in the immediate area for someone with some capability. In the meantime the nurse had told me where Grace was and I'd headed down the tiled hallway. I had to turn around and wait for Anne.

"This way," I said.

"Go ahead, I'm right behind you." So I turned and walked as briskly as I could.

Chloe stood up as we entered the room, and Anne moved around the bed without acknowledging her.

"Mother?" she said, putting her bag down. "Mother?" Grace finally turned to her. Her eyes were so empty they reflected light like the bottom of a bowl. "It's me, Mother." Anne looked at me. "What is this?"

"She doesn't recognize us either, and it upsets her when she tries to speak." I started to go into the details of what had been done so far and the diagnosis, but Anne didn't want to hear it from me. She wanted the doctor and sent me after her. I returned a minute or two later, explaining that the nurse told me the doctor would make her rounds in about fifteen minutes. Anne picked up her purse and threw it across the room.

"I'll get her myself," she said and stalked out of the room.

"She's upset," Chloe said.

"She has the uncanny ability to make me feel incompetent."

"Lots of people can do that to me," Chloe said. I frowned at her. "Give her a chance, Charlotte."

"Grace warned us, Chloe. Next time she steps out of line I'm gonna lay her out. It took her a day and a half to get here and she acts as if we're late."

"Charlotte," Chloe said.

"No, I mean it. What right does she have to imply that we aren't watching out for Grace?"

"She's her daughter. In her eyes we don't have any rights as far as Grace is concerned."

I frowned at her again.

"Who got her here?" I pouted.

"You're not her daughter, Charlotte; you're her boarder."

"Whose side are you on?"

Chloe frowned at me then. "I'm on Grace's side. Fighting with Anne won't help Grace."

"Since when did you become the voice of reason?" I flopped down in a plastic chair, put my elbows on my knees and my chin in both palms. Chloe sat back down too, and we both looked at Grace. We realized she'd been watching us throughout my tirade. It was the first time she seemed really alert since the stroke.

I said, "Hi, Grace."

She looked down at her hands spread on the sheet, and said her name, "Grace." It wasn't clear, but we understood the word as her name. It was like a strange shell on the beach she'd just picked up.

"You've had a stroke, Grace," I said. "It's affected your speech, but you'll get better with practice."

She mumbled. She brought her left hand to her lips and pinched them.

"That was Anne, Grace," Chloe said.

Saliva choked her for a moment. "Who are you?" she said. The corner of her mouth trailed every word like a crutch.

"Don't you remember, Grace?" Chloe whispered. "I'm Chloe, your boarder."

A male nurse stepped into the room and removed the sheets from the other bed in the room. Grace watched him and when he left she turned back to us. She wiped spittle from her chin. Chloe put her hand over her own mouth.

"Grace," I said, "do you know where you are?"

"My arm won't work." Each word was an effort, the last bit of paste squeezed out of a tube.

"You've had a stroke. It affects one side of your body," I explained. "Do you remember me, Grace? Or where you live?"

"No," she said, without much distress. And then, "I'm hungry."

"I'll go get you something," Chloe said and left, almost running into the door facing.

"Grace, we're going to take care of you. There's no need to worry."

"I'm not worried."

"You'll get better every day. I live with. . . ."

Anne entered the room then, with the doctor. I looked at my watch. A petty thing to do. Still, it had been fifteen minutes.

"Grace has been talking. Haven't you, Grace?" I said.

She nodded.

"Mother, how do you feel?"

Grace looked at her and squinted, as if she were looking far into the distance. "I don't know you."

"Grace, I'm Doctor Aktar. Do you know where you are?"

"I'm in a hospital," Grace said.

"That's right. You've had a stroke. It will take some time before your motor skills return to normal. That's why you're having trouble with your speech. You shouldn't let it bother you. Is there anything you want?"

"I'm hungry," she said.

"Chloe's gone to get her something," I said.

"I'll order a tray and have the nurse bring it in. No outside food. If you want to see me at any time just tell one of the nurses, ok?"

Grace nodded. The doctor put her hand on Anne's back and led her into the hallway. I followed them out. "She doesn't remember anything," I said.

Dr. Aktar turned and said, in hushed tones, "The return of her speech, in any form, can only be a good sign. As I said, with some work her motor skills will return, and we've put her on some medication that will hopefully reduce the risk of further strokes, but I am concerned about her memory loss. She's never had any problems with her memory before?"

"None at all," Anne said.

"Well," I said. "That's not exactly the case."

Anne turned to me with an expression of complete distrust. "What?" she asked.

"There's been times when she forgets things."

"Why didn't you let me know?" Anne asked.

"Chloe and I've talked about it," I said. "We haven't known her all her life. We didn't know if it was something new. It was usually minor things, things anybody might forget. But she forgot Pinky's name once, and once, after I'd been living with her for weeks, she asked me who I was. I know it seems odd, but it wasn't any more strange than some of the other things she does."

"What other things?" the doctor asked.

"She talks to herself."

"Her memory may very well return," the doctor said. "She's gone through a great deal of trauma."

"What do I do now?" Anne asked.

"Let's keep her here for a while, get her started on some rehabilitation, then you can take her home."

"I live in Florida," Anne said listlessly. "I'll have to find a home for her there." She put her finger on the lobe of her ear.

"This is her home," I mumbled.

"What?" Anne said, furious with this second interruption.

"This is her home. Grace likes it here."

Anne sighed. "She doesn't even know where here is." She walked back into the room as if the doctor and I were both suddenly superfluous.

"What can we do to help her?" I asked her.

"The mother or the daughter?" she whispered.

"Grace," I said.

"As far as her memory is concerned?" I nodded. "Give her time."

"She doesn't have time," I said. "Doctor, woman to woman here, Grace doesn't get along with her daughter. She loves her life here."

"I'm sorry," she said, "but her daughter, as next of kin, is in control. You might show her some familiar objects, photos maybe. But since she doesn't even recognize her own daughter, I think it's going to take some time."

I couldn't think of anything else to say, so I said, "Thank you." I

waited in the hallway while the doctor gave instructions about Grace's food to the nurse. An orderly brought a tray up moments later, followed by Chloe with a stack of brownies.

"She can't have those, Chloe," I said.

"They're for me," she snipped.

We spent some moments getting Grace adjusted around the tray. Anne and Chloe sat down then to watch Grace eat. There were only two chairs in the room.

"Grace," I said, "I've got to go to work now." She smiled a lopsided smile. "I'll be back at lunch time, OK?" She put a banana slice in her mouth.

"You go ahead," Anne said. "Thank you for everything you've done."

I thought about pulling Chloe out into the hallway and telling her what Anne had said, but it would have been too obvious. And it would have upset Chloe. We still had a couple of days.

"I'll be back," I said.

As I left the room I heard Anne telling Chloe, "I'm going to make some phone calls."

For an insane moment I thought of cutting every telephone line that led into the city.

≈

I arrived at the dig in the same clothes I'd left in two nights before. I excavated mechanically that day, preoccupied with Grace. I'd called Michael the evening of Grace's stroke to let him know what had happened and explained I might be late or absent. That morning he simply touched my arm and said, "I'm glad you're back." Then he told me the thimble and the North Devon sherd we'd found earlier both dated from the mid-seventeenth century. We surmised that our subjects were interred sometime between 1623 and 1671, when the graveyard was enclosed, probably earlier than later since the location of the graves had been forgotten.

The first skeleton was now completely exposed. The arms were bent at the elbow with the hands crossing over the chest. There was

more evidence of Paget's disease here. The bones seemed warped. The skull rested on the occipital looking up. The mandible hung open, and was completely devoid of teeth. Only three molars remained in the maxilla. It was possible that some teeth had become dislodged after burial and had fallen into the cranial vault, and were now hidden by the dirt that filled the skull. The cranium itself seemed very fragile, the parietal bones thinned with advanced age; therefore, the state archaeologist recommended excavating the skull with its fill intact. The contents could better be removed at the lab. At approximate intervals of three inches, along the sternum and neck vertebrae, four brass wire clothing fasteners were found. Michael photographed them in situ and placed them in a plastic bag for later typing. Lab work would tell us much more than we could see in the field. The soil samples we'd taken might reveal various types of pollen or larvae that could tell us what time of year the burial took place.

With the first skeleton exposed it was easy to see that the second grave, although very close by, did not intersect it in any way. This indicated that either both bodies were interred at the same time or that there was knowledge of the first burial at the time of the second. We decided to leave the first skeleton in place while excavating the second in order that we might better record any relationship. While Michael and I broke for lunch, the state archaeologist began work on a measured drawing, which would place the skeleton in a three-dimensional context.

≈

Although I'd slept only in snatches the last two nights, uncomfortably in the hospital lobby, and spent the morning lying stomach down on a two by twelve, I felt a sudden resurgence of energy on my way back to *Rosinante*. There I gathered a box of Grace's personal items, photographs of Sweet George, some of her clothing, and a bottle of perfume off her dresser. Midden's meows were almost screams, so I quickly fed him and Pinky. I thought about putting Pinky in the box too, but didn't think they'd let me in the hospital with him.

When I walked into Grace's room she was eating lunch.

"The other two," she said, "are down in the cafeteria." Her speech

was remarkably clearer. There seemed to be much less drooping at the corners of her mouth and eye.

"How're you feeling?" I asked.

"I feel like I should be somewhere else."

"I brought you some of your things." I took the box to the side of her bed. She was eating predominantly with her one good hand but I noticed the other arm was resting on her stomach instead of at her side. "Can you move your arm?" I asked.

"Yes." She moved it weakly about half an inch.

"That's great," I said.

"It's nothing," she said.

"But you still don't remember any of us?"

"I've seen you before." I didn't know if this was a reference to four months ago or that very morning.

I held up a blouse from the box. "This is your favorite shirt," I said.

She looked at it and said, "It's pretty. I like the color."

I gave her the bottle of perfume. "This is yours too."

She held the open bottle under her nose and then scrunched up the part of her face she had control over. "That's putrid."

"You always hated it," I said. "See? It's full. Here are some pictures. This is me and you and Chloe on the boat." I held it up so she could see.

"What boat?" she asked.

"It's your boat, Grace," I said, somewhat petulantly.

"I'm sorry," she said.

I wanted to shake her by the shoulders and tell her if she didn't start remembering, her life was going to be ruined, but that didn't seem fair either. If she never regained her memory, it wouldn't be right to prejudice her against Anne. Maybe it was another chance for them, mother and daughter.

"Do you recognize him?" I asked, holding up the photo of Sweet George.

"Is that my husband?" she asked.

"Yes," I screeched, "yes. You do remember."

She began to shake her head sadly, more for my benefit than hers. "I just guessed it," she said. "I had to have a husband if I have a daughter. Why hasn't he come to visit me?"

138

"Oh, Grace," I said. My eyes washed over. "I'm sorry, he died four years ago." She tilted her head, as if she didn't understand why my voice was breaking.

I'd walked into the hospital with dirty hands and knees, holding what I thought was a box of love and memory and hope, and walked out with the same box, a loose collection of yard-sale merchandise.

≈

I went back to the dig numbly that afternoon, my hands in my pockets. I didn't know what else to do but give Grace time and keep myself busy. It seemed strange that she should die and breathe at the same moment, that something as seemingly huge and indelible as Sweet George should vanish without trace, as forgotten as the graves we were unearthing. I was, at the time, more baffled than grieved. I suppose it was some form of self-preservation that allowed my body and half my brain to work while the other half lay stunned, unable to comprehend. What bothered me the most was that Grace seemed so unburdened. I wasn't altogether sure that it was my job to help her regain her memory, in the same way that I won't try to reform or enlighten a happy believer in the hereafter. Rational debate either isn't effective or undermines a usually benign contentment. I mean, as long as they don't try to take me along with them by force, I'll let them go unassailed. But somehow, every bone in my body fought against letting Grace remain in her pastlessness. It seemed to me that she was only buried and could be found and excavated. Perhaps it bothered me because I knew if she could forget Sweet George I might also lose Jonah someday, just as easily, just as completely.

"Easy," Michael said. "There's a person under there."

I suppose I'd been using my trowel a little too persuasively. "Sorry," I said.

"Anything else you'd like to say?" he asked.

"Nope."

Bones began to appear soon, almost as if they'd been submerged and were slowly floating to the surface. The second skeleton seemed to be extended as well. I'd begun in the area where I'd originally come into

contact with the skull the week before. Michael worked at the other end of the grave. The bones we were uncovering were in much better condition pathologically than the old woman's. There was no sign of any bone-wasting disease. The degree of closure in the sutures of the skull indicated a fairly youthful individual. The epiphyses of several of the upper body bones also led me to believe that our subject was quite young. This wasn't unusual. In fact most of the grave sites we'd excavated in Kentucky were of children and young adults. Life expectancy wasn't always what it is now. I spent a great deal of time with a bit of bamboo and a small brush cleaning the teeth. It looked to me as if the third molars were in the process of erupting through the gum at death, which indicated an age somewhere between fifteen and twenty-one years. I worked so long on the cranium and teeth that Michael had time to remove the great bulk of earth from the lower skeleton. He discovered the fetus.

His first words were a hushed, "Oh my."

I looked up.

"Oh," I said. My spread fingers strained to support my weight in the dirt.

He pushed himself up. "I didn't expect this," he said.

A tiny white skull, the size of my fist, and a pale humerus lay exposed in the sunlight. I stepped out of the grave and stood on its rim.

"What?" Michael looked up and asked.

I stared at him. The volunteers and crew looked back and forth between us. "It's OK, Charlotte. She probably died in childbirth."

"I understand that," I said.

"OK."

"I need some water," I murmured, and I turned sideways into the volunteers, slipped through them as if they were brush on a shoreline, and disappeared into the interior.

Michael and the state archaeologist continued to excavate. After hours of meticulous work among the tiny bones the fetus lay revealed, still curled in the bowl of the mother's abdomen. I looked over into the pit and lost myself in the fragile shavings of the ribs, the delicate, yet-to-ossify epiphyses, the birdlike long bones. The orientation of the body within the body was one hundred and eighty degrees. The small skull

pointed toward what would have been the pelvic opening. Apparently that opening had proven too narrow, an impossible escape. The skull of the fetus retained a conelike shape received under great pressure. It seemed to me to be the saddest of deaths, a double dying, a loss so great as to be mystifying.

The artifacts contained in this second grave seemed insignificant compared to the discovery of the baby: a button cast with a design proved indecipherable in the field, a fine copper alloy buckle, and more brass wire clothing fasteners.

It took the afternoon and the next day to prepare the three skeletons for final photography, and another day to actually remove, label, and pack the bones for delivery to the university.

I apologized later for removing myself from the excavation.

"It's OK," he said.

"No, I don't know what it was," I lied, sounding defeated. And then I told the truth, "but I had an almost nauseous wave of contrition pass through me when I realized what we'd uncovered. I felt responsible somehow."

"But why, Charlotte?"

"Because I've learned something I'll never be able to forget. Because it was her secret, her sadness, not ours."

≈

In the evenings and on my lunch breaks I went to the hospital. Grace had already begun physical therapy, and was moving around the room with a walker. Chloe and Anne were at her side. I sat for long hours with Chloe in the hospital lobby and cafeteria.

"I miss her," I said.

"But, you know, Charlotte, she's nicer now than she was. She doesn't get upset, and she still has her sense of humor. That male nurse came in today and after he left Grace said, 'I liked his belt. I like a little bit of leather around a man's waist.' She told Anne her fingernails were too long."

"Chloe, she's a Stepford Wife. She's not the same person. She doesn't have her memory."

"But she doesn't seem to care. It doesn't really bother her."

"Well, it should," I squeaked. "It bothers me. Doesn't it bother you?"

"Of course it does, especially since we're about to lose her for good." She looked down. "Anne spends most of the day on the phone. She's getting all the paperwork in order."

"What kind of paperwork?"

"You know, your parents go senile, you get control of their money and stuff. Anne's going to take Grace back to Florida soon."

"I think we should do something," I said.

"Of course we should. What?"

"Look, what do you think Grace would feel like if she gets taken to Florida, put in some crazy house, and then her memory returns? Anne's got her checkbook and complete authority over her."

"She's gonna be wicked pissed," Chloe said. "And she's gonna blame me."

"OK, then. We need to jar her memory. The only thing I can think of is to get her back aboard *Rosinante*."

"Anne won't like that. She's surprised Grace hasn't fallen overboard already."

"Then we won't ask Anne's permission."

"She's going home tomorrow, and she'll be gone for two days."

"What about Grace?" I asked.

"She's staying here, then when Anne gets back she'll move out to some kind of rehab center in Dover for a couple of weeks."

"Then it's off to Florida?"

"Yeah. She might have gone sooner but the place there won't have an opening till the beginning of the month."

"OK."

"OK, what?"

"I'm thinking."

"Oh."

"We'll need a wheelchair."

"That's easy. This place is lousy with them."

"Tomorrow night, after she's eaten, we'll sneak her out and take her home. We can bring her back the next morning."

"We'll get in trouble for sure," Chloe said.

"I know, but they trust us now, so we might as well take advantage of them."

"The old Grace would approve," she said. "But, Charlotte, I've been thinking. What if it's not the stroke? What if it's psychological? What if she doesn't want to remember?"

I didn't answer her, but I thought, almost savagely, that Grace had no right not to remember, that it was her only real responsibility left to the rest of the world, not to forget.

≈

The next morning I had an hour before my second meeting with my attorney, so I walked back to the dig and watched the heavy machinery backfill our site. Michael was there alone: the rest of the crew had been given the day off. The next week we'd begin washing, counting, and labeling the artifacts we'd found. Two weeks in the field is usually followed by two months in the lab. We wouldn't be working on the human remains, but Michael expected osteological reports from the university soon, and archivists were still searching through city histories and records to identify our two skeletons. I didn't hold out much hope for that. If they'd been forgotten during their own century, little could be done to resurrect them three centuries later.

"I never like this part," I told Michael.

"The backfilling?"

"Yeah. I just want to keep on digging."

"Not me. I'll be doing the paperwork on this site for the next six months. I think it works out to about two printed pages to a five-gallon bucket of dirt. Every time you scrape your trowel, I've got to write another sentence. The feds want a report, the city wants a report, Strawbery Banke wants a report."

"But all this work is for nothing if you don't publish," I said. "It would be like we never found them."

"I know," he sighed. "I just wish we were all interconnected somehow, so we automatically communicated with one another: whatever I see everyone else sees, whatever I understand everyone else understands."

143

"Yeah," I said, "that would help, or it would make life pretty boring."

"It's just a dream," he said. "If I didn't write it all down, I'd not only forget it, I'd miss things. Somehow, working all the information into a logical order gives you insights you can't get in the field. I'll start writing a sentence without knowing where it's going, but I always get somewhere. So I'll go up in my office and sit down and see what happens. Sometimes the somewhere you get to is just another question. And with this dig I think we ended up with more questions than we began with. This dig wore me out."

"You take it too personally," I said.

"Personally?" He turned to me. "How else am I supposed to take anything?"

≈

He was right. A bug crawls on the wall across the room and I usually think it has something to do with me. It had been three days since we first uncovered the young woman and her fetus. I couldn't bring myself to tell Chloe what we'd found. It wasn't the kind of thing I wanted to bring up with someone who was pregnant. I had so much earth on my hands I didn't recognize it as dirt. I didn't take it personally enough. At least, not until later.

≈

My lawyer, coming into his office behind me, his breath catching on the back of my ear, pulled my chair out.

"Sit down, Charlotte." I sat in a big red leather armchair that could have held Grace, Chloe, and me comfortably. I slid my rear across its slick surface till I could scotch myself against an arm. My hand found a row of large faceted tacks. Malcolm Laury had accepted my case with an air of, if not distrust, incompatibility. He now seemed to be teetering upon enthusiasm.

"Well," he said. "It's all very strange. I've had a discussion with your in-laws' attorney. I must say their position baffles me. After much con-

sultation I presented your offer. Although you offer every possible financial reparation. . . ."

"It's not reparation," I said. "I'm not admitting any guilt."

"Of course not." He sighed. "The word is, they're not inclined toward a settlement. It's ridiculous. They've been offered everything you have, more than they'll ever get in court. I don't understand."

"OK," I said. "Tell them this." I moved up on the edge of the chair and leaned forward. "If we do have to go to court I won't defend myself. Tell them I won't say a word. If I have to take the stand I'll take the fifth everytime. Tell them they'll never hear another word about Jonah from me if they persist."

"Really?" he said, somewhat perplexed. I don't think Malcolm had handled anything more arduous than a speeding ticket.

"Can I do that?" I asked, somewhat timidly.

"Sure. You don't have to incriminate yourself," he said.

"You don't seem to get it," I said, my voice rising. "I committed no crime. I admit no guilt. I also refuse to discuss it. They can have everything I've got but my past."

"There's no need," he began. "What I mean to say is I'm bewildered. To be honest with you, almost every case I deal with involves saving people money, or getting them money for some offense done to them. I'm not usually put in the position of telling an opposing counselor that his clients can have everything my client owns." He was honestly confused.

"Look," I said. "It's not about money. It's about control. That's what they want most of all. They want to be the top ball bearing in a pyramid of ball bearings so that when they move everyone else under them moves too. It's what makes them feel secure."

"Well, at any rate, it's going to be interesting to see their response. But you also have to consider the possibility that it may not be control they're after. As I have to consider that it may not be money, which, I'm telling you, is a hard thing for a lawyer to contemplate. If it's not control, and if it's not money, it may be revenge."

We both half-smiled at one another, then we both looked for something else in the room to look at. My finger fell off the last tack on the arm of the chair. I stood up.

"I'll get back with you in a couple of days."

"That will be fine," he said. He shook my hand. "And, Charlotte," he added, "There'll be a moderate request for payment with my secretary at your next visit." He smiled.

"What's money to me?" I said, as grandly as I could muster. "Present your insignificant bill."

"You are a frightening woman."

≈

I was a rattled woman. There's nothing as easy to imitate as resolve: step forward righteously, frown continually, assume authority over inanimate objects, and treat them roughly, never notice the incredulous bystander, stare forward with blinding purpose. I moved down the glassy tiled hall of the hospital pushing a recalcitrant wheelchair and turned into an elevator where I could exhale freely once the door had closed. "OK," I said, "you've stolen a wheelchair. Shouldn't be much harder to steal a person." I rolled off the elevator as the doors slid open, then marched down the hallway to Grace's room. The door was open. I didn't have to steal her, I thought: she was free.

Chloe had Grace sitting up on the side of the bed, in her slippers and robe.

"OK," Chloe said, "we're going for a ride, Grace."

"I wish you wouldn't talk to her like that," I said.

"Like what?" Grace asked. We helped her into the wheelchair. "Wait," Grace said. "My tennis ball."

"Sure," Chloe said, and handed her a new tennis ball, put it in her afflicted hand. She grasped it with only a little struggle.

"That's fine, Grace," I congratulated, as she smiled up at me.

"Been working on that all day," she said.

"Got any new memories for me?" I asked.

"None whatsoever," she replied happily. "Haven't got a clue. Drawing a blank. Staring out a window." She giggled.

As we pushed her down the hall Chloe leaned over and whispered to me, "She's still in there, isn't she?"

"I think she's banging on the walls."

Luckily the nurses' station was in the opposite direction of the elevator. We only passed one maintenance worker in the hallway, and he was looking into a closet.

"Another elevator ride," Grace said, tossing her hand nonchalantly.

We stopped at ground level, and, instead of exiting through the main entrance where a receptionist sat, we crossed through the cafeteria and went out a loading dock door that was just off the dining room. My car was parked behind the dumpster.

"Smells bad out here," Grace said.

Chloe forced the wheelchair over the rough blacktop and onto the sidewalk.

"Open the door, Charlotte," Chloe said. "Hurry."

"Why are we in a hurry?" Grace asked.

"Just get in the car, Grace," Chloe snapped, and almost yanked her out of the chair by her armpits. I moved the chair back out of the way, and all three of us worked to get Grace comfortably into the car. Chloe and I shut the car door and collapsed the wheelchair. We'd have to take it along. As we hefted it up over the lip of the trunk we could hear Grace yelling at us. I slammed the lid, and did the animated head jerk to see if we'd been watched, and then jumped into the driver's seat.

"My seatbelt's not on," Grace cried.

"Just forget it for now," Chloe said.

"It's unsafe," she said, holding the buckle in midair.

"Oh, God," Chloe yelped, and wedged herself between the two front seats. She thrashed for the buckle and finally got it snapped to. I was already driving.

"We have to be back for breakfast," Grace told us somewhat anxiously. "Breakfast is at seven o'clock."

"We'll be back," Chloe said. "Besides, breakfast is at 7:30."

"I don't want to miss it," Grace said.

"Grace," I said, "if we miss it, we'll get breakfast somewhere else."

"Well. . . ." she trailed off and looked away uncertainly.

"We're taking you home, Grace," I said. "Maybe it will help you remember. Don't you want to go home?"

"Hospital's my home."

"No, Grace," I insisted. "No, it's not. We're taking you home. The hospital is where sick people live."

"But I'm sick."

"OK," I said. "OK. Just look at it as a night out."

"Breakfast is at seven o'clock."

"OK," I said.

Chloe was slumped into a corner of the back seat and chewing on her fingers. I caught her eye in the rearview mirror and she mouthed the word, "Mistake!" at me. I frowned back at her and drove on.

As we neared Prescott Park and *Rosinante*, I watched Grace's face as closely as I could, looking for any sign of recognition. But she showed no particular interest in her surroundings, seemed almost distracted. When I pulled into the lot at the Smarmy Snail, parking directly under Memorial Bridge, she asked, "Are we here?"

"Yes, almost."

We hauled her back out of the car and into the chair and around the sidewalk onto the restaurant's deck.

"Are we eating here?" she almost screamed. The deck was full of patrons who all looked up at once, their forks suspended in curiosity.

"Excuse me, excuse me," Chloe said in embarrassment, working her way through the tables to the gangway. I unlatched the chain. Chloe nosed the wheelchair over the first rail when Grace reached out with her good arm and clung to the railing.

"Oh no," she yelled.

"Turn around and back down," I told Chloe.

"OK. I won't let you fall, Grace."

Grace gripped the wheelchair and peered out over the wheel into the water. "I don't remember any of this," she said.

"You're used to walking down," I said. "You're coming home backwards."

"I'm tired," she said.

"I know, honey," Chloe said. "We're almost there." Chloe had her stomach up against the back of the wheelchair to slow its descent. "I'm gonna have my baby right here," she wheezed.

"No, you're not," I hissed back. "We haven't got time for it."

With some struggle we got Grace up over *Rosinante*'s coaming. She

could walk now, but only hesitantly. We put her on the settee in the salon and Chloe and I sat down next to her. We were silent for a few moments, settling, listening to each other's breathing, but then we both looked at Grace expectantly.

"What?" she asked.

"Well?" I said. "Does anything look familiar?"

She looked around, her vision lighting on individual objects, then going on. "Not really," she said.

"You're not trying, Grace," Chloe whined.

"I'm sorry," she said.

"Well," I said, "do you feel any sense of home? I mean, do you feel secure here?"

"I feel better than I did coming down the ramp."

"It's a gangway, Grace," Chloe said. Then to me, "She'd never call it a ramp, Charlotte."

"It's OK, Grace," I sighed, and put my arms around her. "It's OK. Do you want anything to eat? Or do you want to go to bed?"

"I'm trying not to be afraid," she said.

"I'll take you back to the hospital if you want to go, Grace," I offered.

She looked at Chloe, whose face pleaded with her to stay.

"No, I'll spend the night. You girls have gone to so much trouble." Midden padded up from our cabin then, mewing, rubbing against my shins. "Is that my cat?" Grace asked.

"No, he's mine," I said. "But sit right there. I've got someone else who wants to see you." I opened the companionway door, and Pinky, who'd been leaning against it, fell out into the salon. He righted himself with much effort, coughed, slurped, and began sliding toward Grace on his own saliva. I looked at her. It was the first time she'd ever seen him, and she grimaced, helplessly. I wanted to scream with rage for Pinky's loss. He put his paws on her calf and she swept them away.

"Oh, he's wet," she said. "Get him down."

I went to Pinky and picked him up, even though he was struggling toward Grace, his tongue slipping from his mouth. He moaned, dropped out of my arms like a dead body to the floor, and puling, slouched toward Grace again.

"No, doggie," Grace said and held out her hand, palm flat and down. Pinky licked her hand and she rubbed it dry on her gown. "Get him away."

I picked him up again, carried him below to my cabin, and shut the door. He barked once and then returned to his laborious breathing. I could hardly speak I was so stunned by Grace's reaction. I rubbed Pinky's brittle coat, tried to soothe him. He writhed. "It's OK," I said. "It's OK, baby."

When I returned to the salon, Chloe was helping Grace to her cabin.

"We're not going to sink, are we?" I heard Grace ask her.

"No, Grace, this boat has been afloat for more than sixty years," Chloe said. "It will float one more night, I promise."

We put her in her bunk, still watching closely to see how her surroundings affected her. But again, it was as if she'd never been on a boat before, or in restricted quarters. She groped, fumbled, bumped.

"What if I need to go?" Grace asked.

"I'll be right here," Chloe said. "I'll help you." She climbed into the bunk above Grace.

"OK," she said, still unsure.

I switched off the lamp, and sat in the galley for an hour or so quietly. I realized this would be the last night we'd spend on *Rosinante* together. Chloe whimpered in her dreams, and I thought Grace had long fallen asleep too, but she whispered into the darkness, "Poor thing."

I kept my silence.

≈

I woke to a muffled yell. For a moment I didn't know where I was. The room seemed strange, as if someone had turned my childhood bedroom ninety degrees. But then I heard Grace, with some strength, call out again. I jumped out of bed, squeezed through Pinky and Midden at the door, and raced forward. I yelled Grace's name as I ran. I hoped that waking at home might somehow startle her memory. It was just dawn, still dim in the galley, but I could tell Chloe's bunk was empty. Grace had pulled herself up into a sitting position.

"Grace?"

"I need to go," she said anxiously.

"OK." I helped her up. "Where's Chloe?"

"I don't know." I opened the door to the head and helped her inside. "I can do it from here," she said.

"OK." I closed the door and waited. Chloe stepped into the salon from on deck.

"Is she up?"

"Yes. Where were you?"

"The baby woke me up."

"Were you sick?"

"No, no. It's just rolling around in there. I think it's a disco baby. It moves to a steady beat. I needed a walk."

I pointed to the head door.

"How is she?"

"The same."

"I also got a letter from Roger."

"Yeah?"

"He left it on the boat." She held it up in the air.

"Well, what does he say?"

"It's incoherent. You'd think he could make sense on paper at least. It's the same old thing. He's sorry and it's our fault, and it's the wrong time and it's my fault and he has no job but he misses me, and probably thinks the baby will look like him, but it's a mistake and on and on."

Grace knocked on the door from the inside.

"Yes?" I answered.

"How do I flush this thing?"

Chloe frowned and shook her head.

"I'll do it, Grace," I said.

She opened the door and we helped her into her robe and up into the salon.

"Are we going to be in time for breakfast?" she asked.

"Sure, we've got plenty of time." After Chloe and I changed, we carried Grace off the boat, and put her back into the wheelchair.

It was August now, and from down river a fog bank approached, darkening the morning, dulling the water. We were silent as we trundled

Grace and the chair back up the gangway and rolled across the deserted deck of the Smarmy Snail. The wheels thumped across the gaps between each plank rhythmically, like a muffled metronome, an ashen passage of time. Grace broke the bluntness with a shrill, tattered wail.

"What, what?" I yelled.

"There." She tried to turn in the chair.

"What?" Chloe asked.

"Wait," she said. "Back there. Just back there. Someone's dropped a ten-dollar bill."

Chloe and I looked at one another. She seemed to feel as empty as I did. I pivoted the chair slowly and wheeled Grace back to the corner of the restaurant.

"Right there. Get it." And she pointed. I rolled her closer.

I kneeled down and put my hand on the bill, drew my fingers together over the plank and lifted my empty hand into the air. "You see, Grace. Someone's painted it on the sidewalk. It's not real."

"Well," she said, sitting back in her chair dejectedly. "They sure fooled me."

≈

We expected all hell to break loose when we returned to the hospital. Grace had been gone for almost ten hours. But the receptionist looked up and smiled as we rolled by. A young man pushed a laundry cart onto the elevator we rode and did nothing more alarming than yawn. We passed no one in the hallway outside Grace's room. The note Chloe had left on the rumpled sheets saying we'd taken Grace for a bit of fresh air was undisturbed. And five minutes after we had her back in bed an orderly stepped in with her breakfast tray. They never missed her. For a few moments, as Chloe and I watched Grace eat, we were unbelievably relieved. We were ready to take responsibility for our actions. We knew we'd risked not only losing visiting privileges but also jail. But then we began to become rather incensed. We'd escaped but only through negligence, Grace's caretaker's negligence.

"I've got a good mind to go out there and let them all have it," I said.

"But you can't do that, Charlotte," Chloe shushed.

"I know, I know."

"We tricked them."

"It wasn't that good of a trick. A note on a bed sheet? They couldn't have read it more than once."

Chloe turned to Grace, "You won't tell anyone you didn't stay here last night, will you?"

"I won't tell."

"Not even Anne," I said.

"That won't be any trouble. She never asks me anything," Grace said dryly. "Are you sure she's my daughter?"

I looked at Chloe and couldn't help grinning.

"You told us she was before you lost your memory, Grace," I said, "but this is the first time we've ever met her."

"Maybe she's not my daughter," Grace said.

"Grace," Chloe whispered harshly, and looked toward the door.

"Well, maybe she's after my money."

"I don't think you have much money, Grace," I said.

"You said that was my boat."

"It is."

"Well, it must be worth something."

I nodded, unsure.

"Things that are mine are mine," she said, closing the subject by shoving most of a wedge of toast into her mouth.

≈

It was a Sunday, and Chloe had to work, but we had enough time to walk down to Karen's Restaurant for breakfast. Watching Grace eat had made us both ravenous. The work of several artists hung on the walls of Karen's, mostly floral treatments or lobster boats cradled in coves. Two of Grace's paintings hung with them: a small canvas that was nothing more than a manila envelope with a Federal Express label, one corner ripped open, and another larger work that seemed to be an exact reproduction of a two by three foot section of brick sidewalk. Lodged between the brick courses were tiny but brilliant bits of trash, a cigarette

butt, a piece of wire, anomalous scraps, all of it on the verge of dissolv-ing, withering, blowing away.

"Why does she only paint things?" I asked Chloe between bites.

"She painted Sweet George."

"But that was unusual," I said.

"I don't know. Maybe because things stand still. She always likes to get stuff just right."

"But that envelope, and those bricks," I said. "They're better than right somehow. There's more there than right. If you took a photograph of either of those subjects, it wouldn't be as right as she has them."

"We should take her some of her paintings," Chloe said.

"She didn't recognize the bill on the sidewalk at the Snail," I said.

"No."

"But we'll try it."

"Charlotte, I'm going to tell Roger what I think."

"What's that?"

"That I don't want to marry him. That I want to raise the baby on my own. That I'd rather he not be a part of our lives. If he wants to see the baby occasionally, we'll try to work something out on a regular basis, the way divorced people do, but that I'd prefer it if we just went separately from this point on. I don't want or expect his help. I'm going to be blunt about it. We've both dillydallied too long."

"Do you want me to be with you when you tell him?" I asked.

"No. He'd be embarrassed."

"You make sure, Chloe," I said, "that there are other people close by. I don't trust him."

"He's just young," Chloe said. "I'll be all right."

"I'd take a poll just to be sure. You may think you understand him, but you're young too."

"I haven't taken a poll in a week," she said.

"Why not?"

"I don't give a damn what anyone else thinks, anymore."

"Chloe," I said, "I think some kind of instinctual maternal enzymes or something are building up inside of you." I smiled. "You're twice as smart, twice as brave, as I am."

"Who cares what you think," she said.

≈

I picked up a couple of MOES sandwiches that evening and brought them to the hospital. I thought it would be a nice, illegal change from the hospital food Grace had been eating. She'd always loved them, big subs packed with pepperoni, onions, green peppers, and black olives. I laid the wrapped sandwich on her bedside table when I arrived and to my amazement she reached for it immediately, saying, "I've been wanting one of these for a month."

"One of what?" I asked, frozen in midfall to my chair.

"A MOES," she said, popping the tape on the butcher paper and spreading it on her lap.

"Grace," I said in a tight whisper.

She looked at me. "What?" I looked down at her sandwich and she followed my eyes down to it as well. She turned back to me, her fingers retreating from the paper. "I recognized it?" she said.

"You sure did," I grinned.

"I could smell it," she said, and began to eat.

I felt my throat hardening so I went out into the hall, leaned against the concrete block. I clinched my fists, pushed away from the wall. I had to tell someone. I marched down to the nurses' station.

"Excuse me," I said. A young nurse looked up from paperwork. "Grace," I said, "down in room 210, she just remembered something. I brought her a MOES and she recognized it. What do we do?"

Her pupils moved toward one another. "Do you want me to call the doctor?"

"Uh, no," I said. "I'm just really glad."

"Maybe you should get her another sandwich," she suggested. "I'll make a note here for the doctor. She'll pick it up on rounds."

"OK," I said. I put my hand over my mouth to cover my perplexed grin. "I'm really happy," I said as I walked away. The nurse smiled at me, her pupils swinging toward each other again as if attracted by her magnetic nose.

By the time I got back to Grace's room, Anne was sitting in my chair.

"Oh, Anne," I said, "she's just remembered something. She remem-

bered a MOES. She recognized the package and the smell immediately, didn't you, Grace?" Grace nodded, her mouth full.

Anne didn't look at her mother, but up at me. "Don't you ever have anyplace else to be? Every time I come in, one of you is here." She threw her car keys into her purse, then bent over and slapped the purse on the floor, shoving it under the chair. Grace stopped chewing.

I was stunned. "I'm sorry," I whispered. "We knew you'd be gone this weekend. I just came down to have dinner with her."

"I'd just like to have some time alone with my mother," she said, leaning forward in the chair and jerking her jacket forward with both hands.

"I'll leave," I said, "but you need to know that she just had some recognition of something she'd only known about before the stroke. Her memory is returning."

"Mother?" Anne said, turning to her brusquely.

Grace said, "When I saw this sandwich, I knew it was a MOES."

"A what?"

"A MOES. It's her favorite sandwich," I interrupted.

"Do you remember anything else?" Anne asked.

"I don't know," Grace said truculently. She didn't like being quizzed.

"What are your grandchildren's names?"

"That's not fair, Anne," I said.

"Can I be alone with my mother, please?" she yelled at me.

Almost instantaneously Grace threw what was left of her sandwich across the room against the wall. We both turned to her.

"Get out, both of you," she said.

"But, Grace," I said.

"Mother," Anne said.

"This is my room. Get out." She picked up a chip of black olive off her bedspread and threw it toward the rest of the sandwich.

"I'll clean up this mess you've made." Anne stepped toward the sandwich that decorated the wall.

"If you both don't leave right now. . . ." and she paused, looking at a nurse in the doorway. "I want these people out of my room, nurse, right now."

"ok," I said. "ok, I'm leaving."

Anne stalked back to her purse. "I'll be here at seven tomorrow morning, Mother. We're moving you to the clinic."

"Come at eight," Grace snapped. "Breakfast is at seven."

Hoping to cool things off, I waited for Anne in the hallway. But as she stepped out of the room, her purse careening, she lowered her head and swept past me. I had an almost irresistible urge to sideswipe her with my hip, knock her up against the wall. Instead I watched her click her way down the tile, and be forced to suffer the humiliation of waiting for the elevator.

≈

At seven the next morning Anne didn't go to the hospital. She came to *Rosinante*. Chloe and I were barely awake. We met her in our pajamas at the salon door. After brief eye contact she moved immediately to her purpose.

"I've placed *Rosinante* on the market. A broker will be coming down from Camden tomorrow morning. I'd appreciate it if you'd keep the place picked up."

Chloe, one finger still rubbing an eye, said, "It's not a 'place'. It's a boat."

Anne paused and shook her head. "Have either of you paid this month's rent?"

"Yes," I said. "I deposited both our checks in Grace's account Friday."

"Well, then," Anne returned, "I'll honor my mother's commitment for this month. Then you'll have to be out."

"Off," Chloe said. "It's a boat."

"Off then," Anne said.

"Chloe will be eight months pregnant at the end of the month," I said.

"I can't help that. I have to put Mother's affairs in order."

"Her affairs?" I said. "She's not dead."

"She might as well be," Anne said.

"Anne," I said and I reached out for her sleeve. "Your mother is just

157

up the bank. Give her some time. Don't lock her up. She'll be back, I know it. If you don't want to deal with her, let Chloe and I. Let her come home, at least for a while. It couldn't hurt her."

"Couldn't hurt her? She can barely walk and you want her down here surrounded by water? No. She's my responsibility."

"If you think she's dead already," Chloe said, "I don't see your point."

For a moment I glimpsed Chloe's mother's side of their relationship.

"Well," Anne said, "I can see you're mature enough to raise children."

"Listen, you," Chloe began, but I gripped her by the arm.

"Listen to this," Anne said, "off this boat by the end of the month or I'll have you thrown off."

"Anne, I'll talk to Grace about this," I said.

"It won't do you any good. Go ahead. I'm her guardian. In effect this is my boat. I won't argue with you anymore." She turned to leave and bumped her head on the salon door frame.

"It's a boat: you have to duck," Chloe snickered.

"Damn it," Anne spit.

So I said it too, but at Chloe, "Goddamn it, Chloe." Then I turned back to Anne, "Please, Anne, please. Chloe and I, we both love your mother."

"Well," she said, "so do I," and she turned up the dock and climbed the gangway.

I stamped my foot on the salon sole like a child. Then I turned to Chloe.

"What a bitch," she said.

"You really helped out a lot, Chloe," I yelled.

"Charlotte, her underwear is so far up her butt it's caught between her teeth. You do remember she just threw us off the boat."

"I remember, but aggravating the situation won't help," I said.

"Aggravating? Charlotte, how can things get any worse? Who cares if she likes us?"

"I do," I said. "I hate it when somebody doesn't like me, especially when they haven't got a reason."

"I'm glad it's me having the baby. You're the most gullible hick I've ever met. People don't act on reason. They just act. They can't even avoid themselves. You were trying to reason with a brick wall. She was beating you with a board and you were giving it back to her every time she dropped it."

"Shut up," I yelled.

"You shut up," Chloe yelled back.

We both did for a moment, then I ventured, "She's taking Grace to the clinic this morning."

"I shouldn't get all worked up like this. It's not good for the baby." She ran her hands over the front of her pajama top, molding it to her stomach.

"I'm sorry," I said.

"Oh, bejesus, you drive me up the wall," Chloe said, throwing her hands up and going below.

"What is with you?" I snapped back at her, and went out and sat on the foredeck in my pj's. I sat in a deep dew, amid thick fog, and before long I was soaked through. The mist was so viscous I couldn't see the far bank of the river. The horizon was a powdery mingling of gray water and white fog, and even sounds were muted, sullen. I could hear the throaty wake of a lobster boat as it passed under Memorial, but could not see it, couldn't tell whether it came or went. Even though it was August my butt seemed frozen to the deck. I pushed myself up and went below to our cabin. Chloe was already dressed for work. Midden and Pinky were both asleep at the foot of my bunk.

"You can't see a thing out there," I said.

"You say she remembered a MOES?" Chloe said.

"Yes."

"I wonder if that clinic has a kitchen." She ran a brush again and again through the half inch of her hair as she stood before the dresser.

I stepped up behind her, looking at her face in the mirror. "You're really pretty, Chloe."

She turned and hugged me, and whispered over my shoulder, "I'm so fat."

≈

159

We decided that morning not to go to the clinic for a day or two, to give Anne some time to settle down. Even then we thought we'd do a drive-by, to make sure her rental car wasn't in the parking lot when we visited.

While Chloe was at work I went grocery shopping for the ingredients to Grace's favorite cake. We were going to force food on her anorexic memory.

≈

I stopped by Malcolm Laury's again, but he hadn't yet received a response to his last fax. He said if he didn't hear anything by Wednesday he'd try again.

"It's possible," he said, "they're playing a little game, letting us sit on a hot plate waiting for their answer. But I'm in no hurry to give them your money. Are you?"

"No, but I do want to get the thing resolved. I want it behind me."

"That's what they're counting on. Just be patient."

"I have another question," I said. "How does someone become a guardian?"

"You go before a judge."

"I have a friend who's confused; she doesn't know what's going on."

"That's the main reason the judge would OK guardianship. Usually it's next of kin. Is there something I can help with?"

"No. At least not yet. My friend's lost her memory and her daughter is now handling her affairs in a way I think my friend would be opposed to."

Malcolm put his hands together on his desk pad, then moved a pencil, aligning it so that it was parallel with the edge of the pad. "Then I would say your best bet is to hope your friend's memory returns."

"But what if her daughter does something that's not in my friend's best interest?"

"It's going to be very difficult to contest a daughter's right to care for her parent, unless you could show some degree of harmful intent or negligence."

"I don't think she's intentionally harmful, just stupid. I mean removed, almost as if it's a bother to be involved. And it's only partly that. She really believes she's doing the right thing."

"It's hard," Malcolm said, and moved the same pencil to the other side of the blotter.

≈

I felt a need for some work of my own, and so that afternoon and the next morning I worked at the Jones House at Strawbery Banke, cleaning, counting and cataloging some of our finds from the upper levels of our site. It was just the kind of mind-numbing, tedious work I desired, counting hundreds of rusty nails, sorting them by size and type. Every sherd of pottery had to be cleaned and numbered by applying a lacquer patch and writing over the patch with indelible ink. In this way if needed, the numbers could be removed or changed by dissolving the lacquer. There were bags and boxes of artifacts, enough to keep three or four of us busy for months. Michael still hadn't received the osteological report, and hadn't yet been able to identify our most important artifact, the metal button found with the pregnant skeleton. There seemed to be some characters, possibly an inscription or figure represented on it. Rather than cleaning it himself, he'd sent if off to a laboratory that specialized in photographic and X-ray methods of information retrieval which wouldn't harm the artifact. Many commemorative buttons made in England during the seventeenth century celebrated royal weddings or military campaigns, and Michael was hoping we had one of these to help date the burial more closely.

I felt my hours in the lab that week were a warm safe bubble. I let my guard down there, tried not to worry about my problems or Grace's or Chloe's, tried to concentrate on the coordination of my eyes and hands, writing legibly a ten-digit alphanumeric code on sherds of creamware the size of my fingernails. I let my guard down. And the bug on the wall, for once, was looking directly at me.

≈

On Wednesday morning we visited Grace at the clinic, which turned out to be simply a nursing home. Instead of intensive therapy, she was receiving a fifteen-minute workout with a volunteer. But we weren't too concerned about Grace's physical ailments. She'd progressed a great deal already, in the hospital and on her own. Her strength and confidence were almost at their pre-stroke levels. What concerned us was the realization that the old folks' home was just a holding tank for Grace, a stop on the way to a permanent room at a nursing home in Florida. It took only five minutes of small talk with a volunteer to discover that Grace would only be with them for a few days rather than two weeks. We asked for the address of the retirement home in Florida and discovered that the community was almost two hours from Palm Beach, where Anne lived.

"Maybe it's the best nursing home in the area," Chloe suggested.

"It's two hours away by car," I said. "Anne flies up here in three hours. It doesn't make sense, Chloe. It's Florida: there must be thousands of good homes in Anne's area. It gives her an excuse not to visit. She never visited Grace here; she's not going to visit her there either. I could just kill her."

"I was going to kill her on the boat and you wouldn't let me."

Grace was in a double room. Her roommate was asleep when we entered. Grace leaped from her chair, where she sat fully dressed twiddling her thumbs when she saw us. She shushed us, putting her finger to her lips, and then whispered, "For goodness sakes don't wake her up. She's crazy." She pushed us out into the hall. "The first night I was here," she said as we moved down the hall, "I woke up and there she was, two inches separating our noses, and when she saw I was awake she leaned even closer and said, 'BOO.' Then she went back to her bed. She says my things are her things, and she takes my things and puts them in her dresser drawers. She tells me she knows me but I've never cast eyes on her in my life."

"How do you feel, Grace?" I asked.

"I feel fine. Watch this." She twiddled her thumbs for us. "And this bad leg, it's almost caught up with my good one. And the best thing is I can wink. It took me an hour to do it but watch." She winked at us three or four times. "I've always wanted to be able to wink."

"That's your good eye, Grace," Chloe said. "You're winking your good eye."

"I am?"

"Yes."

"Oh well. I can still wink."

"You always wanted to be able to wink?" I asked.

She stopped and turned to me, putting her hand familiarly on my forearm, "Yes, always. Isn't that strange?"

"Is always two weeks or seventy-five years?" I asked.

"It seems much longer than two weeks," she mused, and then turning away abruptly, she said, "And this is the community room."

Eight or nine aged individuals sat in a Naugahyde room watching a TV suspended from the ceiling. Chloe noticed immediately that at least half of them held remote controls. Occasionally one of them would draw and shoot and the TV would drop dead, the screen turn dark, and then come back to life on another channel.

"We have activities every afternoon," Grace said. "Yesterday we made bird's nests out of ice cream sticks." She leaned toward us and in a whisper stated, "Everyone here is quite old."

"You're here, Grace," Chloe said.

"But only for a few days, then Anne will be back. I'm moving to Florida with her."

"Do you want to move to Florida, Grace?" I asked.

She seemed to scan our faces for a clue to her answer.

"I don't want to stay here," she said. "I'm doing what people tell me to do."

An ancient man walking with two canes clacked up behind Chloe, and after taking both canes in one hand, reached up with his free hand and rubbed Chloe's cropped head. She shied and turned around.

"Just wanted to feel it," he said.

"Well, ask first next time," Chloe said shrilly.

"Can I feel it?"

Chloe looked at me, smiled, and then stepped back up to him and lowered her head to be petted. The old man lifted his hand again, but in midflight, trembling, it stalled and fell to Chloe's left breast, where it

lighted with a squeeze. Chloe yelped and jumped back. The old man tittered and turned, and clacked back down the hallway.

"I can't believe it," Chloe yipped.

"He tries that on everybody," Grace dismissed.

Chloe still held one hand over her boob. "If he tries it again I'll break his canes."

"He knows no one's going to send him to jail," Grace explained. "He doesn't care what anybody thinks. He's just promiscuous. Everybody in here is old and crazy."

"We brought you some cake, Grace," I said, lifting a sack toward her. It was her favorite, German chocolate. I was hoping for another bleat of recognition. When none came, I explained, "It's your favorite."

"It is?"

"Yes," Chloe said.

"Then let's eat it," Grace said, smiling, and put her hands on both of our backs, pushing us toward the cafeteria.

We stayed for most of the day, having lunch with Grace, watching her physical therapy session and the afternoon craft class, where they glued empty Spam cans together to form a Christmas tree, brushed more glue over each can, then sprinkled them with multicolored glitter. With each step in the building of the tree I became more depressed. Grace participated but did so listlessly. In time she seemed to forget we were there, and eventually she gravitated to a chair in front of the TV, and picking up one of the remotes, aimed at the screen and fired.

The ancient man sat near the exit, and as we left he waved at Chloe with his cane and said, "Come sit on my lap, little girl."

"Put an ice pack on it, grandpa," Chloe said, and slammed through the doorway.

≈

That night on *Rosinante* Chloe and I made dinner but ate in silence. We'd gone through Grace's things again, hoping to find something that might prod her stubborn memory, but it seemed we'd tried everything: old photos, her paintings, perfumes, clothing. I washed up while Chloe readied for bed. Even Midden and Pinky moved about the boat quietly.

Another August fog enveloped us, muffling even the gurglings of the tide and the ceaseless straining of *Rosinante*'s dock lines. I hung the dish towel limply over its hook and switched off the light. As I stepped down into our cabin I heard Chloe speaking quietly to herself, her speech not a whisper but dimpled somehow, modulating, imploring. She stopped when I entered and looked up at me from her bunk.

"Chloe?"

"I was just praying," she said.

I sat down on my bunk. "I don't know that even God can help us now," I said. Midden jumped up in my lap. I stroked his fur.

"Why didn't you tell her, Charlotte, about Florida and about Anne kicking us off the boat?"

"I don't know. I'm not worried about us, Chloe. We'll find a place to live. I mean it won't be like this, but we'll find something. And I didn't want to tell her that she was going to another nursing home in Florida, because there's nothing she or we can do about it."

"Charlotte," Chloe said, "I wasn't praying to God. I was praying to Sweet George."

So I said a little prayer to Sweet George too, and hoped that between the two of us we could summon him up. And as I ended my prayer it occurred to me that I'd never once thought of speaking or praying to Jonah, that I'd never once since his death asked for his help.

≈

Realizing our time with Grace was short, Chloe called in sick Thursday and again we spent the day at the nursing home. Anne had gone back home but would return Friday to pick Grace up. It was difficult to find topics of conversation that Grace could participate in. We talked about Harry and his fishing boat. They'd been out for three days and were due back in the next day, but she had no memory of him. Chloe talked about Roger. She still hadn't had her meeting with him. She told Grace it was supposed to be that afternoon but that she'd put it off because she'd rather spend the day with her. At times Grace was animated, asking questions, insulting the staff or Anne. She seemed to think of Anne as

one of the staff, someone with authority over her, to be minded, but also to be resentful of in ways.

"She keeps fixing my clothes," Grace said. "She refolds them. I've folded them once and she goes and refolds them. It doesn't make any sense." She paused then looked up. "She brushes my hair." She turned to Chloe. "You know I don't like that."

I smiled, recalling Chloe's fingers in Grace's scalp. Then I realized at the same time that Chloe realized, and we both babbled into the beginnings of sentences that were indecipherable. I began again, "Why should Chloe know you don't like that, Grace?"

She looked at me, and then at Chloe, "Because."

"Because, why, Grace?" Chloe asked.

Again she was confused. "I don't know. It just seems she should." She shrugged.

"I wish you could remember, Grace," Chloe sighed.

"But don't you remember, Chloe?" she asked.

"We got in a big fight once. I had my hands in your hair and you hit me."

"I did? I'm sorry."

"No, I deserved it."

"Well, at least you remember."

"It hurts me that you don't, though, Grace," Chloe said. "It's not enough for just me to remember. Both of us have to or it's half-forgotten. It's like it didn't happen. It's not the same."

"Honey, as long as one of us remembers, it's all right."

"Grace," I said, "if you get to Florida and you, for some reason, don't like it, you'll let us know, OK? I've written down my p.o. box. You can write us a letter. And we'll call you from time to time."

"I'm not leaving until Saturday," she said.

"I know."

"Anne and I are going to the boat tomorrow to get my things."

"We'll be there, Grace."

"You don't think someone's stealing the boat while you're here, do you?"

"No," I said. "It's tied to the dock."

"It's my boat," Grace said.

That afternoon, as Chloe and I sat in Naugahyde chairs, each with a remote in our hand, Grace sat across the room in the craft class. A local elementary school art teacher had been brought in. Chloe and I watched TV lackadaisically, flipping through back copies of *Modern Maturity*. The teacher, perhaps three or four years younger than I, enthusiastically passed out cream-colored craft paper and small tin watercolor sets. She then placed a basket of fruit on a tabletop and began drawing circles on a chalkboard, explaining the geometric simplicity of art. *Hogan's Heroes* was on TV. LeBeau had fallen in love with another member of the Resistance. I looked up again and saw that Grace had already dipped her brush in her glass of water and was working, glancing occasionally at the basket of fruit. She worked intently, squinting. At times she seemed to become perplexed, and would pause momentarily, but only to take up her work with renewed speed. Fifteen minutes later the teacher strolled between the tables of painters, commenting on their progress. When she got to Grace, Chloe and I could hear her saying, "What is this?" Grace pointed to the basket of fruit. "No," the teacher said, "You need to start with a circle." She took the brush out of Grace's hand and made a circular motion on the paper. Grace shoved her away with both arms and stood up. Chloe and I were there instantly.

"What is it, Grace?" I asked. She looked startled to see me. I suppose she'd forgotten we were there.

"She marked on my painting," Grace said finally. There were tears in her eyes. "I know how to do this," she said.

I looked at her and then down at the paper. She'd used only a light blue, washed with white, shades of light gray. There was nothing that resembled a basket of fruit in any way. Nothing in line or color, just an anomalous gathering of strokes. Then Chloe, beautiful Chloe, stepped between us, picked up the paper and put it in Grace's hand.

"It's the reflection," Chloe said. "It's the reflection of the TV on the skin of the apple." And in that instant the teacher and I saw it too.

"I know how to do this," Grace said again. "My head hurts." We walked her back down to her room. She cried most of the way there. "Why don't I know where I am?" she asked us. She cried noiselessly while a nurse examined her, and she fell asleep with tears still in her eyes. She was unable to recognize anything more.

And I thought, what a fool I've been. It wasn't her finished works that would bring her back to us, but the process of painting them again.

≈

That night Chloe and I resolved to do everything we could to convince Anne to leave Grace with us. We were sure she was coming around, however slowly. A complete change in environment couldn't possibly help or stimulate her memory. It would make her even more confused, less able to care for herself. We knew we'd only have one chance, when Anne brought Grace by to pick up her things late the next afternoon. All the same we didn't have much hope.

Chloe went off to work the next morning and I went to the lab at Strawbery Banke. Everyone there was very excited because Michael had just run out of the building on his way to the university. The technicians doing the osteological work had found something and wanted him to see it in person. I wondered what could be so important that Michael would have to see it personally, what couldn't wait for the report. I tried to think of something I could have missed in my preliminary analysis of the remains, and went over our photographs of the skeletons again. But nothing new came to mind. So I went back to work with the volunteers. I labeled, counted, sorted, tried to work through life a digit at a time.

I tried to construct an argument for Anne. Unfortunately none of my reasoning got past her hypothetical reaction to each point, "I'm her daughter. I'm in charge."

≈

By lunch Michael still hadn't returned. I wanted to get back to *Rosinante* to clean before Anne and Grace arrived, to make sure that Grace took as much of her past with her as I thought she would want. I left the Jones House with my head down, listening to the hammering of marine carpenters across the sward that used to be Puddle Dock. They were restoring an old wooden boat. I cut swiftly through a group of tourists who were asking polite questions of the Strawbery Banke barrel maker and laughing at his responses. I hurried because I still had on my name tag

and I didn't want to be stopped by someone desiring a detailed history of the city. I was thinking about packing Grace's things, about making her some cookies for her trip. With each step I kicked at the earth. The morning fog had burned off from the inner harbor and it didn't seem right that it could be such a beautiful day. In the parking lot in front of the gift shop I was startled by someone reaching out and grabbing my arm. It was Michael. When I looked up at him he was ducking away and I then realized my arm was in the air, ready to strike.

"Cripes," he said.

"Don't ever do that again," I said crossly.

"OK, Charlotte. Christ, you're temperamental. I thought you might want to know. We've gotten some answers. The button proved to be unreadable. The expert at Williamsburg said the shank could have been made anytime between 1630 and 1750. But you're not going to believe what they found at UNH and what one of our researchers came up with over at the Portsmouth Athenaeum."

"What did I miss?"

"You didn't miss anything. But the skull of the old woman, we took it to them loaded with matrix because we were afraid it would collapse if we cleaned it in the field, right? Among the material, buried in the skull cavity, they found a coin, an English copper, dated 1691." He paused, looking at me.

"1691?" I said. "Inside?"

"Yes," he said, beaming, "Freaking unbelievable. It must have been placed in her mouth or over one of her eyes when she died."

"But if it was over an eye why just one?"

"One of the osteologists said there was some scarring, a slight calcium buildup, on one of the orbits. She may have been injured, blind in one eye."

"But 1691, Michael. Point of Graves was dedicated twenty years earlier."

"Exactly," he said. "Which means these burials weren't lost. They weren't a mistake. They were purposely placed outside the walls of the cemetery."

I began to shiver uncontrollably.

"Which brings me to what our researchers found," he went on.

"The rod through the abdomen. It wasn't, probably wasn't, a surveyor's stake. It's possible that what we have here was a suspected witch. It seems the practice at the time, after a witch died, whether of natural causes or not, was to drive a stake through her, pin her soul to the ground, so she wouldn't come back."

"But the other body," I said. "It didn't have a stake in it."

"I think these burials, Charlotte, might be something like a sinners' graveyard: the folks who weren't good enough to be buried with the righteous. I know this all seems wild, it's just theory, but maybe the young girl's sin was that she was an unwed mother or," he sighed, "would have been."

I nodded, but I felt lightheaded, as if I might faint at any moment. Michael said something else, about showing me the coin later and then he was gone. I stood in the gravel parking lot in front of the gift shop, shaking as if I were chilled even though it must have been eighty-five degrees out. I took a tentative step forward and didn't fall, so I took another. I was trying to work through all the questions but my mind seemed thick, congested, as if I'd just woken from a dream of drowning. I was still in this suspended state, numb, hugging myself with both arms, when I stepped onto the deck of the Smarmy Snail and saw Richard and Mary at a table there.

Richard looked up, Mary turned, and I strode right past them, down the gangway and aboard *Rosinante*. Grace and Anne were already there, packing her things.

"I didn't think you were going to be here till late this afternoon," I said to Anne.

She pursed her lips. "We thought it would be easier if we did this alone."

"You weren't even going to let us say good-bye," I asserted.

"You're making it hard on Mother. Please, let us get on with our lives."

There was a knock on the salon door. "Charlotte." It was Richard. "Charlotte, please come speak with us."

I left Anne, and then slamming open the salon door I forced Richard off the boat and back down to the dock with my upraised palms. "I don't have anything to say to either of you," I said. "I suppose

your detective can tell you where my lawyer's office is. I've offered you everything else."

"You killed our son and you think you're going to pay for it with money?" Mary said. It sounded so strange, the words actually spoken aloud. "You've got another think coming."

"Charlotte," Richard said.

"That's enough," I said.

"We just want to know why," he said.

"Why what?" I yelled. "I didn't kill Jonah anymore than you did. I'm not even sure he killed himself."

Mary was in tears, her hands in fists held at her stomach. "But he loved you," she said. "He wouldn't have been so despondent if you'd done your part, loved him too."

"I won't talk to you anymore," I said, and began to move away when I heard a scream. I ducked and turned to Richard and Mary, who were looking back up at the deck of the Smarmy Snail. Everyone there was standing at their tables, and looking away from the boat. I'd thought for a moment that Mary was going to attack me. Then I heard Chloe's voice. Anne stepped out on deck behind me. By the time I'd pushed my way between Richard and Mary, Chloe was at the top of the gangway, her back to us. Then something struck her and she fell over, her arms flailing and she rolled down the aluminum way, her leg finally catching on a tubular handrail stanchion. Roger stood above her; the restaurant patrons were moving away from him.

I screamed Chloe's name. She began to move, to roll off her back. Her legs and head hung out over the water. Harry's boat had come in that morning and on the chance that he was still belowdecks I yelled for him. I ran toward Chloe then as Roger moved down on her again.

"I love you, Chloe," he said. "I love you," and before she was on her feet he struck her in the face with his fist. Her body spun toward me, blood slinging from her mouth. I heard Anne screaming at Grace, telling her to stay on the boat. I'd bent over by that time, had my hand on Chloe's face when I felt Roger's shoe on my shoulder and then I too tumbled down the gangway, and struck my neck on the last rail stanchion. I was so afraid of falling in the water. I looked up and saw Roger kick Chloe in the small of her back. She slid the rest of the way

171

down the incline and into my arms. We struggled up and I put her behind me.

"Get on the boat," I said.

Roger stepped down the gangway, holding his arms limply at his side. "You're going to protect her?" he said. And almost instantly I was knocked up against *Rosinante*'s lifelines. The side of my face felt hard, wooden. He walked past me. Chloe was already aboard. Anne was now on the dock too, and Richard and Mary stood between Roger and the salon door. "You people get the hell out of my way." There were several seconds of silence as the three of them backed away from the boarding steps. Then *Rosinante*'s engine turned over. I reached down and flipped the stern line off its cleat. As I climbed over the rail onto *Rosinante*, Roger began screaming at Chloe to get off the boat. The incoming tide began to swing *Rosinante*'s stern out into the river's current. The boarding step fell off the dock and into the water. The electric shore supply cords snapped with a bright blue flash from the boat's outlet. Roger stepped past Anne and Mary and Richard, who seemed paralyzed by the authority of his physical violence. He was moving toward the bow of the boat, the only place he could get aboard. I ran forward as fast as I could, but I knew I wouldn't get there before Roger did. Chloe was at the helm, the boat in full reverse, but the line was short, strong. It wouldn't break. Roger put his hand on a piling and stretching out, stepped on *Rosinante*'s coaming. I looked for something to swing. There was nothing. I looked back up. He was still there, one foot on the bow and one on the dock. But his hands weren't on the piling. They were stretched out, straining for *Rosinante*'s lifelines. The bow line was taut beneath him, vibrating. I didn't understand. But then I saw Harry's boat hook, and Harry on the other end of it, in the stern of his boat. He'd hooked Roger at his pants waist with the long pole and was pulling him back.

"A little forward, Chloe," Harry yelled. The boat began moving back toward the dock, threatening to pin Roger between them. At the last possible moment he went with the strain and fell back down to the dock. I raced forward. The bow line went taut again and as I struggled over the cleat, Chloe pushed me aside and cut the line like an umbilical with one sweep of our big butcher knife. When I looked up again Harry

had Roger in a bear hug, holding him up in the air from behind. Roger kicked and screamed for Chloe to come back, and then he began to cry. I went back to the helm and stood there with Chloe and Grace. Chloe held the boat at a speed sufficient to keep us twenty feet off the dock, maintaining position against the current. She was still sniffling, running her forearm beneath her bloody lip.

"I thought he was going to kill me," she said.

I looked back at the dock. Anne and Richard and Mary stood there, a few feet from Roger and Harry. I turned to Grace and Chloe. "Let's get out of here," I said.

They both looked back to me, as if I'd suggested we commit suicide.

Harry uttered an obscenity then. We turned. Roger had Harry's forearm in his teeth. We watched as Harry picked him up bodily and threw him into the Piscataqua.

"NOW," I said.

Chloe pushed the throttle forward and we began to move down-river against the current.

"Mother," Anne yelled.

Grace stepped up to the salon window and waved at Anne. Richard and Mary walked out to the end of the dock, as near as they could come to me.

"Mother!" Anne yelled again.

They all watched us pull away. Roger tried to swim after us in the fifty-four degree water, but the current was too strong and carried him upriver. We watched as he snagged and clung to the stone base of Memorial Bridge.

"Where are we going?" Grace asked.

We motored beyond Henderson's Point, beyond the old Victorian prison, toward the harbor mouth, and no longer could we see the dock or the people on it or even the Smarmy Snail.

"We're going away," I said. "Anywhere we want. We've lowered our mast."

We passed the Coast Guard station, and rounded Portsmouth Light and then, entering a thick fog bank at Whaleback Light, we slipped into the Atlantic Ocean. *Rosinante* rose and fell on swells.

"Can you do this in fog?" I asked Chloe.

For an answer she asked, "How about Prince Edward Island? We could go there."

And Grace said, "I've always wanted to go there."

"We're not running away, are we, Charlotte?" Chloe asked, reaching up and flipping on the radar set and the other instruments.

"No," I whispered. The fog was taking us so thickly we could barely make out the bow of our own boat. "We're not running away. We're escaping. There's a difference."

The three of us stood at the helm, looking forward, but listening to the base warning of the lighthouse foghorns on our stern.

"The foghorns," Chloe said. "They're trying to call us back. But you never move directly toward them because that's where the rocks are."

"Are you OK, Chloe, honey?" Grace asked.

"I think so. My mouth hurts."

"I'll go get a washcloth," Grace said. She stepped carefully, moving from handhold to handhold, and went below.

"I'm scared, Chloe. Tell me what to do. I can't see anything," I said.

"You're scared and I'm just starting to calm down," she answered. "We've got calm seas. The only thing we need to worry about is running into someone or letting them run into us. Quick course in radar." She lifted her hand to the set. "See, I've got the range at one mile. This is us right here in the middle. Each one of these rings is another quarter mile out from us. That smudge right there: that's Whaleback Light. This little dot is 2KR, the buoy at the entrance to the harbor. We just passed it on our port. These two other dots are moving. Those are boats. We want to stay away from them."

"That's not so difficult," I said, looking up into the green glow. "I feel better already."

"Yeah," she answered, "radar's great, but it doesn't show you what's under the water, and sometimes it doesn't pick up small boats or wooden boats."

"We're a wooden boat," I said.

"But we've got an aluminum reflector hung in the rigging," she explained. And then she said, "I suppose we'll have to take it down soon."

"Why?"

"I imagine the Coast Guard will be after us before long. We just stole an old lady and her boat. We're lucky the fog is so thick."

"I'll get it," I said. I stepped out into the weather, a warm, griseous shroud, and climbed up on top of the salon and lowered the reflector from the short mast. The water around us seemed to languish, thick as oil. Bits of seaweed didn't seem to float in it but to be caught there. The foam off *Rosinante*'s bow gelled and collapsed back into the water as if the surface was tacky. We slid slowly past lobster buoys that reclined in a sea without waves, the warp beneath them disappearing into cloaks of dark seaweed. I stepped back down on the deck, felt the thrum of the engine under my feet, and walked forward to the bow. The fog filled the space between me and the salon. I turned and looked forward, my eyes straining to make shapes out of our formless surroundings, and at times it did seem as if something was about to be revealed, to solidify, and I would turn and look back to Chloe and find that she was gone, that I was floating alone on the forward third of the boat. I took hold of the lifeline and walked back to the salon, each foot of the deck reappearing as I walked, surfacing, rising from the cool water slickly and without effort. I found Grace and Chloe dry in the salon.

"How long will it be like this?" I asked.

"Ten more minutes, a week," Chloe said.

"I feel like I'm a kid, under the sheets with a flashlight," I said.

"I'll need the charts from below, Charlotte," Chloe said. "And I think we should put Grace in a vest."

I glanced at her, turned to Grace for a moment, then went after the life jacket and the charts. The engine was louder below, more firm. I could feel it working through the grain of the wood cabinets and sole. The water pulsed against the hull, an intense pressure rather than friction, a hiss rather than a rip, a low enduring moan of contact that sounded pleasurable.

Chloe rolled the charts out on the salon table while I watched the radar screen. The helm was on autopilot; *Rosinante* was churning forward at a consistent six knots.

"Here's the one we want: the Gulf of Maine." Grace sat next to her, looking on. "Straight across the gulf to the southern tip of Nova Scotia, then up the coast. Then we cut through the channel here. Prince

Edward Island is here. Someone's already laid out the entire course in pencil: headings, distances, waypoints. I guess Sweet George did this."

"No, I think I did it," Grace said. I turned from the screen to her. "It's my handwriting. I must have done this," she said. "It seems so strange. I was going here before, wasn't I?"

"It will come back to you, Grace," I said. "Give it time."

She ran her palms across the curled charts, then the point of her index finger along the courses.

"How far is it, Chloe?" I asked.

"Seven hundred miles, maybe," she said.

"What?"

"It's a long way, Charlotte."

"Can we go that far?"

"We've got two hundred and fifty gallons of fuel. Say we make four miles a gallon. There's plenty. We'll run out of food long before we run out of fuel."

"How far is it to Nova Scotia?"

"Day and a half, two days, depending on the seas."

"We can pull into a port there, can't we?"

"We'll have to be careful. The Canadians have a Coast Guard too. I guess I'm going to miss my doctor's appointment next week."

"But if we can get to Canada, won't we be safe? I mean, they protected draft dodgers during the Vietnam War."

"I don't think they'll harbor kidnappers and thieves," Chloe said.

"That's just it," Grace said, "I'm no kid. Anne was going to put me in another nursing home, wasn't she?" Chloe and I looked at her but didn't answer. She went on. "I've forgotten some things, it's true. But I'm not sick. Just because I can't remember her doesn't mean I can't take care of myself."

"We can't do this," I said. "We have to turn around and go back. You're pregnant, and we don't have Grace's medicine. This is crazy."

Grace stuck her hand down into a deep pocket of her skirt and pulled out two pill bottles. "Anne put them there when we packed up at the nursing home." She smiled.

I read the labels. There was almost a month's supply.

"This baby will come wherever we are," Chloe said, and stepped up

to the helm. "OK. I'm going to set us on a course. We're on our way in a straight line now, as the crow swims."

We'd been out perhaps an hour and a half when we first heard *Rosinante*'s name hailed over the VHF radio. We'd been monitoring channel 16, expecting a call from the Coast Guard, a demand to return, a shot over our bow. But instead it was Chloe's father, his foggy, disembodied voice hailing *Rosinante* from his boat, which circled in the haze around us, searching.

"Aren't you going to answer him?" I asked.

The call came again: "*Rosinante, Rosinante, Rosinante*, this is Dorothy Gale." Then, "Chloe, baby, I know you're there. They've got Roger locked up. I know you're there. We're worried about you. You call me, little girl, right now. I'll find you and lead you back into the harbor."

"Chloe," I said.

"I won't talk to him, Charlotte. I'll break up and I don't want to."

The calls came regularly, every few minutes, becoming fainter as we moved out to sea. Chloe stood at the helm stolidly, staring forward into that blinding fog. But she flinched whenever the radio crackled.

"Let's just turn it off," I suggested finally.

"No," she said. "You always monitor 16. It's the emergency channel. Someone may need help."

As we cut further into the sea, Chloe increased the range of the radar set, and at the end of four hours the last bit of land, the Isles of Shoals five miles off the coast, disappeared from the screen. The radar's longest range was sixteen miles, but the circle it roamed over held few signals. We watched the blip of a large ship cross our bow five miles ahead, bound south around Cape Cod, but for the most part the ocean seemed sparsely populated.

At nine that evening we heard the strong signal of the Portsmouth Coast Guard station mention us for the first time, stating strangely enough that we were overdue and asking all boaters to watch for us, a fifty-foot cruiser with three persons aboard.

Grimly Chloe suggested, "Well, we could set *Dapple* adrift and burn some trash, one of the life rings, throw it all overboard."

"I don't want my parents to think I'm dead," I said.

"It was just a thought," she said. "If we were dead, no one would bother us anymore."

"Let's just get away for now, Chloe. Thelma and Louise we're not. We just need some time."

"Sooner or later, they're going to catch us, somebody will catch us."

"Maybe they won't do it in time, though." We sat silently for another hour, listening to the sturdy drone of the diesel. "The fog's not so bad in the dark. It can't be twice as dark as dark," I said. "Two times zero is still zero."

"What?" Chloe said listlessly. "You sound like Alice in Wonderland."

"I'm hungry," I said. "You hungry?"

"I'm famished."

Before I could turn to go below Grace rose from the companionway, balancing a plate of tuna fish sandwiches. "I was lost down there for a while but I finally found everything."

I ate two sandwiches and went below and made myself a third, and brought chips and olives back with me to the salon. My jaw ached when I chewed where Roger had clubbed me. Chloe chewed on one side of her mouth so the cut on the other side wouldn't crack open. When she finished eating I said, "Why don't you go below and get some rest? I'll watch things."

She looked at me.

"I can do it. Grace and I will watch things," I said.

"OK," she said. "I'll go below for four hours. Watch these three gauges. The rpm should stay at nineteen hundred, the oil pressure at fifty pounds, and the water temperature at a hundred and eighty degrees. If you think you're going to come close to anything on the radar screen, come get me. If you hear or smell or feel anything queer, come and get me. The running lights are on, so don't touch any of these switches. If the weather changes, come and get me. If you want something to do, you can take these coordinates off the Loran and plot our position on the chart every half hour or so. The number on the top of the screen is our latitude and the lower one is our longitude. OK?"

"OK," I said.

"OK," Grace said. "I'm not a bit sleepy."

178

Chloe went below rather warily, I thought. Grace and I used a long ruler and a pencil to plot our current position on the chart, in the gulf, on the planet. We looked at the small lead X in the middle of the water for a few minutes.

"That's where we are," Grace said.

"It's sort of comforting, isn't it?" I said.

"Yes," Grace said, putting her hand over my forearm.

"Do you know where we're going, Grace?" I asked.

"By the time I get there I'll know exactly where I'm at."

I smiled. "Do you know what day it is?"

"Would you without a calendar?"

I stepped down to our cabin, crossing to my dresser for my calendar, when Chloe leaped from her bunk, striking her head on the shelf above. "What is it?" she yelled.

"It's nothing, it's nothing," I said, my heart pounding. "I just came down for my calendar."

"You're on watch," she said harshly.

"OK," I said, "It was just a second."

"You're on watch," she said again, so I stepped quickly back up to the helm, and scanned the radar screen, all the gauges and stared out into the void of the night. When everything seemed to check out, I handed the calendar to Grace.

She looked deeply into it, and finally said, "Well, there are a great many days to choose from, aren't there?"

I put my finger on the calendar. "It's this one, Grace. We need to get you caught up. We may have to prove that you can take care of yourself."

"OK, Charlotte. I'll keep up. I'll learn any life you want me to. I made the sandwiches."

"You did," I said and put my arm around her shoulders. Together we watched the screen and gauges, plotted our position from time to time, and listened closely for any suggestion of a change in tone from the engine room. It seemed to modulate from time to time from a deeper bass to a quicker roar, and after a while I realized there was a slight swell running under us, a swell as long as the hull, lifting us a foot or two slowly and allowing us to slide gently back down into the sea. At

2:00 A.M. Chloe's alarm went off and she joined us in the salon. We were sixty-five miles off the coast of Maine, the seas still calm, a few breaks in the fog allowing stars to fall down on us. I walked once around *Rosinante*'s wet deck, and then went to my own bunk.

I found Pinky on my sheets and Midden under them. They both looked seasick. I laid down in the serpentine space they allotted me. Every muscle in my body seemed tense, coiled, trying to maintain my balance continually. The sound of the engine and the sea through my pillow were soothing though, and I slept the sleep of a sailor, soundly in snatches, ready to burst from my bunk at the slightest burp of the engine. I felt the sea's swells move through me fluidly, as if I were a length of warp loose in the water. My dreams were odd, viewed through saltwater. Sweet George and Roger and Jonah were playing cards together, and sitting in the dinghy that hung from davits at *Rosinante*'s stern. They seemed to have known each other for years. At the end of this dream, in the transmogrifying way dreams have of undermining themselves, I was sitting in the dinghy too, looking at my poker hand, which contained at least seventy-five kings and a pair of deuces, when I realized I was Jonah. Roger smiled at me, and laid down a spread of eighty aces on the thwart amidships. I was going to crack his skull with an oar until I remembered I was dreaming and woke up, thirty seconds before my alarm went off.

I put on some clean clothes and clunked up to the helm. Chloe was there alone, leaning into a graying dawn. There were little whitecaps breaking on the sea. The fog had given over to low dense clouds that seemed to mirror the break and boil of the waves below. Chloe turned to me, her face as pulpy as any sailor's who'd spent the night in barroom brawls. Her left eye was bordered by a crescent of lavender and her right cheek was swollen.

"Charlotte," she said. "I need you to make a round on deck and make sure everything's secure."

"OK. Why?"

"It looks like we're going to get a little weather. The NOAA weather forecasts say twenty-five- and thirty-knot winds by ten this morning. We'll have some rain too, but its the wind. . . ." she broke off.

"Are you all right, Chloe?"

"I'm just tired. My eye is sore."

"It's purple," I said.

"Grace finally went to bed. She stayed up with me most of the night. Just make sure there are no loose lines that could go overboard and get tangled in the prop. Make sure the forward hatch is secure. And anything that might blow overboard needs to be brought in or tied down."

"OK," I said, and slid the salon door aside and stepped out. The wind smelled like an empty tin can, and immediately raised the hair on the back of my neck. We were heading directly into it and the small waves, so the boat didn't roll but lunged slightly as if it were a horse jumping over a curb. I stowed the settee cushions away, and coiled up the only line I found loose, the painter hanging off Dapple's bow eye. I looked over into the dinghy to see if there were any cards lying between the ribs. Three fenders still hung off *Rosinante*'s rail, so I brought them aboard and stowed them in the locker behind the church pew. Four of Grace's flowerpots sat on a canister behind the pew. I threw them overboard. I then read the directions printed on the outside of the life raft canister. And finally I lashed the halyards on the little mast down so they wouldn't pop in the wind.

"Everything's secure on deck, captain," I told Chloe.

"OK, do the same for everything below. Everything either in a cabinet or tied down."

"Chloe," I asked, "What can twenty-five-knot winds do to us?"

"We'll be OK. Luckily they're coming from the direction we're headed. They'll slow us down but we shouldn't roll much if we stay on top of the wheel. We may get eight- or nine-foot waves later in the day.

"Really?"

"It will be OK. If this old boat holds up."

"Should we rest the engine for a while? It's been going all night."

"It's a diesel. It would rather work than not. Daddy wouldn't have anything else on his boats."

"OK, I'll see what I can do below."

"Some breakfast too, Charlotte, and a cushion for this bony stool," she yelled after me.

"Boy," I yelled back. "You sure turn captain easy."

Grace was sitting on her bunk, and rubbing her eyes. "I forgot where I was for a minute," she said.

"Well," I answered, "that's better than forgetting who you are for a couple of weeks."

She stuck her tongue out at me, then began to brush her hair while standing uneasily at her dresser.

"Where are the bungee cords, Grace?" I yelled from the galley. I squatted before an open cabinet door and peered in. When she didn't answer, I turned to her. She was staring at me.

"I believe I know," she said, her eyes wide. Her brush hung limply from her head, caught in her hair, while her hands worked one another like clay. "See if they're not in a coffee can under the sink."

I moved to the cabinet, sitting Buddhalike in front of the door, praying in a way. The can was there, and inside, the bungee cords. I knew we hadn't used them since we took the boat up river to Patten's Yard earlier that summer. I held them in the air so she could see.

"Now why would I remember those old things?" she asked.

I shrugged, but smiled. We used the cords to hold all the loose articles firmly to the bulkhead over the galley counter, and to snug the canned foods down in the cabinets. Almost everything else was screwed down or gimbaled. We did take the books from the shelves above my bunk and laid them among the pillows and blankets in case we heeled over too far.

Back at the helm I told Chloe about the bungee cords.

"You made dinner last night. Maybe you saw them then," she suggested.

"I don't remember seeing them then," Grace said.

We watched the ocean, whose horizon was lost in clouds. Pinky and Midden joined us and we realized that we hadn't fed them since the voyage began. But when I put food in front of them they weren't interested. Midden was still tense, as if someone were touching the pads of his paws, while Pinky looked as dry and relaxed as I'd ever seen him. He climbed up on the settee and gazed out the salon window from time to time to check on our progress. He groaned once, as we lurched and rolled out of a swell. There was perhaps a quarter mile of visibility, a hundred-foot ceiling, and we were the only solid object in all that we

surveyed. Raindrops began to patter against the windows of the salon, streaking horizontally across their lengths. The wind built in gusts out of the northeast, each surge leaving a stronger sustaining blow. It was only minutes before I understood that we were all three now straining to hold our balance, gripping the mahogany rail at the helm. *Rosinante* tried to hold her bow above the clamor of the sea, but finally the troughs of the waves became too deep, and as she plunged down into them the next wave would catch her short and slam into her upper strakes and throw spray over the gunwale. Soon there was more salt water on the windshield than fresh. Water ran down the decks, around the cabin trunk, and fell back into the sea through the scuppers. Every third or fourth wave seemed steeper, harder, and as sharp as the stem was, the contact still shuddered the boat as if it had just run into a concrete wall. It was a *Rosinante* unbridled, all spume and mane.

I asked Chloe a question but soon realized she couldn't hear me. The sea was now louder than the engine beneath us. So I yelled, "How much longer will this last?"

"Till it stops," she yelled back.

"Are these waves only nine feet tall?"

"These are only five or six; the nine-foot ones are building now."

"I don't see how it can be so calm and then a couple hours later be like this. It changed so quickly."

"This is nothing," she yelled. "It didn't take Roger ten seconds. I'll take this any day. I think everybody should put on a vest, just to be safe."

We snapped on the big bulky life jackets, in between *Rosinante*'s leaps and ankle-twisting landings. Grace, tired of trying to stand, wedged herself into the corner of the settee. I stood with Chloe, who stood behind the wheel even though she didn't steer. The boat was still on autopilot.

"Would it be smoother if you steered manually?"

"No, these waves are fairly regular. The autopilot can hold a better line than I can. If it gets worse, if we start to spin in the bottom of a trough, I'll take it. We don't want to wallow."

"Is there anything I can do?"

"We're OK. We just have to ride it out. It will end sooner or later."

"I wish there was something I could do," I said.

"It's weather, Charlotte. You know, it didn't hurt as much as I thought it would. I always thought if Roger really let me have it . . . I thought it would hurt like hell. And it did, but it was only temporary. It makes me mad that I was so afraid of him."

"I'll just ride it out," I yelled. "But tell me if you want me to do something, OK?"

"Go down into the engine room and pull up one of those short floorboards. See if there's any water in the bilge."

I bumped my way below. The noise was deafening near the engine. I yanked up a board in the floor and almost smashed my nose with it. Down between the big oak flooring ribs, a trickle of seawater ran through the bilge. I didn't know if this was any more water than *Rosinante* always took on, but it didn't look ominous. I snapped the board back down and crawled back to the engine room door and up the companionway.

"There's a thin stream running, not much," I told Chloe.

"Good. We should check it every once in a while. Poor old boat."

I looked back over my shoulder at Grace. She was sound asleep; her head was lolling back and forth with each breaker. A real sea stomach.

No matter how Chloe fiddled with the controls on the radar it continued to pick up wave crests as tugboats, barges, cargo ships and liners, all of them surrounding and bearing down on us.

"The worst thing," she said, "would be to get caught between a tug and its barge. The steel cable between them would either slice your boat lengthwise at the waterline or hold you in place till the barge ran you down. And even if the tug sees you it can't stop the barge. It just keeps on keeping on, all that foam at the bow and three hundred feet of steel behind it."

"Really," I said.

"We probably won't know it if it happens, though," she said to comfort me.

The waves before us were cresting above eye level now, their bases dark but shimmering. As they rose their color faded, then intensified, and even in the gray light, deep greens and blues and occasionally turquoise curls were shot through with light before they spumed, fell thrash and spoondrift across our decks, and died there, colorless, thin water. *Rosinante* vibrated, gathered herself, stalled in midair as if she

were deciding, then dropped with all her deadweight to a granite-surfaced sea. There were moments when I knew that three-quarters of her keel protruded through the back of a wave, and other moments when everything was either under water or spray except the rudder and prop. The engine roared then without the ocean's resistance and *Rosinante* lost steerage. Finally Chloe snapped off the autopilot and took the wheel herself, gripping the mahogany spokes.

"Jesus," she said. I didn't hear her, but read her lips.

"What?" I yelled.

"The rudder's just a weather vane sometimes. I can tell. The wheel turns too easily."

"We're off course a little," I said.

"Doesn't matter. Bow to the weather. We don't want these waves on our beam. Skinny old boat would roll like a whore."

"Chloe," I screamed, laughing.

"Well," she mouthed, smiling back, turning the big wheel.

"This is ridiculous," I screamed, but my scream barely surfaced over the wail of the storm. "You're seven months pregnant and your're standing at this wheel all day."

"It's got to be easier than giving birth in a rice field. You ever read that book?"

"Yeah."

"She was muy macho."

"She was in a book. You're real," I yelled.

We were in the height of the storm for almost an hour, but it seemed like only moments. At last, Chloe nodded ahead. "Look, the spray doesn't go all the way over the boat anymore."

"Is it dying down?"

"Maybe."

"So these are nine-foot waves?"

"I don't know. Biggest waves I've ever been in were six or seven and these are a lot bigger."

"Why didn't you say so?"

"No way to turn back," she said.

Over the next two hours we watched the storm and wind subside, and by dusk the sun gleamed low on the horizon between earth and

overcast. We sailed away from it into a night of oily seas, swells that could have come from Iceland or South America. Chloe said we could have made Nova Scotia by 2:00 or 3:00 A.M., but thought we'd better hold off the coast till daylight since she was completely unfamiliar with it. So we dropped the rpm on our good engine, and idled, lolling over the slick sweeps. Chloe slept, then I slept, Grace woke and made us a meal of chicken soup and crackers and Oreos. By midnight the sky was completely clear, and we all stood out on *Rosinante*'s drying decks.

"Well, now, that wasn't so bad, was it?" Grace hummed.

The air seemed fresh, sponged, vibrant. We bailed a foot of water out of *Dapple,* who held water as well as she repelled it. The red starboard light of a boat passed us a mile off. Chloe said she thought it was a trawler. By 4:00 A.M. we saw lights on the shoreline. We laid down the chart on Nova Scotia and read underlined passages to each other out of a guidebook from Sweet George's library.

"Isn't it good to be free?" Grace said. "It seems as if I've heard all these things before."

Chloe smiled, but tugged at her underwires, and finally, exasperated, pulled her entire bra off through her sleeve.

"You're going to leave your shirt on, aren't you?" Grace asked.

"Of course," Chloe frowned.

"Fine by me," she said. "I used to have a friend who was proud of her breasts. She was vain. Throw'em right up in your face at the least opportunity. I thought they were too pointed but I never told her so. I just let her go on thinking as she would. Not really even symmetrical."

I looked at Chloe with my jaw hanging loose at an angle.

"And pale," Grace added, "She put bowls over them to protect them from the sun when she laid out. So they always looked like they'd just passed out on her chest."

Chloe and I laughed till we were gagging, as happy as we'd been in weeks. She'd remembered something that wasn't from the last seventeen or eighteen days, something personal, and she'd given it life in her voice, as pointed and satiric as it was. She didn't seem to realize what she'd done and neither Chloe nor I brought it to her attention. It was too good to be mentioned, too rare, as if the sound of our voices might spook her, this deer in the backyard.

≈

Dawn broke fogless, bright. Chloe and I raised a Canadian flag, a courtesy to the broad reach of land off our port. We'd chosen to make landfall at a small cove that the guidebook called "secluded and scenic, if there aren't six other cruisers already at anchor." It was about two miles up the coast from the nearest community. We thought we could anchor *Rosinante* and then take *Dapple* around the point to town for supplies. The coastline was rugged, sparse, fragrant. There were homes scattered along the shore, sitting above wave-washed rocks. We passed the town a mile out to sea, but a tower and two church steeples were easily visible. Two small boats angled out of the harbor, but didn't come toward us. What I perceived as an unbroken mass of rock, Chloe saw as multiple inlets and coves. She picked our destination out with binoculars and turned *Rosinante* toward shore. High tide was within the hour. This would give us a better chance of not running aground in a strange anchorage. I picked up the glasses as we neared the coast. The rocks, waveworn and dark, seemed to undulate. Then I realized there were dogs on the beach, dozens of them, and just as I opened my mouth to say dogs out came the word, "Seals."

Chloe took us in through a wide channel, turned to port behind a small island, and brought the boat to a standstill in the cove. She and I and Grace then went forward and let go the anchor, which fell with a splash and a roar of chain. We were in twenty-five feet of water so Chloe backed *Rosinante* off to lay out more scope and finally we snubbed the chain so the anchor, Old Muddy Beak as Chloe called it, would get a good bite. Then, for the first time in forty hours, *Rosinante*'s engine was switched off. The quiet following, the pall of the cove, was mesmerizing. At first I seemed as deaf as the anchor on the bottom but then I began to pick up the lap of the water against the hull, the hushed scoot of wind over worn rock, and brightly, like a metal bowl dropped, the bark of a seal at the mouth of the cove. There were no homes on the shoreline, only the tide-washed stone and steep hills of conifers. No other boat shared the anchorage. We walked *Rosinante*'s decks for a few minutes, looked up into the trees, and then, after hugging ourselves in the warmth of the sun, we all turned in.

I woke late that afternoon. Chloe was still asleep in her bunk across the cabin. My mouth was dry, so I went forward for a glass of water and to check on Grace. Pinky was up on her bunk. I carried my glass back up to the salon and out on deck. I looked forward. She wasn't there. I looked to the stern and saw that *Dapple* had been lowered off the davits. The cable hung down loosely. I rushed back down below and woke Chloe.

"She's gone," I said. "Grace isn't on board." After helping Chloe roll out of her bunk, we both went back on deck.

"I can't understand why she'd do this," I said, scanning the shoreline for her or *Dapple*.

Chloe yelled out, "Grace," and her voice bottled in the cove and echoed.

"What?" Grace yelled back.

We both ran to the stern and looked down between the davits. *Dapple* was in the water, but still clipped to the cables. Grace was sitting in her with a paintbrush in one hand and a baby food jar in the other.

"What are you doing?" Chloe asked.

"People are looking for us, right?"

"So?"

"So I'm hiding us," she said and gestured toward the mahogany transom. She'd painted over most of *Rosinante*'s gold-leaf name board, leaving a few letters in the center. "We're now the good ship SIN'N," she said. The paint seemed to match the grain, to flow effortlessly into mahogany.

"It's bad luck to change a boat's name," Chloe said.

Grace frowned. "Luck is the little sister of ignorance," she said.

Chloe and I looked at each other, a Stooges' double take.

"What?" Chloe asked.

"No more superstitions," Grace answered.

"OK," Chloe said.

"Haul me back up."

We helped her aboard. "You used to do a lot of that kind of work," I told her. "Grain painting, I mean."

"When I started it all seemed very suspicious. Don't touch it for a while. It needs to dry."

"We should turn the life rings around too," Chloe suggested. "*Rosinante* is on those too."

≈

I left our protected waters late in the afternoon, taking *Dapple* around the point to town. The seals barely raised their heads as I passed. There were ledges close to shore so I took the little boat further out than I wanted, but the ocean was calm and I shipped little water. The two-mile run took only fifteen minutes. The harbor moored two trawlers and fifteen or so smaller boats. A black government wharf protruded out into the bay with many smaller piers lining the shore. I brought *Dapple* to a float that several other dinghies were tethered to. It turned out to be a fisherman's co-op. I walked up the gangway to the solid footing of the pier. There, my legs swayed, and I lurched and caromed off the railing. It took another twenty feet or so before I was sure I wasn't going to fall. A boy, carrying a bucket of crushed ice, asked if he could help.

"Could you tell me where the nearest grocery might be?" I asked.

"There might be one if you turn left outside the shack there and walk for three or four minutes," he said.

"Is it all right if I leave my dinghy at the float?"

He turned and looked at the varnished *Dapple*, bobbing among the painted and battered working skiffs and rubber sleds.

"Can I look her over?"

"Sure," I said and left him skipping down the pier.

I walked past several very small houses, a couple of larger shingled structures that might have been boat sheds and arrived at the town center: Thuly's Market on one side of the street, two churches and a grange on the other. I stepped up the worn wooden risers and inside the small store. Bare bulbs hung down from a tin ceiling. The shelving seemed to be at least twelve feet tall and ran down both walls the full length of the shop.

"Yes, dear?" a young girl said before the door was shut behind me.

"Hello. I've come in on a boat and I'm afraid I don't have any Canadian dollars. Will you take U.S. currency?" There were Visa and Mas-

terCard stickers on the front window but I didn't want to use a credit card till I absolutely had to.

"I can take your currency. U.S. is worth a bit more than Canadian. I'll figure the exchange rate," she said.

"Great, thank you."

"What will you have then?" she asked.

"I need a couple loaves of bread."

"White or wheat?"

"One of each. And eggs, some bacon, canned green beans. . . ."

"We only have French style left."

"That's OK." She walked behind the long counter, and took food from the shelves by using a long, hooked stick to knock cans off higher shelves. She caught them with her free hand.

"And fruit, do you have any fruit?"

"That's out there with you, dear. Center section."

I gathered bananas, oranges to stave off scurvy, apples, but not the grapes, which had gone rubbery. Then I followed her down the counter, and pointed out cans on the shelving that she'd nonchalantly knock down.

"I'll put it all in a box for you since you're in the boat," she said.

"Thanks."

"We don't get too many tourists in here by boat. They come by the road more often. What part of the states are you from?"

"New York," I said.

"You don't seem that way at all, dear," she said.

"It's the boat," I said. "It takes the hurry out of you." I paid my bill and carried my box back to the water. The boy was still there on the float, his eyes running along *Dapple*'s seams, sheer, and stem. He held her steady while I climbed in.

"Thank you," I said.

"She's fine," he said. "What's a . . . '*Dapple?*'"

"A burro," I said, smiling.

"Oh, it's not fair," he said. His eyes seemed so tranquil, so approving. "Are you anchored up in the seal's cove?" I didn't answer immediately, unsure. "But it's the only place to anchor along this part of the coast."

"Yes," I said, "that's where we are." I started the engine. He smiled hesitantly, conscious of in some way undermining me.

He threw the painter in the bow, waved and yelled, "Tie up here anytime."

I waved, but never turned back, sure that everyone in town was watching me leave. I felt faces in windows, in cockpits, following me out of the harbor. In twenty minutes I'd given away my citizenship, the fact that we'd come to Nova Scotia by boat, and our present anchorage. I'd have to do better.

≈

That evening, as we ate dinner on the afterdeck, we made what plans we could. We'd move up the coast of Nova Scotia in eight-hour cruises, leaving at first light so we'd be able to find safe anchorages in daylight. And so it was for the next several days. We were lucky with the weather: the coast of Nova Scotia has an average of twenty days of fog in August. We had four days of sunshine in a row before being trapped, pleasurably, in Shelter Cove. We'd made nights at Port Mouton (a sheep fell overboard in the harbor in 1604—the smallest incidents name the centuries), in Mahone Bay and Ketch Harbour, then bypassed Halifax far out to sea before returning to the coastline at Shelter Cove. Our passages had been smooth and without incident, although anytime we approached shore or passed a boat that looked like it might have something official about it, we literally vibrated. All of our anchorages were in areas sparsely populated, small fishing villages, or inlets, like Shelter Cove, which was completely uninhabited. We woke on our fifth morning in Nova Scotia to another slow-witted fog. For the first time we felt a sense of security. There was no chance that we'd be seen from shore, and we were the only boat in the cove. In the fog there was little chance that anyone would be joining us.

I sat on the forward hatch above the galley and listened to Chloe and Grace feed the animals down below. I could almost hear the tension easing in my body. I was grateful for every day we'd stolen and I felt assured that we had one more. Grace was coming along. There had been no startling moment of recognition; there were still great gaps in her

memory, but occasionally things returned to her, items so inconsequential, found long after they were lost, like combs and pens beneath couch cushions. But these artifacts were so pleasing, as reassuring and startling as waking in the morning. Grace confessed to having no power over their discovery.

She painted every evening, setting up her easel in the salon or on the afterdeck, making a landscape journal of each of our anchorages. We told her that she didn't like doing scenery before, and she was incredulous. Why her skill hadn't disappeared with her memory none of us could comprehend. She never hesitated from palette to canvas.

I'd been afraid for any of us to go ashore after my excursion with *Dapple*, so for the most part we stayed aboard *Rosinante*, aka *Sin'n*. If we had to raise anchor hurriedly, I didn't want a third of the crew on leave. We'd been out of range of U.S. Coast Guard signals since our first night on board so we didn't know how the search for us was proceeding. Chloe hoped that they were looking up and down the U.S. coast. We monitored Canadian stations and kept an almost constant ear to the radio, listening to the chatter of pleasure and commercial traffic, but never heard a word about *Rosinante*.

Chloe had said little more about the attack, only that she'd had her say with Roger, that he'd spoken only in agreement and that they'd parted at the door of a restaurant across town somewhat coldly. And then, as she returned to *Rosinante*, as she stepped on the deck of the Smarmy Snail, she'd been struck from behind. He'd followed her. "He was hitting me and telling me he loved me over and over, and I couldn't get away," she said.

"Why did you start the boat when it was still tied up?" I asked.

"I climbed aboard so fast I fell over the coaming and when I sat up there was the key. I just wanted to get away. I thought the cleats on either the boat or the dock would tear loose. I would have taken the entire dock with me if I could have."

Later, she asked what had given me the idea to leave. "You were so sure," she said.

"I haven't figured out how to tell you yet," I'd said.

I sat on the hatch, looking into the fog and the vitreous surface the boat sat on. I tried to picture myself explaining all this to Jonah and it

just made me laugh aloud. My voice thudded into the fog, like bullets into a mattress. Chloe and Grace each leaned out of a salon door, as if the boat's ears had perked.

"What is it?" Chloe asked.

"Sounded like demonic hell itself," Grace said.

"Let's go ashore," I said. "We've got all day. We can cross that small peninsula. There's a beach on the other side. We'll come back if the fog starts to lift. I need to walk in a bigger circle."

We loaded *Dapple* to the gunwales with a cooler, a basket of food, Pinky, Midden, rain gear, and the three of us. The fog was so thick we couldn't see the shore, but using a handheld compass and a bearing off the chart we found it easily enough since we were almost landlocked in the cove. It was half-tide so we had to drag the tender through mud to get it close enough to tie its painter to a tree. The land was wooded, rugged, but it was only a short walk across the isthmus to a sandy beach. Midden tried to follow along the shoreline, but soon became disgusted with the sand that clung to the pads of his paws and returned to the tree line where he guarded the picnic. Pinky, no wetter than the rest of us in 100 percent humidity, stayed near Grace who sat down above the high tide mark with her lap board and water colors. Chloe walked with me, searching the sand for shells and pebbles. She felt very unsteady, and stepped along the slight incline as if it were frozen. The incoming tide inched forward in wavelets that came out of the fog it seemed with great effort. I stuffed the pockets of my pullover with shells and smooth rocks. The narrow peninsula was completely uninhabited, and although the coast of Nova Scotia had been settled earlier than Portsmouth, this beach had few artifacts to show for it. I didn't find a single sherd. If it weren't for a plastic tampon tube and an empty motor oil container that had washed up, it would have seemed we were the first humans to walk this beach. Chloe and I formed a ring of stones and, while she had a sit-down, I gathered driftwood and started a small fire. The smoke rose and mingled with the fog till we couldn't tell which was which, water or fire. We spread our rain gear on the wet sand and lay on each side of the fire.

"Those people, all those people," Chloe said. "Who were they, the ones I pushed through to get on *Rosinante*, the ones on the dock?"

Pinky joined us, a thin dribble of drool running off his chin to the

fur of his paws and thence into the sand, increasing the volume of the ocean.

"Anne was there, of course, early with Grace. I don't think we would have seen Grace again if we hadn't come home when we did. Anne was on the boat but she got off when we heard all the commotion. She told Grace to stay aboard. The other people were my in-laws."

"Your in-laws? From Kentucky?"

"Yes."

"What did they want? What did they say? That's why you wanted to leave, wasn't it?"

"No. Partly. I mean they were there and I wanted to get away from them, but that wasn't why I wanted to leave. There's something I have to say to them that I don't want to say. I wanted to leave for Grace's sake and for your sake and mine. But what made it so urgent to me at the time wasn't just Roger and Richard and Mary and Anne there on the float. It was the people that we excavated this summer, the ladies in the park. That morning I'd been at Strawbery Banke. I'd talked to Michael. Some things had turned up since we closed the dig. They found that the bodies were buried long after the cemetery had been plotted. They were buried outside its walls on purpose. They were outcasts, the two women. It's possible that the old lady, that she might have been thought a witch, and that the girl was pregnant and died out of wedlock. They were buried outside of the graveyard of those bound for heaven, although I'm sure the same family of mice gnawed on everyone's bones, sinner and saved alike. I know it's three hundred years between then and now, but it unnerved me."

Chloe lay with one hand under her cheekbone, and the other on her rounded belly. Her hair had grown so that it almost began to lay over. Tears began to form in her eyes and soon rolled off her cheek and nose into the sand. "Poor things," she said.

≈

By 10:30 the next morning the fog had lifted, leaving a weary haze over the horizon. The sun through the haze was glaringly harsh. Once we were safely to sea Chloe backed the engine down until we made only

three knots, and turning to Grace and me she said, "I'm tired of looking into the sun and I'm tired of eating out of cans."

"Do you want to pull into a harbor?" I asked.

"We've only got thirty-seven dollars between us," Grace said. "We need to make what we have last."

"We're in the middle of the ocean, girls," Chloe said. "We're going to have fresh fish for supper."

"Oh, good," Grace chirped.

"We don't have any fishing gear," I said.

"There's a roll of monofilament down in the engine room," Chloe said. "There's two or three hooks in that box of junk under the settee."

"What do we use to cast with?"

"We don't cast. We'll use the boat to cast. We'll troll. We'll just tie the line to the boat and pull it through the water."

"What can we use for bait?" I asked.

"Spam, maybe," she said. "Cut it into strips and thread the hook into it. But we'll need something shiny too, to get their attention."

"What about some earrings?" I said. "I've got some that are silver-plated, real flashy. I hate them."

"Let's see what we can rig up."

"I'm glad you're with us, Chloe," I said.

We slipped one of my earrings over the barb of a hook, embedded the hook in a chunk of Spam and, after tying the line to a stanchion, threw everything overboard. When the hundred feet of mono became taut Chloe dragged a few feet back in, tied a loop in it and clipped a bungee cord into the loop. Then she clipped the free end of the cord to another stanchion.

"Now, when the bungee goes taut we'll know we've got a strike."

Staring at the cord, we all sat on the afterdeck as *Rosinante* motored slowly along.

"How will we know?" Grace asked.

"When the cord stretches all of a sudden," Chloe explained.

"What could we catch?" I asked.

"I don't really know," Chloe said. "If this were Maine I'd say a striper or a blue maybe."

"Maybe we'll catch a Spamfish," Grace said, trying not to smile.

Chloe held her belly as if it were trying to float away.

"What if we catch a shark?" I asked.

This brought Chloe up short. "We need something to brain it with," she said.

"I was kidding," I said.

"No, we need a club or a baseball bat. Even if it's just a blue, those suckers have wicked teeth."

"There's a ball peen hammer in Sweet George's toolbox," I said.

"That'll do."

I went below, and as I came back up the companionway to the salon I heard a scream, then another. I held the hammer up in the air as I ran. Chloe was bent over, a turn of the line around her hand.

"What is it?" I yelled.

"Fish on," she screamed back.

"Pull it in," I yelled.

Grace stood in the middle of the afterdeck, bouncing up and down, holding both hands to her mouth. She lowered them to yell, "Don't let it get away, don't let it get away." Then she clamped her hands back over her face.

Chloe dropped to her knees and pulled with all her weight. The line veered out to starboard, pulled her down on her stomach, her hands sticking out through the lifelines.

"Go—kill—the—engine," she said, each word enunciated and exiting separately through the gaps in her clinched teeth.

I rushed forward, turned the key and then rushed back. Chloe was now lying on her side; the line left her hand tautly and entered the water at a steep angle.

"He's going down," she said.

For a moment the line slackened and Chloe pulled six or seven feet aboard. Then she took another turn around her hand. I could see blood on the heel of her palm where the line had cut through.

"Chloe," I said.

"Stings like a son of a bitch," she answered.

I went back inside and finally found a pair of Grace's gardening gloves.

"Here," I said. "Put these on."

"You put them on, goddamnit, Charlotte," she said.

"I don't know how to catch a fish," I yelled.

"Don't let him get away," Grace screamed again.

"He's going under the boat," Chloe said. "He's going under the boat, the wicked bastard." Chloe scooched forward on her side till her arms draped over *Rosinante*'s gunwale. The line shivered straight down and then followed the curve of the hull out of sight. Chloe's arms and hands were now plastered and held firmly against the hull too.

"He's a good'un," she said, straining to look back up at Grace and me. "If he comes back this way, if the line doesn't get cut on the keel or the prop, I'm going to give him to you when the line goes slack. We'll have to be quick. I feel like my arms are going to drop off."

"OK," I said, slipping the gloves on.

Grace picked up the hammer. "I'm ready too, Chloe, honey."

Chloe was still draped over the side of the boat with her legs splayed on deck. She began to pant. "All the blood's going to my head," she said. "I don't know if I can hold on."

I laid down next to her, and reaching down, slipped my fingers between the line and the hull.

"Don't pull, don't pull," she wheezed. "We don't want to cut the line on the hull. Just take the strain so I can unwrap my hand."

"OK," I said, "got it."

Chloe took the turn from around her palm and immediately the line began to burn hotly through my glove. Half of the line she'd pulled in went back out before I was able to get a wrap around the heel of my gloved palm. Within moments the line went slack again.

"Pull it in," Chloe whispered.

I sat up and she and I hauled in on the clear wet monofilament, dropping it in a tangled mass on deck. We were able to work up almost half of the line before it came taut again, breaking out of the water at a sharp angle on our beam.

"He's getting tired," Chloe said. "He's up near the surface."

Grace screamed, "I can see him, I can see him," and she pointed out to sea. A silver glimmer shot across the surface, then submerged.

"He's huge," I said.

"Keep tension on the line," Chloe warned. "Pull some in if you can."

Slowly, over a period of four or five minutes, we worked the fish up near the boat, but when he was close he veered off again. I had to let ten or fifteen feet of line back out. I kept a consistent tension on the line for a couple more minutes when it went suddenly slack in my hands.

"He's gotten off," I said. I pulled in on the line. It curled in limp coils down into the sea.

"Keep pulling it in," Chloe said. "He may still be on."

I hauled in line, as limp and loose as a laboratory skeleton, till I thought there could be little left under water. At any moment I expected to see a bare hook or the bitter end of the monofilament. We all stood hanging over the lifelines, peering down into the slate gray water. Grace, holding the hammer at her side, dropped it suddenly on the deck. The retort made me jump, and at the same moment I saw what she'd seen, a sleek glimmering slowly moving down alongside the hull of the boat.

"FISH ON," Chloe screamed.

I could have slugged her. I jumped again, feeling queasy all over, and I began to shiver. The line went taut in my hands again, but there wasn't any real strength behind the pull, just weight. I gathered in more line, till the fish skimmed along, back and forth, just beneath the surface, only a few feet off *Rosinante*'s beam.

"He's monstrous," Grace whispered.

"It's a blue," Chloe whispered. "He must be three feet long."

"What do I do now?" I asked. The line moved back and forth in my hands, as if a leaden kite tugged on it.

"He's wasted," Chloe said. "See how he rolls over on his side?"

"It feels like he's a car battery," I wheezed.

"OK," Chloe said, "OK." She held her arms out at her side, palms lifted, as if she were holding back two crowds. "If we try to lift him up over the side, the line might break. He's a lot heavier in the air than he is in the water. And we don't have a gaff. I'm going to lower *Dapple*. Charlotte, when I get the boat in the water, you give the line to Grace and come help me. Bring the hammer."

"Oh," Grace said. "Oh."

Within moments *Dapple*'s hull slapped the water and Chloe was calling. Grace took the line from me, wrapping it around her gloved hand.

"Easy," I said. "Don't let go."

"I won't. Oh, he's pulling. He's alive." She looked down into the water and back to me. "Poor thing," she said.

I climbed down the stern ladder into *Dapple* with the ball peen. Slowly Chloe and I worked the dinghy around to *Rosinante*'s starboard side, to close in on the blue. He made an effort to pull away from *Dapple*'s bow but finally came alongside, exhausted. Chloe took the line from Grace.

"OK," she said. "Here's the plan. I'm afraid if I lift him up he'll break loose. So we're going to dip him out of the ocean with the boat. We're going to put our weight all on this side of the boat, the gunwale will dip into the water, and I'll pull him aboard. Then we'll need to right the boat before she fills. OK?"

"It's cold water, Chloe," I said.

"He'll try to break free when I jerk on him and he's got wicked teeth. Watch your feet and hands. You'll have to hit him in the head to kill him. OK?"

"OK, but let's not capsize the boat."

"Let's not lose this fish, Charlotte."

"OK," I said.

We moved to each side of the center thwart. Chloe maneuvered the blue alongside, and I put my hands on the gunwale and leaned over. Chloe pressed too and water began to roll over the mahogany. I was soaked from the waist down almost immediately. In the moment that I felt my balance going, Chloe heaved backward and brought the big fish swimming aboard, and *Dapple* rocked back over, water up to her thwarts. The blue thrashed, thumping against the dinghy's delicate strakes and ribs. His jaws were snapping among our legs till we raised them up out of the water into the air.

"Jesus, Jesus, Jesus," Chloe shrieked, trying to move away to a place that didn't exist on the little boat.

"Hold him still, Chloe," I screamed and took three wild swings with the ball peen, all of which caromed off his slick skull and splashed saltwater back up into my eyes.

"Hit him, hit him," Chloe screamed again. The blue made a leap for the hem of Chloe's pants and bit instead the center thwart, gnawing into

the mahogany. I flipped the ball peen sideways and brought it down on his head directly above the eyes with a heavy dull thud. He let go of the thwart and flipped forward once, bouncing his nose off the gunwale, and rolled over on his side.

Chloe rose, staggering upward, and screamed, "Take that, you vicious son of a bitch," and she shook both of her fists at the dead fish.

I reached forward gingerly, water dripping from my hair and eyebrows, and touched the part of the fish furthest from the teeth. The fin moved, but only with the current in the dinghy.

"You've killed him," Chloe said. "Hail to Charlotte. The wicked fish is dead."

I reached down with both hands and took the blue by the tail, and standing, lifted him up in the air with a struggle. "Look, Chloe," I said, "all the color is going out of his body."

She bent down and looked, and sadly said, "It's just like when Dorothy goes back to Kansas."

I looked up at Grace and smiled. Then I looked back down at the blue, and with a silken gurgle he vomited the lump of Spam and the remains of a half-digested mackerel into the dingy. My lips curdled, and I leaned away, out over *Dapple*'s side, and I vomited too, half-digested eggs.

"I'm pregnant and everybody else is throwing up," Chloe said.

I dropped the blue back down into the foot of water in the dinghy and ran both sleeves over my mouth.

"Jesus, it was alive and we killed it," I moaned.

"We'll eat good tonight," Chloe trilled. "Blue is wonderful. Some butter and lemon, grill it till it flakes. Look." She pointed at the fish, my earring hanging from its chin. "Lucky thing. He caught himself under the chin. If he'd stuck the hook in his mouth he could have eventually bitten through the line. Throw us a bucket, Grace, so we can bail this boat."

We rowed heroic *Dapple* back to *Rosinante*'s stern, fought the weight of the fish aboard, and Chloe gutted and cut steaks out of our catch.

"If we had a fish scale," Grace said, "we could weigh it. It might be a record."

"We don't believe in scales anymore," Chloe said.

"No more scales," I said.

Grace smiled. "I suppose he weighs just enough."

≈

We anchored near the Ecum Secum inlet that night, and in Webb Cove in Isaac's Harbour the next, enjoying blue for dinner both evenings. We offered the fins and head to Midden, but he preferred the steaks. Pinky however, carried off the flat, lifeless skull by the drooping gills to the chain locker, where we had to fish it out a second time the next day. It was cached among gnawed and whitened steak bones, his stuffed animals, and one of my shoes I'd missed for over four months.

The heel of Chloe's hand had been sliced deeply by the line, but it had finally stopped bleeding and seemed to be healing with a constant application of Mycitracin and Band-Aids. Her spirits had lifted considerably with the catching of the blue. She cooked with great depravity. Verbose, but laudatory toward the fish, she praised his courage and struggle, and thanked him for honoring us with his presence at each meal.

At the only store in Isaac's Harbor, we spent almost all of our remaining funds on a tank of gas for *Dapple*'s motor, batteries for flashlights, and food. The proprietor never looked up from the countertop, never said hello or good-bye, which we appreciated. On the run back to *Rosinante* in *Dapple*, Chloe scanned the buoys of the harbor. "We'll have to keep fishing," she said listlessly.

We'd begun reading Sweet George's old hardback copy of *Anne of Green Gables* aloud to each other in the evenings. Sitting in the salon or on the afterdeck, Pinky and Midden tucked along our thighs, we took turns over the short chapters, reading about Anne's adventures with Marilla and Matthew and Diana, her absorbing and peculiar view of relationships. She even pooh-poohed praying, a wildly courageous act for a young girl of the nineteenth century.

"They say the Japanese and the Polish are wild about her," Chloe said. "They identify with her. There'll probably be millions of tourists on Prince Edward Island when we get there."

"Japanese tourists?" Grace asked. "But she had appallingly red hair."

I shrugged. "It's her spirit everyone likes, her ability to imagine a different life than the one she lived. She was an orphan, and she found a family. She was smart. She made a place for herself."

"If it's my turn to read when Matthew dies, I'm going to pass. I won't make it through," Chloe said.

≈

That night, in Webb Cove behind Hurricane Island, Chloe and I both woke to a sound. For a bright moment of fear I thought someone was boarding us, but when Chloe snapped on the light in our cabin Grace was standing there in her nightgown. She was sobbing in a low, deep hum, her eyes moist with pain.

"Grace?" I said, standing up.

Chloe and I took her shoulders and led her to my bunk. She sat down on the edge.

"I was afraid you weren't here," she cried softly.

"Where would we go? What is it, Grace?" Chloe asked.

She looked from one to the other of us, her lips wet and trembling. "I had a dream about George and when I woke up I knew who he was," and she broke down, leaning forward into her own lap, her body heaving with her sobs. She brought the hem of her nightgown up to her face and pressed it into her eyes.

"It's OK, now," we offered. "It's OK."

"No, no, no, it's not," she said, jerking up and collapsing forward again. After a few moments she was able to sit up. "I feel so unsure," she said. "And I feel so guilty. I tell you the truth, Chloe, when I walked in here I wasn't sure if you'd had your baby or not. How could I forget George? And Anne?"

I wrapped my arms around her and pressed my face into the cloth on her back.

Chloe said, "Oh Grace," and I heard her begin to blubber and so I let go too, hidden as I was, and we all cried together there, the first time I think all three of us had wept in unison since we'd met. Somehow we all ended up sitting on the cabin sole, drying our eyes with my crumpled

bedclothes. Midden and Pinky blinked in the artificial light, and tilted their heads in confusion.

"It's so strange," Grace said. "It still seems as if great chunks of my life are missing, like I have tunnel vision or I can't see in spots. How long have I been this way? I mean I remember the last few weeks, but. . . ."

"It's been weeks, Grace," I said. "You had a stroke."

"I know, I mean I remember, I mean, how could I have forgotten? It seems so obvious now, so apparent, so. . . ." She held her hands palm up in the air, "So lush."

"It was the fish," Chloe said suddenly. "We should have been feeding her more fish. I remember reading somewhere that fish is memory food."

"Brain food," I corrected.

"Same thing," she said.

"I'm so happy, Grace," I said. "I was afraid we were going to lose you."

"I feel so guilty," she said, looking down at her hands. "How could I forget?"

"It wasn't your fault," we told her. "It was the stroke."

"I shouldn't have had the stroke. I should have been stronger than the stroke. It could happen again. I could lose everything again. How did I come to know you, Charlotte?"

"I'm your boarder, Grace. I rented this cabin from you."

"Oh yes, of course you did." She looked around the cabin. "I remember Anne as a little girl, and in high school, but suddenly she's middle-aged. She has children, doesn't she?"

"Yes," I said.

"Maybe I'm not remembering. Maybe these memories are dreams."

"No," I said.

"My husband's name was George and he loved me," she said. "It feels so good to remember him." Her eyes glistened. "He had a bin with nuts and bolts in it out in the garage."

I didn't know what to say. Chloe and I simply rubbed and patted her, the way we would an animal we couldn't communicate with.

"I'm so tired," she said. We took her back to her bunk, and when

Pinky jumped up next to her she snatched him to her breast saying, "Oh Pinky, I'm sorry." We left her stroking his bristling fur.

And back in our bunks Chloe whispered across the darkness of Webb Cove to me, saying, "Charlotte, it doesn't seem like we should let her sleep. What if she's gone again in the morning? What if she doesn't know us?"

I paused, numbed, and finally answered, "Oh, Chloe, go to sleep."

≈

Grace knew us in the morning. She woke up angry, wanting to rave, but at the same time she was waiting for her brain to explode.

Over breakfast I said, "We could go back now, Grace. If you want."

But she said no. "I want to go on to the island. George and I. . . ."

"You used to call him Sweet George," Chloe said.

"I did?"

"Yes, but just for the last few years."

"Oh." She looked doubtful, like a dog who's been told to jump up on the bed. "Well, we were going there when he died, so I want to go on. I don't care what we do afterwards, but I want to go. We can call Anne from there."

"We'll still need to keep a low profile," I said. "If anybody is looking for us, we might get held up."

"You girls have treated me real well," Grace said, looking out into the harbor. "I want to thank you for not giving up on me."

"It was the fish that did it," Chloe said.

"Oh, Chloe, shut up," I said.

"It was," she insisted.

"Maybe it was just enough time to heal," I said.

"Look at it anyway you want," she said and looked away, tapping her fingers on the rim of her plate.

"I'm so happy, Grace," I told her and I took her hand.

"Me too," she whispered, but she didn't return my caress.

≈

By midmorning we were rounding the headlands and going northwest through the Canso Causeway, the strait that separates the mainland from Cape Breton Island. By late afternoon we had entered St. George's Bay and were searching for one of our last anchorages in Nova Scotia before heading out across the Northumberland Strait to Prince Edward Island.

"I really didn't remember you," Grace said.

Because of the inflection of her voice, I couldn't tell if she'd asked a question or made a statement. A quick glance at her, as she looked out at the entrance to a cove at Cape George, revealed that she wasn't sure either.

"Grace," I said, "it's just going to take some time to straighten things out in there. You can't do it all in one day."

"I feel anxious," she said.

"About what?"

"I don't know. Everything."

"We passed a lot of boats today," Chloe said. "But no one seemed to pay particular attention to us. I don't think we're in danger of being caught tonight. This cove is fairly secluded. Just a few lobster pots."

"I'm not worried about being caught," Grace said.

"We've got food for five or six days. We should be at Prince Edward Island in two days if the weather holds," I said.

"It's nothing in particular," Grace said. "Should I drop the anchor now, Chloe?"

"What's our depth?"

"Thirty feet."

"Lower away."

Grace and I went forward and chained ourselves to the planet. I took an extra turn around the capstan.

"George used to go around the other way with the chain," she said. "Should I. . . ?"

"No, it's all right. It will hold just as well. I just remembered he went around the other way. Why did I remember that? What makes that so important? I can't remember his middle name."

"Give it some time," I said.

"And I don't remember being a child," she went on. "Or being pregnant. It seems as if I've always been this age."

"We've been on the water all day. Why don't you go have a lie-down?"

"All right, but it's harder to be alone."

"Why?"

"Because," she smiled. "I may walk back up into the salon and find a bunch of strangers there."

"Then you'd better stick close by."

"Do you know what the oddest part is, Charlotte?"

"What? What's the oddest part of all this oddness?"

"I'd somehow forgotten it. But I've remembered now. I've remembered that I'm going to die."

"Grace, you're not going to die."

"Oh, I don't mean soon, just eventually. Somehow, after the stroke, I'd forgotten that I wasn't immortal. My memory humbles me." She put both hands to her face, covering her eyes. "I am tired," she said. "I think I will go to bed for a while."

"Do you want me to wake you for dinner?"

"Yes. Chloe wants me to have the last of that bluefish." She smiled and touched my forearm.

≈

We sat in our cove for the next three days, watching the tide ebb and flow, the advancing and receding mud, socked in. The fog never attempted to rise, but seemed to settle in like fall leaves among the stubble of the garden. Weather forecasts reported that the entire Gulf of St. Lawrence was shut down, blanketed in a dense layer of humidity. We played cards, finished reading *Anne of Green Gables*, and fished for hours at a time off *Rosinante*'s beam. Our only company was a low, dark lobster boat that cruised in and out of the cove. The lobsterman was checking his traps, as if there were no fog at all.

"He knows the coast," Chloe shrugged. "My dad can go from Portsmouth to York blindfolded."

We listened enviously as he motored out of the cove on the first and second mornings, almost always out of view. On the third morning he came alongside. We all leaned on the rail, curious to hear and see another human. Even at ten feet away mist fell between us so that he

seemed ashen, shy. He throttled down and held his bow to the ebb with one hand on the wheel. With the other he cupped his mouth and shouted, "Foggy, eh?"

"Hello," we yelled, "Foggy."

"Will you be needing anything?" he asked, with the perceptible lilt of a Scottish accent.

"Just for the fog to lift," Chloe said.

"Yes, and me too," he said. "It's thicker than relations at supper. Slows me down considerable. It's a fine old ship." He threw his hand toward *Rosinante* and throttled forward for a moment to remain on our beam.

"Thank you," Grace said. "How far is it to town?"

"If you take your dinghy as far up in the cove as you can, beach her there, it's a four-mile walk unless you get a ride. All by yourselves?"

The hair on the back of my neck bristled. "For now," I said, stupidly.

His pale brow furrowed. "I have more traps to check, but I could stop back by on my way up and give you a lift into town if you're short of supplies. You could stay the night in one of the B and B's and I'd bring you back in the morning."

"We're OK, but thanks anyway," I said.

"Bound for PEI?" he asked.

We didn't answer immediately. Finally Chloe said, "We're just cruising."

"Almost everyone's bound for PEI, the tourists, I mean. Everyone goes to see that little girl's place. My wife and daughter's been there. Well, if you need anything, most of us are on 9." He lifted the mike of his radio.

"Thank you," we all yelled back, as he disappeared into the mists.

"I wonder who 'most of us' means?" I said.

"Probably the fishermen," Chloe said.

His visit saddened me somehow. I turned to Chloe and Grace. We all lingered on the rail, listening to the bloated fading of the lobster boat's exhaust. "We're all going to the home of someone who didn't even exist," Chloe said. "She was made up."

"God's made up, Chloe," I said. "Plenty of people visit his houses."

"He is?" Grace said. "It's hard to know what's real and what's not, speaking from some experience."

"I just wish this damned fog would lift so we can get the hell out of here. I really don't want to have my baby in this cove. I can't believe his wife and daughter have been there."

"You didn't think we'd be the first ones to visit?" I asked.

"Of course not. There's all those Japanese and Polish. It just makes me a little nervous, like your in-laws and Grace's daughter and Roger are all going to be waiting there for us, up in Anne's bedroom at Green Gables."

"That guy," I nodded off into the fog, "he'll go back to town now and talk about us."

"I say we leave here in the morning, fog or no fog," Chloe said. "If we move slowly along the coast we can get into Caribou Harbor. It looks easy to enter on the chart, plenty of fog signals. From there we can cut across the strait the next day to Charlottetown."

With our decision made, we rested easier.

≈

I rowed *Dapple* ashore later and began beachcombing for a shipwrecked God, a battered and wave-broached deity; a God which now mingles with grains of sand and supports only the most rudimentary of life: seaweed and sucking periwinkle, barnacle and boring worm; a God whose only infinity is one reaching into the past. I came upon the bleached curve of a whale's ribs and stood in the airy cavity where Jonah wept. I came upon the black oak of a boat's ribs where fish once gasped and birds now nested. It seemed that everything came into shore at last, every last buoy and board and feather, every cloth and bone. The land laid out sand to soften the blow, to accept even the most fractured and diminished, things so inconsequential they float: a seagull, a seal, a log. The dead all float, naturally seeking a higher ground. I walked along this margin between worlds, a tidal zone, neither land nor sea and at times both. It seemed to occupy the present, a present as recent and as soon as the last and next wave, a trough of time, abundant as contact but constantly depleted. My foot slipped off

a slick stone. It felt good to walk, to search, to have some memory of God as a whole, to trust that the earth has given its welcome, to hope that for God too there is a heaven, a place as good to rest and disintegrate as a beach.

≈

We were singing TV sitcom themes to each other that evening, asking trivia questions about Jethro and Ellie May, Jeannie and Major Healey.

"Stupidest Professor?" Chloe asked.

"Who?" I asked.

"The professor on *Gilligan's Island*. He could build a radio out of coconut juice but couldn't patch that boat. OK, most heinously chauvinistic theme lyric?"

I thought and thought but couldn't come up with anything.

"Give up?" Chloe asked.

"I've got it," Grace said, sheepishly. She hadn't played much.

"What?" I asked.

"*Green Acres*," she said, and then sang, "'You are my wife—Goodbye city life.' I'd have told him to ride that tractor into the sunset."

Tears gathered along our noses; our legs failed to support us. Grace continued to open a can of peas.

≈

"I can't get my shoes on, Charlotte."

I woke from a sleep as dense as fog. "What?" I asked.

"My feet are swollen. I can't get my boots on. I knew this would happen. I've been waiting for it. Not only am I fat but now I'm swollen. I'll be pregnant and barefoot for the next month."

"Wear your slippers."

"It's varicose veins next, you know, or hemorrhoids. I already have to pee every ten minutes. Flatulence, indigestion, that's my lot."

"What about irritability and impatience?"

"I've got those already."

"It's still foggy," I said. "Do you still want to risk going?"

"I feel like I'm going to burst, Charlotte. I need to get where there's people."

"Chloe, you're still more than a month off."

"I know, I know. It's just that I liked my doctor, and I had the hospital all lined up. I'm just nervous. I'll feel better when we get to Charlottetown. It's been nice not having to worry about Roger. Do you think the baby will be pretty, Charlotte? I'm hoping that it will be just right; you know, I've always been heavy, and Roger is too skinny. Maybe the baby will be perfect."

"I'm already jealous because your baby's going to be so perfect, Chloe."

"I've thought about giving it up, but I can't. We've gone through so much. I'm going to do my best to be a really good ma."

"You'll be great," I said.

"I already love it so much. I shouldn't complain about my feet."

"Complain all you want. I don't listen."

"Thanks a lot."

"It's nothing."

We found Grace in the galley, turning her famous pancakes. She pointed toward them and said, "It's so strange, finding all these old things in my head again. I was standing here over the stove and of a sudden there was this way of making pancakes in my head, like a postcard someone slid under the door. I took it right up and it felt so familiar. I was so elated for a moment, and then I was just afraid again."

"Why?"

"It just seems that once you find something all there is left to do is lose it. I mean, you can't find it again, can you?"

"There are new things too, Grace. Finding stuff you didn't lose. Brand new things," I said, trying to comfort her.

"But I'm too old to find new things."

I frowned at her, and Chloe patted her stomach, "Tell her she's nuts, Baby It."

We took a compass line out of the cove that morning, and found the fog dissipated a mile off the coast into an eye-fatiguing haze, miserable but not dangerous cruising conditions. We had to reenter the bank late in the evening to find Caribou, but luckily we fell in behind the

ferry returning from Prince Edward Island and found our way to an anchorage rather easily.

I raised my glass that evening at cocktails, "Tomorrow at Prince Edward Island," and Grace and Chloe both smiled wearily, but clinked away.

"If it's still foggy we'll try to follow the ferry out in the morning," Chloe said. "She'll lose us quick but it'll be nice to have a pilot out of the harbor."

"You think it runs everyday?" I asked.

"Sure. The ferry probably makes the run in two hours or less, fat with tourists." She popped her empty cocoa cup down on the table and rubbed her itching belly with great sweeps of her fingernails. "You know what I've been craving all week?" she asked, then answered, "Lobster. Lobster and a vat of butter to dip it in."

"We don't have any money left," I said.

"I know," she said. "And I can't believe I'm suggesting this, but there's two lobster buoys barely ten feet off the bow. The fog is so thick no one would see us. It will be low tide in an hour. The traps will only be ten or fifteen feet down. If we're lucky they'll have three or four big fat beasts inside."

"That's stealing," Grace said.

"Chloe, your own father's a lobsterman."

"I'm a bad seed," she said.

"But if we get caught," I said. "You told me once that they practically lock you away forever for poaching traps."

"They do," she shrugged. "But not for nearly as long as they do for kidnapping."

No one spoke for moments. "It sure is easy to get hooked on a life of crime," I said.

"I can see the crook's viewpoint," Grace mused. "Get it while you can. Who knows what's going to happen to you tomorrow."

"The fog seems to be thicker at times," Chloe said. "We'll wait till it's so thick we can't see our own sins. We'll have an alibi: we couldn't see our own hands' dirty work."

We left Grace aboard, boiling water and melting butter. As I rowed *Dapple* around *Rosinante* toward the buoys, I told Chloe I'd never been

so nervous in my life. The brume was so thick, swirling with ominous portent, that I felt we were in the grip of a Hollywood fog machine. I felt that Chloe should be holding high an old oil lantern, peering into the mists.

"Can't you row any more quietly?" she whispered.

The water's surface was as dull as clay.

"I can hear a boat," I said, and held my oars. Just outside the anchorage, on the edge of the channel, the slow revolutions of a big diesel engine thumped by. Within moments a wake appeared from the fog and we rode the rolling water in silent dips. When we were sure the boat wasn't turning into the anchorage I rowed on and we came up on the first buoy, lying gently on its side in the slack water. I shipped my oars, reached over the gunwale, and brought the red and white buoy aboard. Chloe put her foot on the slimy warp while I hauled, hand over hand. I brought in perhaps forty feet of line before I felt the trap's resistance.

"It's heavy," I huffed.

"It's just a couple of bricks," Chloe said.

Dapple heeled over with my exertions, but before long I could see the green wire cage through the opaque sea. It broke the surface knocking against *Dapple*'s strakes, each bump sounding like a gunshot.

"Shh, shh," Chloe said, and she reached over and helped me haul the trap aboard.

"Jeez, it stinks," I said.

"That's just the bait, or maybe the muck at the bottom of this harbor," Chloe said. Within seconds she popped open the wire gate. There was so much moss hanging off the trap that I couldn't tell if there was anything inside. Chloe bent over, looked through the door and plunged her hand into the opening. "Gotcha," she whispered, and pulling her hand back out brought with it a big, dark, claw-waving lobster. "Pound and a quarter easy," she measured, and dropped it into a bucket.

I peered into the trap door in the same way I'd look over the edge of a cliff. "There's another one down there," I said.

"He's underweight," Chloe answered.

"What do you mean? He looks fine. We're stealing them. You can't be queasy about size limits."

"If you take the small ones, you'll damage the reproductive cycle. I may be a thief but I've got scruples."

"Jesus," I said.

"No," she said, "just common sense." She locked the door back down on the trap and we dropped it and the warp and the buoy back over. The second trap contained two more lobster above the legal limit. Chloe put them in the bucket as well. When I started to drop the trap overboard, Chloe stopped me.

"What?"

"Here." She slipped her watch off her wrist and clasped it to the door of the trap. "I can't help it," she said. "It's a fair trade."

"Chloe, if you leave that they'll know someone's poached the trap," I said.

"We'll be gone early in the morning. Most lobstermen only check their traps every couple of days. He won't know it was us."

"Are you sure?" I asked. "It's your watch. We could go back to the boat and get something else."

"Charlotte," her eyes opened widely. "We could put a pair of panties in there. Wouldn't you die to see him when he pulled those out?"

"Chloe," I said.

"No, we'll do it," she insisted. "It will make his week. That would be worth the three lobsters. He'll have this story to tell his whole life."

"OK," I said, and dropped the trap overboard.

"I mean it," she said.

"I know, OK," I repeated.

And so we spent the next half hour rowing back to *Rosinante*, sorting through our underwear and finally choosing a pair of mine with little pink hearts all over them, a pair that Jonah had given me when we were first married.

"Jonah wouldn't mind," Chloe said. "He'd think it was funny too."

"They're worn-out, anyway," I said, wadding them up and putting them in Chloe's hand.

She smiled broadly, her face full of the happiness of giving a stranger something he'll always remember. "Doesn't it make you feel good?" she asked.

"We're robbing the poor sod," I said. "And you're making out as if we've blessed him somehow."

"The watch makes it a fair trade," she answered. "It's waterproof to a hundred feet. And the underwear is a sort of blessing, now that you say so. He can fly them from his mast for the rest of his fishing career." Then she suddenly stepped back, placing her hand on her stomach.

"What?"

"Whoa," she said.

"What?"

"Big kick, soccer style," she said.

"Give me the panties," I said. "I'll do the Blessing of the Fleet. You help Grace with the lobster."

"You're a good person, Charlotte, to take on someone else's quest like this. You'll look back later and see this as one of your best works." She'd never been more sincere in her life. So I frowned at her and went on my way.

≈

Fogdogs punctuated the bank as we trailed the Northumberland Ferry out of the harbor next morning. So we followed at times in patches of clear blue sky and at others only by radar; the big ferry was a constant blip reaching out before us. We listened to her frequent radio calls on the VHF. The captain seemed to know every ship bound in and out of the harbor. We lost sight once again between Caribou and Pictou Islands, a few miles offshore. I kept an eye to the radar while Grace steered. We didn't want to run up on the ferry if she slowed or stopped. She showed to be a couple miles out ahead of us. I watched the screen as several other boats left the harbor and struck out at various points of the compass. I pointed out a small boat that had fallen in on our heading.

"They must be going to Prince Edward Island too," I said.

"We'll have to watch them," Chloe said. "They may not have radar. If they come up close we'll start sounding our horn every few seconds."

A few minutes later the radio crackled again, and Chloe and Grace and I stopped breathing.

"Northumberland Ferry, this is Caribou Harbor Police." The ferry returned the call asking how they could be of service. "Northumberland Ferry, can you provide us with any information on craft in your area?"

The ferry answered, "Caribou Harbor, we are presently fogbound a mile beyond Pictou Island, but we do show several craft on radar."

"Northumberland Ferry, we're interested in an old cruiser, approximately fifty feet in length, white hull, which we believe followed you out of the harbor this morning."

"Caribou Harbor, I believe that vessel is approximately two miles off our stern."

"That may be us, Northumberland Ferry. We're on your course," the police returned.

"We show two vessels on our stern, captain, at two and four miles distant."

"Jesus Christ," Chloe said.

"It was those goddamned panties," I yelled.

"Get that reflector down, Charlotte." I climbed back up on the salon deck and lowered the aluminum reflector as I'd done earlier coming out of Portsmouth Harbor. When I went below the radio began to buzz again with official voices. It was the Caribou Harbor Police, but this time they weren't calling the Northumberland Ferry.

"*Rosinante*, *Rosinante*, *Rosinante*, this is Caribou Harbor Police boat."

We all stood motionless in the cabin.

"Caribou Harbor, this is Northumberland Ferry. We now are getting only one signal at our stern. No, no, there's another, but now it's gone again."

"Northumberland Ferry, please keep us advised."

"The police boat either doesn't have radar or it's not working," Chloe said.

"What do we do?" Grace asked.

"The ferry is pulling away from us pretty quickly, so our signal will get less and less clear." Chloe stood over the charts. "If we go behind Pictou Island, get in close, any reflection we're presenting will merge with the island's. But I think we'll have to do something else too."

"What?" I asked.

"Pray that the fog doesn't lift for one, and we're going to have to sacrifice *Dapple*."

"I don't understand," I said.

"When we get behind the island we'll stand an oar up in *Dapple*'s bow, and tie the radar reflector to it, then we'll send *Dapple*, with her motor running and tiller lashed, out on the other end of the island. Hopefully they'll get a good signal off her and the police boat will follow. They won't be able to follow fast because the fog's thick and they'll have to check in with the ferry that's constantly moving further away. We'll stick close to the island for an hour or so. The ferry should be well beyond radar range by then. The police will have *Dapple* but they won't have us."

"Is that OK, Grace?" I asked. "Can we leave *Dapple*?"

"We'll get her back later when everything's been cleared up," she said.

"I hate to give her up," I said.

Chloe turned toward the island a half mile off our starboard beam while we listened to the ferry and police boat return each other's calls. *Rosinante*'s wooden hull seemed to fade in and out of their radar and so the ferry could only give reports occasionally. We shuddered each time the police boat called our name, always in threes, "*Rosinante Rosinante Rosinante*" as if he were calling us up in a seance, and asking us to materialize out of the fog.

"It wasn't the lobster," Chloe said. "They know our boat. They've been looking and somehow someone spotted us."

"The lobsterman at the cove," I suggested.

"Yeah," Chloe nodded, "maybe. We should have lured him aboard and clubbed him."

We motored in behind the lee of Pictou Island, rigged up *Dapple* as our false signature, and sent her puttering off alone into the Gulf of St. Lawrence. They picked up her signal almost instantly.

"Caribou Harbor Police, we have a good signal off the eastern shore of Pictou Island heading northeast."

We waited a hundred feet offshore while the search continued, watching the police boat closing in on *Dapple* on our radar set while the ferry disappeared from it. When the police were almost upon her, we

scooted away to the west at full speed, making a long arc out of the ferry's radar range, hugging Caribou Island and the Nova Scotia coast before turning once again northeast toward Prince Edward Island.

We seemed to feel no elation at our narrow escape, thinking instead on the loss of our loyal little tender, her signal merging with that of the police boat's. They now had solid proof that we were in these waters.

"They know we're bound for Prince Edward Island," I said.

"Well, we won't go into Charlottetown for sure," Chloe said. "We'll look for a smaller harbor, and we won't go in unless it's foggy or it's dark."

I got out the coastal guide and looked for a likely spot along the southern coast. "Listen to this," I said, and read, "The town of Victoria just off Blue Heron Drive is a quaint fishing village with craft and antique shops, art galleries, and live summer theater at the Victoria Playhouse."

"It sounds wonderful," Grace said. "Like a little Portsmouth."

"And we can get a tour bus to Green Gables from there," I told them. "It would be nice to have just a couple of days before. . . ." I didn't know how to finish the sentence.

Chloe pushed *Rosinante* hard through the strait. Victoria was another two to three hours further west than Charlottetown. The fog lifted and dropped, rose a hundred feet off the flecked water and descended to its surface with a crushing mist again. We sliced through fog-dogs that brought glaring sunshine down upon us, perhaps five minutes of warmth and fear. We were sure the Canadian Air Force, Coast Guard, and Mounties had all their spotter planes searching for us. Late in the evening, as we neared the coast, the fog completely abandoned us. Prince Edward Island appeared suddenly before us in dense folds of field and forest; dusk draped the countryside, stars above reflected in solitary porch lights of farmhouses. We found Victoria, a cluster of stars in a cove, at midnight, and slipped quietly in taking up a vacant mooring ball between two lobster boats with our boat hook. The village seemed to be asleep. We stood out on deck as *Rosinante* adjusted to her stall, to the end of her hard run. Her timbers popped and groaned and heat rose from her exhaust. She was as solid as a sidewalk under our feet.

"Good boat," I said.

And Chloe said, "Good boat."

And Grace said, "I wish Sweet George could be with us."

We stood silently, looking at the lights of the town reaching out to us across the water.

"How will we get to shore in the morning?" Grace asked. "Swim?"

"We could pull *Rosinante* into a dock, but that would involve asking permission and everything that goes along with it. And we couldn't leave her there. The tide falls so much here she'd be sitting on the bottom."

"There's the life raft," I suggested.

"That's what we'll do," Chloe said.

"An early start then?" Grace asked.

"Best if we get in early, with everything we'll need for the day," I said.

"What about money?" Chloe asked.

"We can get some cash at an ATM. Those things are everywhere. They'll know we're here, but we'll be at Green Gables by then."

"What about Pinky and Midden?" Chloe said.

"We'll leave them here," I said. "They'll be safer here."

"I feel like we're abandoning ship," Chloe whispered.

≈

Early the next morning, after a quick cereal breakfast, we closed all the through hull valves, shut off the propane at the bottles, and locked down the helm. We filled Midden and Pinky's food and water bowls, and left the salon door cracked so they could get out on deck. When the life-raft canister hit the cove with a cold splash, a water-activated switch opened a compressed air tank and the bright fluorescent octagonal raft billowed out below us, complete with emergency rations, flares, and paddles. We hugged the animals and then we dropped aboard the raft with our jackets and backpacks, Grace's medicine, a picnic for lunch and all of our identification. Chloe and I paddled somewhat awkwardly the one hundred yards through the moored boats to a pier where we tied the raft to a float. It looked very strange among the sharp-stemmed dinghies.

I fully expected a dozen Canadian Mounties on the pier, but there were none there, not even an early rising fisherman. We staggered into town and found an ATM mounted on an old storefront, and it issued me two hundred Canadian dollars without even blinking. I even read the receipt to see if it didn't say, "You're under arrest." For almost two hours we wandered through the village, as lights began to glow from house windows and shops began to unlock their doors. We saw fishermen and tourists on the ends of several piers looking out across the water at *Rosinante*, easily the largest craft in the water.

The first van left on a tour to Green Gables at 9:00 A.M. and we were on it, holding our bags in our laps and smiling stupidly at one another across the bench seat. Only two others were on the van, a woman and her daughter. The elderly driver asked if anyone would like the tour conducted in French or Japanese, along with English. Grace whispered that he was showing off.

"He looked at you, Grace, when we boarded," Chloe said. "I think he winked."

"Shut up, girl."

The woman in the front seat turned from her daughter to us and whispered, "Have you heard anything about this Green Gables place?"

"You haven't read the books?" I asked.

"No. We've already done all the other tours. But I've heard it's very pretty."

"It's the setting of a book about a girl your daughter's age," I said.

Chloe leaned over and whispered in my ear, "That almost took all the wind out of my sails. I say we kick her off the bus."

"Shh," Grace said. "Look out the window."

Chloe put her teeth over her bottom lip and her cheeks bulged with suppressed laughter. She poked me in the ribs every few seconds.

"Will you stop that?" I hushed. But this only made her clamp her palm over her mouth and shriek.

"You're an embarrassment," Grace said, folding her arms.

Chloe's face reddened till it resembled the body of a ladybug, and finally she uttered an almost obscene guffaw, which brought the disapproving eyes of the driver up into the rearview mirror. Then, wiping her eyes, she apologized, and said, "I'm just so relieved." Then she began to

cry, at first silently, then with unremitting clumps of boo hoos, hands over face, caught breaths, remorseful sighs.

Grace shook her head and rolled her eyes. She leaned forward to the woman and her daughter and said, "I'm sorry, she's pregnant."

Which made Chloe sit up straight, run her forearm under her nose, and cascade into laughter again.

Occasionally the driver would point out a farmstead as "typical" of Anne Country or "typical" of the province or "typical" of the period, and before long Chloe had taken it up. Everytime he'd speak she'd follow his remarks with, "That's just typical," or "Typical, typical, typical" in a singsong of syllables. The driver wasn't pleased. At last she asked him if it wasn't "typical of tourists to be annoying?"

"That's enough, little girl," Grace snapped. "Just because you're nervous is no excuse to be rude."

Chloe crossed her arms over her baby and turned away, looking out the window. Then she turned back to us, and with her palms planted on her broad thighs, said, "I'm on a pilgrimage with infidels."

"Chloe," I said. "Shut the hell up. What is wrong with you?"

"She sees this little girl here and it makes her nervous," Grace said. "I know how it is."

"You do not," Chloe said.

The girl turned around and faced us with a scowl.

"It's all coming back to me now," Grace said. "I remember you, Chloe. You're the one who can't make up her mind, much less tell somebody what to do. You can pilot a boat but you're afraid you can't raise a child. I've got your number. This little girl before us is daunting. You're afraid of her."

"I am not," Chloe said, almost shrieking.

"It's something you grow into," the girl's mother said, turning her shoulder to us. "I was scared too, at first. But they're not born twelve years old. You get to grow up with them. I've got a good idea of how Millie's mind works by now."

"Mother," the girl said, twisting around and hiding her face in her hands.

"Oh, Jesus," Chloe said. "No advice. Don't give me advice."

"Fine with me," the mother said, and turned back around.

The driver, trying to break the thick silence that followed, couldn't help himself. He said, "The small schoolhouse on your right is typical of those constructed on the island at the end of the nineteenth century." His voice trailed off and he sighed heavily, as if all his confidence had been undermined.

Chloe spoke to the window. "I don't know where she comes up with this crap." Then she swung back around, her weight bouncing on the bench seat and testing the springs of the van. "You know what I'd forgotten, Grace? I'd forgotten how annoying you can be. All kinds of crap from completely nowhere."

"That's enough, Chloe," I said.

"You're always on her side."

"Typical, typical, typical," Grace sang.

"That's enough, Grace," I said.

"God, I hate her," Chloe said again to the window.

The woman and her daughter turned slightly, looking at me askance, commiserating with my situation. I stuck my tongue out at them.

Before I thought possible we were in Cavendish, the Avonlea of L.M. Montgomery's books. Our driver pointed out landmarks that suggested Avonlea School, the post office, the Presbyterian church, and Orchard Slope. But when we passed over a small bridge Chloe yelped, "The Lake of Shining Waters."

And Grace said, "Where?"

"We're right on top of it," Chloe said.

We parked in a gravel lot with other buses, large and small. The driver opened the sliding door with the pronouncement, "Just up the path to Green Gables, ladies. Take all the time you need. I'll be ready at your return."

"Isn't it beautiful, Grace?" Chloe asked.

"That must be the Haunted Wood," I said, and pointed to a grove of pines.

"There's the creek," Chloe yipped. "Dryad's Bubble."

Parks Canada maintained the old house, once owned by Montgomery's cousins. We joined a line purchasing tickets, a long line of elderly men and women interspersed frequently with young girls. I

looked for men in dark suits and sunglasses speaking into their lapels, but couldn't spot any. A Parks Canada employee, with a silver badge, took our money and smiled evenly. Oh, you're good, I thought. If she was looking for us, I couldn't tell.

"Are either one of you as nervous as I am?" I asked.

"About what?" Grace asked.

"I thought they might be here waiting for us, like Chloe said."

"I'm not nervous," Grace said, and she, quite awkwardly I thought, bent forward and slapped at her lowest jacket pocket.

"What does that mean?" I asked.

She turned to me, lifted the flap on her pocket, and reaching in pulled out the blunt chrome nose of a gun. And then dropped it back down.

My backbone curled and fused. I scanned the faces of the others in line near us. They hadn't seemed to notice. I bent forward from the hip and whispered into Chloe's ear, "She's got a gun."

"Who?" Chloe shouted, scanning the horizon.

I clamped my hand over her mouth and narrowed the slots of my open eyelids till dimes couldn't have gotten through. I nodded at Grace. Then I held my hand out, palm out, and looked at Grace.

"No," she said aloud.

"Now," I whispered. "Give it to me."

She shook her head fiercely.

Chloe stood there with a gap in the line ahead of her. We were only eight or ten paces from entering the door of Green Gables.

"Give me the gun," I mouthed, and pushed Chloe and Grace forward.

"It's mine," Grace said.

"Why did you bring it?"

"We might need it," she said simply.

"Where did you get it?"

"It's George's," she said. "We kept it hidden in the ceiling above our bunk. In case anyone ever tried to board us. It's common in the Caribbean. I've been packing it all week."

"Keep it in your pocket, Grace," I said, "no matter what."

"Jesus," Chloe said.

I held the front door open for Grace and Chloe and we shuffled into the house behind the rest, in front of the others, links in a continuous human chain of sightseers who entered the front door and exited out the back. The two screen doors never clapped to. Velvet ropes hung across the entrances to most of the rooms, which were decorated to the descriptions in the novel. We looked into the parlor, the sitting room, and Matthew's room, walked through the kitchen, and then returned to the front hall and climbed the stairs to Anne's room. A low white bed occupied one corner of the gable room. The window looked out at a cherry tree, the Snow Queen as Anne called it. It seemed very spare. It seemed all that was required. It seemed odd, the three of us peering into the little room, the hot breath of other tourists on our necks impatient to have their look and be off.

"They wanted a boy," Chloe said. "They kept Anne but they'd asked the orphanage for a boy."

We lingered in the doorway as if it were a bus stop, leaned against the casings. There was a wicker rocker in one corner, a bookcase filled with old spellers and grammars, and a small mirror with cupids and purple grapes painted on its arched crest.

An old woman behind me coughed. We moved on then, down and out the back door. Small signs pointed the way to the Birch Path and Lover's Lane and Violet Vale.

"I'm a little tired," Grace said. "You two go on. I'll sit on this bench here."

Chloe glanced at me. "No. I'm pooped too. Let's just go back to the van," she said.

"I need to walk down there," I said.

"Of course," Grace said. "You go ahead. We'll wait. You can tell us what you see."

They sat down together. I looked at them, pursed my lips, and then spun on my heels. I walked down the path, turning occasionally and walking backwards. Chloe and Grace seemed to be just sitting there, looking off into the fields and orchards. They weren't watching me leave. When I entered the wood, and lost sight of the bench and Green Gables, I let myself have the thought, clearly and without hindrance: I could leave them there. It would be the last place I saw them, sitting

peacefully together outside Green Gables. There weren't any violets in Violet Vale. Perhaps the tourists on Lover's Lane did love each other. Birch trees did rise over the Birch Path, though they looked to be of the same vintage as Park Canada's custodianship. I knew Chloe and Grace would get back to Portsmouth without me. I stood among the birches where Anne and her bosom friend Diana played, imagined other lives as their own. I wanted Jonah to be there but I knew he wasn't. I tried to imagine a life other than the one we lived together, but it wouldn't come to me. I couldn't transport myself in the same way a fictional character could. And so I decided to go back to Portsmouth too. I knew Grace and Chloe were ready. They were waiting for me to be just as prepared. I wanted to live there with them again in some kind of peace. There were things, hurtful things, that needed to be said when we got home. And I, I knew, would be hurt the most, although for months I thought I'd been protecting Richard and Mary from the truth. I'd only been protecting myself. Bones littered the earth. It seemed about time to start picking them up. Yet if anyone, at that moment, had kicked a gravel, uttered a boo, I think I'd have disappeared into the Haunted Wood forever.

I walked back to Green Gables, my hands in knots in my jacket pockets, and sat down between Grace and Chloe.

"How was it?" Grace asked.

"It was pretty," I said. "But it's not as wonderful as Portsmouth."

"All the same," Chloe said, "I'm glad we came."

"They'll probably be waiting for us," I said. "When we get off the tour bus."

Grace turned to me. "I know we're being chased, but I can't remember by whom." She squinted.

Chloe and I looked at each other. My lungs felt like they were going to collapse.

"Your daughter," I said, "after your stroke, was legally responsible for you. She was going to put you in a nursing home. We took you and your boat away so she couldn't. It wasn't premeditated. Remember Chloe was being beaten on the dock and my in-laws were there too. I'd been hiding from them."

"Of course," Grace nodded. "It just seemed fuzzy for a moment."

"Don't go out on us now, Grace," Chloe whispered.

Grace clinched her teeth and looked down at the bare earth between our feet. "We'll get everything straightened out," she said at last. She shook her head. "No matter how long you live you never expect this." She didn't elaborate and we didn't press her. We rose from the bench as one.

It seemed that our bus ride back to port lasted no longer than a few minutes. Grace nodded off from time to time, while Chloe ran her hands again and again over her crystal stomach. When we stepped off the van and began to walk together down the street toward the pier, we all felt unusually conspicuous. *Rosinante* still nestled at her mooring in the harbor and at the end of the pier the brilliant life raft still bobbed among the other dinghies. It was inconceivable that some sort of authority hadn't discovered us. We continued onto the pier itself, walking three abreast.

"That's it," Chloe said. "I'm going to start robbing banks. It's too easy to get away."

We stopped at the head of the gangway. The tide was out and it would be a steep walk down.

"Maybe we should go give the police a call," Grace suggested.

"You don't want to embarrass a cop," Chloe said. "That really pisses them off."

We stood there, baskets and bags hanging off our arms like boat fenders. Then the lumber of the pier groaned behind us and before we could turn, Chloe and I had been separated from Grace. Our baskets and bags scattered over the pier. Someone behind me had both of my arms.

"OK," I yelled. A handcuff slapped over my wrist.

"Stop," I heard Chloe scream, "you're hurting me." I wrenched my body around and saw the policeman struggling with Chloe, trying to bring her arms behind her back.

"She's pregnant," I yelled.

Grace stood alone on the edge of the pier. As the policeman put the cuff on my other wrist I watched Grace take the gun from her pocket and point it toward the policeman behind Chloe. She took three quick steps forward, and jammed the gun muzzle into the policeman's neck. He froze. She said, "You're hurting her. Stop hurting her."

The cop didn't twitch. "OK," he said. He let go of Chloe. My cop still held firmly to my cuffs. When Chloe moved off a few feet, Grace said, "She's pregnant and you were hurting her, twisting her arms behind her back like that. Now, I'm going to give you this gun." She dropped the gun to her side, then held it back out to him in the flat of her palm. She turned to me and stuck her tongue out as far as she could.

"Yes, Grace," I sighed.

The policeman, still moving tentatively, took the gun from her. "Very sorry," he said.

"Now, if you're going to handcuff the girls, I'll want a pair too." She proffered her wrists.

"I didn't bring a pair for you," the cop said.

"Why not cuff Grace and I together?" Chloe suggested.

Two more men, in suits, were striding down the pier by this time. The policemen seemed to be at a loss. He put one cuff on Grace.

"No, no, no," one of the suits yelled. "She's the victim."

"She pulled a gun on me, sir," the policeman tried to explain, and he held up the weapon.

Chloe brought her arms up and rested them on her stomach. She smiled broadly at me, and then turning to the two suits she nodded at Grace, and said, "Thank goodness you've found us, officers. This woman kidnapped us and forced us to take her to Green Gables."

I began to giggle, and Grace smiled and harrumphed, and we were all summarily hustled off to the lockup.

≈

We spent two nights in a Prince Edward Island jail, a place never described in *Anne of Green Gables*. We explained our actions to detectives there, but they were only interested in holding us till U.S. agents arrived to take us back to New Hampshire. They were kind enough to see that Midden and Pinky were seen to, and promised Grace that someone would watch over *Rosinante*, and that *Dapple* would be returned to her davits.

The president of the Anne Country Society heard of our story and

interviewed Chloe over the phone. She asked if it had been worth it all to see Green Gables and she promised to send along a copy of the next society newsletter which would carry our story.

Once we were back in the States there were lengthy interviews with agents and officers. We'd been charged with not only kidnapping but in addition grand theft (of *Rosinante*), and numerous other infringements. But within a few hours after Anne met with Grace we were set free. Chloe's father and Harry and two of his deckhands flew up to Prince Edward Island and brought *Rosinante* and *Dapple* and the animals home in a round-the-clock cruise that lasted several days.

Within ten days of our capture we were all back aboard *Rosinante* at her berth beneath the Smarmy Snail. It was a victory that we celebrated with a late dinner on *Rosinante*'s afterdeck, in a Tuesday twilight, as the last of the light dimpled the river's length. Cars rumbled over the steel grating of Memorial Bridge and two tugboats were easing up river on the flood tide. There was so much to watch and listen to that we talked very little early on, but as the river darkened and lamps struck out across the water from Badger's Island, we began to wander in and out of conversation, disconnectedly, as if we were three different lobster boats working the same cove.

"Is there anything you need, Grace?" I asked.

"Why, no," she said, "I'm fine. I'll get up and do these dishes in a minute. I'm just a little tired."

"The doctor said everything was fine with the baby," Chloe said. She was due in three weeks and was feeling more and more uncomfortable.

"I thought you were on fire when you jumped out of your bunk last night," I said. "I thought Roger was back on the boat."

"Well, my toes were trying to touch my heel. I've never had a cramp that wicked in my life. I had to stomp on it three times. Roger won't bother us. There's the restraining order, and I think my father threatened to kill him."

"You're standing in the middle of a roomful of people," Grace said, "and suddenly you realize you're the oldest person there. It's odd, because you reach this level without any experience, and you're expected to know your role. And you expect, expected, yourself to be wise as well, and it comes as a great letdown to know you're just the same per-

son, but older. So you go by the old standbys, advise moderation one day and vision the next, because some days you're satisfied and happy, and some days you feel there are too few days left to seize. You have to take old age personally."

"Where did all that come from?" Chloe asked.

"The doctor said you were fine," I told Grace. She'd just had her second checkup since we'd returned. But she wasn't fine. There were occasional lapses in her short-term memory and the doctor had acknowledged that although her medication would reduce the risk, it wouldn't altogether prohibit another stroke.

With great effort Pinky climbed up Grace's shin, dragging his tongue behind him. Midden soon followed him from below, and jumped up in my lap. I scratched him under his chin, where there seemed to be a permanent itch. Grace reached down and petted Pinky, and then began to rise to clear the table but I stopped her.

"Wait, Grace. There's something I want to tell both of you. I mean I want to test myself with you two before I meet with Richard and Mary on Friday. I'm going to tell them the same things and I think it would be best if I practiced."

I held Midden firmly to my chest. Grace sat back down and Chloe put her hands together, as if in prayer, and then released them to roam over her stomach.

"I know I've always told you that I loved Jonah." My voice caught, and fluttered, like trash hung on a fence.

"It's OK," Chloe said. "You don't have to tell us. It doesn't matter."

"No," I said. "You see," I rubbed the water out of my eyes and Midden jumped down. "I need the practice, because I don't want to break down in front of all the lawyers and Richard and Mary and my folks."

I went on with my confession, and Grace broke in once, saying, "How can you be sure? No, I don't think you can be sure."

But I shook my head, and continued, and concluded at last with, "Sometimes, I'm such a goddamned coward, I think if I really loved him, I would have died too. But I haven't, have I?"

"We don't want you to die, Charlotte," Chloe said.

"Don't be ridiculous," Grace said. "Don't be ridiculous. It's all in the past, dear. It's gone."

"But it's not, is it? If it was, I wouldn't be sitting here crying about it. I remember it all."

"I'm sorry," Grace said. "You're right, but would you rather not remember him at all?"

"I don't know what I'd do if I couldn't think about him."

"Of course. Don't let the past take your future, Charlotte," Grace said. "Do you know what's strangest about all the things I've forgotten and remembered?"

"No," I said.

"I have the queerest sensation now that I remember God, as if he were some real person in my past."

"But God's not someone you remember," Chloe said. "He's someone you trust." Grace shrugged. "You're giving me the creeps, Grace. I hope none of this is affecting the baby."

"You're going to have a beautiful baby," Grace said. "I can see it."

"You deserve a beautiful baby," I said, and then, "I'll do the dishes. I feel the need to get my hands into a sink."

"When do your folks get in?" Chloe asked.

"Thursday morning," I answered. "I'm going to put them up at the Sheraton. They'll need a good night's sleep after they hear everything I've got to tell them."

"Have them here Friday morning for pancakes," Grace said. "Then at least when you meet with your in-laws later, you'll all be throwing up the same color. And Charlotte," she paused and touched my forearm, "you know, dying isn't such a bad end."

I don't know why, but whenever my hands are full of dishes I find it almost impossible to speak.

≈

I picked up Mom and Dad at the airport, and after they were settled into the hotel, we went to the Dolphin Striker for dinner. We sat in the back room at a window that looked down Ceres Street to the tugboats. I went step by step through all that had happened since I'd left home. It seemed odd that it had been only six months since I'd packed up and found Midden at the rest stop. My folks hardly touched their meals, just

looked at me as if I were telling them that I'd been working for the CIA in Casablanca. When I told them what I was going to say to Richard and Mary in the morning, my mother began to cry and my father looked away. Somehow they'd known.

≈

I couldn't help but smile at how hesitantly Mom and Dad stepped aboard *Rosinante* the next morning. As I introduced my parents to Chloe and Grace, I saw my shipmates suddenly through their eyes: a fragile old woman and a robust, enormously pregnant girl, one head blue and the other shaved. We all sat at the salon table and talked about Chloe's due date, our voyage to Prince Edward Island, and the work I'd done at Strawbery Banke that summer. My father went down below and helped Grace with her pancakes. He is a great pancake lover. I showed my mom through my cabin, and her only comment was that it would be easy to pick up. She asked Chloe and me how we slept with all the rocking the boat did, and if we weren't worried about it sinking as we slept. I felt so odd, acting the host for my folks, acting as an intermediary between them and Chloe and Grace. I'd been worried Mom and Dad would think they were strange, as if my folks had never known other humans outside of me. My father had on a new short-sleeved shirt that morning. He rarely bought clothes and I don't think I'd ever seen him in short sleeves. So much can happen in such a short time. Was his new shirt just between him and me, or him and Mom, or could I mention it in mixed company? It's difficult sometimes to know where to draw the line of confidences. But I knew that my folks could tell that Chloe and Grace were my friends, and that was all they seemed to need to appreciate them. My mother smiled often and my father touched *Rosinante* once under Grace's eyes and said she was a fine piece of craftsmanship.

When we'd finished breakfast and were about to leave for Malcolm Laury's office to meet with Richard and Mary, Grace and Chloe both hugged me in front of my parents. My father took my shoulder under his arm and my mother took my hand and we walked away, leaving them standing on deck. It was good to think of them there, waiting for me to return.

Richard and Mary were already at the office, sitting at a conference table with clinched knees and folded arms. After I returned from Prince Edward Island, I'd called Malcolm and asked him to set up the meeting. I asked my folks not to say anything. I just wanted them to be there. I sat down directly across from Mary, between my parents. Malcolm sat at the head of the conference table. He made some prefatory remarks concerning his opinion of Richard and Mary's case, and finally said we'd agreed to hold this meeting in hopes of some reconciliation.

"May I ask," Malcolm said, "why your lawyer isn't present?"

"We'd just like to speak in private," Richard said.

"How do you feel about that, Charlotte?" Malcolm asked. "Would you prefer that I leave you alone?"

"It's OK, Malcolm. But I want my folks here."

"That's fine with us," Richard said.

"I'll close the door, but if you need anything, Charlotte, I'll be available." Malcolm left the room. The latch clicked to, leaving a dust-mote-ridden silence.

My father coughed and spoke. "Well, I'll just say, Richard, that I think all this is cowardly and unforgivable and. . . ."

"Daddy," I said and grabbed his forearm. "That's enough." Then I turned to Richard and Mary. "I have some things to say."

"That's all we've wanted," Mary said. "An explanation. Why this had to happen." She stopped or she would have begun to cry. She put her hand over her open mouth, and exhaled through her fingers.

"It wasn't Jonah's fault," I said. Mary nodded, her eyes filling with tears. "But it wasn't mine either. You're wrong about how I felt about your son. I loved him and I still love him. And I really don't know if it was an accident or if he was trying to hurt himself. I don't know. You know how he was. Things made him sad and he wasn't able to share them. Maybe he didn't know how. I never thought he was thinking about killing himself. But they say you can't tell sometimes. Sometimes people who think about dying really do want to die and don't want anyone in their way. But there is something I do know and I've been keeping it from you, and my parents too, and I even kept my knowledge from Jonah. And for the selfishness with which I held my knowledge I

am in some way guilty and responsible. It wasn't that I didn't love Jonah. It was that he didn't love me."

"That's a goddamned lie," Mary screamed and she stood up, both of her hands in fists. Richard stood too and put his hand on her arm. She flung him away. "How can you say that?" she shrieked. "It's a lie."

Malcolm opened the door behind us. Mary looked at him, sat back down, and buried her face in her palms. Malcolm closed the door again.

"I wish it were," I said. "I still fantasize that it isn't true. But I know it is. He liked me I think. He desired me at times."

"Stop," Mary whispered.

"It's been hard to say because I feel guilty about it, that he didn't love me, and now I've betrayed him by telling you that he didn't. He was a good person. He was just unable to cope with letting other people down. He felt some need to love me, but he didn't, he couldn't. It wasn't his fault that he didn't. And I don't think it was mine. We were trying, over and over again. I don't know if he killed himself, but if he did it was because he was Jonah, and I didn't know how to stop him from being Jonah, or how to stop loving him, or how to leave him. He didn't want anything from me, not even his freedom."

"Did he ever tell you he didn't love you, Charlotte?" Richard asked.

"Of course not," I answered. "You don't understand. He never would have done that. I think he trapped himself with his decency, and I wasn't brave enough to let him go. I knew he wasn't in love with me, but I loved him so much. I thought about it at times, that perhaps I should force a confrontation, force him to confess but I didn't have the courage. We just moved along in our lives lying to each other, trying not to hurt each other's sensibilities. I think what's bothered me as much as Jonah's lack of love was my lack of courage. You may be right. Maybe he died to escape from me."

My mother put her arm on my back. Mary watched her.

"I'm sorry," I said.

"Just tell the truth," Mary said bitterly.

"I'm trying to."

Mary slammed the table with her opened palms. "You were pregnant," she yelled, "just admit it. You left when I spoke about children. I saw your unused pills."

"I was pregnant," I said softly.

"And you're not pregnant now, are you? You aborted the pregnancy."

"He didn't know," I said.

"What? No. You stopped the pregnancy and he killed himself because he knew you'd leave him."

"No," I said. "He didn't know I was pregnant. I didn't tell him. He didn't want children. You knew that. I became pregnant secretly, hoping it would release him, bring him out of his depression. Then I couldn't tell him. I'd deceived him. I thought it might break our marriage. I was a coward. There were four weeks of terror. After he left for work that day I went into town and had the abortion. It's true. I was waiting for him that evening. I was going to tell him what I'd done. I was going to tell him I hated him, and hated myself, for what I'd done. But he never came home."

"I don't believe you," Mary said, staring at me.

"I'm sorry," I said. "I wish none of it were true."

"He's dead," Mary said, "and you're still here."

"That's enough," my mother said.

"I've been sorry for that too, but not anymore," I said.

"Let's go, honey," Richard said. "Let's go." He helped her up from her chair and they left the office without looking at me or saying another word.

I turned to my mom and started bawling. "I tried to give them everything else but they wouldn't take it," I cried.

"They thought you still had Jonah somehow," she said.

"Where did he go? How can things change?"

My father put his hand on my knee. "Charlotte," he said, "there's no telling how your memories will change. You'll get older and see things differently." He lifted his shoulders inside his new shirt.

"What's the deal with you and short-sleeved shirts?" I asked, still crying, and I leaned toward his shoulder, falling into his bare arms and the comforting musk of my childhood.

≈

I'd always thought it would kill me to tell anyone that Jonah hadn't loved me. I was so ashamed, for myself and Jonah both, that I was unlovable, that he was incapable of loving, that it took his death to resolve our marriage. My pride and shame were too large. I won't say my confession made the past easier to bear, but it made me feel less vulnerable. I'd lived in mortal fear of someone making the accusation before I was able to turn myself in.

≈

My parents stayed in Portsmouth through the weekend, extracting a promise from Chloe and me that we'd come to Kentucky for Thanksgiving. Grace told them she'd been on enough trips for one year, and that she wouldn't be able to stand two days in the car with Chloe and a baby anyway. Which brought a whoop of surprise from Chloe, who exclaimed, "Hey, I'll have a baby by Thanksgiving," as if she'd just received an announcement in the mail.

≈

It was early September now, and the deck of the Smarmy Snail was less crowded since most of the summer tourists had departed. After my folks went home, Chloe and Grace and I spent almost an entire week restocking and cleaning *Rosinante*. Grace wanted all the exterior brightwork sanded and revarnished, ready for the winter to come. We spent long days scrubbing and painting, buffing and polishing. Harry had filled the diesel tanks and Grace added huge amounts of stabilizer, following Sweet George's example. In the evenings we languished on the afterdeck, weakly chewing take out food, too weary to cook for ourselves.

Chloe and I hadn't been privy to Grace's conversation with Anne when we returned from Prince Edward Island. Anne had left abruptly after relinquishing the guardianship. At the time it seemed too sensitive, too personal, to indulge ourselves with questions. But we were tired, and couldn't now hold ourselves back. Late in the week of our overhaul, over half-eaten MOES, Chloe leaned forward over her stomach, and

asked, "Grace, how did Anne take it? You know, when she found out your memory had returned?"

I stopped eating.

"She thought that I was lying, that I'd been coached. So she asked me questions, things that you and Charlotte probably wouldn't know."

"You're kidding?" I said.

"No, she's not," Chloe said.

"What did you say that convinced her?" I asked.

"She sucked her thumb up until she was almost nine," Grace said.

"But you could have told us that before your stroke," I said.

"Yes," Grace acknowledged.

"So?" Chloe said.

Grace cleared her throat, and looked back up river, between Chloe and me. "She asked me," Grace said softly, "what the name of the man was that I left Sweet George for." She kept her gaze averted from ours, as if she were a lower-ranking female in the group. "When Anne was seventeen, when she was your age Chloe, I had an affair with a man named Pat Webb, and I left George for almost a year. It didn't work out and George took me back, but Anne never did. It was such a stupid thing. It was all my fault. I can't tell you if Anne was glad that I came back or not."

"Which time?" I asked.

"This time," Grace said. "All it meant to her was that I'd left her for the second time."

I clasped my hands between my knees and opened my mouth, but I had absolutely nothing to say.

"I don't understand," Chloe said. "If you loved Sweet George, how could you leave him?" She was clearly angry.

"Chloe," I said, and I put my hand on her forearm.

"It's all right," Grace said. "She's right. I was just bored, Chloe. I let myself become bored. And there was this man, who wasn't anyone in particular, just a way not to be bored. And after a few months I was bored with him too, and this also wasn't his fault, in the same way it wasn't Sweet George's. So I left Pat and lived alone for several months. That's when I began to paint, and when I finished the first painting I was proud of, I wanted to show it to someone and the someones I

thought of were George and Anne. And George took me back but I'd hurt Anne too deeply and she couldn't."

"I cursed her for you," Chloe said.

"I'm sorry," Grace whispered.

Chloe pushed herself up and left the boat. When she was halfway up the gangway I yelled after her, "Where are you going?"

"I'm gonna go have a cigarette," she yelled back. "And I'm going where you and Grace won't see me smoking it."

"She'll be all right," I told Grace.

"Anne just got up and left too," Grace answered. She took the remains of her sandwich and with the butcher paper it came in folded it up into a small package. Her shoulders sloped deeply into her breast the way a bird's wings fold. Her clothes seemed suddenly to billow with excess fabric. Her wrists and ankles, exposed, reflected the night's light like fish just beneath the surface of the water. They seemed sickeningly weak, but they held her as she rose from her chair, grasping the edge of the table. "Can you. . . ?"

"I'll clean up," I said.

She moved slowly off to her cabin without answering, the soles of her shoes scraping the teak deck in little coughs of contact.

≈

Through the next week Grace and I revisited all of her outdoor work in Portsmouth. She'd wash the dirt from the oils and touch up any wear. She also looked for a site for her long-planned water work, and finally chose a depression in the sidewalk on Vaughn Street, not too far from the Whalen Wall, the huge blue whale mural covering the entire side of a building. Grace had watched it go up the summer before and said it was nice for what it was, but that it wouldn't fool a seal.

"I want dogs to try to drink out of my puddle," she said. "I want children to jump on it and feel sure they've made a splash. I want young bankers to try twice for the nickel under the puddle's surface."

We went so far as to sweep the depression, set a line level to see how big the swale would be if it was full of water, and even applied a fixer to seal the concrete. But the following morning Chloe and I both

rushed to the galley at the sound of breaking glass. Grace stood next to the sink; her hand was still trembling; there were shards at her feet; and the corner of her mouth and the lid of one eye were slipping away. She slurred our names.

≈

It turned out to be a minor stroke. We took her to the hospital and she remained throughout the day and overnight, but her speech soon became clear and she quickly regained the use of her hand. There was no memory loss this time, except for the short period before she broke the water glass. She couldn't remember how she got to the sink, or even putting on her bathrobe when she got out of bed. She asked us not to worry Anne. She stayed on the boat for most of the next week, wary of another stroke, resolved in some way to prepare for it, to ward it off. Grace spoke to us only remotely. She seemed to be involved in some internal struggle that left her without any desire for much conversation, and for that matter without any hunger. We cooked huge amounts of food in attempts to entice her, but she'd only eat a bite or two, say how good it was, and retire to her cabin. Only Pinky was invited to join her. We tried to draw her out to work or to paint, but she'd shuffle on deck from below, then complain about the brightness of the sun, the glare off the water.

≈

It took the baby to drag her from her lethargy. It intruded upon Grace's life as strongly as it did Chloe's. Chloe's water broke a week and a half early. Grace seemed to regain all her old energy helping Chloe get up the gangway to my car. By midnight Chloe was screaming for a Pepsi, her parents sat in the waiting room with one chair between them, Grace paced in front of the birthing room doors, and I, as coach, was offering Chloe instead of Pepsi an ice chip. With her first strong contraction she'd clamped onto my wrist and demanded, "Call my mother. Now."

"Now you want me to call your mother?" I asked, incredulously.

"NOW," she yelled, lifting her head off the pillow. So Grace had

called her parents and they'd come at once. When they arrived, I asked Chloe if she wanted to see them.

"Are you out of your mind?" she yelled. "I'm about to have a baby, Charlotte." I was ready for this. Coaches, I'd been warned, weren't always treated with equanimity.

The doctor wasn't two paces into the birthing room before Chloe went over the terms she'd negotiated. "No enema, no shaving, no stirrups and no episiotomy until we see how much the perineum is going to stretch. And I get drugs as soon as I ask for them."

"Right, Chloe," the doctor murmured.

"ok," I said, grasping the stopwatch that hung around my neck. "You should be getting another one just about. . . ."

"NOW," Chloe said, her teeth meeting and her chin dropping onto her sternum, her whole body cramping.

"Just get through them one at a time," I said. "That's good. Just a few more seconds. There. Good girl." I mopped her brow with a cool damp cloth.

"ok," she said, once she regained her breath. "You can cut the praise and encouragement crap. The baby's coming no matter what you say."

"ok, I'll shut up," I said. "Want another ice chip?"

"I want a Pepsi," she yelled.

"Chloe, you can't have a Pepsi. You know that."

"By God, I'll get up and go get it myself. There's a machine just down the hall." She lifted her trembling leg off the gurney but another contraction snapped her leg back onto the bed. "Oh, Jesus," she cried, and tears rolled down her round cheeks. When the contraction was over she said, "I'm going to start pushing."

"No," the doctor said, "not yet, Chloe."

"I've got to get it out," Chloe cried. "Charlotte. . . ."

"What, sweetie?"

"It's that bluefish we caught. It's inside me."

I smiled and wiped her face. "No, it's not, Chloe. It's a baby, just a baby. Concentrate now."

"This is where my husband is supposed to tell me he loves me," she strained.

We worked through another half hour of labor and finally the doc-

tor said, "OK, Chloe. You're there. Let's have a good push with this next contraction."

"I haven't had the drugs yet, have I?" she yelled.

"No," I said.

"I'll wait a bit," she said, and grunted into her pain. She squeezed my hand through the contraction until I thought it would burst. Then we had a moment to rest. I pried my hand from her grip and shook it out in the air. "I'm having a baby and you can't even hold a person's hand."

"I'm squeezing back next time," I said.

"Is my mom outside?" Chloe asked.

"And your dad too," I answered. "I already told you that."

"That's good." She seemed to visibly relax. "I want them here in case anything should happen."

"Something is happening, Chloe. You're having a baby."

"Oh yeah."

"Another ice chip?"

"I'll give you the money for the Pepsi. Oh, wicked Jesus Christ."

I put my hand under her back to help support her.

"Very good, Chloe," the doctor said and stood up, encouraging her. "I think we'll see a crown here in a couple of minutes." Chloe slumped back into the bed. "It doesn't feel like the contraction is stopping," she cried. "I'm not getting to rest."

"Breathe, Chloe," I said. "Breathe. Don't forget to breathe."

She exhaled heavily and sweat streamed off her hairline.

"I can do this," she said. "But I get to kill somebody for it. I have a baby: I get to take a life. It's only fair."

"OK," I said. "We'll pick somebody out after the baby is born."

We grunted through three more contractions. When Chloe couldn't grunt, I grunted for her. The crown of the baby's head appeared for a moment then retracted.

"It was the baby's head," I told Chloe. "Did you see it in the mirror?"

She looked at me and rolled her eyes. When she got her wind again, she said, "Not another word."

"OK," I said. "OK."

"We shouldn't have eaten the fish, Charlotte," she said. "Now it wants out."

"Chloe," the doctor stood up again between her legs. "We're just not getting enough stretch. You're beginning to tear. I'm going to make a small incision. I'll do it at the peak of your next contraction. You won't even feel it."

"Goddamnit," Chloe cursed.

"Are you sure?" I asked the doctor.

"Yes," he said, without even looking at us, already in preparation.

At the height of the contraction, Chloe's face a red rubber ball, the incision was made in the perineum. A nurse tilted the mirror away so Chloe wouldn't see the additional surge of blood. The baby's crown slipped forward and remained there at the end of the contraction. I looked back at Chloe. She'd passed out.

"Chloe?" I said.

A nurse pushed me aside, scanned Chloe's pupils, and then passed ammonium nitrate under her nose. Chloe coughed and shook her head to get away from the salts.

"You fainted, Chloe," I told her.

"OK, big push this time, Chloe. Do you hear me, Chloe?" the doctor asked.

She nodded. I took her hand again. My tears began to fall onto her forearm. "I love you, baby," I said. And she rammed into her contraction. "Push, Chloe," I yelled. And she screamed back at the ceiling and suddenly the baby's head was in the doctor's hands and Chloe screamed again and the baby, blood splattered, slate blue, cheesy, gushed into the doctor's arms. A nurse vacuumed the nostrils and the baby coughed, inhaled, and began to cry, silently at first, then in great inherited gusts of weeping. Chloe had fainted again.

"A little girl," the doctor said proudly. Then he looked up at Chloe. I touched her cheek. Her eyes rolled open.

"You did it," I said, smiling, wiping water from both our faces. The nurse brought the baby to Chloe and laid her in her arms. "It's a little girl," I said. "She's perfect. She has more hair on her head than you do."

Chloe lifted the baby up to her face and kissed her and said, "Look who's here," somewhat sadly, then she dropped off again.

The nurse took the baby, and the doctor after looking at Chloe, said, "Let her rest for a moment." Then he said, "Here's the placenta. We can get her sewn up now."

I left the room, and taking Grace's hand I told everyone it was a girl, and that mother and daughter were both well. Grace sat down. Her lips compressed and her eyes swung away from me, then she took in a great gulp of air and looked up. "There's nothing left to worry about now," she said.

≈

Chloe brought Shirley Dapple home to *Rosinante* two days later. In the meantime Grace and I had rushed around rounding up a crib and stroller and other paraphernalia. Grace seemed to have regained her composure. She didn't paint but she was active and never had to be reminded to take her medication. She was attentive to Chloe and the baby, getting them settled back into the life of a boat.

"This is where you got to be as big as you are now," Chloe told the baby.

"You grew up here too," Grace said, nodding at Chloe.

We sat in the salon, the last warmth of September on our skin. Chloe, opening her blouse, brought Shirley up to her breast to feed. Her nipple was engorged, dark and wet.

"Do you remember, Chloe, the first night I stayed here? You didn't even want me to see you in your nightgown."

"How was I to know you weren't interested?" she said, but she blushed as well.

Grace sat with her head back, her eyes closed. "I remember," she whispered, and paused.

Chloe and I looked across the salon at her face. "You remember what, Grace?"

She brought her head upright slowly, turning it so that her ear was almost on her shoulder and with her eyes still closed, she said, "So many things, so near."

"Don't get mystical on us, Grace," Chloe said, holding Shirley's head.

Grace opened her eyes and sighed sweetly, without concern. "The doomsayers may be right some day," she said, "but they'll never have the satisfaction of saying so."

I looked at Chloe and raised my eyebrows. I was so stupid.

Chloe winked and said, "A dog chasing his tail finds happiness close to home."

Grace frowned at her, but said, "She's so beautiful, Chloe, all promise, no memory."

"I think she must remember this boat, living in the water and on it," I said. "She seems so comfortable."

"The rocking soothes you, doesn't it, Shirley?" Chloe whispered into her scalp.

Grace pushed herself up, swept her fine hair off her brow, and descended to her cabin.

≈

She chose her time, I think. A few days later, after making us pancakes for breakfast, Grace told us a joke as we prepared Shirley Dapple for her first day of shopping. Chloe felt she was strong enough to walk a bit, so we were going to take a ride to the mall.

"I have a joke," Grace said.

It was so unlike her. Chloe and I were smiling already. "What?"

"Why do witches ride broomsticks?"

We couldn't help smiling. We smiled rapturously. "Why?"

She snickered, put her hand over her mouth and, blushing, she answered, "Because nature abhors a vacuum."

"Grace," we screamed. We leaned on things. We touched each other. Grace smiled.

"We'll be back in an hour or two," I said as we walked up the gangway.

What obvious oversight am I making right now? In pre-Columbian Mexico they added wheels to toys but never carried the idea further, never built larger useful carts. What am I missing at this very moment? I've missed so much in the past. It always seems I'm backing into the future, as if I'm rowing a boat.

Grace stood on *Rosinante*'s stern, holding her arms across her chest. "Have a good time," she shouted. And I turned without thought to Chloe and Shirley, our first outing. I wanted to buy Shirley her first pair of overalls, tiny and blue.

We stayed longer than we'd planned, eating lunch in the food court. When we returned, *Rosinante* was gone. Pinky and Midden were leashed to the dock. We were at a loss. I ran into the Smarmy Snail and asked if anyone had seen the boat go out. One of the waitresses said it had left that morning.

"Did you see who was aboard?" I asked.

"No," she said. "I just happened to look up and the boat was crossing the river."

I went back out to Chloe and said, "I just don't understand."

≈

The Coast Guard found *Rosinante* late that evening, a few miles out to sea beyond the Isles of Shoals. Her helm lashed and engine running, she swung in a wide arc on the ocean's surface, spanning deep water. No one was aboard, but there was no mystery: Grace had left a note. In her crippled cursive, raggedly poised like linen torn, she explained, "I won't go to heaven without my memory."

≈

Chloe and Shirley and I attended a funeral last week: not for Grace, her service was held months ago, but for the ladies of Prescott Park, the ones we excavated over the summer. The repatriation, after much debate, took place at Point of Graves, within consecrated ground. We still know little about them. No written word seems to have survived. Lab analysis revealed that both burials took place in the spring. Pollen from several varieties of wildflowers was found in soil samples taken from among the bones. I ask myself: is this evidence of love?

We never found Grace, although for days after the official Coast Guard search we looked for her in Harry's and Chloe's father's boats. Harry offered to trawl for her but we all, including Anne, decided

against it. Grace wouldn't let her future take her past. I have to smile now at her self-imposed burial at sea. She has a chance of surviving in a way, of becoming a fossil, stone replacing bone through the ages to the drifting music of whale song. Some future archaeologists, heaven help them, may disturb her bones.

I've been trying to understand this yearning to go along with the dead. I dream of coffins shaped like dinghies, riding the tide out to sea. At night, they bump lightly against *Rosinante*'s hull, wood on wood. Jonah is in one of them. Would he want me beside him? I keep wondering if all those gone before us have anything to say, but sadly dissolve to the conclusion that the dead could care less, while we strive still for love and acceptance, some reconciliation, to be forgiven for not dying with them. The burden is going second, going last. Perhaps Grace has been allowed, for a second time, to rejoin Sweet George.

In her note, Grace asked her daughter to let Chloe and me buy *Rosinante*, and Anne was gracious enough to comply. Shirley has grown so much in the last few months. She's fat and oblivious, puff and bladder. At her baptism, holy water mixed with her tears. And Chloe, in a curious reversal, has immersed herself safely within her child. She seems to have taken no notice of Grace's departure. I try to remember that we're young, and that the only thing as strong as Grace's death is our memory of her.

All I have from Richard and Mary since our meeting is a letter from Mary stating, "My son is no martyr. I believe in the slick road."

Michael stops by now and then, sits on the bow with Chloe and Shirley and me. I admire his persistence.

Harry, in from days at sea, brings us a big fish wrapped in paper, and grinning sheepishly, says, "Now, girls, don't tell the wife."

Midden, infuriatingly enough, has taken lately to using *Dapple* for a litter box. I'm thinking of changing his name.

Pinky struggles on.

I'm back in school, at UNH, taking classes in marine archaeology. *Rosinante* should be able to take us to historical sites all along the Atlantic coast and throughout the Caribbean. And so I've been taking diving lessons too. The water's not so bad once you get used to the numbing cold. It seems to help the arthritis in my wrists. At an open-

water class, fish nipped at my exposed ears and followed me as I roamed the bottom, circling the remains of an old sunken boat. It was strange to come eye to eye with a fish as flat and narrow as the space between my eyes. It was strange to look up at the sun through thirty-five feet of water and the air bubbles I'd just exhaled, but I didn't feel as much alien as prodigal: the fish and I both got to thirty-five feet with our own gifts. The fish didn't appear surprised to see me; he almost seemed to have been waiting. He acted as if I was late, that I was dumber than he'd thought.

There are days when the night stays with me like the aftertaste of milk, all reflection on the tip of my tongue. Something seems to be going bad in a thin layer. I wonder then what it is I'm almost remembering, the same way I'll sometimes reach for a doorknob and close my hand on air. I yearn for knowledge but all I know is others have come this way before.

The leaves have lost in a last swoon of pallor or blood. Submerged, embroiled in ebbing waters, they're carried past, rushed downward. I suppose I've become a familiar sight to those on the waterfront by now, sitting at dusk or dawn on *Rosinante*'s capstan, watching the water flow and recede. I hope I don't appear melancholy. A yellow tooth moon rises through skeletal tree limbs, slowly disentangling itself, like an old woman picking her way out of unfamiliar bedclothes, removing sheets from her legs as if they were nets. The river reflects this light. I won't go to heaven without my memory. It seems to me now that faith and memory are one and the same thing, or at least that they can't exist without one another. I feel suddenly able to pray to my own past, to ask for some deliverance, a place to abide. The water before me takes on the color of everything I remember, and it moves.

Acknowledgments For their courage, brains and heart, I give great heaping spoonfuls of thanks to my manuscript readers: Linda Coomer, Eleanor Eidels, Beverly Hutton and Margaret Ryan. Martha E. Pinello and Mary B. Dupre, archaeologists at Strawbery Banke Museum, Portsmouth, N.H, were most kind with their time and advice. Thanks to Aunt Dot for her pancake recipe. Fiona McCrae makes the acknowledgments once again. In the past it's been for editorial help, but this time it's for carrying me in the glove compartment all the way from Boston to Saint Paul. Mary Ann Cooper, Hazel Ranck, Linda Petrikovic, Kathy Podolsky, Bonnie Dunlap, Barbara Self, Pat Hiett, Dale Cawvey and Martha Stewart, all employees of the Azle and Burleson Antique Malls, gave me the time and peace of mind to write this book. And finally, thanks to the Fates for allowing me to be born while it's still possible to know and love a wooden boat. JOE COOMER